THE WINTER SOLDIER

COLD FRONT

MACKENZI LEE

Los Angeles　New York

First Hardcover Edition, February 2023
First Paperback Edition, April 2025
10 9 8 7 6 5 4 3 2 1
FAC-004510-25016
Printed in the United States of America

This book is set in MrsEaves
Designed by Kurt Hartman

Library of Congress Control Number: 2022938443
ISBN 978-1-368-02616-1

Visit www.HyperionTeens.com
and www.Marvel.com

SUSTAINABLE FORESTRY INITIATIVE

Certified Sourcing

www.forests.org
SFI-01681

Logo Applies to Text Stock Only

For Mom, Dad, Zach, McKelle, Q, and Kenai

The Living Room Residency
2020—2022

And Chief—my favorite Soviet sleeper agent

When you wake, the only thing you remember is dying.

The crack of the ice as your body struck it, louder than antiaircraft fire. The cold that drove all the breath from your lungs. The water that flooded them when you gasped in shock. You had fallen hard but landed weightless, the world going white around you as you floated, too cold to swim, too cold to breathe. Too cold to do anything but die.

You don't know how, but you were certain you were dying. It had always been different before—though you can't remember what exactly that "before" looked like. Before, you had flirted with death like a drunk at a bar, reckless and giddy but with no intention of following it home. You had stood on the knife's edge. Sucked last chance after last chance to the bone. They had been endless. Until they weren't.

But you aren't dead, are you? So then, what is this?

Your eyes are crusted shut, and when you crack them open, the light burns. Spectral clouds dot the corners of your vision, fog gathered and made flesh. Here are the ghosts coming to collect you. You can't recall their names. But surely you had a mother and a father once. Perhaps it's them, beckoning you over the threshold with hands outstretched. Maybe a friend who didn't survive childhood—doesn't everyone have one of those? The first time you learned that people really die, and the thing to fear is not the loss but the losing. Maybe the ghosts are soldiers. You remember soldiers. Maybe it's them, your band of brothers, gone into the deep, frigid water before you, now waiting on the other side.

The ghosts wear white caps, and their faces are covered. You can't see their eyes, just the light overhead reflected in them. It refracts through the glass bottles hanging above you, long tubes snaking down from them like kite tails before disappearing under your skin.

You can feel their contents draining into you, and your body seizes against the added weight. Your chest constricts, a spasm like those raised by the cold. Suddenly you're back in the water.

You're afraid, but you don't know why.

You want to fight, but you don't know what.

You're not sure you could, even if you tried. Your limbs don't feel like your own. Your whole body is a foreign landscape, treacherous in its strangeness. There is pain in places that don't exist. Weakness in muscles that never relax. The water is gone, but the cold remains.

"What is your name?" a ghost asks.

You can't see your legs, but you try to move them. It's like trying to break through a shell of thick ice.

"Do you understand me?" the ghost asks, and you do. You understand him, but you still can't move your legs. You try your arms, but only one of them obeys. Your fist closes and opens and closes again.

Is it yours?

A fist. A hand. You try to look, but something holds your head in place, and the light is still in your eyes. You want to stand—you always thought you'd die on your feet, rising to meet the bullet. But here you are, drowning in light and full of water, with nothing but a hand that isn't yours.

"What is your name?" the ghost asks again, and you know the answer.

Don't say it, you think, and you clench your jaw until you feel the pain. Your whole body trembles with the effort it takes not to answer, to keep your head above the current when it would be so much easier to give in and let yourself sink.

"Almost finished," the ghost says, and you feel the soothing press of fingers against your forehead, pushing back your hair. Someone else had done that, once. Someone else had touched your hair with tenderness, but when you reach for the memory, there's only empty air. You can feel the absence of whoever once occupied that space inside you. It steals your breath, the enormity of that chasm. Your heartbeat stutters, the tremor echoing in a rising electronic beep.

"Tell me your name," the ghost says.

The ice cracks under you. The water funnels in, frothing and studded with glacial ice, and you can't fight it. You can't swim. You can't wait on a tide that will never turn, and it's not just water as far as you can see. It's farther. It's all that's left.

Through a mouthful of cold water, you gasp your reply, gagging up each word like it's a sharp-edged fractal of frost. "I don't know."

"Good," the ghost replies. "Good, that's perfect."

CHAPTER 1
1954

The agent flinches when Rostova rips the hood from his head. The room is dim, but the agent has spent the last few days in darkness, blindfolded as he was shuttled between basements and transport trucks and freezing concrete cells. Even the sickly-yellow glow of the single overhead bulb must feel like a spotlight, bright enough to make him recoil. Either that, or he had been anticipating a blow.

The bare bulb overhead flickers, and all the shadows in the room jump like static on a television screen. The chair the man is chained to is bolted to the floor, so that when he starts to rock, wheezing with fear, it doesn't move with him. The metal cuffs dig into the raw skin at his wrists, his old wounds already weeping. His lips are chapped and crusted with badges of blood. Fresh streaks coat his teeth and run from his broken nose into his mouth. One eye is swollen so big it looks like a halved grapefruit has been shoved under his skin.

Rostova steps back, surveying the agent without blinking as he drools and sobs. She had been a sniper on the Eastern Front and had spent the bloodiest days of the war lying motionless, covered in pine branches and buried in snow, her breaths shallow and her heartbeat slow until the moment she squeezed the trigger. Now stillness and silence remain her weapons. Only the battlefield has changed.

When Rostova doesn't move, the agent starts to blubber in Russian, the blood and snot in his throat clotting his words. No one stays silent for long after weeks of isolation and waiting, no company but their own grisly imaginations. By the time they reach this room, a few seconds of Rostova's stillness are enough to send them tumbling, unprompted, into confessions.

"Alexander Fedorov," Rostova says suddenly, and a strangled gurgle of surprise slips from the agent. He looks up at her, and she smiles, showing her teeth. "Can I call you Alex?" she asks in bright Russian. "Or Sasha? Does anyone call you Sasha? And yes, I know"—she waves a hand at an objection he hasn't raised—"Alexander isn't your real name, but why not keep up appearances? You've come this far."

Fedorov digs his feet into the tile floor, trying to push himself back in a chair that won't be moved. "Who are you?" he asks, his voice pitched. "KGB?"

Rostova's smile widens. "No, no, we're much worse."

Fedorov's foot catches the drain in the floor, and he recoils from whatever slippery mess is still trapped there from the last man who had been chained to this chair. "I'm n-no one," he stammers, staring at the ground. "I don't know what I'm doing here. I'm a student. I don't know anything—you have the wrong man."

"Now, we both know that's not true." Rostova tugs at one of her gloves, pulling it off a finger at a time. "You work for MI5, don't you?" She flicks her eyes to Fedorov, but he is still staring determinedly down. "You've been in Russia a long time, but every mask slips eventually. Your mother—she *was* Russian. Your father was a British soldier. They kept in touch after he went back to England, and when you were old enough, he recruited you into his clandestine activities. You don't have to pretend," she says when Fedorov shakes his head. "He told us himself. Before we shot him. Well, not us. The KGB. And remember—we're worse." She finishes peeling off the first glove and takes a step forward, letting the fingertips drag across Fedorov's greasy hair. "You should be so proud, Sasha. You've lasted much longer than he did."

A sob shudders free from Fedorov. Rostova bends at the waist, peering into his face. "You have an assignment, don't you? That's exciting! Your first assignment! You've been waiting for—what?—almost a year undercover. Do you want to tell me about it? Or where you were traveling?" Fedorov is trembling, the sweat and blood on his neck beading and sliding off. In the silence, each drop hits the tile with a *plink*, like the pulled pin of a grenade. Rostova drops into a crouch before him, twisting her head as she forces her face into his line of sight. "It must be such a hard secret to keep. You didn't even tell your girlfriend—wait, fiancée, isn't it now? You proposed on Prechistenskaya Naberezhnaya this past New Year's. Near the river. Didn't you?" Fedorov says nothing. Rostova stares at him, that eerie stillness settling through her again. "Didn't you?" she repeats, her voice sharp enough to shave with.

Fedorov's teeth rattle as he shakes, but he doesn't say anything.

Rostova grabs him with her still-gloved hand, pinching his face as she shoves him up and backward. His neck wrenches as she slams him upright in the chair, the back of his head smacking the headrest. "Sasha, if we're going to be friends," she says, her tone a disconcerting combination of bright and dangerous, "you're going to have to look at me." She straddles him, her weight on his knees, then twists his face to hers. "Is it the eye?" She rams her elbow against his windpipe as she leans forward, giving him a clear view of the patch she wears over her right eye. "I know, it's confusing. Some people don't know where to look."

Fedorov's face gleams with a mixture of blood and spittle and tears. "I don't know anything. I'm just a student." The words come out pinched by Rostova's grip. "I read economics. I was born in Leningrad. My father was—"

"I have a question for you, Sasha." Rostova lets his face go and instead loops her arms around his neck, still sitting on his lap so their faces are very close together. "In all your time in my country, did you ever hear about something called the Winter Soldier Project?"

Fedorov blinks, momentarily disoriented by this conversational pivot. "It . . ." He swallows hard, struggling not to look away from Rostova's face. "It doesn't exist."

"That's what you heard?"

Any color left in Fedorov's cheeks drains. "It's a story."

"Tell it to me." She pushes a strand of hair off his forehead. "I love stories."

"The Winter Soldier . . ." He looks again to the door, then back to Rostova. His breath hitches. "He's an assassin. Mindless and cruel. Unfailingly loyal to the Soviet Union and impossible to sway. Impossible to fight."

Rostova gives a theatrical shiver. "You didn't tell me it was a scary story."

"He's a Super-Soldier. Like Captain America."

"Not quite." Rostova holds up a finger. "That part *is* just a myth. Our soldier did not need any chemical enhancements to make him deadly."

"He doesn't exist," Fedorov whispers.

"A ghost story, then." Rostova slides off his lap, retrieving her dropped glove from the floor and pulling it back on as she surveys Fedorov. "I'm impressed, Sasha. I assumed the Winter Soldier Project would be above your pay grade. MI5 is farther along than we thought. *Were* they paying you? MI5, I mean. Don't believe any of their *do it for the experience* garbage. Never"—she points a finger at him—"work for free, Sasha. I'm telling you that as a friend. Nothing looks *that* good on a CV." She grins at him. One of her molars is gold.

Fedorov takes a sloppy breath. "I don't have anything to do with the Winter Soldier Project."

"I know that. Don't you think I know that, Sasha?" She laughs. "They didn't tell me you were funny. Next you're going to tell me you thought we were alone this whole time."

Fedorov looks wildly around the room. A shadow near the door shifts, and he snaps backward against the chair, cowering. The manacles around his wrists rattle, a sound like coins dropping through a pay-phone slot.

Rostova glances over her shoulder, following his gaze. "Oh, I'm so sorry, I forgot to introduce you." She slaps her forehead, then steps back, giving Fedorov his first unobstructed view of the figure leaning against the room's only door. "Alexander Fedorov," Rostova says, with a grand flourish. "This is the Winter Soldier."

The soldier steps forward.

Fedorov thrashes in his chair, kicking hard like he might be able to push himself away. A thread of blood from the reopened scabs on his wrist drips between his fingers and puddles along the rim of the clogged drain.

"Quite a ghost story, isn't he?" Rostova says, and the Soldier feels her thump him on the shoulder, close-fisted, so that it rattles his body armor. Somehow, she is always stronger than the impact-resistant fibers they tell him are woven into his vest. "Should I leave you two to talk more about your new assignment and all the many things you don't know?" Rostova asks, looking from the Soldier to Fedorov, who's still squirming. He mewls like a frightened kitten but goes abruptly silent when the Soldier rests one hand on the back of Fedorov's chair. The cybernetic fingers shine, even in the poor light.

Behind the Soldier, Rostova is already heading for the door. "We thought we'd let you in on one more Soviet secret, Sasha." She turns on the threshold, leaning lazily into the room with one hand hooked around the handle. "Otherwise you won't have anything left to take to the grave."

───────────

When V emerges from the interrogation room, Rostova is waiting for him, rolling a toothpick between her teeth. She pulls back her sleeve, making a show of checking her slim wristwatch. "Twelve and a half minutes." She taps the face with her nail, like she's testing a sheet of ice before stepping onto it. "Disappointing, Agent Vronsky. I was hoping you'd get it done in under ten. If it *is* done."

"It's done."

"He really didn't know much, did he? What a waste." She pushes herself off the wall, and he follows her into the room behind the cell; it's narrow with a long counter stacked with electronic equipment. A squat television screen in one corner displays a live feed from the interrogation room, the picture green-tinted and fuzzed with static.

Rostova picks up a set of earmuff headphones and plugs them into the recorder, pressing rewind until the tape screeches. "Any cleanup?" she asks, glancing at the screen. "Did he piss himself? He looked ready to, and all

I did was take off my glove." V shakes his head. Rostova swipes off her fur hat so she can press the headphones to her ear. Her dark hair, threaded with white, is cut into a choppy, cropped style that is shorter than V's. His own hair has grown long—it brushes his chin. He's certain it's the longest he's ever worn it. Every time it sweeps the back of his neck, his body registers the strangeness.

Rostova looks up from the slowly spinning reels of the tape deck to where he's standing in the doorway, then flaps her hat at him. "Don't stare at me like that. It makes me itchy."

"He didn't have a name for his new contact yet," V says.

Rostova rewinds the tape showily, like he drowned out the audio. "How are you so sure? They were pulling his teeth out in Moscow for two weeks, and you think just because he didn't give it up to you in thirteen minutes—"

"Twelve and a half."

"—he didn't have a name?"

"I know when a man is telling the truth."

"Really? You're a lie detector now?" She traces the shape of his bionic arm in the air with her finger. "Does that thing make pancakes as well? Pick up radio signals? Actually, that could be useful. Remind me to mention that to Karpov." She punches a button on the recorder, then drops backward into the rickety swivel chair pushed up to the counter. When he doesn't say anything, she continues, with one ear of the headset still clamped against her shoulder, "I wonder what that would cost, to give you some kind of antenna. You could feed every man, woman, and child in Russia three square meals for the price of that tech hanging off your shoulder, so what's a few million rubles more?" She folds her hands behind her head and stretches. "It's just as Marx would have wanted it."

"Who?"

"Shush!" Something on the recording catches her attention and she puts up a hand to silence him. She stares forward, listening hard, then shivers. "You're really scary, you know that?" she says, her gaze flicking to him. He doesn't say anything as she returns to the tape. The room is silent except for the tinny audio piping through the headphones.

Rostova frowns suddenly, then rewinds the tape and plays it again. She flips the toothpick against her front teeth. *"Metropole."* She repeats the word Fedorov had kept screaming, over and over for most of their twelve and a half minutes. *"Vida Metropole.* What is that?"

"I don't know. That's all I could get him to tell me."

She unwinds the headphones, then tosses them back into their cradle. "All right. Anything else?"

"He was undercover as a student—"

"We know that," she interrupts. "What did he tell you about his assignment?"

When V doesn't say anything, Rostova bites down on the end of her toothpick too hard, and it splinters. She spits, then tosses the end on the floor, grinding it under her heel. "So close," she murmurs, running a hand over her face.

"Close to what?" he asks. "That isn't nothing."

She gives him a smile, though it sags around the edges. "No, it's not nothing," she agrees. "But it's just not quite enough."

"It isn't nothing," he says, his voice pitching in frustration. "*Metropole* isn't nothing."

"Then what is it? A code name? A cipher? A drop location? His dog's name?"

He resists the urge to roll his eyes. "That's a stupid name for a dog."

She rewinds the audio again, her finger lingering on the playback button for a moment before she pops reels out of the machine and starts to yank the tape, wrapping it around her fingers and pulling until it turns into ribbons.

"You look disappointed," he says.

"It's just my face." She drops the tape into a wastebasket under the counter, followed by a match that she strikes against the bottom of her shoe. The flame turns bloodred, accompanied by an acrid smell rising off the tape as it blackens and curls. "Comes from a lifetime of people letting you down." She slaps her fur hat back onto her head. The shadow of it makes the patch over her missing eye look like a bullet hole. "Come on, Vronsky. We need to get back to base." She pushes herself to her feet with a heavy sigh but stops when she realizes he's still blocking the doorway. "Let's go."

"It's not nothing," he says, the frustration simmering in his voice like anger on a low heat. Somehow, even after months of staring down man after man, each as pathetic and terrified and babbling as Fedorov, this particular failure, this nothing—or not nothing, but this *not quite enough*, this *so close*—salts a wound. Something in him is certain this is the end of a line. He doesn't know what it is exactly that stops with Fedorov, or even where his own certainty springs from. Maybe it's the tilt of Rostova's smile. Maybe it's a muscle memory from a fight long ago, one he must have lost. Otherwise he wouldn't feel so tense and bristling.

"Hey." Rostova claps a hand against the side of his neck, turning his face to hers. "It's not your fault he didn't know anything."

"I know it's not—" he starts, but she shushes him.

"I've been doing this longer than you," she says, "so I can tell you from experience—it doesn't do you any good to dwell. All it will do is fester. Leave it, and move on."

She pats him on the cheek. "We'll find another way in. And you." She pokes him in the chest. "Get some time off."

"I don't want time off," he mutters.

"Take it anyway," she replies firmly. "Enjoy it on my behalf."

"You'll look into it."

She squints at him. "Into what? Vida Metropole?"

"It's not nothing," he says firmly, then adds, "Please."

"You're blocking the door," she says, that same soft growl from Fedorov's interrogation creeping into her voice.

He isn't afraid of Rostova. He has no reason to be. He's at least a decade younger than she is, as well as six inches taller and likely fifty pounds heavier. He has a bionic arm. She has one good eye and a right shoulder weakened by years of rifle kickback. He'd dislocated it twice by accident in their last round of combat training. And they both know that if she damaged him—the Soviet Union's most valuable soldier—she'd be driven to a field outside Moscow and shot through the back of the head. If he hurt her, she'd be marked collateral damage and filed away like a traffic ticket.

But V steps back, and Rostova shoulders out of the control room, the moment of tension shaken off like a dusting of snow. She holds the door open for him, and as he passes, she whistles the Soviet anthem, squeezing out the high notes between the gap in her front teeth like she's spitting apple seeds.

"How have you not been shot yet?" he mutters.

"Because I shoot first!" She holds up two fingers and her thumb in the shape of a gun, and levels it with the space between his eyes before pantomiming a kill shot. "Bang! They never see me coming!" She starts whistling again as she trots down the hallway, but pauses outside the interrogation room door. "You really think he doesn't have a name?" she asks.

"Everything he knows, he told me."

"Well then." She nods toward the door in wordless instruction. "I'll meet you in the truck. Make sure there's no mess. This building doesn't have a janitor, and I'd hate to have to bus in some poor grandmother from Moscow only to shoot her when she's finished mopping."

"And you never miss."

She laughs. "Good work, soldier." She pops into a quick salute, fingers to her brow. "As always, your country thanks you."

CHAPTER 2
1954

The physical is routine. He has one after every assignment, all administered by the same surly nurse with
bottle-red hair and a lazy eye. She makes notes in the file
folder she always has. V strips down to his undershirt
and boxers, then sits on the examination table without
being asked.

"ID number?" she asks, still staring at the paper,
and he recites it. When he's finished, she looks up for
the first time, like she hadn't recognized him until she
heard the numbers. "Welcome back, Agent Vronsky. I
trust your mission was a success?"

"It went as planned," he says simply, like he could

have told her anything else, and she nods at the stock reply.

"Very good. Lie back, please." She jams the file folder into the crook of her elbow as she pulls on a pair of white latex gloves. Their dusty smell is familiar incense in the exam room.

V stares at the ceiling, the light over him somehow too bright even when switched off. The physicals are never eventful. The nurse makes a visual assessment, takes his vitals, asks a few questions, then clears him for his next assignment—or signs off on his leave. The only time it has ever deviated from routine was after a job in Omsk, a motorcade assassination that went wrong when a policeman managed to get a concealed blade in between V's shoulder and the joint of his bionic arm, prying a paralyzing gap between them before Rostova was able to take the man out from a rooftop across the street. Doctor Karpov had come himself then to complete the reattachment operation, and had stayed several days after for observation.

The nurse snaps the latex, and his muscles tense in anticipation of pain. The hair on the back of his neck stands up, though he isn't sure why. Perhaps it's the lingering adrenaline and still-elevated heart rate from Fedorov's interrogation. *There is no danger here,* he reminds himself.

He jumps when the cold metal of a stethoscope touches his skin, and has to stop himself from reflexively grabbing the nurse around the wrist and twisting her hand away from him. He takes a deep breath through his nose, counting his heartbeats.

The nurse frowns. "Did that hurt?"

"No."

"When was your last stress test?"

Check your copious notes and tell me.

He blinks. He was not made to be insubordinate. He was made—trained—to be compliant and obey. The thought had flashed through his mind like a hidden frame in a film reel, gone before he had the chance to properly examine it.

"Please relax," the nurse says, and pinches the skin at his elbow, searching for a vein. "This will all be standard." He feels a prick as the needle goes in.

He's tired. He could fall asleep on the exam table except for the electric charge that sizzles through his whole body when she attaches a diagnostic machine to his bionic arm. The electricity maps his nerves, and his throat smacks of metallic bile. This is taking too long—longer than usual—and the lights overhead are blinding. When did she turn them on? How many hours has he been without sleep? Too many, he guesses, as he watches the light bounce through the glass bottle connected to the IV drip in his arm. He feels like a fish in a bowl. Somewhere overhead, a vent switches on and he shivers, his skin breaking out in gooseflesh.

"Are you cold?" The nurse doesn't wait for him to answer. She pulls a blanket over him, so heavy and unyielding he suspects it's for protection from radiation rather than warmth. It feels like she's stacking stones on his ribs, pressing the air out of them in a slow hiss. The light turns blue where it collects and then bends through the IV bottle.

Don't fall asleep.

His body jerks, a sensation like missing a step. He had thought for a moment he was starting to tip off the table. The blanket slithers to the floor, landing softly. Not heavy at all.

At the counter, the nurse turns. She's holding an ampoule jutting from the top of a vial, half-full of liquid. "Relax," she says again, her voice pinched.

"What are you giving me?" he asks. His mouth is dry, and he can still taste copper.

"It's glucose," she replies. "Your blood sugar is low."

His vision flickers, and he blinks. He knows something . . . something about glucose and cold. Maybe he read it once, though he can't even remember the last book he picked up. Maybe someone told him when he was young. Though he doesn't feel as though he was ever young. His chin dips, and he closes his eyes. Behind his lids, someone is smiling at him, bright red lipstick framing her mouth.

"Wait!"

V jerks awake. The nurse startles too, almost dropping the vial.

Rostova has careened around the door, panting, one hand on the frame to steady herself. "Not yet," she says to the nurse, holding up a hand as though directing traffic. "You have to wait."

The nurse glowers. "Excuse me, agent, we are in the middle of a physical exam."

"You have to wait. You can't . . ." She glances at V, laid out on the exam table, then turns back to the nurse. "Please. I have information that may change things. He'll need to be awake."

The nurse flicks the side of the ampoule. "We're on a timeline."

"I understand that."

"And we've already started."

"I understand that too."

"I have orders—"

Rostova throws up her hands. "You have orders, I have orders, we all have orders, everyone I know has damn orders, you're not special."

V tunes out the argument as he stares up into the light

again, trying to remember what it was he had known about glucose. The light through the IV drip looks less like a bowl now, and more like . . . He can't remember. A plane, maybe, the lights at takeoff skidding through the starless sky and him watching from beneath a sheet of glass. Was it glass?

He's jerked back to the conversation when he hears the name of their director. "Karpov signed off on blank slate," the nurse is saying, "before you left—"

"What's blank slate?" V manages to push himself up on his elbows, though his limbs feel swollen, his skin too tight. "What did Karpov tell you to do to me?"

The nurse gives Rostova a pointed look. "That," she says, jabbing the ampoule's tip at him, "is exactly why it's time."

"He's not . . ." Rostova flexes her fists at her side. Her jaw is clenched so tightly that a vein in her forehead pops out. "You can't undo the procedure once it's underway, but you can wait. Please." The word comes out pinched, her lips barely moving. "Just. Wait."

The nurse glances at the readout slowly printing from the machine hooked to V's arm. "You have until the diagnostics are finished. Then I'm following through with *my* instructions."

V closes his eyes again. The light pressing against them is making his head throb. *Just let me sleep,* he thinks.

He doesn't care what they do to him. Let them pump him full of sugar. Let him freeze to death. He doesn't have enough energy to wonder why those two things are related. The current is already pulling him under.

Then someone slaps him across the face.

He startles, almost falling off the exam table. The nurse is gone, and Rostova is leaning over him, his face in her hands as she shakes him gently. "Come on, Vronsky, wake up, it's not bedtime just yet."

He tries to push her off him. "I'm on leave."

"Not quite yet, lucky boy." She hooks an arm under his, pulling him into a sitting position. He sinks back down as soon as he's straight. His whole body feels heavy as lead.

"I'm tired."

"I know; so am I. We're all tired. This whole damn country is tired, but we carry on anyway." She pinches the tube of the IV drip, then slides the needle out of his arm, pressing a gauze pad over it before it can bleed. "Hold this." Rostova grabs his bionic arm and presses the fingers over the gauze, then turns back to the counter. His head falls forward, chin to his chest. "No, no, none of that." Rostova slaps him again, gentler this time, then retrieves his clothes from a bin beside the exam table. She tosses him his shirt, but he doesn't react fast enough to catch it. It hits him in the chest, then falls to the floor. Rostova sighs. "Come on, you're the great pride of the USSR. I need you firing on at least a few more cylinders before we see Karpov."

V retrieves his shirt. He feels like he's pushing back against a high wind. "Karpov isn't here."

Rostova flashes him a grin. "He just arrived."

V rubs his forearm against his eyes. "Why is Karpov . . . ?"

Rostova answers the question before he can finish. "Because I called him. Because you were right—Metropole wasn't nothing. You were—" She notices him struggling to pull on his thermal shirt, with one hand still holding the gauze in place. "Oh, you're so pathetic," Rostova says with a fond laugh. "Here."

She helps him pull his shirt over his head, and he rests his forehead against her shoulder. "I want to sleep."

"No you don't. You've just been drugged so you think you do."

His head lurches up. "What?"

"Don't listen to me—I'm lying to you." Rostova pinches his cheek hard enough to bruise. "Come on, eyes open. Deep breaths. How many fingers am I holding up?"

"None."

"Good, that was a trick question." She slaps him one more time, a quick, sharp tap with the back of her hand, then grabs him by the neck and plants a kiss on the top of his head. "We're almost there, Vronsky. Now put your pants on, and let's go."

Karpov is waiting in the briefing room when they arrive, sitting at one end of the long conference table and flipping through a folder. He's always smaller than V expects, especially when he isn't framed by operating-room lights and looming over a surgical table. He's bald, with a neat goatee clipped to a point, and the build of a soldier who hasn't seen the battlefield in years but never lost his military posture. Even alone, he sits straight as a blade.

He looks up when Rostova and V enter, but points only V to the chair beside him. "Agent Vronsky, please, sit down."

V sits, while Rostova lurks behind Karpov, trying to catch a glimpse of the file on the table before him. V tries not to stare too. Is it a medical chart? *His* medical chart? He still feels cold and soupy from whatever the nurse gave him—*had* she drugged him? Had Karpov told her to? Had Rostova? His bionic fingers twitch against the table.

"I apologize for the abrupt change of plans," Karpov says, his voice cutting through V's thoughts. "How are you feeling?"

"I'm fine," V replies without hesitation. Behind Karpov, Rostova gives him a thumbs-up.

"I know this is"—Karpov glances at Rostova, who quickly clasps her hands behind her back—"longer than we usually keep you in the field without a break."

"He can handle it," Rostova interjects. Karpov ignores her. He pulls a sheet of paper from the folder, a blurry photo clipped to one corner, and passes it across the table to V. V pushes the photo aside so he can read the name printed at the top.

"Agent Rostova's initial assessment of Alexander Fedorov's confession was that he was saying *Vida Metropole*," Karpov explains. "We thought at first it may be a cipher phrase, or a code name. What has become recently clear is that what he actually said was *Riga Metropole*."

V looks up from the folder. Karpov and Rostova are both watching him read, Rostova with a knuckle pressed against her teeth. "Does that make a difference?" he asks. It still doesn't mean anything to him.

"The *Metropole* is the name of a hotel in *Riga*, Latvia," Karpov says, over-enunciating the two key words. "It was not initially flagged as consequential, until one of our agents photographed this man outside it." Karpov reaches across the table and taps the photograph.

V tips the photo, trying to make out some distinguishing feature that will make it more than just the blurry shape of a man on a rainy street. "Who is he?"

"An English intelligence agent," Karpov replies. "He was high up in British Special Operations during the war. He recruited young men and women finishing secondary school to attend university in Germany under false credentials, then report on political movements within the institutions. MI5 has been testing the program in the Soviet Union; Alexander Fedorov was one of their moles. Fedorov has a reservation at the Hotel Metropole bar for tomorrow night. We believe he was going to meet this man."

V scans the information. The man's name, age, height, address—none of it means a thing to him, but he knows that by the time Karpov asks for the paper back he'll be expected to have it memorized. The last line of the dossier lists the man's known affiliations: the Special Operations Executive, MI5, MI6, Project Fugue.

Project Fugue.

V blinks.

"Agent?"

V looks up. Karpov prompts, "You know drop protocol."

"Of course," V says. He wants to ask what it is he's picking up from this man, what Project Fugue is, but that's not his concern. The reason behind his work doesn't matter. What matters is he does it.

But it reminds him of something. Something he can't remember. Something from before he was here, from his . . . youth? Is that right? He feels older than that. And younger. How is he both older and younger?

His brain feels like it's rolling around in his skull, and when he looks down at his hands, for a moment, they seem like someone else's. That same prickling sense of unease from the exam room is creeping up his neck.

Nothing's wrong, he tells himself firmly. *You're just tired.*

He's exhausted, and he hasn't seen the sky in so long. He goes between strongholds, straight into windowless rooms where men are chained to radiators, already marinating in puddles of their own urine and blood before he ever touches them. His handlers drive armored trucks with tinted windows. He sleeps in the back seat with Rostova at the wheel, and when he wakes, he often can't remember the trip at all. He couldn't point to their home base on a map, and he suspects they prefer it that way. There's never a way to mark the time in any of those dark cells—it could be midnight, or noon, or three in the afternoon. It could be next year. Another century. What does it matter?

"You'll take Fedorov's place for the drop," Karpov says. "His MI5 contact has been out of Britain since before Fedorov was recruited, so we believe they've never met. Pick up whatever information he had for Fedorov and return it here. Then we'll give you that well-earned time off you've been promised." Karpov smiles, though it looks like a poor imitation of an expression he once saw demonstrated but can't yet convincingly reproduce. "Do you have any questions, agent?"

Project Fugue. It's stuck in his head, like a song. Karpov is still talking, but for a moment, V can't understand him. It's like he's forgotten every word in Russian.

"Agent?"

"I think I know this man."

V looks around, wondering for a moment who had spoken before he realizes it was him.

Behind Karpov, Rostova stills. For a wild moment, V imagines her reaching into her jacket, drawing out a pistol, and pressing it to the base of Karpov's skull. He'd never see her coming.

Karpov's dead-eyed smile doesn't falter. "What's that?"

"Do I . . ." V looks down at the dossier again, the photograph sharpening like he's adjusting the lens on a scope. He can make out the shape of the man's nose. A prominent chin. Eyeglasses. "Did I know him?"

"Why would you know him?" Karpov says, his tone rendering the phrase unquestionably rhetorical. "This man is an English agent. He's never set foot on Russian soil."

"Before—" V starts, but Karpov interrupts.

"There is no before, agent. There is only now. There is only this work."

"But this man—Edward Fleming—"

Rostova takes a sharp breath. V glances at her, and she shakes her head, though he isn't sure what he's done that he shouldn't have.

Karpov fixes V with a frigid stare. "What did you say?"

"That's his name, isn't it?" He looks down at the file, but it's like the letters have rearranged themselves. Whatever name he just plucked from the air is not the name on the file.

"What name did you give, agent?" Karpov asks.

"I don't remember." He looks to Rostova, but all she does is shake her head violently, as though he hasn't already realized he's stepped on a land mine. "I was confused."

Karpov snatches the paper from in front of V. The photo comes unclipped and flutters to the floor. "It's off."

Karpov stands, straightening his coat, and turns sharply for the door, but Rostova steps in front of him. "Wait—wait."

Karpov's hand flexes on the folder. The paper crinkles. "Move, agent."

Rostova glances at V, and he looks down at the table obediently, pretending he can't hear them. She lowers her voice, but the room is too small for a truly private conversation. "It was a slip. Just a slip. A mistake. Even your soldier isn't infallible, he gets confused sometimes."

"He's compromised," Karpov says, but Rostova shushes him like he's a child. Karpov's neck turns red. "It's been too long. You know the half-life."

"He's not compromised," Rostova says. "I'll go with him. I swear, nothing will go wrong. He's not compromised."

"I'm not compromised," V says.

They both turn to him. Karpov clenches his jaw, studying V for a moment, then pivots back to Rostova and pokes a finger in her face. "One slip—"

"I know."

"He cannot make mistakes. *Our soldier* cannot make mistakes. You are too tolerant. You encourage him."

"So assign someone else," Rostova says bitterly. "In the time it takes to swear them to secrecy and teach them how not to piss themselves with fear, this opportunity will have come and gone."

Karpov thrusts the folder into her chest, hard enough that she takes a step back. "If anything goes wrong, you'll be a secretary in Lubyanka Square before the end of the week. If you're lucky."

Rostova nods. "I understand."

Karpov stares at her for a moment, then turns back to V, retrieving a briefcase from the floor and setting it on the table. "It would appear you have an advocate, Agent Vronsky," he says as he unclips the latches. "It's amazing the impact a good handler can have."

"I'm not compromised," V says.

"We know, agent. But as a precaution." Karpov withdraws a blister pack of pills from his briefcase and pops two out—one red, one white. They land on the table with a gentle plink, and V thinks of marbles on blacktop, a cat's eye gleaming in the punishing sunlight of late August—

V blinks.

"Since we can't give you leave, these will keep your strength up," Karpov explains. "Help with your stamina in the field. Agent Rostova will make sure you take them twice a day."

V stares at the pills. Something is nagging at the back of his mind like a snagged trip wire. The pills remind him of something. Something he can't quite make out through the rain-fogged lens of his memory. Something about a nightingale.

"Soldier." Karpov's voice cuts into his thoughts. "What's your purpose?"

"To comply," V replies.

"Exactly."

V shuts his eyes. His throat closes.

"Take the pills, soldier," Karpov says. "Comply."

V picks up the two pills and dry-swallows them both. He feels them all the way down his throat.

CHAPTER 3
1941

When Bucky received an official summons to Commander Crawford's office—on US military letterhead and from an Army messenger who, in spite of the fact that they'd played poker together in the rec room the night before, would only call him *Mr. Barnes* when he made the delivery—he knew he was in trouble.

Off the top of his head, he could think of a half dozen things he had done in the past week that might earn him a stern talking-to from the commander. It could be that he had "borrowed" Crawford's Cadillac to take Jenny Menzel swing dancing, then brought it back with the gas tank empty. Or that he hadn't done any of the high school coursework he had promised to complete—maybe

Crawford had found the blank math workbook Bucky had stashed under the mattress in his bedroom at the Crawfords' house, his promise to diligently homeschool quickly broken when he remembered how aggressively uninteresting he found almost every subject. Or, if not the empty workbook, the enlistment papers he had tried yet again to slip into the camp roster, complete with the registrar's signature forged at the bottom.

He did not expect that, when he entered Crawford's office, the usually neat desktop would be strewn with liquor bottles, magazines, candy wrappers, and a green glass bottle of expensive aftershave. The wide eyes of a pin-up girl posing with an arched back against the nose of a bomber stared up at him from the front of a magazine, red lips parted in a cherry-round inhalation. *Uh-oh*, she seemed to say. *You caught me.*

We're going down together, Bucky thought.

Crawford didn't look up when Bucky sat down across the desk from him. The commander was leaning back in his chair, feet wedged against one of the desk drawers as he studied a crossword printed on the inside flap of a copy of *Adam*. He'd cracked the magazine's spine and curled the cover around so a curvy blond stared out from an advertisement, the words GIRLS FIT TO FIGHT! and a phone number lettered along the curve of her back.

Crawford tapped a pencil against his chin in an exaggerated show of consideration, then asked without looking up, "What's a nine-letter word for a formal rebuke or warning for bad behavior?"

Bucky resisted the urge to roll his eyes. "That's not in there."

"Starts with an *R*," Crawford went on like Bucky hadn't spoken. "So long as I have Duke Ellington's hit song '*Blank* Little Words' right."

" 'Three Little Words,' " Bucky supplied. His father used to sing it to his mother in the front seat of the car when he and his sister were tucked into the back. He'd take her hand when it came on the radio and hum his way through the lyrics he never remembered, no matter how many times he'd heard them.

Crawford let the front of the magazine tip forward so he and Bucky were facing each other across the desk. "James."

Bucky returned the commander's grim expression and replied with equal severity, "Nicholas."

Crawford sighed, then flipped the cover of the magazine shut and tossed it onto the desk on top of the rest of the contraband. "How long have you been running this grift?"

"What grift?"

"You can't fool me, Buck. Everything you know about trouble, you learned from your old man, and everything he knew, he learned from me. You think this doesn't have his fingerprints all over it? He sold pennies for dimes when we were still in elementary school. Told the other kids they were worth a fortune because they were minted on the first day of the new century."

"Is that how you two met?" Bucky asked, though he knew the real story—Chicago-suburb yards that sat back-to-back, a loose board in the fence, a dog that would never stay penned, and the two boys who chased him back and forth until they lost track of which boy belonged to which house. "You spent all your savings on centennial pennies? Did you flatten his nose when you found out he had taken you for a ride?"

Crawford snorted. "The only reason I would have popped your dad is if he wasn't cutting me in. But we both grew out of nonsense like that by the time we were your age." He waved a hand over his desktop. His uniform cuff caught the neck of a Bayer aspirin bottle, and it wobbled. "Come on, Bucky. Where did all this come from?"

Bucky surveyed the contraband, trying to look like he was seeing it all for the first time. "Did you stock up when you and the missus were in town this weekend, sir?"

Crawford folded his hands and rested his elbows on the desktop. A fly was doing circles next to his ear, flirting with the shoulder strap on his uniform. "One of our brand-new privates came by to tell me he visited the company library."

Bucky nodded sagely. *Don't give them an inch,* his father always told him, wisdom that had served George Barnes from middle school cafeterias to the tunnels under the Somme. "Smart. I hear basic training wears a man down if he doesn't find a way to keep his mind engaged."

"He said he found a bottle of Bacardi behind *Madame Bovary.*"

Bucky widened his eyes, the picture, he hoped, of shock. "Strange."

Crawford slid a finger under the knot of his tie and wiggled it a few times. Sweat had left a dark band under his collar. It was only June, but the Virginia air was already soupy. "And when he asked one of the other boys about it, he said they had a company kid sneaking into town for them and picking up all the contraband goods they can't get on base. Only fifty cents a trip. And I can only think of one company kid who likes to ride into Arlington every week for comic books I've never seen him read." Crawford leaned forward, smashing a pack of bubble gum under one elbow. "So I'm asking you again," he said, "how long have you been running this grift?"

Bucky stared up at the ceiling fan. The motor clunked with every feeble rotation. "It's not a grift, it's a business."

"All right. A business, then." Crawford picked up one of the whiskey bottles and weighed it in his hand, studying the label. "This isn't cheap liquor."

"Only the best for our boys in uniform."

"So, fifty cents a trip." Crawford traced numbers in the air, feigning multiplication. "How much have you made?"

Bucky shoved his hands under his thighs. "Does that matter?"

"Give me an estimate. Ten bucks? Twenty?"

Bucky rubbed a hand over his chin. The fly that had been lingering around Crawford's shoulder was now riding the breeze from the ceiling fan.

"Fifty?" Crawford prompted. "Please tell me it isn't more than fifty." When Bucky didn't answer, Crawford sighed and clasped his fingers around the bridge of his nose. "You're going to be the death of me, Buck."

"Don't say that, sir," Bucky said. Then he added, "It's going to be a heart attack because you eat so much butter."

Crawford's mouth quirked. "Okay, smart-ass. You want to make a deal?"

"I thought the Army didn't negotiate with enemy combatants."

"You tell me about this business of yours, and I'll let you keep whatever money you've made. Deal?"

Bucky considered this. He was pinned to the wall, that was clear, and there was little chance he'd ever be able to restart the operation, even once a new platoon of privates had cycled through Camp Lehigh—the library was compromised, and Crawford had Bucky in his sights. He'd tell the drill sergeants to keep their eyes peeled too—the ones who always seemed hopeful their troops would do something wrong just for an excuse to exercise government-sanctioned punishments would be giddy. And he *almost* had enough to put a down payment on a motorcycle. He didn't have a license, but one of the milkman's sons in Arlington was willing to sell it to him under the table.

The fly landed on the lip of a Cracker Jack box, wings spasming.

"Fine." Bucky swiped an unopened bottle of Coca-Cola from among the detritus and popped the cap on the edge of the desktop. He would have gone for the whiskey if he thought he could get away with it, but Crawford's eyelid was already twitching. Better not press his luck. "What do you want to know?"

"Who else is in on this?" Crawford asked.

"No one. It's just me."

"Then which soldiers in my camp are you rum-running for?"

Bucky shrugged, taking a long drink of the Coke. It was room temperature and flat, more medicinal tasting than a bottle brewed this century should have been. "I don't know." Crawford gave him the look again, but Bucky held up his hands. "I mean it! I'm not holding out—I don't have any names."

"Now how is it possible you don't know the names of the men you're smuggling for?" Crawford pointed a Chick-O-Stick at him like it was a baton. "You know every soldier in this camp."

"The boys each have a book in the library." Bucky raised the bottle again, thought better of it, and set it down on the desk. Crawford slid one of the Vargas-girl prints under it, a makeshift coaster. "They put their money in every week, and I get what they want."

"And how do you know what they want?" Crawford asked.

"They fold a page corresponding with the listings in the directory."

Crawford rubbed his temples. "There's a directory?"

"Inside front cover of *War and Peace*. Figured no one would ever check that one out. It feels a little too ironic right now. So, say one of the boys wants a pack of Mike and Ikes. They check the directory, see Mike and Ikes are page seven. Then they find their book, fold down the corner of page seven, and put it back on the cart to be re-shelved. If you want two boxes, you fold it twice. Easy."

"And who's selling you liquor? You're only—you know what, never mind. I don't want to know." Crawford tossed the Chick-O-Stick on the desk. The wrapper crackled as it rolled. "So what I'm to understand is that you've been running a covert operation inside my camp for months, using a code you developed based on library books, to smuggle non-requisition items to my soldiers?"

Bucky stretched out his legs, staring at the dusty cuffs of his slacks. The seams were starting to fray. If Mrs. Crawford saw them, she'd leave three new pairs folded up on his bed before the end of the day, whether he asked or not. And he wouldn't ask. "Sorta seems like a waste, not letting me enlist, huh?"

Crawford slumped backward in his chair so hard that the swivel bounced. "No. No chance. We're not having this conversation—"

Bucky sat forward in his chair, knees bumping the desk. "I want to be ready. When it happens—"

"*If,*" Crawford corrected.

Bucky rolled his eyes. "The US won't stay out of this war for long. When the call comes, I want to be ready to fight."

Crawford rubbed a hand through his thinning hair. "You're too young. You're sixteen—"

"Seventeen next month."

"And seventeen is still too young. This isn't a discussion. For god's sake, you're a kid."

"You've got a camp full of *kids* going through bayonet training right outside." Bucky flung a hand to the open window. The shouts of drill sergeants as their platoons ran laps were carried in by the hot wind. "You think half of them didn't lie about their ages to get here?"

"Too bad for them no one got in their way." Crawford stretched over the desk and yanked the window shut. "There will be plenty of time for fighting. You'll be fighting the rest of your life."

"The war will be over before I'm old enough to enlist."

"If you're lucky."

"You were my age when you signed up. You and my dad lied about how old you were."

Crawford leaned back against the window frame, his chair wobbling on two legs. "Your pop and I also put firecrackers in our neighbor's mailbox, so we aren't exactly examples of good judgment."

"I want to fight," Bucky insisted.

"Why?"

The question caught him under the chin. "What do you mean?"

"You can say *patriotism* and *America* and all that until you're blue in the face, but there is no sixteen-year-old who gives a fig about that." The commander let his chair fall forward again and he leaned across the desk toward Bucky. "You don't want to fight a war, you want to be a war hero. And there's a hell of a difference between those two."

"That's not fair."

"Play stupid games, win stupid prizes. As your commanding officer—"

"You're not my commanding officer," Bucky snapped, then added, though he knew how childish it sounded, "And you're not my father, either."

Crawford straightened abruptly, turning away to stare out the window. Bucky pressed his fists into his knees. He almost apologized just to fill the excruciating silence. It hadn't been untrue, but it was mean. He hadn't had to say it. He didn't always have to reach for a switchblade when he felt cornered.

But then Crawford turned back to him and said, "You're right. I'm not. But I'm as close as you've got to either, so shut up and listen to me. You gotta quit this." He gestured at the contraband on the desk. "No more Vargas girls and Bacardi and peppermint patties. You're gonna rot this company's teeth before they ever hit France. Is that clear?"

Bucky tried to suppress an eye roll. "Yes, sir."

"And," Crawford added, his hands flexing on the arms of his chair, "if you're so keen on helping with the war effort, you'll take every cent you made off this scheme and use it to buy defense bonds."

"What?! You said—" Bucky started to protest, but Crawford raised his hands, interrupting him.

"You can keep it if you want—I know we made a deal, and I'll honor that. But if I were you, and if I really, truly wanted to do whatever I could to aid the war effort, not just to feed my own ego—"

"Okay, I get the picture." Bucky slumped in his seat, trying not to scowl. "Can I go now?"

Crawford stared at him for a moment, then said, "I worry about you, Bucky."

Bucky folded his arms. "Well, don't. I can take care of myself."

"That's what worries me. You got a mind all your own. It'll make you a lousy soldier." Crawford swept a stack of magazines off his desk and into the trash can. Bucky winced when the Lik-M-Aid followed it. If his operation was blown *and* he was going to be guilt-tripped into donating the profits, he hoped he'd at least get to keep the spoils. "Your dad was just like you when we were young."

"He didn't turn out so bad."

"No, he didn't. But he also knew when to shut up. You haven't mastered that one yet." Crawford stared down at one of the Vargas girls with an almost academic curiosity. "You really been running a whole contraband operation out of the library?" he said, almost to himself. "And none of us had any clue? I'll be damned."

Bucky slid one of the packs of bubble gum off the desk and into his jacket pocket. "It wasn't hard."

Crawford laughed, shaking his head. "We gotta find you a hobby."

"Let me enlist—"

"That's not what I meant," Crawford interrupted. "You should be in school. What do you think about trying a summer term? Arlington High hasn't started theirs yet."

"Remedial classes," Bucky muttered.

"Well, you're out of practice."

"At school?"

"And at sitting still. You should be playing baseball or going to the prom, not selling pin-ups to soldiers. You're bored, and when people get bored, they get stupid."

Bucky felt his cheeks redden. "I'm not stupid."

"I didn't say that."

"I'm not going back." The single term of high school he'd tried after his father died had been a series of compounding humiliations—he'd already been in classes a grade lower than everyone else his age, and even then he couldn't keep up, so he'd stopped trying. Homework was easy to ignore with Camp Lehigh outside his bedroom window; the yells of the drill sergeants and the tandem clomp of heavy boots on dirt were more appealing than stumbling through *The Scarlet Letter*. He was still having trouble sleeping at the Crawfords', and would drift off in class, waking to a teacher barking his name and demanding he recite the year the Treaty of Paris was signed. Most afternoons he passed in detention, either for sleeping in class, or for telling that teacher she could shove the Treaty of Paris up her ass, or for starting fights with the upperclassmen who called him slow because he was still struggling with seventh-grade math. By the time summer came, he'd been fed up. Crawford was legally his guardian, so Bucky had forged the commander's signature on the drop-out paperwork before his humiliating report card showed up in their mailbox.

Crawford selected a palm-size bottle of gin off the desk and squinted at the label. His insistence that he didn't need reading glasses was getting harder to swallow. "You ever dip into these before you deliver them?" he asked.

"No. They'd notice if the seal on the caps was broken."

"Don't you know the trick?" Crawford glanced up at him. "Your dad and I figured out how to get around that when we were your age."

Bucky leaned forward, waiting. "Well, are you going to tell me?"

"Absolutely not." He set the bottle in the top drawer of his desk, then slid it shut. "Now, go get your cash. There's a bin for defense bonds in the front office."

Bucky stomped across the training field toward the Crawfords' house. Mrs. Crawford had insisted on keeping a room just for him, even though it meant all three of their girls had to share. But Bucky preferred to sleep in the barracks with the soldiers instead of a house with a family that wasn't his, no matter how many times they'd insisted they were as good as. Some days, their earnest kindness only reinforced how poorly he fit with them, like an extra book jammed on an already packed shelf.

He paused as a platoon of new recruits jogged past him with their empty rifles held over their heads, their sergeant behind them red-faced from blowing his whistle. More than half of them were struggling to keep up. A few had given up entirely and were walking instead of running, their limbs flopping like they were made of string. Bucky wanted to join the sergeant in shouting at them to pick up their pace. He could keep up with the greenies in any of their drills—he'd done it plenty of times. Some of the sergeants let him run the courses with their platoons, and sometimes he did it at night on his own, timing himself on his father's old stopwatch.

Being sixteen shouldn't have been a barrier. He didn't know many kids his own age, but he didn't feel sixteen. What he felt was trapped, a goldfish in a teacup. He could have grown to twice his current size if he'd only had a bigger pond to swim in. Some days, even the ocean felt like it would be too small for his restlessness.

The Crawfords' house was empty—the girls were at school, and Mrs. Crawford had gone into Arlington for the day to get her hair set, so there was no one to avoid when he stood on the toilet in the shared bathroom, jimmied the air vent out of place, and retrieved the roll of bills hidden there. It was thicker than he remembered, and, for a moment, he considered what Crawford would say if he didn't turn in the cash. Probably nothing. Which would be worse than any rebuke.

He trudged out of the house and back to the commander's office, plucking at the front of his sweaty T-shirt as he jogged up the steps. It came away from his skin with a wet suctioning noise.

In spite of the open windows and electric fans chugging away on every available surface, the tiny office was somehow even hotter than the outside. Crawford's secretary looked up from her typewriter and gave Bucky a warm smile, but he ignored her. He crossed to the defense-bonds collection bin, a color poster above it proclaiming YOU SERVE BY SAVING! accompanied by an illustration of Captain America, grinning, with one hand fisted on his hip, the other smashing through the middle of a Nazi flag. His pose looked more ballet class than boot camp, and the artist had painted his grin so wide it tested the limits of his face. His perfect white teeth looked too straight and too crowded. Bucky would have knocked all those teeth out if he could.

Bucky rattled the collection bin until Crawford looked up through his open office door. He held up the roll of bills, making sure Crawford could see as he dropped it into the bin. It landed with a resonant *thud*, the echo betraying its emptiness.

"Oh, James, that's so generous of you—" the secretary started, but stopped short when Bucky gave Captain America a middle-finger salute, before he about-faced and stomped out of the office.

CHAPTER 4
1941

There was no reason for Bucky to go into Arlington with the Friday grocery truck now that he had no clandestine purchases to make, but he went anyway. He had a handful of change he hadn't dropped at the feet of America's favorite airheaded Adonis, and there was a girl who worked weekends at Molokov's Drugstore and Soda Fountain who he wanted to see. Linda. Lydia? No, definitely Linda. Lydia was the senator's daughter from DC who he had met at a Christmas party the Crawfords had taken him to. Her mother had caught them necking in the pantry and dragged Lydia away by her pearls. The Crawfords made their exit quickly after, and Bucky had decided it was best not to ask the commander if he would violate his nondisclosure agreement with the US government and give Bucky her phone number.

The Friday-night rush was just beginning to die down when Bucky arrived at the soda shop. Crumpled paper napkins and empty malt glasses littered the tables, their insides coated with gelatinous rings of half-melted ice cream. He had hoped the approaching summer would keep the high school regulars away for the weekend, glued to their textbooks in preparation for finals, or distracted by plans for the senior formal, but a crew of rowdy juniors from Arlington High School were holding court at the end of the counter, blowing bubbles in their milkshakes and making jokes that they all found loudly hilarious. He knew a few of them from his miserable term at school, and saw the rest around town enough to know they weren't worth getting worked up over, but he would get worked up anyway. It didn't take much.

He spotted Linda behind the counter, pouring a root beer from the goose-neck tap. Her fingers left streaks in the condensation on the glass. She looked up at the sound of the bell over the door, and her face lit up when she saw him. She gave him a little wave, then crooked a finger toward the counter, eyebrows raised in invitation.

And she really was so pretty. Pretty enough to ignore the Arlington High crowd for.

Bucky waved back, then chose a stool as close to her but as far away from the high-schoolers as possible.

Linda delivered the root-beer float to a booth by the window, then slid down the counter toward Bucky under the pretext of wiping down the napkin holders. "Hey, Bucky."

"Hey, you." Her cheeks dimpled. Sometime between dropping off the float and returning to the counter, she had undone the top button of her blouse, and when she leaned around the soda fountain, reaching for an empty glass, he caught a sliver of her lacy brassiere. "Are you wearing lipstick, or are your lips always that pretty?"

She blushed happily. "Maybe a little. Mr. Molokov said I had to take it off when I'm behind the counter, but I couldn't blot it all without soap."

"What's the occasion?"

"The show choir performed today. I did my hair up for it too." She pumped a hand under her curls. "My mother helped me."

"It looks nice."

"She makes this pomade out of beeswax—she put so much in, I don't know how I'll wash it out. Here, feel it."

He caught one of her curls, twisting it around his finger as she leaned forward with her elbows on the counter. "What did the show choir sing?"

"'You're a Grand Old Flag.'"

"Very patriotic."

He could smell her pomade, along with the zing of spearmint on her breath. "Well, that was the idea."

He shifted his fingers to her earring, a small gold hoop with a pearl dangling from it like a bubble. "Do you have a lot of assemblies about America?"

"Now and then." When she reached over the counter for an abandoned spoon, her fingers brushed his—and, yes, they'd definitely get to second base in the alley behind Molokov's tonight. Maybe rounding third, if he swung right.

Then, from down the counter, someone called, "Hey, Barnes!"

Linda straightened so quickly he almost yanked out her earring. She quickly refastened her blouse before turning back down the counter to where the Arlington High crew was sprawled. "Johnny, do you want another Coke?" she called, trying to plant herself between him and Bucky as best she could from the other side of the counter.

Bucky considered pretending he hadn't heard. Let Linda sedate them with another round of malts and fries and maybe they'd forget he was here. If he let Johnny Ripley under his skin, he'd be itching for days. Johnny, who had loudly corrected Bucky's pronunciation of *antipodes* when he was called on to read aloud from *Great Expectations* in their shared English class, and told the musical director that Marsha Perry had missed her entrance in *Pirates of Penzance* because she and Bucky were making out behind the auditorium during rehearsal.

Johnny Ripley, who had asked the biology teacher if he could switch lab partners for dissections because he was afraid Bucky was bringing down his grade.

"Barnes!" Johnny called again. "I'm talking to you. Did you go deaf, or just get dumber?"

Bucky didn't quite turn to face him, just pivoted enough on the stool to acknowledge he'd heard. He kept his elbows on the counter, digging the nails of his left hand into his right palm. "Do you need something, Johnny?"

Johnny grinned, showing off crooked front teeth. He was leaning on the counter, one of the girls from their group sitting on the stool behind him with her chin on his shoulder. The rest were pretending not to listen but fooling no one. Their obnoxious laughter had gone too quiet too quickly.

Johnny stuck the end of a straw between his teeth. "How hard up is the Army that your old man had to come to the high school today to give a speech about joining up once we graduate?"

"He's not my father," Bucky said.

"Really?" Johnny twisted the straw, his grin pulling wider around it. "You both got the same wide-set eyes and big ears. Kinda reminds me of a caveman. You see the resemblance, don't you?" he asked the girl behind him, and she giggled.

"Hey," Linda said quietly, pressing the frosted side

of a Coke bottle against Johnny's bare arm. "Cut it out. You're being a bully."

Johnny dragged a foot along the underside of the counter, leaving skid marks on the mirrored surface. "The commander pulled me out of class," he said, leaning over the counter to address Linda but still making sure Bucky heard. "Me and a couple of the other top juniors—ten highest GPAs in the class. Him and this English man wanted to talk to us in particular after the assembly."

Why did knowing this was bait not make the trap any easier to sidestep? All his life, Bucky had been told to *just ignore them*, but that always felt too much like conceding. His father had lectured him about battles and wars, and how sometimes giving up a fight was the bravest thing a man could do, but Bucky had never believed it. He always had to trip every snare. Pick every scab. Touch his fingers to the burner, even though he knew it was hot.

He turned to face Johnny. "What did Crawford want with you?"

Johnny twirled the straw around the neck of the bottle. Pearly water droplets beaded along the ridges in the glass and trickled down, puddling on his napkin so that it stuck to the bottom of the bottle when he lifted it. "He was recruiting us for some special team the Army is putting together. Something more important than just running drills and digging holes. Apparently it requires a superior intellect. He said something about cream always rising to the top."

"You think soldiers are stupid?" Bucky challenged.

"Think you can spell *superior intellect*?" Johnny replied.

"Okay, Johnny, quit it." Linda swatted her rag between them. "I'll kick you out if you don't shut up."

The other high-schoolers weren't even pretending not to listen anymore. They were all piled up behind Johnny as he swiveled on his stool, staring at Bucky. One of the girls cupped a hand around her friend's ear and whispered something that made both of them laugh. Bucky felt the color rise in his cheeks.

"Your brother was there too," Johnny called to Linda.

Linda looked down at her hands, twisting a discarded napkin around them. "Tom doesn't want to enlist. He's going to go to college."

"Me too," Johnny said. "Tom and I are too valuable to waste as cannon fodder."

"And you think other men aren't?" Bucky was standing—he didn't remember standing up, but suddenly he was on his feet. His elbow hit one of the straw-dispensers and it tipped. Linda caught it just before it spilled.

"I'm just saying," Johnny said with a withering look at Bucky's clenched fist, "there's a certain caliber of man you don't waste in the trenches. Apparently your pop knows that too, since he recruited us for his special team."

"So what will you tell them when your ass gets drafted?" Bucky demanded. " 'Sergeant, there's been a mistake—I'm too special to be here'?"

"I don't have to register until I'm twenty-one," Johnny said. Then he muttered into the neck of his bottle something that sounded suspiciously like *idiot*.

"Johnny," Linda said loudly. "Why don't you all go sit at the booth? I'll bring your drinks over. Bucky—"

"He can leave if he wants." Johnny swiped his hand over the hatch marks of facial hair struggling on his upper lip. "Need me to help you make change, Barnes? It must be hard to count higher than ten with your shoes on."

Bucky punched him.

He didn't think it was a hard swing. It wouldn't have wobbled the punching bag at camp. But when his fist connected with Johnny's eye, Johnny went flying backward like he was on a yanked wire, glasses flying off and skittering under a nearby table. He bounced off one of the spinning fountain stools, sending three empty glasses flying off the countertop. Two of them broke against the linoleum, and the third sprayed the foamy remnants of a malt across Linda.

The soda shop went quiet. Bucky could hear the ice cream dripping off the mirror behind the counter. He flexed his hand, and his knuckles throbbed. His head was pounding, and he felt too hot. Everyone was staring at him.

Bucky couldn't think what to do, so he bent down and picked up Johnny's glasses. "Here." Johnny stared at Bucky, frozen in shock. Then he reached up and touched his split eyebrow. The cut was already flooded with blood. "Sorry."

"Sorry?!" Behind the counter, Linda spluttered. She swiped a hand over her face, trying to mop off the malt and instead smearing it like sunscreen. "What the hell, Bucky?"

Bucky wasn't sure he'd ever heard a girl curse. It was somehow more alarming than Johnny bleeding on the floor.

Bucky stuck his throbbing hand in his pocket, staring at his shoes. "I should go." It sounded much less casual than it had in his head, but he started for the door anyway. Then he realized he was still holding Johnny's glasses. He turned again, just as Mr. Molokov appeared behind the counter.

"What's going on out here?"

And he was caught. He dropped the glasses without thinking, and the lens, still intact, popped out of the frame, wobbled on its edges, then hit the floor, cracking neatly in two.

When Crawford arrived at the soda fountain, Bucky was waiting in the supply room, banished there by Molokov to wait for his parents or the police, whoever showed up first. A smart retort about the unlikelihood of his parents coming for him had bubbled up inside Bucky, but the adrenaline had all funneled out of him, leaving him as wrung out as wet laundry. He waited, wedged between vats of condiments, a greasy dish towel from the kitchen pressed to his bloody knuckles, until Crawford's silhouette darkened the doorway.

"Let's go" was all Crawford said before disappearing, leaving Bucky to stagger after him, his shoes sticking to the greasy floor.

Crawford was already in the driver's seat of his Cadillac, idling in the parking lot behind the soda fountain, when Bucky toppled into the passenger seat. The streetlights overhead had burned out, and in the darkness the windshield looked oiled. The moment Bucky shut the car door, Crawford cranked the gearshift. The headlights flooded the cab with yellow light, and Bucky's head snapped back as Crawford hit the gas, sending them hurtling onto the street.

Crawford didn't say anything the whole ride back to Camp Lehigh. He was still in his uniform, so Bucky wasn't surprised when the commander parked the Cadillac at a careless angle next to the company office building. There was a single light still on inside. As Crawford cut the engine, Bucky saw a figure step up to the window, the dark silhouette like a blot of ink on white paper. Whoever it was stayed there, watching as Crawford stomped up the steps and inside, Bucky trailing behind him.

In the staff kitchen, Crawford rooted around in the icebox until he found a package of frozen vegetables, which he tossed to Bucky. "Put that on your hand," he said brusquely. "If it's still hurting tomorrow, you should see the doctor."

"I didn't hurt myself," Bucky grumbled, though he still pressed his fist against the crystallized cardboard. "I'm not that stupid."

Crawford stopped in the kitchen door, massaging his forehead for a moment before rounding on Bucky again. "You're stupid enough that I got called out of an important meeting because I had to pay for damage done by my kid—"

"I'm not your kid," Bucky muttered, staring down at the thin cut along his thumb from Johnny Ripley's glasses.

"If I'm covering the cost of your misdemeanors, you're my kid."

Bucky rolled his eyes. "You're so dramatic."

"I'm not the one who couldn't keep my hands to myself over some barb about dropping out of high school." Crawford slammed his fist into the wall, and Bucky jumped. He'd seen Crawford mad before, but not like this. And not at him. "If it's that easy to get a rise out of you, you're going to get picked on by jerks like that Ripley kid your whole life because it's only fun to poke a dog that bites."

"He called me stupid!" Bucky retorted, jutting out his chin.

"Lots of people will," Crawford snapped. "Pick your battles."

The cardboard box was melting into pudding in his hand as the peas defrosted. "I pick my battles."

"Then you've picked too many," Crawford amended. "Put some back."

"You'd rather have some bully like that working for you than me?" Bucky demanded.

Crawford folded his arms. "Excuse me?"

"I heard you were at the high school today recruiting him for some special project."

"That's not—"

"So it's not that you don't want underage men to enlist, you just don't want *me* to enlist."

Crawford pinched the bridge of his nose. "Don't do this right now, Bucky."

"You know I'd be a great soldier," Bucky said. His voice was rising—partly with passion and partly with the excess adrenaline still sloughing off him, leaving behind a desperate embarrassment that made him sound like a kid. "The best you've got. I learn fast. I work hard. I want to fight. Half the boys who leave this camp would rather be anywhere else, but I'd be in France right now. First ship tomorrow, I'd be on it if you'd let me."

"Bucky—"

"If you weren't so scared of something happening to me or losing me like you lost my dad, maybe you'd realize that. Whatever you want those meatheads to do for you, I swear I can do it ten times better and faster and smarter. Just because I don't have a five-point-oh GPA and nobody's lining up to get me on their debate team—"

"Hey, cool it, okay? Take a breath." Crawford pulled the other chair out from under the small table and sat down across from Bucky. Their kneecaps knocked as Crawford scooted forward. Bucky looked away, trying to breathe but instead gulping at the air, like the room was filling up with water. He could feel his chest constricting, and he didn't want to cry, though the harder he tried not to, the hotter and sharper the tears starting to gather at the corners of his eyes grew. He didn't want to feel so brittle and coiled up, his skin so thin that every blade slipped between his ribs.

"Let me see your hand." Crawford pried the box of peas from Bucky's fist and tossed it into the sink. It missed and instead hit the counter with a wet *splat*. Bucky stared up at the ceiling as Crawford prodded a thumb in between each of his bruised knuckles.

Bucky sniffed, sucking a wad of snot into the back of his throat, then wiped his nose against his shoulder. "I'm okay."

"I know you are," Crawford replied, but didn't stop his examination. They both knew Crawford wasn't really checking anything, just giving Bucky enough time to pull himself together.

"Really." Bucky pried his hand from Crawford's and clamped it under his opposite arm. It was still throbbing so badly he was sure Crawford could see it, like a wound in a cartoon short, red and pulsing. The knee of his slacks was soaked from where the peas had melted into it. "Stop fussing."

Crawford raised his hands. "All right, I'll let Marcy take care of that tomorrow morning."

"Don't tell Mrs. Crawford about this. Please. Don't tell anyone."

Crawford looked down again at Bucky's bruised knuckles, then sighed. "You owe me."

"I know."

"I mean that literally. You're going to have to pay for that kid's glasses."

"Too bad I'm flat broke."

"Is that so?"

"It's been a tough week. I lost my job—"

Crawford snorted. "Your *job*."

"And I got harassed into giving my life savings to some idiot in blue pantyhose."

"*Harassed* is an exaggeration. So is *pantyhose,* come to think of it."

"What would you call them, then?"

Crawford considered this for a moment. "Aerodynamic combat . . ." He trailed off, waving a vague hand, so Bucky finished for him.

"Sausage casings?"

"All right, enough of that. The poor captain isn't even here to defend his fashion choices." Crawford stood, knees cracking. "Let's get you home." He turned, but stopped, and Bucky raised his head. A man was standing in the kitchen door, his knuckles poised over the frame like he had thought about knocking but had been eavesdropping instead. He had thinning hair and thick glasses, their lenses smudged with fingerprints. They made his eyes look double their actual size.

Bucky thought he heard Crawford swear under his breath, and he looked between them, trying to remember if he'd seen the stranger around camp before. "Sorry to keep you waiting." Crawford took Bucky by the arm and pulled him to his feet, dragging him toward the door. "I'm just about finished."

The man waved the apology away. "Think nothing of it. Is this the young man who required you to post his bail?" His accent was English, posh like Leslie

Howard's, and his voice so soft Bucky couldn't imagine he ever raised it—he couldn't possibly have the lung capacity.

"This would be the deviant in question." Crawford clapped a hand on Bucky's shoulder, using the grip to pivot so that he was between the two of them, like he was trying to block Bucky from the stranger's view. "Thankfully they never made it as far as the police station. Let me drive him home—"

Bucky rolled his eyes. "It's barely a mile, I can walk—"

"Let me drive you," Crawford said firmly. His grip tightened, and Bucky wondered if Crawford was keeping him from seeing the Englishman, or the other way around. And what exactly he was trying to hide.

The Englishman peered around Crawford, owlish eyes fixed on Bucky. His magnified irises were the same tortoiseshell color as the frames of his glasses. "Actually, Commander, I finished reviewing the transcripts while you were away, and I'm not sure we've found what we're looking for."

"Can we discuss this—" Crawford started, but the man interrupted him, addressing Bucky.

"Mr. Barnes, was it?"

"James Barnes," he confirmed, then added, just because he knew it would annoy Crawford, "sir."

"I'm sure you're quite exhausted from a night of crime, but might I have a quick word?" The man set his hat on the table, then gestured to the chair Bucky had just vacated. "I'm afraid it can't wait—I'm on a plane back to London tonight."

"Sure, I got a minute." Bucky started to sit, but Crawford hooked him by the collar, dragging him back toward the door.

"Oh, no. Absolutely not."

The Englishman unbuttoned his suit jacket as he sat, legs crossed. "It's just a chat, Commander."

"I said no." Crawford planted himself at the end of the table, pressing his hands flat against it as he stared down the Englishman. "Not him."

The Englishman folded his hands around his cocked knee, hardly glancing at Crawford. "He fits the profile perfectly."

"What profile?" Bucky asked.

Crawford ignored him. "Bucky's not part of this."

"Part of what?"

"He's off the table."

"What table?"

Without looking, Crawford reached over and clamped a hand over Bucky's mouth. Bucky considered biting his fingers but resisted. "I'm telling you, he's not a good match. He almost got arrested tonight. He *should* have been arrested."

The Englishman blinked. "Precisely."

Bucky ducked out from under Crawford's arm,

collapsing into the chair across from the Englishman. "I want to hear what he has to say."

The Englishman inclined his head. "Commander?"

Crawford glowered at them both, arms crossed.

The Englishman smiled. "Brilliant." He removed his glasses and polished them on the end of his tie before replacing them on his nose and giving Bucky a careful up and down. Bucky sat up a little straighter, still unsure what suit he was being measured for but certain he liked the cut of it, if only because of how determinedly against it Crawford seemed to be.

"Mr. Barnes," the Englishman said. "My name is Mr. Yesterday."

"No it's not," Bucky said.

Mr. Yesterday's mouth quirked. "Well spotted." He reached into the inside pocket of his jacket and withdrew a small notebook with a pencil nub hanging from the binding by a red ribbon. He licked his finger, then flipped to a clean page. "A few questions, before we chat. Have you graduated from high school?"

Bucky felt his shoulders sink. Strike one. "Not yet, sir."

"So you're currently enrolled?" When Bucky didn't answer, Mr. Yesterday prompted, "Are you in school?"

"Depends what you mean by school," Bucky replied. Behind Mr. Yesterday, Crawford pressed a fist to his forehead.

"Are you currently attending a secondary school in pursuit of your high-school diploma?" The tip of Mr. Yesterday's pencil hovered over the page of his notebook. "It's a yes-or-no question."

"Not necessarily."

"There were extenuating circumstances," Crawford cut in, his gaze flicking to Bucky's bloody knuckles, as though concerned he might haul off and punch this posh Englishman like he was a bonehead in a soda fountain. "His parents both passed within a few years and his sister went off to boarding school."

Mr. Yesterday ignored Crawford. "It's a yes or no, Mr. Barnes."

"No." Under the table, Bucky pushed his heel into the top of his opposite foot. "I'm not in school."

Mr. Yesterday made a small note in the book. "So your sister is attending school, but you had to stay here?"

"I didn't have to," Bucky said. He was gripping the sides of his chair like it was the jump seat of a plane. "But there wasn't money for both of us to go, and Becks— Rebecca—my sister. She was always the better student."

"You could have both attended public school in Arlington, could you not?"

"But she got a scholarship, if we could cover the room and board." He hated that he was arguing. He hated having to defend his choice to drop out of school yet again—he'd already broken someone's glasses once that night over this same question. He was tired of being treated like he was too young to make his own decisions. And if this Englishman had met his sister, he'd understand it was clear which of them got the brains. Rebecca was a walking encyclopedia, carrying books around the way most girls carried purses. "I already knew what I wanted. It doesn't really require a fancy school."

"And what is it you want, Mr. Barnes?" Mr. Yesterday asked.

"I want to be a soldier," Bucky said. "Growing up here seemed like the best place for that."

He waited for Mr. Yesterday to stand up, put his hat back on, and thank Bucky for his time but explain that he was looking for someone who could at least do eighth-grade math. But instead, he made another tick. "Do you speak any other languages?"

Bucky tried not to stare at the notebook. The man hadn't written enough for it to be a word—was he keeping a tally of something? And had Bucky's lack of schooling been the *right* answer, or simply not a disqualifying factor? "Russian and German," he said.

Mr. Yesterday looked up from his book in surprise. Crawford, who had been mashing his face into the side of the refrigerator, looked up too. "Where the hell did you learn German?" Crawford asked incredulously.

"I have the same question," Mr. Yesterday said, waving his pencil in Crawford's direction. "But in regard to the Russian."

"My mom's family was Russian," Bucky said. "My grandma emigrated from there to live with us. My mom taught Becks and me both Russian when we were kids so we could talk to her." He hadn't spoken it in years, and always struggled to write it, but this didn't seem the time to mention either of those things. "And one of the delivery-truck drivers is Swiss," he said to Crawford. "He's been teaching me German."

"Any French?" Mr. Yesterday asked.

"I'm sure I could learn—and I know, it's a yes-or-no question," he added.

Mr. Yesterday chuckled, making another tick in his book. "Do you have a job with this delivery driver who is teaching you German?"

"Bucky has been creating his own jobs around the base," Crawford said. "Selling pin-ups to the soldiers."

Mr. Yesterday's pencil snapped against the paper.

"Well, not *just* pin-ups," Bucky said quickly, realizing as soon as he spoke it was a mistake. None of the other vices he had been helping indulge would make him look any more aboveboard. He glared at Crawford—why had he even brought it up? "Booze and candy and aftershave and cond—things they can't get on the base."

"Things they aren't *allowed* to have on the base." Crawford pulled a handkerchief out of his jacket and wiped his face.

"It boosts their morale," Bucky argued. He could spin this as righteous if he needed to. He could say five nice things about Captain America if absolutely pressed.

Mr. Yesterday stared down at his notebook, like he wasn't sure what to write or even how to write it now that he'd snapped his pencil. Bucky's heart sank. Whatever it was he was being profiled for, he suspected that smuggling contraband onto a US Army base would be a disqualifying factor.

Crawford seemed to agree, for he was already leaning forward again, reaching for Bucky's arm to pull him out of the chair and fling him out into the night, away from this strange Englishman and whatever lock he was searching out a key for. But Mr. Yesterday held up a hand to stop him. Crawford fisted his hand around the back of Bucky's chair.

"How did you get these items into camp and to the soldiers without detection by commanding officers?" Mr. Yesterday asked.

"I . . ." Bucky glanced at Crawford. If he lied, the commander would correct the record. Then he'd be a smuggler *and* a liar. "I had a system worked out in the camp library." He hoped he could leave it there, but

Mr. Yesterday raised a bushy eyebrow. It barely cleared the wide frames of his glasses. Bucky sighed. "All the boys had a book, and they'd leave me cash on a page that corresponded with what they wanted me to get for them. Then they'd put the books on the shelving cart so I knew to collect them, and I'd put them back on the shelf when I got them what they wanted."

Mr. Yesterday cocked his head. "Interesting."

Is it? Bucky thought desperately. *Or is it treason?* Maybe not full-on treason, but light treason. Aiding and abetting, at the least. Could it be considered military sabotage? Should he mention the motorcycle? He was planning on driving it illegally, but that might shed necessary light on the clandestine nature of his operation.

"How long did you run this business?" Mr. Yesterday asked.

Bucky could practically feel the heat of Crawford's gaze on the back of his head. Any minute now, his hair would catch fire. "A year next month."

"Good god, Buck," Crawford muttered under his breath, and Bucky realized Crawford thought this enterprise had been in its infancy when it was busted.

"A whole year you evaded detection?" Mr. Yesterday asked. "Right under your commander's nose?"

Bucky glanced at Crawford. "Yeah, and it's a pretty big nose."

Mr. Yesterday flipped backward through the notebook, then strung the ribbon down the center and closed it around the pencil. "Nicholas, I'm disappointed in you."

Crawford's jaw flexed. "I don't think it was a year, it probably started—"

"Not about that," Mr. Yesterday interrupted. "I'm sure there are far worse violations of United States military code of conduct happening within your hallowed halls. No, I'm disappointed that you've been hiding this exceptional young man from me. He's exactly what we're looking for."

Crawford mashed his fingers against his eyelids. He couldn't seem to decide if he wanted to fight or concede as he slumped backward against the counter. "I know," he said.

"Frankly, he's perfect," Mr. Yesterday said.

Crawford wiped his forehead again. "I know."

Bucky looked between them. He pressed his elbow into his knee to stop the bouncing from shaking the whole table. "What are you talking about? What am I perfect for?"

Mr. Yesterday tucked the notebook back into his pocket. "Mr. Barnes. I'm with the British Special Operations Executive. Are you aware of the nature of our work?"

Stay calm, Bucky reminded himself, though his heart was hammering with excitement. "That's spies and stuff, isn't it?"

"In so many words," Mr. Yesterday replied. "Our purpose is to conduct espionage, sabotage, and reconnaissance missions in Europe, as well as assist resistance groups within occupied territories. Based on our intelligence, we estimate that this war will not be brief. We will likely be feeling the repercussions for decades to come. And in anticipation of that, we have begun preparing the next generation of special agents. The ones who will finish the war we started. Therefore, the SOE is training young operatives to infiltrate universities and schools in occupied territories, live and study under an assumed identity while collecting and passing political information back to us. We have already placed two agents through this program, ages eighteen and twenty, respectively, though they both began training with us when they were sixteen. How old are you, Mr. Barnes?"

"Sixteen," Crawford interjected. "He's sixteen."

"Seventeen in a month," Bucky argued. Crawford glared at him.

"We have been working with the US State Department here in hopes of adding several Americans to our program," Mr. Yesterday continued. "Since the United States has yet to enter the war, American students will attract less attention in German-controlled cities than British ones. Your Commander Crawford has been aiding us in our search."

Bucky twisted around in his chair toward Crawford. "You're a spy?" he demanded.

"No. Not exactly." Crawford tugged on his collar. Had he been wearing a tie, Bucky was sure he would have loosened it. "I have been . . . on the State Department's payroll. When we have good men with real promise come up the ranks, I point it out—that's all. For this job, they wanted to recruit close to DC but not in the city itself, which is how it landed on my desk."

"You never told me!"

"That would rather defeat the point," Mr. Yesterday said lightly.

Bucky gaped at Crawford. "You've been a spy all this time—"

"I'm not a spy," Crawford said. "I'm heading up the American arm of a covert operation that involves the United States military."

"Sounds like a spy," Bucky muttered.

"May we proceed?" Mr. Yesterday interrupted. "We still have a lot to get through, and I don't have time for you to get bogged down in technicalities."

Bucky mouthed *Spy!* to Crawford, then gave him a thumbs-up before turning back to Mr. Yesterday. Crawford rolled his eyes.

"Mr. Barnes," Mr. Yesterday said. "If this is a project you'd be interested in being part of—"

"Yes," Bucky said.

Mr. Yesterday held up one finger. "Let me finish."

"Sorry." Bucky sat on his hands. "But yes. I'll still probably say yes."

"You'd be sent to London," Mr. Yesterday continued. "Then taken to a secure facility where you'd undergo six months to a year of training in espionage techniques, languages, et cetera. Perhaps eighteen months in your case—we'd need to enroll you in some secondary-school classes to catch you up academically. And see where your languages are. At the end of that period, you'll be evaluated for fieldwork."

Bucky, who had been nodding through the entire speech, blurted, "Great. Yes. Absolutely."

"I'm still not finished." Mr. Yesterday brushed a melted pea that had escaped the packaging off the table with his thumb. "Before we proceed, I need to know that you understand the risk associated with this work. Not all applicants are given field placements. Some quit. Some are deemed unsuitable after a few months. Some make it all the way to the end of their training before they're dismissed."

Bucky clenched his teeth to stop himself from cutting Mr. Yesterday off. He'd do it—he'd do anything. He'd give them years of his life. He'd speak perfect German. He'd speak German backward. He'd swim the ocean all the way to London.

"And if you are placed in the field, the work is dangerous, to put it mildly." Mr. Yesterday took his glasses off and polished them again, this time on the cuff of his coat. "I tell you this because I know if I don't, your commander will: most of our undercover agents in France don't last more than two weeks in the field. Wireless work is very different than what you'd be doing, but once you're in, there is no extraction. If you reveal yourself or are captured, the British government will deny any association with you. We will not be able to send you aid. Neither will the United States. You'll be trained to endure interrogation. We expect that is a skill you will have to use. You'll be expected to die for the cause. You cannot enter this job with anything less than a perfect understanding of that fact. There are no exceptions. Once you enter the field, you will be alone."

Bucky swallowed. His initial enthusiasm began to deflate like a punctured balloon. "I understand."

"You don't," Mr. Yesterday replied curtly. "You can't. No one truly can until you have carried a cyanide pill in your pocket and had to consider taking it. I say this not to frighten you away from the work, but to be sure you grasp the gravity of your choice. It's not like it is in films and adventure novels. And it's not like whatever war games you played in your backyard as a child that ended when you were called in for supper."

"I'm not scared," Bucky said.

"We'll fix that." Mr. Yesterday picked up his hat and unhooked his coat from the back of the chair. "I suggest you take some time to think it over. Perhaps discuss things with the commander here. It is not a small decision, nor one that should be made lightly, or on a whim." He slid a card from a silver case and passed it across the table to Bucky. "This is my office number, should you ever need it. Ask the secretary for the weather on the Isle of Wight and you'll be put through to me."

There was no name or address on the card, just a too-many-digits phone number in embossed navy script.

"Any questions, Mr. Barnes?" he asked.

Bucky looked up from the card. "Do I get a gun?"

"Okay, that's enough for one night," Crawford interrupted. "I think your car's here, sir."

Mr. Yesterday stood, re-buttoning his suit jacket. "Very good. Always a pleasure, Commander." He offered a hand to Crawford, then said, "I don't think it will be necessary for you to follow up with those boys from the high school."

Crawford frowned. "Are you sure?"

"Quite. I believe we've found our man." Mr. Yesterday

turned to Bucky. "Think about my offer, Mr. Barnes."

"Yeah, I definitely will." In spite of the somber warning, he knew he wouldn't have to. He'd have signed anything Mr. Yesterday gave him right then and there. His whole body was buzzing, an idling motor inside him suddenly kicking into gear.

As soon as Mr. Yesterday was gone, Crawford rounded on Bucky. "Absolutely not."

"Absolutely yes!" Bucky leaped to his feet, holding the card over his head. "This is exactly what I want to do."

"So you can wait a few more years before you do it."

"It'll be too late by then."

Crawford folded his arms. "Too late for what?"

"To join this mission!"

"It's not a mission," Crawford corrected him. "It's a dangerous, untested, undercover training program."

Bucky flicked the card between his fingers like a magician. "What would you have done, when you were my age, if someone gave you a chance like this? A real chance to do something important?" He knew this was his only ace, and he played it cautiously. "My dad told me stories about what you were like when you were young. He said you helped him lie on his enlistment forms, so you could join up together before you were old enough."

Crawford looked unmoved. "That doesn't mean he would have wanted you to do the same."

"But he would have understood!" Bucky said. "And I think you do too. You know how crazy it makes me to sit here, doing nothing."

"Wait until you're eighteen," Crawford replied. "Then at least I'm not legally responsible for your impulsive decisions."

"So you'd rather I wait around until I'm drafted to be used as cannon fodder?"

"There's no draft—"

"There will be," Bucky said. "The US is gonna get involved for the long haul, and you must think it will if you're helping find recruits for this long-term project. You can't hide me from this forever. It's not *Everybody do your part except my best friend's kid who could be an amazing undercover agent in training but I'm too scared to let him out of my sight.* You know I'd be great at this work. Keeping me from doing it would be, frankly, unpatriotic."

They faced each other. Crawford was still a few inches taller than Bucky, but the gap between them had been closing over the past year. If his father were still alive, Bucky would have been taller than him. His father, who, out of the pair of them, had always been the one to run headfirst into trouble while Crawford covered his flank, grumbling all the way but never faltering. His father, who had always been the first to step up and volunteer, to stick his neck out for a stranger and stand up for what was right. They both remembered him that way, and

Bucky was sure the only reason Crawford was holding him back was because he saw that same flinty gleam in Bucky's eye.

Crawford rubbed a hand over his eyes and blew out a heavy sigh. "You," he said, shaking his head, "are a real pain in the neck, you know that?"

Bucky saluted. "Learned it from the best."

"This isn't me saying yes."

"You aren't saying no either."

"This is a *We will make this an ongoing conversation. Don't argue.*" He held up a hand. "That's the best you're going to get from me right now. You've put me through enough tonight." He gave Bucky a playful shove, cuffing him around the neck and ruffling his hair. "Your dad would have been proud of you."

Bucky shoved him in return, dealing Crawford a slowed-down punch that the commander caught with his palm. "Guess you'll just have to be proud of me instead."

CHAPTER 5
1954

The Hotel Metropole's bar is paneled in dark wood, with polka-dotted floors and burnished copper ceiling panels, a relic of old-world decadence miraculously preserved amid the gray concrete and clean lines of the Soviet buildings that surround it. Windows with gold script line the booths, giving the patrons a view across the Aspazijas Bulvāris. The glass is spotted with rain from a morning storm, each drop illuminated by the headlights of passing taxis and streetcars. The sparse bulbs are shaded in amber, turning the light warm-toned and syrupy, like the bar sits in the belly of a whiskey bottle.

V smooths the lapels of his suit, feeling more

conspicuous than he knows he looks. He can't remember when he last wore something other than bulky combat gear or the breathable athletic clothes for training with Rostova. With his hair combed back and the leather gloves to hide his metal hand, he feels as slick as an otter, oiled by the sea. Surely someone will look around and realize he isn't native to this landscape. When was the last time he was at a bar? When was the last time he was anywhere that wasn't soundproof and underground, cold leaking through the walls and drains in the floor of every room?

The flight here had been equally strange. Rostova had piloted a decommissioned bomber left over from the war, laughing every time she noticed him clutching the edges of his seat, his teeth clenched.

"I've never flown before," he had shouted to her, his voice barely audible over the engines.

She had smiled, eyes on the windshield. "Yes, you have."

"I don't remember it."

"Those are two different things, aren't they?"

The earpiece he's wearing now crackles suddenly, and he feels the buzz of static in his eardrum like a fly caught there. "Don't spill anything on that suit." Rostova's voice is tinny. "It cost more than your arm."

He resists the urge to glance around, as if he could see

her from where he's standing in the doorway of the hotel bar, though he knows she's where he left her: perched behind a sniper's rifle on the roof of the apartments across the street, watching him through the scope. *She's here to protect you*, he reminds himself, but the back of his neck itches.

I am not compromised. He almost says it aloud. He's been wanting to say it to her since before they left. He wants to look her in the eye and know she believes it. If they thought he was compromised, they wouldn't have sent him all the way here. Karpov would have shot him back in the bunker, or let the nurse slip a pillow over his head or mix arsenic into his IV drip. There are easier ways to kill him than bringing him all the way to Riga just for Rostova to shoot him in the head. They don't need a public scene to spin a false narrative around. There's no one to miss him. And even if there were, people disappear every day.

"Stop doing that," Rostova says in his ear, and he realizes he is unconsciously fastening and unfastening his suit jacket. The earpiece crackles again. "Try to look like a human being and not a robot that doesn't know what tailoring is."

He feels like an exposed nerve, too sensitive to a world this unfamiliar and new—the sound of ice clattering in glasses behind the bar, the soft laugh of a woman a few tables away, the smell of the floor polish, and the glow of passing headlights through the black windows. The horns on the street. The song over the radio. The world is so much more alive and raw and exuberant than he had been prepared for.

"Can I help you?" someone asks in Russian, and he looks up. A maître d' in black and white has paused before him, an empty tray clamped under one arm. When V doesn't answer, he prompts, "Do you have a reservation?"

"Fedorov," he says. "My name is Alexander Fedorov. I'm meeting a hotel guest for a drink."

"Very good, sir." The maître d' checks a list of names at the host's stand, then says, "Feel free to sit at the bar until your party arrives."

As the maître d' disappears into the kitchen, V tugs on his gloves like they might fall off, then smooths the front of his suit again before heading for the bar. He hasn't done undercover work like this before, and his existence as a creature of the darkness feels written all over him. The way he stands. Breathes. Walks. It's all community theater. What is he supposed to do with his hands? Should he put them in his pockets? Should he look people in the eye? Don't they all smell it on him, the blood of the men he's killed?

But no one gives him a second glance as he pulls up

one of the tall stools and perches upon it. He glances around. The tables are crowded, but the bar itself is almost empty. There's a couple at one end sitting with their heads pressed together, the man palming the woman's thigh under her dress, and a second man drinking alone, his face red from too much vodka.

V forces himself to take a deep breath. *This will be easy. Drops are easy.* The other agent—whatever MI5 suit he is meeting—likely hasn't had any combat training, let alone training that could compare with V's. He won't even be armed. *Drops aren't dangerous.* Drops are newspapers, a brown paper sack tossed into a park rubbish bin, the difference between a FOR RENT and a FOR SALE sign in an apartment window.

So why does it feel as though a piano wire is slowly cinching around his throat? The room is too hot. He's sweating—how is this suit heavier than any of the tactical gear he wears?

A man takes the stool two spots down from V and places his hat on the bar. V glances up, like he's looking for the bartender. The hat is MI5's signal that the agent wasn't followed. If he had hooked it on the back of his chair, it would mean he'd been tailed and V would have had to turn and leave without collecting what he came for.

His earpiece fuzzes again. "All clear from where I'm

sitting," Rostova says, then adds, "Take your time."

He feels a sudden surge of gratitude she's here with him. Rostova can be mean. She can be hard on him. She can be mocking and cold. But she's also his teacher and his friend. She's iced his bruised ribs and taught him the Russian songs he had forgotten from his youth. She smuggled him pirozhki from her trips to Moscow when he was in lockdown, though they didn't fit into his scientifically calculated diet. She's been his only companion, and even if she does nothing but sit on the roof and watch, he is glad she is here. She won't betray him. Not for Karpov. Not for anyone.

"Stop touching your suit," Rostova snaps, effectively smothering any warm feelings toward her.

He folds his hands across the bar, his gloves squeaking as the leather pulls against itself. The man beside him waves over the bartender. He hasn't looked at V. If this goes well, he won't.

The bartender delivers a wine list to the MI5 agent, then turns to V. "For you, sir?"

"A gimlet on the rocks," he orders in Russian. His signal in return to the hat on the bar between them—he has not been followed. Not compromised. Beside him, the MI5 agent fiddles with the creased corner of the wine list.

"Vodka or gin?" the bartender asks.

V pauses. He hadn't anticipated a follow-up. If this is a code, he doesn't know what it means.

Dear Ginny with a hint of lime.

The words write themselves across his mind, inexplicable but clear. The handwriting so distinct, even in his mind's eye, that he can trace the blocky capital letters in English. Cold washes suddenly over him, like a torrent of snow cascading off a roof and onto his head.

He blinks.

"Sir?" the bartender prompts. When V still doesn't answer, he says again, "Vodka or gin?"

"For god's sake," he hears Rostova say in his ear. "It's not a trick, just pick one. You don't have to love it."

"Gin," V blurts.

"Very good, sir." As he turns, V presses his fingers to his eyelids, not sure if he wants to erase the words or call them back to him. The letters and their meaning are already slipping away like a handful of sand.

Focus.

V opens his eyes. The MI5 agent is holding up the wine list as he asks a question about the reds, and the bartender leans around the taps to hear him. The agent's eyes never leave the bartender's as he flicks a coaster down the bar with his pinky. V glances at it. The side facing up is printed with the hotel's coat of arms. It hadn't been there before, but he hadn't seen the man pull it out of a pocket or slide it from his sleeve. He must have taken advantage of V's momentary distraction and slipped it out.

"Gin on the rocks."

V looks up. The bartender has returned, chilled rocks glass in hand. V snags the coaster and slides it under the glass before he can set it down. "Thank you," he says, and hands the bartender the money Rostova had given him before they left the bomber. V raises the glass to his lips, the sharp smell of lime hitting him behind the eyes.

And that's it. It's done.

The MI5 agent returns the wine list to the bartender as he picks up his hat. "Nothing catching my eye—thank you." He heaves himself off his stool. Sweat glistens around the collar of his shirt.

V takes a sip of his drink. It's over. He can relax. Try to twitch off the creeping cold.

"Easy peasy," Rostova says in his ear. "Finish your drink and let's get out of here. Next time, I get to be the one drinking on the KGB's dime and you can freeze your ass off in the rain."

Next to him, the MI5 agent catches his shoe on the leg of V's barstool. Without thinking, V glances up, at the same moment the man looks at him. His apology dies on his lips as their eyes meet.

The man pales, color leaching from his face like someone pulled the stopper from a drain. His eyes, still locked with V's, are wide and flooded with panic.

"Oh god," the agent whispers.

"Get out of there," Rostova says suddenly, the teasing shucked from her tone. In the background, V hears the click of the bolt-action on her rifle. "The drop's done."

"It's you," the man says.

"I said, get out of there," Rostova repeats. He can imagine her on her belly, eye to her scope, lining up a shot with the barrel of her gun level with . . . with the agent. Not him.

V doesn't move. "Pardon me?"

The agent gapes at him. Half his front tooth is missing, and he looks wild, like an animal pulling back its lips to snarl. "Oh god. Oh god, all the ghosts in hell back to haunt me."

"I'm sorry, do we—" V starts, but the man lunges across the bar and yanks the coaster out from under V's drink. The glass tips, cracking against the bar top before rolling in a tight circle, dribbling cloudy gin over the dark wood.

"Abort," Rostova says. "Vronsky, get out of there. Now. Forget the drop."

"Wait—" He reaches for the agent's arm, but the agent staggers backward, smashing into a table and upsetting a tureen of gravy. The two men sitting there leap to their feet and begin scolding him loudly. The man pushes himself up, stammering apologies in English before he seems to catch himself and switches to Russian. He lurches for the door, leaving a trail of greasy footprints.

"Wait!" V calls again, but the man is already darting from the restaurant and into the lobby, the stained tails of his jacket sticking to his trousers.

"I'm not kidding, V," Rostova growls in his ear. "It's off."

The bartender reaches to mop up the spilled drink, rescuing several now-sopping napkins and apologizing, offering another drink, this one on the house. But V isn't listening—he stares through the door into the lobby, following the MI5 agent's progress as he stumbles through the crowd. The agent's foot snags a suitcase and he almost falls, but a bellhop pushing a luggage trolley catches him. He shoves the bellhop off him, then turns almost a full circle before he reorients himself and starts jogging for the door out onto the street.

"Don't follow him," Rostova says in V's ear. "I'm going. Sit down and take a new drink. I'll be back before you finish it."

And he should. He knows he should. He is not compromised and he knows what he should do.

Comply, he thinks.

But the look in the man's eyes when he saw V was . . . not fear—he's used to fear. Fear and panic and hopelessness are all familiar dance partners; he knows the way their hands feel in his. But this man had looked at V with fear that had nothing to do with his bionic arm or tactical gear or the stories that had preceded him.

This man recognized him. He had looked V in the face and *he knew him*. Not as the whisper of a faceless legend or a classified project. He hadn't recognized the Winter Soldier.

The man had known *him*.

No one has ever looked at him that way before.

It shouldn't be possible. No one should know him, particularly not a sallow Englishman completing a dead drop in Riga. Maybe MI5 has photos of him—but *how*? Is there a double agent among Karpov's team? *Impossible.* V doesn't look like everyone else here—he must have stood out, some unconscious tell marking him as a pretender— *but Rostova would have noticed.*

The agent had known V, before. Someone he used to be before . . .

Before what?

"Apologies, sir." The bartender sets a new glass on the bar. "No charge."

V looks at the bartender, who smiles, apologetic, like V is just another customer. In this room, in this suit, V is another face in the crowd.

But the MI5 agent had known him anyway.

And V has to know why.

The bartender nods toward the lobby, just as the agent throws himself through the hotel doors and out onto the street. "Must be some kind of lunatic."

"Must be," V replies, then reaches for his earpiece.

"Don't—" he hears Rostova say, her voice cutting off abruptly as he crushes the tiny bug between his metal fingers, then drops it in the glass of gin. "Have a good night," he says to the bartender, and follows the agent across the lobby.

Outside the hotel, a gust of cold air hits V in the face, and he feels suddenly more awake than he had in the bar. Water fans from the gutter as a car pulls away from the curb, and he feels the drops against his face. He pulls off his gloves—too tight and too clumsy—and shoves them into his pocket as he searches the pavement for the man. A show has just ended at a nearby movie house, and the crowd is jammed up on the sidewalk, slow and loud.

V spots the agent standing on the curb, desperately trying to flag down one of the taxis pulling into the hotel drive, but they all speed past. V starts toward him, shouldering through the crowd as fast as he can without attracting attention.

The agent seems to sense him, and turns, his face white in the glow of passing headlights. He sees V coming toward him and abandons the cabstand, taking off down the street at a run. V can see the coaster mashed in his fist and pressed to his heart, like a letter from a lover.

A footrace will be a stalemate. V is probably faster, but he doesn't know this city, and he remembers from the agent's file that he's been stationed in Riga for the past two years. He'll know alleys to duck down and pubs he can hide in, the places where the right phrase spoken casually to a shopkeeper will open a secret room where he can hunker down until the unnamed danger passes. He'll have somewhere to go and someone to shelter him. If V chases him, there will be a scene. One of them will be stopped. Probably him. There may be police involved. It will be so easy for the agent to slip away.

V glances over at the apartments across the street, resisting the urge to look up, like he'd be able to spot Rostova on the roof. There's a motorbike idling at the curb, the courier it belongs to on the doorstep, leaning hard on the bell as he waits to be buzzed in. V has never ridden a motorbike before. He's never driven anything, not that he can remember. But he also can't remember who wrote the words *Dear Ginny with a hint of lime* and tucked them so deep into his memory even he hadn't known they were there.

He darts across the street, ignoring the car horns that blare in protest, and swings himself onto the bike.

He flips the kickstand with his heel—a gesture so automatic he almost doesn't realize he does it.

"Hey!" he hears the courier yell, just as V depresses the gas and the motorbike plows forward into traffic. Several cars have to slam their brakes to avoid hitting it, and he hears tires screech on the wet pavement. The traffic is too thick to weave through, even on the nimble bike, so V turns sharply and pulls into the empty tracks of the streetcar running the opposite direction and flies down the road in pursuit of the MI5 agent.

The motorbike has no learning curve. Somehow he knows where to reach for the clutch without thinking. He can tell the difference between the gauges, and knows what they all mean—speed, fuel, oil, water. He spots the British agent on the sidewalk, walking fast, looking over his shoulder to see if V is following him on foot. The lenses of his spectacles are spattered with rain, and he wipes them fruitlessly, the sleeve of his coat only further smearing the existing smudges. He reaches into his pocket with the hand not clutching the coaster—for a weapon? A cyanide pill? A tracking device?

A horn blares, and V looks up. A streetcar hurtles toward him, its headlight a smoky column through the damp air. He swerves, pulling into oncoming traffic without thinking. He almost hits the nose of a taxi and leans away just in time. The spokes of his front wheel chatter as he pulls up along the streetcar, hugging its side as it passes going in the opposite direction. He's so close that one of the bike's mirrors clips the side, snapping off and shattering under the streetcar's wheels.

V scans the sidewalk and sees the agent turn down a pedestrian thoroughfare leading to an old stone arch that marks the entrance to the old town. There's a brief pause in the traffic, and V plows over three lanes and onto the sidewalk after him, ignoring the shoppers and diners who leap out of his way, screaming and swearing at him. The pavement changes to rough cobbles under V's tires, and his teeth clack as he follows the man up the hill. When the engine stammers, he shifts gears without thinking, kicking up a spray of stagnant water from between the stones.

The streets of the old town are too narrow for cars, and almost empty of pedestrians. The agent is running at full speed down the middle of the cobbled lane, arms slapping his sides. He takes every turn possible, leading V down backstreets that seem to be growing increasingly narrow. V leans into the handlebars, cursing every tight corner that forces him to slow or else tip. One alley is so skinny his handlebars are almost wedged between the building walls. Raindrops pelt his face, cold and stinging as flicked coins.

A flock of chickens scatter from the road ahead of him as he takes a turn too hard and clips a stack of chairs under a café awning to protect them from the weather. He overcorrects, and his back tire skids on the wet stones. The tire screeches, and his stomach drops. His instinct is to bear down on the brakes, but instead, without understanding why or what part of him knows this, he lets go. The back tire wobbles, then straightens, and the bike jerks upright again. The front wheel leaves the ground for a moment before V leans forward and slams it into the pavement.

Ahead of him, the agent takes a sudden left, disappearing from sight. V follows, only to smash into the back of a taxi sitting in a bottleneck at another entrance to the old town. The front wheel of the bike crumples against the bumper, and the back tire pulls up, flipping the bike sideways. V jumps, sliding across the cab's trunk and into the back window hard enough that the glass cracks. He grabs a handful of the roof, his bionic hand crumpling it like it's cloth, to keep himself from sliding off the back and into passing traffic. The soles of his dress shoes are tractionless against the slick metal.

V clambers to his feet, the car's roof bowing under his weight. The agent is now almost a full block ahead of him. The man doesn't look back as he turns at an old garrison tower and enters a sprawling park, the dark, lampless paths swallowing him.

The car shudders beneath V as the driver climbs out, slamming the door and shouting incoherently as he points to the cracked window and the dent in his trunk. V ignores him. The motorbike is pinned under the car, the handlebars tangled with the bumper and the engine sputtering. His neck throbs, and he cracks it with a wince.

The driver grabs him by the ankle, trying to get his attention, and V kicks him. The man stumbles backward, clutching his bloody nose. All around them, cars swerve to avoid the shattered pieces of the motorbike on the ground. The drivers lay on their horns. V takes one long stride onto the hood of the car, then back to the pavement, dodging in between the stopped traffic. Another man opens his door so abruptly that V runs into it, grabbing it with his metal arm and ripping it off its hinges, but he doesn't stop. Ahead of him, the garrison tower looms.

Beyond the tower, the park lawns slope down to the water, dewy blades shimmering in the moonlight. The paths are mostly empty, and V easily spots the agent running toward the city canal. When the footpath splits, the agent takes the lower trail and a moment later is swallowed by a tunnel leading to the paths along the water. V chases after him but instead takes a bridge that crosses over the footpath and jumps. As the agent emerges from the tunnel, V lands in front of him in a crouch. He has learned how to jump and fall, letting his bionic arm make contact with the ground first so it absorbs most of the shock.

The agent reels backward with a cry of surprise. V kicks out, hooking a foot around the man's ankle and pulling sharply. The man's legs go out from under him, and he lands flat on his back, wheezing. As V stands, the agent fumbles for the inside pocket of his suit, the same one V had seen him groping at while he ran.

There's a sudden *pop*, the sound so unexpected and sharp that V almost looks up for the tree limb that must have broken overhead.

Then he sees the pistol in the man's hand, small enough to carry in a coat pocket.

The man has shot him.

V's never been shot before, except with the pellet guns he and Rostova use for target practice that she occasionally likes to pop him in the back of the head with to try and break his focus. She had once threatened to shoot him with an *actual* gun after he had failed to find a concealed pistol built into the shoe of a KGB double agent they had captured; the only thing that had saved him was the man's inability to aim with his toes. She had said that once he knew how much it hurt to take a bullet, he'd be more careful.

But it doesn't hurt—not at first. There's only the impact, which knocks him backward, and the sensation of blood soaking through the leg of his pants. Running down his leg. It fills his shoe. These stupid dress shoes. The insole squelches.

But no pain yet. He has to act now, before it has the chance to get on top of him.

He hears the man cock the gun again, but this time when he shoots, V throws out his bionic arm, palm forward, and the bullet flattens against it. The man lets out a cry of shock, then fires again, but the hammer clicks, falling on an empty chamber.

V grabs the barrel of the pistol with his bionic arm and bends, twisting until it's pointing upward. The agent tries to cling to the grip, but V wrenches it from him, flips it in his palm, then slams the butt into the man's ear with enough strength to knock him sideways onto the path. Spit and blood spray from the agent's mouth and splatter on the gravel.

Before the agent can recover, V straddles him, seizing him by his lapels. The agent squirms, whimpering, until V delivers a hard punch across the jaw that snaps his neck back. The remaining half of his broken front tooth snaps off, leaving only a sliver clinging to his gums.

"Please," the man mumbles.

V adjusts his grip, pinning a nerve in the agent's neck with the thumb of his bionic arm. The agent's body curls up like a question mark, and he gurgles, eyes bulging. V roots around in the pockets of the man's coat with his free hand, searching for the coaster he had taken from the bar.

"Please," the man says again, this time in English. Blood mists from his lips, stippling the front of his shirt. "I'm sorry. Please, Lieutenant—"

V stops. "What did you call me?"

Snot drips over the man's lips, and he struggles to take a deep breath through it. "Lieutenant, please, please, let me go."

V stares down at the man's shaking shoulders and bloodshot eyes. He must be lying. Trying to buy himself some time, or distract V so he can get away.

But the way the agent had looked at him in the bar . . .

He pulls the agent up by the front of his jacket again, their faces close together. This man isn't a killer. He probably isn't trained for any kind of fieldwork. He has soft hands and smells like expensive aftershave. His suit is corduroy, the material thin enough that the lapels tear in V's grip. "You know me," V hisses.

"Of—of course," the agent stammers. His eyes dart across V's face, like he's searching for the right answer or waiting for a tell that will betray the farce. "Of course I remember you. And god, you've hardly aged—" He reaches up with a trembling hand to touch V's face, but V knocks it out of the way with his elbow. The agent shudders at V's bionic arm.

"I don't care that you remember me," V interrupts. "You *know* me."

The man snuffles, sucking a mess of blood and snot into the back of his throat. "Yes."

"Tell me who I am."

The man shrinks backward into his suit. The material bunches around the armpits, pulling his shoulders up to his ears. "Wh-what?"

"Tell me who I am."

"I don't understand."

"Do you know me?"

"Yes."

"Then tell me my name."

The question is deceptively simple. In their line of work, a name is the most precious thing. Names are guarded and protected. Names cost lives. V has never had a name. Or, rather, he did—he can see it in the agent's eyes now, as he looks him up and down. He had a name, and this man knows it.

"Tell me," V growls.

The agent's lips part, that snaggled front tooth catching on his lip. "Your name is—"

There's a *bang*, and the agent's neck snaps backward. His body tenses, then goes slack. There's a bullet hole between the agent's eyes, a slow trickle of blood bubbling up from it and dribbling down his nose.

V releases his grip on the man's body and slides off him. Someone is here—someone with a gun. Someone just shot this man. V should already be gone. He struggles to his knees, his injured leg suddenly throbbing. He hasn't noticed it until now. He hears footsteps on the path behind him, and he turns just as a hard kick connects with his side. He feels the heavy metal toe hook him under the ribs, driving all the breath from his lungs and tugging him like a fishhook. He's already woozy from blood loss, and, without his impact-resistant tactical gear to protect him, he topples sideways, skidding along the gravel. His cheek stings.

"Are you stupid?"

He looks up, gasping. Rostova stands over him, her rifle slung over her back and the pistol she had just used to shoot the agent now trained on him. He doesn't move as she bends over the agent's body, pawing through his pockets until she comes up with the coaster. She shoves it into her own pocket, then swivels her pistol back to V.

"Get up," she snaps at him.

V raises his arms, hands in front of him. At least one of them will do some good if she really is going to shoot him.

She pulls back the hammer on the pistol. "I said get up."

"I can't."

"What do you mean, you can't?"

"He shot me."

Rostova glances down, seems to notice the blood leaking from V's leg for the first time, and swears. She shoves the pistol into her belt, then retrieves the agent's wallet from his coat pocket. After a moment of thumbing through it, she pulls out the bills and his ID card, then removes his watch and wedding ring. She tosses the empty billfold onto his chest, then pockets the valuables. V knows this trick. When the police find him in the morning, it will look like a robbery gone wrong.

Rostova grabs V by the elbow and hauls him to his feet. His whole body is throbbing now, not just his leg, and his heart is pounding in his ears. He tries to lean on Rostova, but she shoves him off, and he nearly collapses again before catching himself on the arm of a nearby park bench. His injured leg shakes under him.

"Walk it off, soldier," Rostova says bluntly as she turns down the path. "I'm not carrying you."

He doubles over, elbows on the bench, begging his vision to stop swimming. At his feet, blood is still dribbling from the bullet hole in the agent's forehead like a leaking faucet. Rostova never misses.

"Vronsky," she calls, and he raises his head.

He wants to tell her. He wants to say, *He knew me. He knew my name.*

I had a name. I have *a name.*

I was someone before I was this.

But maybe she knows that already. Maybe she's known it since they met and has never told him.

With a grimace, he eases his weight onto his injured leg and hobbles down the path after her.

CHAPTER 6
1954

Rostova leaves V in the controller's office at the dingy airstrip where they left their plane, tossing him an ancient first-aid kit unearthed from one of the rusty desk drawers before disappearing to complete the pre-flight checks.

Despite the first-aid training he's had, when Rostova returns, V is still slumped on the floor, pale and too shaky to have done anything more than tear open the bullet hole even wider with blunt-nose surgical scissors. The concrete floor is streaked with blood. Rostova curses under her breath, then snatches up the scissors from where V's dropped them. She pulls a lamp off the desk by its cord and points the bulb at the wound, squinting at it for a moment before she pushes him onto his side. "Don't move," she instructs, then digs the rounded tip of the scissors into the bullet wound.

He shouts in pain, his whole body convulsing, and Rostova snaps, "I said don't move!"

"It hurts!"

"What did you expect?" She sits on his feet, pinning him to the ground, and he grabs the legs of the desk, muscles shaking. As Rostova digs into the wound again, he bites down on the sleeve of his jacket, trying to focus on anything but the pain until he hears the soft plink of the bullet dropping onto concrete. Rostova eases her weight off him, and he rolls onto his back, gasping. His vision blurs.

"Here." Rostova thrusts a bottle against his lips and he takes a swig without knowing what it is or where she got it. The flammable taste of alcohol burns his raw throat, but he keeps sucking it down until Rostova tugs the bottle from his hands. "I only need it for a second," she says, easing his hands away from the neck.

"Why?" he chokes.

"There's no antiseptic," she says, then douses his bullet wound in the vodka.

V screams, the sound throaty and strangled by pain. He shoves his fist against his mouth, breathing so hard his chest hurts.

Rostova grabs a strip of gauze from the first-aid kit

and binds the wound, then hands him the vodka again. "Good man." She clasps the side of his neck, giving his head an affectionate shove. "You took that like a champion."

He presses the back of his head into the concrete floor and takes a drink, though it only dries him out. The back of his throat feels scorched, the vodka doing little to wash away the ferric taste of blood lingering there. He wants water. He wants to sleep. He stares up at the tin ceiling, panting like a dog. Rostova wipes her hands on her trousers, then tosses the first-aid kit into the bottom drawer of the controller's desk. The desk leg V had been gripping with his bionic hand is so splintered it almost snaps under its own weight.

Rostova sweeps off her fur hat and runs a hand through her hair, pushing it off her face. Sweat holds it in place like pomade. She pulls her knees up to her chest, resting her elbows on them, then says softly, "You can't do that again."

When he raises his head to look at her, he feels the twinge in his neck from the motorcycle crash. "Do what?"

"Go off mission."

"He still had the information."

"And I told you to abort." She wrings her hat between her hands like she's trying to dry it out. "Not steal a motorcycle and run him down and get yourself shot. My god, what were you thinking?"

V lets his head fall backward again. A speckle of rust across the underside of the tin roof is illuminated when a light on the controller's desk flashes green. "I didn't know he had a gun."

"Like that would have changed anything." Rostova balls her hands into fists, then rolls forward onto her knees so that she's leaning over him. "Hey, look at me." She catches his chin between her thumb and forefinger and turns his face to hers. He tries to push her off, but she sits on him, shoving the nearly empty vodka bottle away as he raises it to his mouth. "Look at me, you psychopath."

He relents. Her remaining eye is deep amber, and she told him once that her other eye, the one she'd lost in the war, had been as blue as a glacier. He still doesn't know if he believes her. "You can't take out your earpiece in the field," she says, squeezing his cheeks gently between her fingers. "You can't ignore me. The whole reason I was there was to see things you couldn't and help you make decisions. I won't let you get hurt." She pats his cheek, ending on more of a slap that makes him squawk in surprise. "But I can't protect you if you don't trust me."

"I don't need you to protect me."

Her eye patch is sitting low on her cheek, and she tugs it back into place, hooking the strap behind her ear. "Right. You had the whole situation under control."

"I did." V grabs the underside of the desk, pulling himself up with a wince. The front of his shirt is stuck to his skin with blood and vodka, and he strips off his suit jacket, then the shirt. His thin undershirt isn't enough to keep out the cold, but it's better than feeling like his clothes are pasted onto him.

"What did he say to you?" Rostova asks.

V looks up from a blood spot on the suit jacket he had been scratching. "What?"

"The MI5 agent." She's still fiddling with her eye patch, looking away from him. "What did he say to you before he ran?"

V looks down at the gauze wrapped around his leg, rouged where the blood is starting to seep through. "He thought I was someone else."

"Who did he think you were?"

"Why would I know?"

"He didn't give you a name?"

For a moment, he thinks she must have heard him ask the agent for *his* name, and he looks away from her too quickly. "He was scared," he replies. "He wasn't making sense."

Rostova considers this, running a thumb over her

bottom lip like she's scrubbing something away. Then she says abruptly, "Did you finish all the vodka?"

He holds up the mostly empty bottle. "There wasn't much after you baptized me."

"Desperate times, darling. Here." She reaches into her coat pocket and pulls out a silver-backed blister pack. "Hold out your hand." He does, and she pops two pills into his palm. "Take those."

"With the vodka?"

She shrugs. "Everything goes down easier with vodka."

He tips his hand, letting the pills roll along the lines of his palm. One red, one white. "What are they?"

"For the pain."

It isn't an answer. He almost says so—what will she do if he refuses to take them? Probably pin him to the ground, shove them down his throat, then hold his nose until he's forced to swallow them. He could overpower her, but he's too tired for a fight. His leg is throbbing and his head hurts and his throat scratches like he's been drinking salt water. And he isn't trained to fight *her*. His job is to comply, to follow orders from his superiors, no matter what.

So why had he ignored her command to abort the drop and stay at the bar while she hunted down the agent herself? Why was he still staring down at the pills in his palm? What loophole in his conditioning had he unknowingly darted through?

"Take them, Vronsky," Rostova says quietly.

He sits up, drops the pills on his tongue, then washes them down with the vodka. Rostova watches as he swallows, her eyes following the bob of his throat. He sticks out his tongue to prove he swallowed them, and she pulls away with a scowl. "You're disgusting. Come on." She stands, brushing her palms off on her trousers, then extends a hand to him. "We need to go, before the sun's up."

He lets her pull him to his feet. The rush of blood to his leg knocks him more off-balance than he expected, and he stumbles. She catches him, tossing his arm over her shoulder.

"Don't drink so much next time," she says, and he feels her dig an elbow into his ribs.

"Thank you," he says. "For coming after me."

She nods gruffly. "I have your back, Vronsky. Even when no one else does. I swear to that."

CHAPTER 7
1941

The Bell-Sharp wing of the British Museum was a sea of teenagers in too-big suits and plaid bow ties that made them look like drips. In contrast, Bucky arrived in a leather jacket he had bought in Camden Town the day before, which was perhaps not the best decision for blending in, but it was undeniably cool. Subtlety could come later. His ship from the United States had gotten in a day earlier than anticipated, and in spite of his soon-to-be-undercover status, he'd taken the day to explore the parts of the city he suspected he wouldn't get to see while pretending to be a teenage chess champion. Or after, while becoming a real spy.

A sign in front of the museum informed visitors that

the catalog was being moved into storage in case of a German airstrike, but the wing where the tournament was being held still hosted a few Norse swords and helmets, tagged and sitting alone in their cases. Tables had been set up between the displays, each with a chair on either side and a chessboard in the middle. When Bucky arrived, matches were already in progress. The players with the highest rankings sat in the center of the room, crowds gathered around their tables. Over their heads, large wooden chess grids had been mounted along the walls and men on ladders watched the opponents below them, moving the corresponding pieces. The whole room buzzed with the low murmur of conversation, like a nest of wasps.

Bucky waited in line at the registration table, trying to look around without appearing too conspicuous, but obvious enough that, were his new SOE handler watching, they would note how observant he seemed. He tried to take in details for later. The way the light fell through the high windows in four parallel stripes over the floor. The particular *click* the clocks made when reset after each move. The sporadic bursts of applause, interrupted by arbiters reminding spectators to please remain silent while matches were in progress. The perfume of the woman at the registration table. She was young and pretty, and the neckline of her bird-print blouse dipped every time she bent over to fill out a new card.

Focus, Bucky scolded himself. *Be a spy.*

But spies had drinks with pretty girls in bars too, didn't they? Wasn't that part of the job? Sharp suits and cocktails he didn't have to pay for and a blond bombshell on his arm? He'd read about those sort of spies in comic books, and the stories must have had at least some basis in reality.

"Excuse me? Are you listening?"

Bucky snapped from his reverie. He'd been staring at the woman without realizing she was calling him up. He stepped forward and gave her a smile.

She didn't return it. "Name, please."

"Barnes. James Barnes."

It had been disappointing learning that he'd be entering under his own name and not a fake one. He'd had a list of possibilities ready, but when his instructions had come from the SOE, it had been to enter with his own name and passport, and tell them he was there for the Oswald Shelby Memorial Chess Tournament. The British government would do the rest.

The woman flipped through a tabbed file in the middle of the table, searching for his name. He held his breath. He hadn't considered what would happen if he arrived and found something had gone wrong, some kink in the line of communication that kept him from ending up on the SOE's list. This opportunity had seemed so perfectly crafted for him—suddenly it felt too perfect, like maybe someone was pulling a prank. . . .

The registrar pulled a card out of the stack. "James Barnes."

"Yes," he said, sounding more relieved than he meant to.

The registrar gave him a queer look, but didn't comment. "USA," she said, reading off the card. "Age seventeen."

It felt like she shouted the last part, and Bucky winced. He hated being young. He hated not being taken seriously. At what age were you adult enough that saying the number out loud didn't serve as a reminder to everyone else of how little you knew and how little time you'd had to learn it?

The woman peeled the second sheet of copy paper off the form and stabbed it through on her document spike, then retrieved a number from the stack at her elbow and held it out to him. "Table twelve. The next round starts on the hour. Clocks are on the table. Pads and pencils to your right."

He hesitated. He had expected at least one door would open for him when he gave his name—literal or metaphorical door, he was flexible. Nowhere in the SOE's summoning papers he'd been sent had it mentioned he would have to actually sit down and play chess. He'd expected someone would have pulled him down a secret corridor by now. Was he supposed to go somewhere? Or do something? He'd read the dossier they'd sent him. He'd also left it back at Camp Lehigh by accident, but he was sure he remembered most of it.

When he didn't take the paper, the registrar asked, her tone pinched, "Did you need something else?"

"Were there any . . ." He struggled for discreet phrasing. "Any notes on my registration?"

"Yes," she replied.

Oh thank god.

But then she added, "It said you were liable to waste my time."

Bucky scowled at her as he snatched the card and turned. "Gee, thanks, you're a huge help."

Table twelve was tucked in the opposite corner of the wing, behind a case so tall it must have contained spears or javelins or the tusks of enormous elephants before it was cleared out. A girl about his own age was already there, sitting hunched over a book that could have doubled as a paving slab. Her hair was the soft blond of homegrown honey, set in waves and brushed out so it hit just above her shoulders. She was wearing slacks of all things, and a red sweater with elbow patches over a button-up shirt that looked like it was made for men.

She didn't look up as Bucky slung his jacket around

the back of the chair across from her. "You better find somewhere else to sit," he said. "A game's about to start."

"I know," she said, flipping the page. Her accent reminded Bucky of Mr. Yesterday's, pinched and crisp and reeking of money. "I'm playing it."

He laughed, and she finally looked up, though her glance was witheringly brief.

"Is that funny?" she asked.

"With all due respect, miss, you don't seem the type."

"What type is that?" she asked.

It was obvious why she didn't belong here—there were no other female players at any of the tables—but saying it aloud felt somehow rude. Even if it was a fact. She stared at him like she was daring him to vocalize it, just so she'd have an excuse to punch him in the nose. He scrubbed a hand over his chin. Was every woman in England determined to make him feel like an idiot? "Well . . ."

"Go on." She dog-eared her page and shut the book, then leaned forward with her elbows on the table. "What is it about me that makes you think I'm not a chess player? Am I too short? Not bookish-looking enough? Is it my hair? Oh god." She pressed a hand to her mouth in delicate horror. "Wait, I know, it's the lipstick. Serious chess players never wear this shade of red."

He glared at her. "You gonna make me say it?"

"You're American." She cocked her head. "That's

interesting. I didn't know they were accepting international competitors this year."

"I didn't know girls liked chess."

"Yes, well, I would wager there's quite a lot you don't know about girls." She checked her slim wristwatch, then twisted around to compare it to the large clock hanging over the registration table. "Shall we get started?"

"We're supposed to wait for the hour."

"Why?"

"It's the rules."

"What are they going to do? Toss us out?" She flipped to the first page on the logbook and scribbled the date and time before squinting at him. "Where's your number?"

"In my pocket."

"You're supposed to wear it." She pointed to her own, pinned to her sweater.

But I'm not supposed to be here! he wanted to tell her. That and, when the SOE did show up, he hadn't wanted their first impression of him to be with a chess-tournament number pinned to his chest like a square.

"Not really my style," he replied.

She gave him a slow up and down, then made a note in her logbook that somehow—irrationally—he was sure was about him. "The tag is still attached to your jacket."

"What?" He swiped at his collar, fumbling to catch the tail of the price tag while simultaneously glaring at her. She looked down at her notebook, but he still caught a glimpse of her smug smile.

"You know," he said, snapping the tag and shoving it into his pocket, "you'd be pretty if you didn't smirk like that."

"Who says I want to be pretty?" she replied.

"That's what all girls want, isn't it?"

"No, we just want to play chess." She pushed one of the pawns forward, then pressed one of the buttons on the top of the clock. The timer started, a loud clicking that set his teeth on edge.

He stared at the board, trying to look like he was thinking and not panicking. The instructions he'd gotten from Mr. Yesterday's office had included a brief primer on chess tournaments and game play, but he hadn't thought he'd actually have to play. Was something wrong? Was there some reason he hadn't been extracted yet? Was *extracted* even the right word? What would he do if no one came for him, other than lose badly at chess? He glanced around, hoping someone would be rushing toward them with an urgent pretense that would give him an excuse to abandon the game.

"It's your move," the girl remarked dryly.

He didn't know what to do, so he pushed his corresponding pawn forward, meeting hers. When he didn't switch the clock, she did it for him with an arched eyebrow.

She moved her knight, and he mirrored her, sliding his own forward before she had a chance to reset the clock.

Her eyes narrowed. "Are you copying me?"

He shrugged. "I'm playing chess."

"No, *I'm* playing chess," she snapped. "You're playing mimic. Don't tell me a symmetrical defense to my English opening was intentional."

He stared at her for a moment, then said with as much confidence as he could muster, "Yes. Yes it was."

"Why not play a Slav's defense?" she countered. "Or a reverse Sicilian? They make the center much easier to control."

He didn't know what either of those were—none of this had been in the introduction materials, so he said, fully aware of how stupid it sounded, "I'm American."

"There's a reason there are no chess moves named after your country." She moved her opposite knight, and he did the same. She sucked in her cheeks, and he wondered how much longer he could get away with this before she overturned the board in frustration.

"Excuse me," said a voice, and they both looked up.

A tall man with precisely combed dark hair was standing at the end of their table, the green ribbon pinned to his lapel designating him one of the tournament arbiters. He was thin and sharp-featured, with a crooked nose and eyebrows that were overgrown but still combed with the same precision as his shellacked hair. He leaned in confidentially, like he was about to discreetly inform them they had food stuck in their teeth. "I'm sorry to interrupt, but you seem to be at the wrong table."

Bucky leaped from his chair in relief, already pulling on his jacket. *Finally.* "I figured there was some kind of mistake—" he started, but the Arbiter cut him off.

"Not you." He pointed to the girl. "You."

She looked as surprised as Bucky, even glancing around like there was a chance he might be talking to some invisible spectator. "I am not," she said. "This is table twelve. I was told my first match was table twelve."

"Then you were told the wrong table," the Arbiter replied. "You need to come with me."

"We've already begun," the girl said, gesturing to the board. "Let us finish."

"He's not at your level."

"Clearly," she replied. "But it's against the rules to force players to vacate a game."

"You could resign," Bucky offered.

"I don't want that on my record." She glared at him. "*You* resign."

"Absolutely not." He couldn't leave this table. If this man was telling him to stay here, he would glue himself to the chair, he was so desperate for someone to give him a set of concrete instructions.

The girl picked up her pencil, turning back to the board. "Well then, we have a game to finish."

"If you had waited until the hour like you were instructed—" the Arbiter started, but the girl cut him off.

"Well, we didn't. No use dwelling on the possibility we might have. Spilled milk, water under bridges, all that. Now may we please proceed? If there's a problem, address it at the registration desk."

The Arbiter stared at her, his caterpillar eyebrows inching together until they met in the middle of his forehead. "I believe I will," he said, turning back to the entrance of the wing. "Excuse me."

Bucky almost called after him. If this obstinate girl refused to move from her chair, surely there was some military law that would allow them to pick her up and dump her into a nearby trash can so the SOE could do its work.

But then she said, "Sit down, you're not getting out of this so easily."

The leather of his jacket squeaked against the chair back as Bucky sank back down. "So you really like this table, huh?" he asked as she considered her next move.

"No, I'm simply not too proud to turn down an easy win." She moved another piece, then depressed the timer with her thumb. "Check."

"Check what?"

She glanced up from her notepad, face creased like

she wasn't sure if he was joking. "Your king is in danger. You have to either defend it or you move it."

"Right. Obviously." Check, yes, of course, he had known that one. He was losing focus again. He cupped his hands around his eyes, forcing himself to stare at the board, but he couldn't resist another glance around the room, trying to take in the crowd without looking like he was—

"Are you waiting for someone?" she interrupted. She had her arms crossed, fingers drumming theatrically against her elbow.

Had it been that obvious? *Am I bad at this?* he wondered. Or . . .

Suddenly it made sense.

"It's you, isn't it?" he said.

She raised an eyebrow. "Excuse me?"

This ring he'd been recruited for—they were training university-aged students. It made sense they would send one to pick him up. She'd fit in perfectly at a youth chess tournament, even if she was a girl, and it would be a low-stakes test for a junior recruit. He leaned forward, his heart fluttering with excitement. "You're supposed to pick me up," he said. They hadn't given him any code word or secret cipher phrase—all he'd been told was that his handler would find him—but surely if she knew, she'd *know*. "That's why you wouldn't leave the table. We're supposed to leave here together. You're here for me."

Her mouth dropped open. "Are you *flirting* with me?"

"What?" He pushed his chair back. "God no, don't flatter yourself."

Her cheeks had gone pink, and she looked around, half raising a hand to call over one of the arbiters.

"What are you doing?" Bucky lunged forward and clapped his hand over hers, pinning it to the logbook.

"Don't touch me." She yanked her fingers from his, then pushed back her chair and stood up, its legs scraping against the polished floor with an earsplitting screech that turned heads at the nearby tables.

He stood too. "Where are you going?"

She was already shoving things back in her bag—the paperback went in along with the logbook and the pencil stub, and then she was sweeping it all flat-armed into her knapsack, even the empty water glass at her elbow, careless in her haste. "To ask for your removal for making suggestive comments toward me." She yanked her bag shut, then glared at him across the table. "If you're trying to ruin my concentration, it won't work. Believe me, I've played men far better at innuendo than you. And they were a lot better at chess as well." She turned sharply away and started for the registration table, the heels of her oxfords clicking against the tile.

"Hang on!" Bucky chased after her, dodging between the crowd of players waiting for their matches to start and almost overturning one of the flimsy tables when he clipped its edge with his knee. "Hey, stop! Wait!" He caught up to her at the wing entrance, just before the registration desk. One of the registrars must have stepped away, because the line was backed up. The girl was studying it like she was debating whether to wait or explore other options for having him removed when he seized her wrist. "Wait!"

She twisted sharply, grabbing his fingers with her free hand and trying to pry them open. "If you touch me again, I will knock your teeth straight out of your head—don't think I won't."

"Stop it, listen." He pulled her closer to him, which only made her fight harder, then said in a low voice, "I think I'm supposed to go with you."

"Oh, now you *think*? How gentlemanly."

"I'm sorry if it's a blow to your ego, but I'm not flirting with you."

"Leave me alone!" She kicked him in the shin—hard. He doubled over, his grip loosening enough for her to pull away and dash for the ladies' lavatory.

He paused for only a second of consideration before pushing in after her, the swinging door hitting the wall with more force than he'd meant for it to. "What the hell—?"

She had stopped just inside the lavatory door, and he smacked into her. They both stumbled, and he had to grab her shoulders to stop himself from falling. His feet slid under him, the floor somehow too slick for just tile, and he looked down. A dribble of bright blood was smeared under his shoes.

His stomach heaved, and he looked up. A woman was sprawled facedown on the salmon-colored tile, blood leaking from her slit throat. Her hair had caught in the drain at the center of the room, clogging it up, so that the dark blood seeped along the grooves in the tile, running toward the door.

It took him a moment before he recognized the bird print of her blouse.

The registrar was dead.

CHAPTER 8
1941

Bucky felt light-headed, and he was worried for a moment he was going to pass out. He'd never seen a dead body outside a funeral home, and there was *so much more blood* than he could have imagined. He reached out blindly until he found the wall and sagged against it. Beside him, the girl was frozen, staring at the woman's body with a hand pressed over her mouth.

There was the sound of a flush lever, and then one of the stall doors opened. A man appeared. His tie was tucked between the buttons of his dress shirt to keep it clean, and he had his suit jacket folded over his arm, though Bucky could still see the green ribbon pinned to the lapel. It was the Arbiter who had tried to hustle them from their table.

The Arbiter looked from the body on the floor to the two of them in the doorway staring at it. His eyes darted over their shoulders to the bolt on the lavatory door. He must have fastened it, but the screws were loose enough that half of them had been ripped from the wall, likely when the girl slammed into it to escape Bucky. The Arbiter swore under his breath, then fumbled for the pocket of his jacket. The light over the sink caught something metallic, and Bucky could see it perfectly in his head, the knife across the woman's throat, the blood unfurling down her front like unbolted silk. The feeling returned to his legs, a survival instinct he'd never tapped into before activating like a thrown switch. He yanked open the washroom door and ran, dragging the girl out after him.

Tournament players swarmed the hallway. The sole registrar left at the desk looked frazzled as she alternated between scribbling on registration cards and craning her neck toward the lavatory, and Bucky guessed she was searching the crowd for her missing partner. Bucky considered asking her for help, but what was there to say? *Your fellow registrar has been murdered in the bathroom and I'm pretty sure her murderer is also still in there and now coming for us because somehow, in spite of being here all of ten minutes and having no idea what the hell is going on, I already know too much?*

His shoe squeaked against the stones, and he looked down, realizing too late he'd left a smudged red footprint. He jammed his toe onto it, trying to rub it away, but only smeared it around. A boy who looked barely out of grade school gave him a curious look.

The girl grabbed his arm, nearly pulling him off his feet as she dragged him toward a closed door. "This way!" He caught a glimpse of the word JANITOR before she wrenched the door open and dragged him through.

The closet stank of bleach, and a faint haze of soap powder seemed to hang in the air. Bucky tripped over a stepladder that hadn't been properly folded and landed with his foot in a bucket, his shoe wedged so tight he wasn't sure he'd get it free without surgical intervention.

The girl locked the door behind them, and he wondered suddenly if she was somehow in on this too and had ushered him into a closet with the intention of finding a more discreet place to off him than a public lavatory. He groped backward through the darkness, searching for what he hoped would be a mop handle with an improbably sharp end. But, in the faint light seeping in from under the door, he could see she was bent double, gaping in shock. She looked like she was crying.

He reached out and put what he thought was a gentlemanly, albeit shaking, hand on her shoulder, but she immediately slapped it away. "What are you doing?"

Definitely not crying.

"Ow!" Bucky yelped, yanking his hand back. "I don't know! Comforting you!"

"By trying to feel me up?"

"Come on, that was your shoulder."

"Oh god, I don't have time to explain anatomy to you as well." She tried to stand straight, and wobbled instead, then slumped against the wall, hand pressed to her chest. "We have to tell someone."

"Who are we supposed to tell?" Bucky asked.

"The police? The museum? Anyone!" She thrust a hand at the door, as though to emphasize the dire situation waiting for them on the other side. "There is a dead woman in the public lavatory!"

"I think she was here for me."

"What do you mean she was here for you?" she asked flatly. "She was working—she was here for the tournament. Not every woman in London is coming on to you—your accent isn't *that* charming."

Bucky gave up trying to un-wedge his foot from the bucket and instead started unlacing his shoes. In his stocking feet, he wouldn't leave bloody footprints marking his path when he slipped out of here. "I can't explain."

"Well, try."

"I don't mean I can't, I mean I'm not allowed to."

"That doesn't make sense," she replied flatly. "A woman has been murdered and you're saying it was because of you—"

He straightened. "I didn't say *because of me*—"

"Because of you, for you, in your place, what the hell is the difference?"

"A lot, actually," he mumbled, prying his foot from his stuck shoe.

"Well, I'm not going to stand here and wait for you to feel like explaining." She turned, reaching for the closet door, but he grabbed her elbow.

"Wait."

"If you touch me one more time, I swear to god, I will aim higher than your shin."

"Sorry, sorry!" He stepped back quickly. His head was swimming. He wanted to sit down. He needed to think. He didn't have time to think. He didn't know what to do. There hadn't been anything in the introduction packet about what to do if you stumble upon a dead body while waiting for your retrieval, particularly if it seemed likely it was the body of the woman meant to *do* the retrieval. "Just . . . give me a minute." He closed his eyes and jammed his hands hard into his pockets, but all he could see was that pool of dark, clotted blood.

Something poked one of his palms hard enough to draw blood, and he yanked that hand back out of his pocket quickly. He thought it was his chess number, or even the stupid tag from his stupid jacket, but when he fished it out, he realized it was the card Mr. Yesterday had given him in case of emergencies.

And this certainly qualified as one.

"I have someone I can call," he blurted.

"So do I," the girl said. "The police."

"You can't call the police!" He took as deep a breath as his constricted chest allowed, and made a decision. "I'm here with the SOE," he said, the words tripping over each other. "I'm supposed to meet my handler here and I think it was her."

There was a sharp *click* and a bare bulb overhead flooded the room with yellow light. Bucky flinched—it felt like a searchlight beaming down on him after that confession, and for an irrational moment, he wondered if this was all part of the training.

The girl was hanging off the light-bulb chain, scrutinizing him. Her breathing had begun to even out, and when she spoke again, she sounded more like she had back at the chess table. Namely, bossy and irritating. "You bloody liar."

"I'm not lying!"

"Are they recruiting from primary schools over in America now? You look twelve."

Bucky glared at her. "I do not."

"Your socks don't match."

He resisted the urge to shove his feet under a nearby mop. "I'm twenty." A pause, too long, as he tried to work out how much of a lie he could get away with. "Five."

She had already been shaking her head, but the

amendment made her snort. "And I'm the queen of bloody Sheba."

"I don't care if you believe me—that man has seen our faces and will be coming for us. We have to get out of here. I can make contact with my handlers." He held up the card. "I have a phone number—someone to call in case I get in trouble."

She snatched the card from him and studied it, tipping it in and out of the light as she ran her fingers along the embossing.

Bucky huffed an impatient breath. "Okay, give it back—you're not checking for a forgery."

He held out a hand, but she jerked the card away, holding it over her head. "You're really an American spy?" she demanded.

There wasn't time to get into technicalities, so he just nodded.

"And you work in intelligence for the United States?"

Again, no time. He nodded.

She sucked in her cheeks, then handed him back the card. "I saw a phone bank on my way in. I can show you."

"Okay. Okay, that's good. I'll start there." He considered putting his loafers back on, but the soles were still sticky with blood. Instead, he pulled off his socks and tossed them into the bucket with his stuck shoe. The closet was absent of anything that could conceivably be used as a weapon and also carried discreetly, so he handed her a spray tin of cleaning powder for protection. "Stay here."

"What? Absolutely not." She tried to shove the tin back into his hands, like whoever ended up holding it would have to be the one left behind. "I'm not hiding in a broom closet while some killer is looking for me."

"Well, he'll technically be looking for *me*."

"He didn't even see you!"

"I'm the spy!"

"Allegedly."

Are we arguing about which of us is in more danger? He was ready to brave the Arbiter just to get out of this closet with her.

"Fine," he said. "But don't slow me down."

"Really? That's your concern?" She snatched the tin from him and shoved it into her bag. "You're the one not wearing shoes."

He looked down, ready to make a comment about her heels, but she was wearing a pair of oxfords with the laces double-knotted—decidedly unfeminine but ideal for fleeing murderers in pursuit. They were likely more practical than his slick-soled loafers would have been.

Bucky reached past her for the door handle, but she stepped in his way. "Wait! What do I call you?"

"My name is—"

"Don't tell me your name!" She clapped a hand over his mouth. "You're a bloody government agent; you can't tell me your real identity! Don't you have a code name? Or something?"

"They, um . . ." He wished he'd been faster with the door. Or ignored her protestations not to be left behind. Or, better yet, never sat down at table twelve to begin with. "They haven't given me a code name yet."

"Well, you can call me Gimlet," she said.

"Gimlet? Like the drink?"

She nodded.

"You came up with that fast."

"Oh, please. Like you don't have a whole list ready."

He did. Though, in his defense, he had a reason to. Something sexy and cool would be preferable. A reference to America. Osprey, maybe, or Hale—he'd read a biography of Nathan Hale once—half a biography—the first chapter and then skimmed the rest. It had been for school. But Nathan Hale had been a patriot, and Bucky liked to think that his service to his country was based primarily in patriotism—

"Would you hurry up, please?" the girl snapped. "Before he finds us."

"Fine." He threw up his hands. The water was murky enough without a fake name muddying it further. "Just call me Bucky."

"Bucky?" she repeated, and he nodded, then added quickly, "It's not my real name."

She pressed a hand to her chest. "Oh, thank god."

He thought she was worried he'd compromised himself, but then she said, "That would be awfully cruel of your parents. Bucky?" she repeated, wrinkling her nose. "Really? Are you married to that?"

"What's wrong with it?" he asked hotly.

She shrugged. "Might want to workshop it a bit, that's all. Bucky." She wrapped her lips around it, then said, "Sorry, I just don't like it. It sounds like the name of a cartoon squirrel."

"Well, your accent makes it sound stupid," he snapped. It was suddenly very hot in this tiny closet, and he plucked at the front of his shirt.

"Just wait until you see it engraved on your Medal of Honor," she replied. "You'll rue the day." She reached up and tugged the chain on the light bulb, plunging them into darkness again. "Now come on."

"You are not in charge of this."

"I am until you prove you're capable of leadership." She reached over him, unhooked a latch he hadn't noticed, then shoved him out the door.

The hall was still crowded with competitors waiting for table assignments. The registration looked like it had halted entirely—a small knot of officials, all with green ribbons, were gathered around the desk, conferring about something. Bucky glanced up and down the hall, searching for the Arbiter they had seen in the lavatory, but he had vanished. When he turned again, the girl—*Gimlet*, he thought, though he felt like an idiot calling her that, even in his head—was already rounding the corner and out of sight. Bucky picked up his pace, struggling to catch up with her.

You don't have to help her, he thought. *You could run the other way right now and leave her to fend for herself.*

But he didn't know where the pay phones were.

Bucky caught up to her at a door at the end of the hall marked STAFF—NO ADMITTANCE. "Do you know where you're going?" he hissed as he followed her.

She turned to him, pushing the door open with her shoulder and then holding it for him. "There's a back way. Don't worry, I won't get us lost."

He clenched his jaw, trying to ignore how much he hated that there was any *us* to this situation.

Behind the door, a high-ceilinged office opened into wide aisles that snaked between stacks of drawers, like a giant card catalogue in a library. "There's a stairway here," Gimlet said, her footsteps far too heavy for someone who was trying to avoid detection.

"How do you know?"

"Because there was a photographer at the main entrance this morning, and I didn't want to have my picture taken, so I found a different way up. They make everyone pose on this step and repeat when they're coming in—you hold up a trophy and pretend you're the champion."

"Why didn't you want your picture taken?" he asked. "What would they run in the papers if you won?"

"Well, no chance of that now, thanks to—"

They had reached the end of a row of shelves, and, with Bucky on her heels, Gimlet turned the corner . . .

And crashed into the Arbiter.

Gimlet stumbled backward, stepping hard on Bucky's bare foot. The Arbiter looked as shocked to run into them as Bucky felt. He must have heard their voices but not known exactly where in the room they were, until they fell into his lap—almost literally.

The Arbiter recovered quicker than they did. He already had his knife out, and he swiped at them. Without thinking, Bucky grabbed Gimlet by the back of her cardigan, yanking her out of the way. The Arbiter swiped again, the blade whizzing so close to Bucky's face he could see a freckle of blood along the curve.

"Get out of here!" Bucky shouted over his shoulder to Gimlet. He hoped she might raise some protest or cry *I'm not leaving you here!*, but she took off at once, dashing back down the aisle and out of sight.

Which was fine. This was fine. He was fine on his own.

Bucky faced the Arbiter, raising his fists like this was a fight between teenage boys behind Arlington High. He was already regretting his moment of heroism. With Gimlet behind him, they had at least had the advantage of outnumbering the Arbiter. Now Bucky was alone, facing a man who was likely some kind of professional assassin or spy or, at the very least, a soldier—with nothing but his bare knuckles.

The Arbiter flipped the knife in his hand, then took another stab at Bucky. Bucky jumped backward, misjudging the distance and smashing into the shelf behind him. A set of heavy encyclopedias rained down on them and Bucky threw his hands over his head. The Arbiter swiped again, but he stepped on one of the books and his legs slid apart. The Arbiter staggered, one knee slamming into the ground and twisting under him. Bucky seized on the momentary distraction and threw a punch, but, even in a half split, the Arbiter managed to catch Bucky's wrist and twist it. Bucky shouted in pain, his shoulder popping in its socket.

A book flew suddenly off the shelf, landing between them.

"Hey!"

The Arbiter turned. Through the hole she had created, Gimlet raised the tin of powdered soap and blew it into his face. The Arbiter reeled backward, his grip on Bucky slackening as he clawed at his eyes. His foot caught the edge of the bookcase, and he teetered, reaching out blindly to try to catch on to something. Before he could, Bucky grabbed the bottom of his shoe and shoved hard. The Arbiter toppled backward, his head striking the tile and bouncing off with a sharp crack. He twitched with a low moan, his red eyes still streaming.

Bucky staggered to his feet and hurtled down the aisle, nearly running into Gimlet as they both turned to each other at the end. "Are you all right?" she asked before he could.

He nodded, shaking the pain out of his arm. "I thought you took off."

"Surely you haven't already formed that poor of an opinion of me."

"I probably would have left *you*."

"Yes, that scans."

Behind them, the Arbiter rolled onto his stomach, mashing a hand over his eyes. Gimlet swiped a finger under her lip, fixing a lipstick smudge at the corner of her mouth. "Quick, before he gets his vision back." Bucky followed her out of the shelves and through a side door, into a narrow stairway. Their footsteps bounced up and down as they ran, and Bucky kept looking back, sure the man was chasing them. His bare feet stuck to the polished stone.

They burst from the stairwell door and tumbled into the basement foyer of the museum. It was mostly empty. A few stragglers from the tournament were still hanging their coats in the cloakroom. A man waiting for the lift gave Bucky and Gimlet a curious look as they lurched out of the stairwell. Across the room, a museum's information desk sat empty, and next to it was a bank of red pay phones.

Bucky yanked the door of the nearest phone booth open and squeezed inside, only to find Gimlet squeezing after him. There was barely enough room for them both, and Bucky had to stretch around her just to get the receiver. He wedged it between his shoulder and his ear, only to be met with a scolding tone insisting he insert coins.

"You have to pay!" Gimlet said.

"I don't have any money. Will they take a collect call?"

"Who? The State Department?"

He shrugged. "Worth a try."

"Here, I think I've got some change." She swung her bag into her lap and shoved her arm in up to her elbow, rooting around. "Hold this." Before he could protest, she started dumping the contents into his hands: buttons, hairpins, half a biscuit, an earring, two tubes of lipstick in the same shade of poisonous red she was wearing, the book of chess maneuvers, a coin that turned out to be not a coin but a token to a fairground. . . .

"What kind of day were you planning when you packed this bag?" Bucky asked as she pulled out what appeared to be a set of birthday candles and two playing cards from yet another pocket.

"I haven't cleaned this out in ages. Oh, here, look!"

She held up a brass coin, and he snatched it, shoving it into the slot.

Bucky had no idea what he'd shoved in—it could have been the fairground token for all he knew about English coins—but the voice scolding him to insert change had switched to a bright dial tone. He clamped the phone under his arm, fishing in the pocket of his jacket until he came up with the card from Mr. Yesterday. "How do phone numbers work here?" He flashed Gimlet a look at the card. "Why's there a plus sign? What do I push for that?"

"That's a country code, you don't need it; just enter the last eight digits." She snatched the card from him and began to punch in the numbers so forcefully the whole phone booth shook.

"Okay, take it easy."

"You owe me a penny."

"You owe me a pair of shoes."

"How was that—"

There was a click on the other end of the line, and Bucky clapped a hand over Gimlet's mouth. A pause; then a woman's voice asked in a prim English accent, "This is Jane, how may I help you?"

Relief flooded him, and he sagged against the wall of the phone booth, narrowly missing putting his hand into a wad of chewed bubble gum someone had stuck to one of the windows. "Thank god. Hi, I'm at the British Museum," he stammered, looking to Gimlet for confirmation, and she nodded vigorously. "And there's a dead woman in the bathroom and a man with a knife chasing us. Someone gave me this number and said to call if I got into trouble—"

"Do you have an appointment?" Jane interrupted.

Bucky paused. "Do I . . . what?"

The woman repeated with more emphasis, "Do you have an appointment?"

He looked to Gimlet, but she just widened her eyes at him in return, mouthing something that looked like *What are you waiting for?*

"No, I need help!" His palm was so slick with sweat, he almost dropped the receiver. "I'm an American, I was sent—"

"Don't say it!" Gimlet whispered. "Didn't someone explain the meaning of the word *covert* to you?"

He covered the receiver. "She wants me to make an appointment."

"So make an appointment!"

"Did you dial the right number?"

"I think so." She flipped the card over, but the opposite side was blank. "Unless this is actually some secret code—"

"Oh my god, the code." He almost smacked his own

forehead, a cartoon gesture of realization. He pressed the receiver to his mouth again, half expecting the long-suffering woman on the other end to have hung up on him. This certainly sounded like the start of a prank call. "I need to talk to Mr. Yesterday. He told me to ask about the weather on . . ." What was it? He hadn't thought he'd ever have to use it. That night in the commander's office, his head swimming with spies and secrets and the possibility of going abroad, felt like it had happened to someone else.

Think!

"I'm afraid I can't—" Jane started.

And then it came to him. "Wight!" he practically shouted into the phone. "Isle of Wight! What's the weather on the Isle of Wight?"

Across the booth, Gimlet made a *What the hell?* face at him.

There was a long pause on the other end of the line, then a click. For a moment, Bucky thought he'd been disconnected, but then a new, female voice said, "Thank you for holding. This is Jane. From where do you require extraction?"

"The British Museum. We're— I'm in the basement. There's two of us—she's not with me—"

"But I'm coming with you," Gimlet hissed. "You aren't leaving me here."

He flapped a hand to silence her. "But she's—"

"We'll send a car," the new Jane interrupted. "For now, stay where you are."

Across the foyer, the stairway door they had entered through banged open, and they both jumped. Bucky caught a brief glimpse of the Arbiter emerging from the stairwell, looking around wildly. His eyes were red and still leaking tears.

Gimlet and Bucky both dropped into a crouch under the receiver as the Arbiter veered into the now-empty cloakroom and began pawing through the coats. He had to pause every few seconds to wipe his eyes.

"Staying put isn't really an option," Bucky hissed, his hand cupped around the receiver.

"Then proceed to your next rendezvous point," Jane replied.

"No, you don't get it, I'm not . . ." He glanced at Gimlet, then hissed into the phone, "I'm not actually an agent." He felt the color rising in his cheeks. "Yet. I was supposed to meet someone here and start training. A handler. Someone was supposed to pick me up. I haven't . . . I've never done this before."

Gimlet let out a tense sigh through her nose and Bucky stared determinedly away from her. He had a sense that, when he hung up—*if* he hung up before the Arbiter found them—the first words out of her mouth would be *I knew it.*

Another pause. So many pauses for a phone call that was so clearly urgent. On the other end, he heard something tear, and the scratch of a pen on paper. Then Jane said, "Meet at the Red Lion Pub, in Westminster, due south of your current location. Tell the bartender you're with Mr. Yesterday. Someone will pick you up from there."

"Great. Fantastic, thank you."

"How do we get out of here?" Gimlet whispered as Bucky replaced the receiver in its cradle.

Bucky glanced through the booth door. As soon as the Arbiter discovered they weren't hidden in the garment racks, he'd look to the bank of phones and discover them staring back at him through the glass door like portraits in a gallery. "Same way we came in."

"I can't believe you haven't even got any money of your own."

"I'll tell the government to set aside fifty cents from my paycheck for you."

"*First* paycheck," she corrected.

"There it is," he muttered.

Bucky eased the door open, knowing there would be no better moment, but the hinge squeaked loudly. He froze. The Arbiter turned. His eyes locked with Bucky's.

Then, from the other side of the room, someone shouted, "Hey! What are you doing in there?"

A man in a museum-security uniform was stalking

toward the Arbiter, glowering. "Thought you'd help yourself to some pocketbooks, did you? Oi, I'm talking to you! Sir!"

As the security guard planted himself between them and the Arbiter, Bucky shoved the phone booth door the rest of the way open. His bare feet squeaked on the tile as he struggled to stand. Behind him, Gimlet hoisted her bag over her shoulder, knocking him in the back of the head. It felt slightly too hard to be accidental.

Together, they fled the basement and hurtled up into the main lobby of the museum. A curtain had been assembled on a rickety frame, the tournament seal stitched onto it. A pack of reporters crowded around, listening intently to a monologue being delivered in Russian by a boy who looked about twelve, then recounted by a translator who seemed to be significantly summarizing what the boy was saying.

They were almost across the lobby when one of the reporters stepped into their path, pointing to the number still pinned to Gimlet's cardigan. "Are you the winner?"

Gimlet shook her head. "No, no, just ducking out for a—"

But the reporters were already swarming them. A flashbulb popped too close to Bucky's face, and stars burst in the corners of his vision. Gimlet grabbed his arm, trying to hide her face against his shoulder as the reporters lobbed questions at them.

"Can you tell us your name, sweetie, and spell it nice and loud."

"Did your boyfriend here win and let you wear his number?"

"I didn't know they were letting girls in the circuit."

"Why aren't you wearing shoes? Is that to do with your game play?"

"Hey, you're a cute couple! Look this way!"

Another flashbulb. Gimlet was practically climbing Bucky's arm, trying to hide behind him. She seemed more terrified of the reporters than she had been of the knife-wielding Arbiter.

"Hey, get out of the way. Out of the way!" Bucky threw out his arms, trying to shield Gimlet and push forward. This was hardly the subtle exit he had hoped for. "Move it!"

"He's American!" he heard one of the reporters shout. "Is your girlfriend American as well, mate?"

"She's not—" Not an important point to correct right now. "Can you get out of our way, please?"

The reporters followed them out of the lobby, finally beginning to dissipate as Gimlet and Bucky jogged down the museum stairs. The wind was cold, and the sunlight reflecting back off the pavement looked gray and dull. The sidewalk was crowded with pedestrians. Men in trench coats and fedoras walked quickly toward the Underground stop, while women changing shift at a department store powdered their noses in the reflection of the front window, their faces lining up with the blank mannequins displaying new hats. Motorcars clogged the intersection, and a line of black cabs idled at the curb.

Bucky led Gimlet to the cab at the front of the line, and they slid together into the back seat. For a disorienting moment, Bucky thought the car didn't have a driver, then realized one was sitting where the passenger seat would be. Of course he was. Bucky had read about this. He'd seen the traffic the day before. He had to get his head on straight, even as everything caught up to him. He was breathing heavier than he felt he should have been.

The driver folded up his newspaper and peered at them in the rearview mirror. "You all right?"

Bucky leaned over Gimlet to shut the door. "Yeah, we're grand," he replied without conviction. "Do you know somewhere called the Red Lion?"

"The pub?" the driver asked. His hedgerow mustache muffled his words. "In Westminster?"

"Yes, that one! Can you hurry, please? We need to get out of here." Bucky waved a hand, trying to gesture for the driver to merge into the traffic as fast as possible, but the man twisted suddenly around, one hand hooked around the opposite car seat.

"You all right, love?" he asked, pushing back the peak of his cap to look at Gimlet. She was slumped down, knees pressed against the seat in front of her and her cardigan rucked up as she ducked below the line of sight of the window.

"She's fine," Bucky said.

"Not asking you," the driver snapped, and Bucky scooted into the door, away from Gimlet. "Has this lad hurt you?" the cab driver asked her seriously, leaning in between her and Bucky like there was any kind of confidentiality in such a small space. "Are you being taken somewhere against your will?"

"I'm fine," Gimlet choked out. She had her cardigan pulled up almost over her mouth, one of the buttons clamped between her teeth. "Really. Please just drive."

The driver didn't look convinced, but he rattled the gearshift and pulled into the street. He kept glancing into the rearview at Gimlet, his eyebrows twitching.

As the traffic swallowed them, Bucky tipped his head back against the seat, struggling to catch his breath. Beside him, Gimlet pulled her sleeves up over her hands and pressed them to her face. The cardigan was too big for her, and starting to unravel along the neck.

"You all right?" Bucky said quietly. When Gimlet

didn't answer, he touched her arm lightly. "Hey." She startled like he'd grabbed her, and he pulled his hand back quickly. "Sorry." Bucky swallowed. "Can I—"

"Don't talk to me," she snapped.

"Fine." He threw up his hands. "Sorry for trying to help."

"I don't need your help," she retorted, the words undercut by the fact that she was still chewing on the top button of her cardigan like she meant to eat it.

A pause. He knew he should leave it alone, but Bucky couldn't resist adding in low tones, "You'd be dead without my help."

"I would never have been in this mess in the first place if it weren't for you," she said sharply. "You'd be the one with your throat slit on the bathroom floor because you didn't know how to use a bloody pay phone."

Silence again. Then the driver turned up the radio.

CHAPTER 9
1954

V waits in a room with a drain in the floor and a chair bolted down.

This is where it happens, he thinks, studying the tendrils of dark hair dried into the grout. *This is where they kill me.*

He doesn't know how long it's been since Riga. Time has been distorted by drugs and pain. Whatever possessed him to rip out his earpiece and chase down the MI5 agent has faded so far into the recesses of his memory that it almost feels like the pursuit order came from someone else and he was only doing what he had been taught to—complying.

They could kill him for this. They *should*. He's seen them kill others for less. He's done the killing. His bionic arm had been removed sometime after their return, while his bullet wound was being treated and he was drunk on a numbing cocktail of opiates and narcotics. They haven't given it back to him yet. Maybe they're afraid he'll use it against whoever they send to kill him. Or maybe they just don't want their real investment damaged.

When he hears the heavy lock unfastened—*they locked him in*—he stands. He won't fight, but he doesn't want to die sitting on his ass either. They can force him to his knees, but he won't wait for them there, head bowed like a penitent.

It's Rostova.

Her fur hat is missing, and both her boots are unlaced. Her eye patch sits slightly askew, and he can see the red imprint on her forehead of where she must have been wearing it instead of over her eye. She looks like she hasn't slept. Her skin has a pale, waxy quality to it.

She arches an eyebrow when she sees him, tipped onto the balls of his feet with a fist clenched at his side. "What are you doing?"

"I don't know."

"Are we going to fight? Hold on, let me change into my other pants." She sinks down onto the floor across from his chair, either ignorant to the stains there or apathetic. "Sit down, you maniac." She nods toward the chair. "You're making me nervous." He perches on the edge, but he cannot make himself relax. A siren is blaring in the back of his mind, and he can't switch it off. Rostova watches him, her legs kicked out in front of her, chewing on her fingernails. "How's your leg?" she asks.

"Fine." He presses his thumbnail into his palm.

"Are you operational?"

"Am I—" He must have misheard her. "What?"

"Are you ready to go back in the field?"

"You're putting me back in the field after what happened in Riga?"

"What happened in Riga?" She picks at a piece of skin along her nail, then bites it between her front teeth. "You took a bullet because the target panicked. I eliminated him. His death was reported by local police as a failed robbery. Isn't that what happened?" She raises an eyebrow, then looks deliberately at the upper corner over the door. He had seen it too—the camera.

Why are you lying for me? he thinks. Hers should have been the first signature on his death certificate. He'd disobeyed her direct orders. He'd compromised them both. He'd put himself in danger and almost ruined their whole mission because . . . because what? A man in a bar had thought V looked like someone. It feels idiotic now.

Rostova catches the edge of her nail and rips it off, leaving a raw edge. "So. Are you ready for your next assignment? Or do I need to go alone while you convalesce here?"

"What's the assignment?"

"Do you know where Norway is?" She reaches into her pocket and pulls out the coaster he took from the MI5 agent, crumpled and battered from being clutched in the rain. She wedges a finger in between the two heavy pieces of paper and pries them apart, showing him the numbers written there.

"That doesn't say Norway."

She toes his knee. "Smart-ass. That's latitude and longitude." She presses the two halves of the coaster back together. "Norway. Well, near Norway. Off the coast."

"What's off the coast?"

"A laboratory. One we've been searching for for a long time. So have MI5. The agent you met in Riga was passing off the coordinates to one of his men, who was then going to infiltrate it. But now that we have the information, we'll get there first."

"Is it on an island?"

"It's on a boat. Big one—the size of an aircraft carrier. That's how they stay off radar—keep to remote international waters and their work then belongs to no government. They answer to no one. These coordinates are their last known location, and based on some complicated math I won't explain, because I don't understand it, we know where they'll be next."

"Who are they?" V asks.

Rostova pinches the bridge of her nose. Her eye patch slips. "Don't ask."

"What research in this lab is so valuable and secret that it has to be kept off the map?"

"You don't need to know that."

V resists a petulant scowl. "Then when do we leave?"

"Karpov wants to look you over, and he wants a brain scan to make sure you're all right. Once he clears you, we'll schedule the plane. Any questions?"

A dozen, at least. Most importantly, *Why did you lie for me?*

"None," V says.

"I have something for you." She unclips a hard case from her belt and hands it to him. "You can add it to your tactical gear. Think of it as an upgrade."

Upgrade. The hair on the back of his neck rises as he unlatches the case.

Inside is a dome, curved like the top of a clamshell. It feels like it's made of the same materials as some of his tactical gear, tough but breathable. He picks it up, running his thumb over the soft mesh along the sides.

Rostova is chewing her fingernails again. A thin crescent of blood rises along her nail bed, and she sucks it. "This way no one will see your face and think you're someone you're not."

He realizes suddenly what the item is and holds it

up to his face. The mask fits perfectly over his nose and runs along his jawline like it was made for him—*it was*.

"Protection as well," he hears Rostova say. "There's an air filter built in, and it's flame-resistant. Here." She reaches over and fastens it for him, two straps around the back of his head so that it covers his face from the eyes down. He can breathe through it, but he can't. It feels like a muzzle. His chest constricts, some wire tripped inside him at that feeling of the mask against his skin—*fight it*. He wants it off, and he hasn't even put it on properly.

"It looks good on you," Rostova says, but he's already reached up, peeling it off and gasping like she'd had him by the throat. "You'll get used to it." He tries to hand the mask back to her, protests rising in his throat, but she shakes her head. Her eyes flit again to the camera. "Don't fight it," she says quietly.

Fight it.

But he owes her. She saved him—twice. Once in Riga, and again when they returned. Whatever peace of mind the mask offers that he won't career off their script again, he can give her that.

Rostova pushes herself to her feet and stretches with her hands behind her head. Her back pops. "Get your brain in shape for Karpov. I wouldn't want to give him any reason to keep you here." She turns for the door but pauses on the threshold. A shy smile creeps across her face as she looks him up and down. "Can't believe you got yourself shot."

V snorts. "Piss off."

"That's so embarrassing for you. I was on the front lines for ten months and never got shot."

"But then you poked your eye out."

She flicks a broken piece of her fingernail at him. "The wind changed—haven't I told you this story before?"

Had she? He can't remember.

"I told you," she says. "You don't listen to me."

"Maybe you don't say anything worth remembering."

She hooks her fingers in her back pockets and cocks her head to the side, studying him. He shifts, the heat of her gaze making him feel like she has him in her rifle scope. "Why are you looking at me like that?"

"I'm thinking."

"What about?"

She rests the side of her head against the doorframe. "Someday I'm going to lose you."

"You're morbid." He drops his head back with an exasperated sigh. "It was one bullet to the leg—"

"That's not what I mean." She sticks her bloody nail in her mouth again. "They'll split us up eventually. They always do. You get too comfortable with a partner, you get complacent. You get attached, and you do stupid things. You miss your shots. Or you don't take them at all."

"Well, it's not happening tomorrow, so stop looking at me like I'm going to be murdered in my sleep."

"If anyone murders you in your sleep, it's going to be me." She holds up her thumb and first two fingers in the shape of a gun and points them at his head. "Bang."

"When they send you to eliminate me," he says, "at least wake me up to say good-bye."

She laughs again. "Believe me, Vronsky, if I shoot you, you'll never see me coming."

It's too hot.

No, it's too cold.

When did you stop being able to tell the difference?

Maybe it's both—the two pulsing spots on your temples are so hot that everything else feels cold in comparison. But it's not the cold your body had been braced for. It's not the ice.

A hand on your face. Something wedged between your teeth.

It's hot again, and someone is screaming. It sounds like pain.

You breathe through your nose, as deeply as you can, but something is constricting your chest, holding you in place, like they think you might try to run.

The ghosts gather. One in white, one in black, opposing pieces across a chessboard.

"I'm trusting you," the white king says, and the black queen replies, "We don't need blank slate. Don't make him start over."

"This is a far bigger gambit than you seem to believe," the king replies.

A queen's gambit, *you think. But a queen's gambit isn't a true gambit. Someone taught you that once. Long ago. Maybe in another life. Maybe in a dream.*

"She's got to be dead," says the queen. "The English wouldn't be planning to bomb it otherwise."

You must be dreaming. There's a woman, and a river, and when a song begins to play, she laughs with her face to the sky. She offers you her hand, and says she'll show you the North Star.

"I'll take precautions," says the queen.

"Be sure you do," the king says. As he drifts from your vision, you hear him say, "You'll need a higher voltage or we'll be here all night."

And then heat returns. The screaming starts again.

You close your eyes and wait for the cold.

CHAPTER 10
1941

The Red Lion was an oak-paneled pub with rickety chairs crowded between small tables. The whole place looked slick as oil, a thick lacquer disguising years of grease stains and spilled beers that had never been wiped up. Bucky stood at the bar, Gimlet next to him. They both fiddled nervously as they waited for the men in front of them to finish their argument with the bartender. They hadn't spoken since the cab. The ride hadn't been long, and Gimlet had paid the driver with more coins unearthed from her archaeological dig of a purse. Bucky had expected some smart remark from her about making sure President Roosevelt himself approved an expense report for her cab fare as well as the pay phone.

But she'd dropped her change into her bag—without looking where it landed, he noticed, which explained the state of it—and opened her own door before he could come around and do it for her.

The men settled their tab and departed, leaving Bucky and Gimlet staring down the aggravated bartender. He had a gray rag wrapped around his hand and was aggressively drying an empty pitcher, scrubbing stains that didn't look likely to budge. "What do you want, then?" he barked at them.

"We're here to see Mr. Yesterday," Bucky said with as much unearned confidence as he could muster.

The bartender glanced up, scrutinizing them for a moment, before letting out an exhausted sigh. "Bloody hell, are you really?"

Bucky glanced at Gimlet, but she was staring at her shoes. "Yes?" he said tentatively, then cleared his throat and said with more certainty, "Yes. Yes we are."

Bucky had expected some kind of stealth or an air of secrecy—or, at the very least, exclusivity. Surely British agents didn't arrive daily seeking asylum in a dive bar where every surface was sticky. Two undercover operatives here must be like film stars arriving at a crowded restaurant, granted the best table with only a word. But instead the bartender dropped the dirty pitcher on the bar, then flung the rag down after it with performative annoyance. "All right. Come on, then."

Bucky and Gimlet followed him into a dim back room, the walls lined with kegs waiting to be tapped and shelves of wine bottles frosted with dust. The air smelled fermented and musky. The bartender heaved one of the kegs out of the way, grunting with exertion. "Don't help me or nothing," he muttered. Neither of them did.

The bartender shifted a second keg, revealing a square outline and a heavy metal hook, which he took a wide stance to grab, then heaved. The trapdoor opened with a cracking sound, and the darkness beyond expelled a stale puff of air. "Go on, then," he said, nodding them down the steep stairs. "Get a wiggle on."

Gimlet went first, Bucky behind her. "Is there a light?" he called, feeling his way down with one hand along the wall.

"Fuse box," the bartender replied unhelpfully.

"Where—" Bucky started, but he was cut off by the thump of the trapdoor shutting overhead. Bucky clenched his jaw. Under his bare feet, he could feel a coat of chalky dirt on the concrete stairs, and he shied at the thought that he might step on something sharp. He slowed his pace, pausing to feel each next step carefully with his toe before putting his weight down. Sticky threads of cobwebs clung to his fingers as he dragged them along the wall.

Below him, he heard a shuffle, then a clatter that startled him so badly he slipped, and had to grab the rail with both hands.

"Found the fuse box," Gimlet said. The wince in her voice made it clear she had found it by running into it. There was a pause, then the *clack* of a heavy switch being thrown. Jaundiced light illuminated a table with a wireless set on one end and a telephone on the other. An icebox was wedged under low shelves stacked with sagging boxed games and a stained set of dishes.

"This is pretty lousy for a secret hideout," Bucky commented, easing himself the rest of the way down the stairs. The floor was soft dirt, so fine it felt like feathers.

"It's not a secret hideout." Gimlet sat down heavily on a cot pushed against the wall, the distance farther than she must have anticipated, for she landed with an *oof*. "It's an air-raid shelter. Or a cellar that became an air-raid shelter when the Germans started dropping bombs. I suspect the difference is that this one gets money under the table for being on call for any agents who need help in London."

"Still. Not quite what I imagined." Bucky toed an empty mousetrap in one corner that had long ago been sprung, the bar crusty with rust and blood.

"Be sure to request the Ritz next time." Gimlet dropped her head between her knees, rubbing the back of her neck.

Bucky took a quick inventory of the room, pretending he couldn't see her distress rather than admit he didn't know what to do with it. The icebox expelled a puff of rancid air when he opened it, and one of the dishes was in two pieces laid side by side. The pack of cards was comprised of so many different decks cobbled into one it seemed unlikely there was a complete set. "Hey." Bucky held up one of the board game boxes and shook it. The pieces inside rattled like tin cans tied to a bridal car. Gimlet jumped. "Sorry. There's chess. I just wanted—sorry, that was stupid." He set the box carefully on the table so it didn't clatter. "I figured it might . . . Are you okay?"

"I'll be fine." Gimlet took a deep breath, then smoothed the front of her cardigan. One of the elbow patches was coming unstitched. She leaned backward on the cot, then sat up quickly when the thin sheet crunched under her hand. "How long do you think we'll be here?" she asked.

Bucky shrugged. "They didn't exactly give me a schedule."

"But your people know we're here?" she asked. "They're coming to get us out? Both of us?"

"As far as I know."

"But you really don't know much, do you?" She flicked the ends of her hair between her fingers, the ghost of a smile dimpling her cheek. "As this is your first assignment."

"So I might have fudged the details a little." Bucky shoved his hands in his pockets. "It was easier than explaining."

"What?" She pressed a hand to her chest in feigned surprise. "Next you're going to tell me you're not actually twenty-five!" Bucky rolled his eyes. Gimlet laughed. "How old are you *really*? Old enough to drive? Or vote? What's the rule about that in America?" She swiped a finger at the corner of her mouth, fixing her lipstick. "What about drinking? Do you even know what a gimlet is?"

Bucky ground his teeth. He was already regretting letting her come. "I know it's a drink." She gave him a small round of applause. "You make it with gin," he said, resisting the urge to pin on an *I think*. He doubted it as soon as the words left his mouth.

Gimlet smirked. "Well done, Sherlock."

"God, you're obnoxious." Bucky turned away from her, searching again for anything he might have missed—like maybe a door to a second room so he wouldn't have to be stuck here with her until the SOE decided to show up. The adrenaline from the museum was fading, but he still felt nervous and twitchy, like a cat released into a new setting. He wanted to stay low to the ground, suspicious and hackled. "Well," he finally said, "what are we going to do while we wait?"

"We could play chess."

"Oh, ha-ha."

"I mean it."

"You'll cream me."

"I know. It'll make me feel better." She heaved herself up from the cot, retrieved the box, and dumped the pieces out on the table. When he didn't move to help, she arched an eyebrow at him. "Do you even know how to play?"

"I know the basics."

"Meaning?"

"I know how the pieces move," he said, then added, for fear of her follow-ups, "Some of the pieces."

"They really should have prepared you better if your cover was a chess tournament."

"I wasn't actually supposed to play."

"Clearly."

"Teach me, then." He pulled out the chair across the table from her and sat down.

The board was missing two pawns and a knight, for which Gimlet substituted a tube of her red lipstick and two silver coins. She pulled her hair out of the collar of her shirt, then shook out her hands, studying the board like she'd never seen the formation before.

Bucky stared down at the black chess pieces assembled before him. "When we played at the museum—"

She scoffed. "I'd hardly consider that *playing*."

"Okay, well, when we started a game back at the museum, what should I have done instead of whatever I did?" She flicked her gaze up from the board, and he added, "I need to know for the next time I'm undercover at a chess tournament. Consider it your patriotic duty to teach me."

The corner of her mouth twitched. "Do you really want to learn?"

He shrugged. "Nothing else to do, is there? Unless you're one for crazy eights and gin rummy."

"Fine," she sighed. "For king and country." She spun the board so the white pieces were in front of him instead of her. "White goes first."

"Why?"

"Who knows? Probably imperialism. I usually start with the English opening. Pawn from C-two to C-four." She reached over to his side of the board and moved a pawn two squares forward for him. "It's a flank opening to stake center control of the board. And if you move there, I'm going to move here." She pushed her own pawn forward. "Your turn."

He hesitated, considering the board like he had learned enough in one move to make an educated decision, then pushed another pawn forward.

Gimlet nodded. "The queen's gambit."

"Yes," he said, like that meant anything to him. She raised her eyebrows and he amended, "No. What is that? Is it right?"

"There is no right or wrong in chess," she replied. "Just different choices."

"Okay. Well." He pressed his finger into the top of the pawn, so hard the piece wobbled. "What's a gambit?"

He braced himself for a laugh or yet another biting remark, but she answered with the explanatory tone of a schoolteacher. "A gambit is an opening in which you sacrifice a piece for an advantaged position. The queen's gambit isn't a true gambit, because black can't hold the pawn. But if you move there, I'm going to play a Slav defense. Meaning black, which is me, accepts the gambit." She hooked her fingers around the head of his pawn and swept it off the board, replacing it with hers.

"Hey, no!" He made a snatch for his captured piece, but she held it over her head, out of his reach. "You can't do that."

"Yes I can. I'm taking your piece."

"Then I don't want to move it there."

"Too late, you already did."

"You didn't tell me you were going to take it if I moved there."

"I *just* told you what a gambit is—weren't you listening?"

"Kind of?" He rubbed his temples. "This is a lot to think about."

"A gambit is a sacrifice. You're giving up your pawn"—she held up the piece—"but now you have control of the center of the board."

Bucky sank down in his seat, his leather jacket squeaking against the chair. "I hate this game."

"No you don't—you simply don't understand it. Here, look." She set his pawn back on the table, then moved the other pieces back into the opening setup. "Start again. I won't take your pawn this time. Go on."

He pushed the same pawn forward, which she mimicked. He didn't know what else to do, so he pushed the one next to it forward as well.

"You're committed to the gambit," she said with a smile.

"You said you wouldn't take my pawn."

"So it's an educated gambit." She moved the pawn in front of her king up one square. "Gambit declined. Or"—she moved it another square forward—"the Albin countergambit. What will you do now?"

She folded her hands on the table and fixed him with a cold gaze, chin tipped down so she was looking at him through her lashes.

He mimicked her posture and returned the stare. Her eyes were a grayish green, like the new boughs of a pine tree, and her lashes were long enough that they cast a shadow on her cheeks. She wasn't pretty, not in the way the girls he'd pick up at the soda fountain back home in Arlington were, but she was interesting to look at. Less obvious and more boyish than most of the girls he knew, with thick eyebrows and a cleft in her chin. She wasn't small, but her clothes all looked too big on her, the cardigan and trousers both shapelessly oversize on her frame. Their flight from the museum had mussed her curls, and her bangs were tucked haphazardly to one side of her face. But her lipstick was still immaculate, and he thought of the blotted cosmetics Linda had been wearing at the soda fountain the night he punched Johnny. He hadn't seen her since then. He'd never gone back to Molokov's, and she'd never returned his calls. It had seemed for the best, but now, the thought of her tapped a vein of loneliness inside him. He knew he'd be in this work alone, but it would have been something to have a girl back home waiting, someone to write letters that would reach her striped with censor marks like a prison jumpsuit.

The phone on the table rang. Bucky and Gimlet both jumped, then looked at each other sheepishly. Bucky picked up the receiver, not sure who to expect on the other end of the line. "Hello?"

"Mr. Yesterday has been made aware of your situation," the bartender's voice said on the other end of the line. "He's coming to pick you up."

"Oh, swell." Bucky flashed Gimlet a thumbs-up. "Thanks, that's fantastic."

"But," the bartender continued like Bucky hadn't spoken, "he's not sure when he'll be able to get away from the office. You may have to stay the night."

"Oh. That's . . ." He tried not to glance at the single cot, hardly wide enough for one of them, let alone both. "Fine." Of course it was fine, why wouldn't it be fine?

"He offered to buy you dinner. I'll bring the special. Anything else?"

"Let me ask—" he started, but the bartender had already hung up, the question apparently rhetorical. "Uh, thank you," Bucky said, like it was he who had ended the call, though as he set down the receiver, he was painfully aware of how loud the tone was. "The British government is buying us dinner," he said to Gimlet, who was sitting with her hands pressed together.

"Responsible use of taxes."

"The bartender's bringing the special."

"How very forward of you to order for me."

He glared at her, and she wiggled her eyebrows. "What, you think this is a date?"

She brushed a layer of fossilized crumbs on the table-top into a neat pile. "When does the cavalry arrive?" she asked.

"He said it may take a while before they can get someone here to collect us."

"I meant dinner."

"Oh. Hopefully sooner than that."

"Good. I'm starving. It just hit me all at once." She shook out her hands, then said, "Do you want to finish the game?"

"Not really."

The brackets at the corners of her mouth reappeared. "Go on, we can start over. I won't trap your pawn this time." She started to reset the board but stopped suddenly and began to set up a different pattern instead, only a few pieces scattered across the squares. White had both knights and their king, while black had only a king and a pawn.

"Is this some kind of variation?" Bucky asked, studying the board.

"This," she said, considering the black pawn for a moment before moving it one square left, "is the endgame of my favorite chess game in history."

"I didn't know people had favorite chess games," Bucky replied.

"Serious chess players do," she said. "So if anyone asks you next time, you can claim this one. Think of me as helping you with your cover." She silently counted the squares on the board, lips moving, then nodded. "So this is Kleinman versus Fleming, 1908. The game was between world champion Rolf Kleinman and a scrappy teenage nobody called Edward Fleming. He was new to the professional circuit. So no one knew quite what to expect from him."

"And he's the good guy?" Bucky asked.

Gimlet gave him a pointed look. "There aren't good guys and bad guys in chess."

"Well, I figured Kleinman's a German name, and nobody roots for the Germans."

She swatted at him. "Let me finish before you cast judgments." Bucky held up his hands, and Gimlet continued. "Now, Eddie, being rather green, was not the chess player he would someday be, which is why he found himself down to a single pawn to Kleinman's two knights."

"This one is still your favorite?" Bucky asked. "Even though the English guy lost?"

"I didn't say he lost." Gimlet started to move pieces, alternating each side of the board. "Though any other player in this position would have resigned. Likely, they would have resigned several moves previous and never let themselves get this far with nothing but a pawn. But Eddie played all the way until the end. He forced Kleinman to chase his king around the board for nearly two hours."

"Thrilling stuff," Bucky replied. "Who won?"

"That's such a boring question."

"Seems kind of crucial in a competition."

"What do you think happened?" she asked flatly. "Edward lost."

"That's disappointing."

"No it's not!" She closed her fist around the black king. "Because he kept going! The arbiter asked him to stop. Just give in and resign. But Fleming refused. He'd clearly lost. Kleinman grew so tired that he got sloppy. He lost a knight. To a final pawn!" She knocked the piece off the board. "By the end, he was offering Eddie a draw—a draw! He just wanted it over."

"He should have taken it," Bucky said, but Gimlet shook her head.

"That wasn't the kind of player Eddie Fleming was." She set the black king in the center of the board, then leaned back in her chair with a heavy breath. "I've always hoped to be the sort of person who never stops fighting. No matter how stacked the odds are against you."

"So that's your favorite chess game?" Bucky asked.

She nodded. "And now it's yours."

CHAPTER 11
1941

The dinner was cold, and the beer that accompanied it warm. Bucky hadn't had much alcohol in his life, but the taste always reminded him of the Indiana wheat fields he had grown up among on a sweaty August day. The water the bunker's rusty tap spat out was brown and ferric, and he was so parched he downed almost half the glass before he'd taken his first bite.

The bartender forgot to send utensils, so both Gimlet and Bucky ate with their hands, scooping mashed potatoes onto roast beef and licking gravy off their fingers. When they finished, they were both exhausted, the long day capped by full stomachs, but neither wanted to sleep. Every time Bucky started to doze off, he'd jerk awake, certain someone was banging on the door. Gimlet kept yawning, though when he offered to stay up so she could rest, she pointed out that the army cot smelled of cheese, and he didn't bring it up again. They played half a chess game, then abandoned it and restarted and finished and began again.

Gimlet gave up when Bucky tried to jump his rook over a pawn. "You can't do that!" she said with a laugh, swatting his hand out of the air.

"Sure I can. It's a brand-new chess move. You wouldn't have heard of it, it's really new."

She rubbed her eyes with her fists, a drowsy smile flirting with her lips. She'd rubbed off her lipstick on the back of her hand, and her mouth was faintly stained, like she'd been eating cherries. "What's it called, then?"

"The Leap Frog."

"Shall we consult the rules?" She retrieved the book of chess plays she had been reading at the British Museum from her bag and opened to the glossary, making a show of scanning the page. "That's odd, I'm not seeing it here."

"So strange."

"A frankly irresponsible exclusion."

"Maybe your book's . . . old." Bucky rested his chin on his fist. His thoughts felt slippery as fish, impossible to hold on to for long enough to properly voice them. He wasn't sure he was being as clever as he sounded in his head. He wasn't even sure he was putting words in the correct order. But there was no one here to impress. "There's a whole new set of frog-based chess moves that just got approved by the official board."

"The official board?" she repeated.

He swallowed a belch. "The Official Board of Chess."

She let her head droop over the back of her chair, humming softly. "I had frogs when I was young."

"Is that some kind of slang?"

She kicked him under the table. "No, I mean frogs! Real frogs, as pets! My father and I would catch them together."

"Are they good pets?" he asked. He'd begged his parents for a dog when he was young, but his mother had already been sick by then. Her limited energy had been exhausted chasing him and his sister around. "Affectionate? Really snuggly? Do they like to play fetch?"

"I didn't keep them for affection," she replied with an eye roll. "If I want affection, I'll get a boyfriend. Did you know—"

"Probably not," he interrupted, then grinned at her scowl. "I don't know a lot of things like you do."

She rolled her eyes. "I do not know lots of things."

"You do. You're real smart."

"Knowing things and being smart are not the same. But did you know"—she leaned forward and tapped him on the back of the hand—"there is a type of frog in the

Arctic tundra that freezes solid in winter and then thaws
out in the spring and goes on living?"

He put both hands flat on the table and gave an exaggerated performance of astonishment. "No kidding."

"No kidding!" She slapped her palms against the
table to mirror his, then laughed. "I know you're mocking me, but I don't care. It's fascinating. They raise their
glucose levels enough to keep their cells from breaking
down and to replace the water in their bodies."

"I'm not mocking you," he said. "That's pretty neat.
It's neat you know that."

"And"—she tapped the table—"there's a type of poisonous frog from . . . somewhere in South America.
Can't remember. But they purposely ingest poisonous
plants in the jungle because their bodies are capable of
synthesizing toxins and weaponizing them. The frogs
are protected from the poison by one single amino acid
mutation in their sodium ion channel protein. Isn't that
incredible?"

"I only understood about three words in that sentence," he said, and she slumped back in her chair with
another laugh, reaching for the mug of beer she'd drained
hours ago. "Does your dad still catch you frogs?"

"No, he died," she replied.

"Oh, geez. Sorry." He swallowed. In spite of being
on the opposite end of years' worth of these conversa-
tions from well-meaning strangers, he found himself

following the same well-tracked path he had loathed after his parents died. "Was it . . . a long time ago?"

"A few weeks, actually."

"Oh, damn. I'm . . . Do you want to talk about it? Or . . . not? I don't know what to say."

She shrugged, pressing her empty beer glass against her cheek. "There's really nothing to say. He sent me to boarding school when I was young, so I never saw much of him. He was a scientist—a chemist, specifically. His work kept him away."

"My mom died, when I was pretty young," Bucky said. "And then my dad a couple of years back. So I'm not just talking out of my ass when I say I'm sorry and I know what it feels like to lose your parents."

She arched an eyebrow at him. "Do *you* want to talk about it?"

"Not really." He hadn't talked to anyone about it. He'd hardly talked to his father when his mother died. Commander Crawford had never given him much beyond a shoulder squeeze and comfortable silence. That was all Bucky thought he wanted, but suddenly he wanted to tell Gimlet about the perfume his mother wore and the competitive streak that came out when they played cards. The way his father loved to take them to movies, and always laughed late at every joke, just as the rest of the theater would start to quiet. How Bucky had packed up his loneliness so tight, it was bound to burst open like an unfurled parachute, and he'd be pulled off his feet. He just hadn't expected that rip cord would be pulled in a British pub basement by a stranger. "My mom was sick," he said without knowing what was about to come out of his mouth. "For as long as I could remember. I think she sort of knew she wasn't going to be around for long, and she prepared my sister and me as best she could. Not that you can ever be prepared."

"What about your father?" she asked.

"He was in the Army. There was an accident at the camp where he was stationed."

"Oh god, that's awful. And you still want to be a soldier?"

"Sure. Why should that change anything?"

She shrugged. "If it were me, I think I'd be a bit resentful."

"It wasn't anybody's fault," he said. Then, since the air in the room was starting to feel hot and pressurized, he added, "And some of us are mature enough to understand that."

She rolled her eyes, though a faint smile was still playing about her lips. "You are a paragon of magnanimity."

"Hell yes I am," he said, though he didn't know what either of those words meant. "What about your dad? What happened?"

She swiped her thumb under her nose. "He was murdered."

"Geez. You really don't have to talk about it," he added quickly, though he offered less out of altruism and more because he didn't want to hear it.

"There's not much more to say."

"Did they catch whoever did it?"

"Well." Her forehead creased. "That's complicated. The perpetrator isn't a secret, but they're an agent of the British crown, which makes them hard to prosecute."

"The government killed your father?" Bucky asked, stunned.

"Something like that." She traced a pattern in a puddle of spilled beer that had collected under her glass.

"So, what did he do?"

She raised her head, glaring at him. "What makes you think he did anything?"

"The government isn't gonna kill people for no reason. America doesn't."

"Or perhaps it's just not being reported on the radio."

"Look, maybe you just don't know all the facts," Bucky argued. "I'm not saying he deserved it or anything, but . . . maybe there was more going on than you knew about?" His voice peaked into a question under the heat of her stare.

"Do you actually believe that, or are you required to defend the establishment at all costs as an operative? Is this one of those interrogation techniques where you shout nothing but *I love America* as some German psychopath pulls out your fingernails?"

"At least we're not fascist jerks trying to take over the world. We're not the bad guys in this war." He saw her purse her lips, and demanded, "What?"

"Nothing."

"Say it."

"Say what?"

"Whatever it is you're thinking."

"I think I'll keep it to myself."

"Yeah, right. You can't keep your mouth shut."

"Good job it's not my fingernails being pulled out, then."

He knew he was picking a fight, but the momentary warmth he had felt for her upon discovering they were both in the Dead Parents Club was already evaporating. "Come on, just say it. Tell me about all the classified work your dad did that proved how awful America is."

"Oh, good lord." She threw up her hands, almost upsetting the chessboard. "Have you ever met a scab you didn't pick?"

"Who am I going to tell?"

"You literally work for the government! The most I ever knew was that he worked on Project Rebirth."

"You mean Captain America?" Bucky asked. "That's not classified."

"Yes, well, it's hard for anything to stay classified when it's wearing stars and stripes on propaganda posters." She smoothed her hair back from her face. It was starting to lose its curl and hung in limp waves around her face. "Project Rebirth was the code name for the development of the Super-Soldier Serum that created Captain America. After it was successful in America, Britain attempted its own version. Four scientists from Abraham Erskine's team, including my father, were brought over in hopes of duplicating the process."

"What happened?" Bucky asked.

She shrugged. "He never talked about the British project to me. The only reason I know it was shut down and he was moved to a different project is because I switched schools."

Bucky studied her across the table, watching as she twisted the sleeves of her cardigan around her hands. "I can't tell if you're leaving things out or if you really don't know anything."

"Even if it wasn't classified, he wasn't . . ." She let go of her sleeves, and they sprang backward up her arm. The cuffs were so stretched out she could have fit both arms in one. "I was never high on his list of priorities. The only time he came to see me at boarding school was just before he died."

"Really?" Bucky cocked his head. "What did he want?"

"He wanted to come with me to my next chess

tournament. I didn't think much of it at the time. I was just excited he was interested in my life for the first time ever." She sighed, and her bangs fluttered. "And he gave me this book and told me to study it."

"What book?"

"This one." She tapped her book of chess plays, which still lay on the table between them. "It's so basic—I guess he thought I was a far worse player than I am. A little insulting. And look here." She flipped to the first few pages and showed him. "He made these little scribbles all over it, though I can't make sense of them."

Bucky squinted at the book. She had it open to the first chapter. A half dozen words were underlined seemingly at random under a section titled "The Sicilian Defense." "No kidding." Bucky traced his index finger between each marked word. "*Master, immediately, asymmetrical, left, retribution.* What's that mean?" When she didn't answer, he looked up. "Gimlet?"

On the other side of the table, Gimlet had gone rigid, her previously sloped posture ramrod straight. She had both hands pressed flat against the table as she stared ahead, her gaze focused on nothing in particular but so intent that Bucky turned around to make sure there was no one there.

"Gim—" he started, but she interrupted suddenly. Her voice had gone flat, like she was spouting facts for an oral exam.

"Project Rebirth UK test subjects were recruited from prisons. Prisoners in for minor offenses were offered reduced sentences if they submitted to medical testing. Contracts were vague and offered under false pretenses. Men from low-income communities were targeted, as were men who had had few or no visitors while in prison."

"Oh, are we talking about that again?" Bucky asked, but Gimlet kept going like she didn't hear him.

"Of the eighty-seven prisoners recruited, forty-three died."

"Gimlet?"

"Additionally, twenty-five experienced chronic complications."

"Okay, you don't have to rattle off statistics."

"Twenty-five prisoners total. Strangeways, Manchester. Grey, Michael Morton. Age twenty-three. Arrested twenty-five December 1938 for public indecency. O'Neill, Oliver Daniel. Age twenty-nine. Arrested ninth September 1935. Assault and battery."

"Hey, that's enough."

"Shepton Mallet, Somerset. Dainton, Charles Pierpont, age thirty-nine. Arrested sixteenth September 1937 for minor drug offense. Dartmoor, Princetown, Devon. Chamberlain, Henry Owens. Arrested—"

"Hey." Bucky reached across the table and put a hand

on Gimlet's. When she didn't react, he shook her slightly. "Gimlet. Stop. Hey!"

He squeezed her hand hard, and she sagged suddenly in her chair. He sprang to his feet, catching her before she fell and propping her up at the table. Her chin was to her chest, hair in front of her face, and when he touched her again, she didn't react. She felt limp as cloth in his arms.

He didn't know what to do. He crouched next to her chair, frantically trying to remember the meager first aid he had learned when he was twelve and had been enrolled in the Boy Scouts for two weeks before he was dismissed for punching another kid in the stomach.

But then Gimlet sat up suddenly, her cheeks flushed and eyes bright again.

"What are you doing?" she demanded, swatting him away. "Unhand me."

He lurched backward, so surprised by how abruptly she had returned to herself that he sat down hard. She glared at him, like she hadn't just turned into a dictionary and ignored him. Somehow she still found the audacity to look at him like he was the one behaving strangely. Was this some kind of elaborate show meant to make him look like an idiot? But she had looked so sincerely gone, it had been like she was talking in her sleep.

"What was all that?" Bucky demanded. "Everything you said?"

"What did I say?"

Bucky stared at her.

She stared back, widening her eyes. "Well?"

"Are you messing with me?"

"What are you talking about?" She snatched the chess book from the table and shoved it back into her bag.

Bucky picked himself up, gaping at Gimlet like she might spontaneously combust. "What exactly just happened?" he asked, resisting the urge to take a step back. "From your perspective?"

"I don't know what you're playing at, but I'm not falling for it."

"Indulge me for a second."

She pinched the bridge of her nose with a sigh. "We were talking about the last time I saw my father. I showed you the book he gave me. You were reading one of the sections and then suddenly you were manhandling me. It was . . . a bit odd, actually." Her forehead creased. "I don't remember you standing up. Or . . ." She pressed her fingers to her temples. "God, I've such a headache. Maybe I should sleep. Though those sheets crunch when you lie down on them."

"So, you don't remember anything you just said?" Bucky asked. "Nothing about Rebirth . . ." He struggled to remember her exact words, he was so dazed with shock. "Dartmoor?"

"The prison?"

"What do you know about it?"

"Nothing." She pulled her cardigan around her, folding her arms over her stomach. "Please stop looking at me like that. It's making me nervous."

"I think . . ." He pressed the heels of his hands against his eyes. "I think I just hallucinated. Or whatever a hallucination is but when you hear things that aren't there instead of seeing them. Or maybe I blacked out or had a dream or . . ." He sank back into his chair, feeling suddenly dizzy, and put his head on the table. His skin stuck to the gummy top.

"Do you need to lie down?" Gimlet asked, and he was surprised by how careful she sounded. He must have looked truly rattled. Maybe it had been all in his head. "Bucky?" she prompted.

"Just give me a second."

Silence. After a moment, Bucky heard a fuzz of static, and then the last bars of a Fats Waller jive filled the small room. He raised his head. Gimlet was fiddling with the dial of the wireless, but she froze when he sat up, like he'd caught her in an illicit act. "Do you mind?" she asked. "I thought music would be nice."

"Tired of hearing my voice?"

"Tired of my own, mostly," she replied with a half smile. "And just . . . tired."

"You like jazz?" he asked, trying not to sound too relieved at the change of subject.

She nodded. "Do you?"

He shrugged. "I'm more of a traditionalist."

"Is jazz too modern for you? Here I thought you couldn't be more than fifteen, turns out you're secretly fifty."

He snorted. "It's just not my style."

"So what is, then?"

The song on the wireless changed, and Fats Waller was replaced by a familiar arpeggio. Bucky grinned. "This—I prefer this." He stood up and held out a hand to her. "Come dance with me."

Gimlet wiped at her eyes with the sleeve of her cardigan. "No, I don't dance."

"Everyone dances," he said. "All you have to do is stand up and sway."

"Really? Is it that easy?"

"Easier than chess. Come on." He wiggled his fingers at her. "I love this song."

She took his hand reluctantly and let him lead her around the table into the space between the putrid icebox and the wireless. "What song is it?"

"You don't know it?" He wrapped an arm around

her waist, expecting she'd tense or try to push him away. Surely she'd insist on keeping a chaste distance between them. But to his surprise, she leaned into him, her chin resting on his shoulder. He was a lousy singer, but he knew a perfect moment when he saw it, and picked up the lyrics with his mouth close to her ear. *That certain night, the night we met . . ."*

"Oh god." Gimlet pressed her forehead into his shoulder. "Is this a love song?"

"The best kind."

"I didn't peg you for a sentimentalist."

"Yeah, well, there's a lot you don't know about me." He brought their clasped hands down and put a finger under her chin, tipping her face up to his.

"This doesn't feel much like dancing."

"How would you know? You don't dance." He hummed tunelessly along with the song, and to his surprise, Gimlet sang the next line.

"It was such a romantic affair."

"I thought you said you didn't know this song."

"I might have heard it." She hummed the next few lines along with him, her voice faint, and then they both began to sing again at the same time. *"And as we kissed and said good night, a nightingale sang in Berkley Square."*

Had they met in a different world, in a different way, he would have asked her to dinner. Or taken her to the soda fountain. He would have spotted her across the floor at an Army dance and they wouldn't have sat down all night. They would have had a few too many drinks at a proper bar, argued about politics, and flirted shamelessly. Maybe they would have shared a cab back to her apartment and fallen into bed together. Maybe he would have woken up before her and snuck out and never called. Maybe she would have.

"Tell me your name," he said, only realizing how close his mouth was to her ear when a strand of her hair caught on his lips. She laughed, and he prompted, "Come on. I'm not a real spy yet."

"So you don't need my real name."

"Why does it matter?" he asked.

She rested her chin on his shoulder, humming quietly. "You know when you find an animal—"

"Are we back to the frogs?"

"—and you want to keep it but you know you can't?"

"Sure," he replied. Rebecca used to drag kittens home from under their neighbor's barn, and Bucky had hidden lizards in shoeboxes under his bed when he was little.

"What's the first rule? Of finding an animal you can't keep."

"Uh, poke air holes in the box?"

She straightened, pushing them apart, though they were still holding each other. "The first rule," she said seriously, "is you never give it a name. As soon as you name something, you get attached to it."

"Am I the frog in this story?" Bucky asked.

"There are no frogs," she said. "And you're not the frog—you're the one who will get attached."

CHAPTER 12
1941

"O_i!"

Bucky jerked awake at the shout from the top of the stairs. He hadn't realized he'd fallen asleep. On the cot beside him, Gimlet sat up, wiping her mouth with the back of her hand. "Did you hear—" she started, but was interrupted when the bartender's voice called, "You still alive down there?"

"We're here!" Bucky shouted, disentangling himself from Gimlet. She was already fishing under the cot to find her shoes.

"There's a car for you," the bartender called. Then he added, "Clean up before you go."

Gimlet glared around the room as she wedged one

of her shoes back on. "Yes, I'm sure that will make a lot of difference."

"What was that?" the bartender called.

"We're coming!" Bucky replied quickly. "Thanks!"

Outside the pub, the clouds from the day before had dissipated, and the sky was such a bright, crisp blue that both of them had to pause on the steps of the Red Lion, hands up as they blinked the sun out of their eyes. A black car was parked next to the curb, idling. The driver was a man in a tweed suit with dark sunglasses obscuring his eyes, his window cracked as he watched people pass on the street. The bartender ushered them out to the car, even opening the door, before accepting an envelope the driver passed him through the window.

The driver pulled out into traffic without a word, accelerating so quickly Bucky was thrown back into the seat. Bucky realized he'd just gotten in a strange car with a strange man in a strange country, and he felt the hairs on the back of his neck rise. Should he have asked for some kind of ID card or a code word or something? Ask him about the weather on the Isle of Wight and see how he reacted? For all they knew, this man could be working with the one from the museum and they were being driven to be shot and dumped in the Thames.

Gimlet seemed to be thinking the same thing, for she nudged Bucky with her knee, then tipped her head toward the driver.

Bucky cleared his throat, leaning forward between the two front seats. "Uh, hi."

The driver nodded.

"Are you with Mr. Yesterday?"

Again, a silent nod.

"Do you . . . Do you need to see the card he gave me? Or anything?" Bucky asked, then immediately kicked himself because he had meant to ask the driver for *his* ID, not the other way around. They were the vulnerable ones here.

Beside him, Gimlet was frowning at the back of the man's head. In the sharp light glinting through the car windows, her skin looked ashen. She had twisted her hair back into a tiny knot held precariously in place by pins she had dug up from her bag. A few strands had slipped free and fell around her face in greasy waves.

"Who is this man we're meeting?" Gimlet whispered to him as Bucky sank back into the seat beside her. "This Mr. Yesterday fellow."

"He recruited me," Bucky said. "Back in Virginia."

"So he's your boss?"

"I guess so."

"And he must be quite high-ranking in the United States government."

"Well, the SOE, but yeah, I guess."

Gimlet had been fiddling with the cuff of her sleeve,

but stilled suddenly, like a rabbit that heard the snap of a twig. "The SOE?" she repeated. "Not the . . ." Her eyebrows puckered. "But you're an American."

"Yeah, but he's not," Bucky replied. "He's English. British. Can you explain the difference between those to me?" But she wasn't listening. Her eyes were darting around the cab of the car, like she was looking for an exit. "What's the matter?"

She bent her head toward him, a few more strands of hair coming loose and falling in front of her face. "You said you were recruited."

"I was."

"In America." She gritted her teeth. "And that your program was—"

"I think it's best," the driver interrupted, and they both jumped; his voice was resonant and deep, "if you do not discuss the details of your assignment."

Gimlet turned away from Bucky, pressing her forehead to the car window. She had the strap of her bag wrapped around her hand so tightly her fingers were turning white.

He thought about touching her, but in spite of the fact that they'd danced together just hours ago, her cheek against his neck and the smell of her perfume overwhelming his senses, even a tap on the knee suddenly felt too intimate.

"Hey—" Bucky started, just as Gimlet turned back to him, saying, "Can I give you my address?"

"What for?" Bucky asked.

"Because I want you to write me love letters from whatever secret base you're stationed at." She dug around in her bag, handing him the same tube of lipstick they'd used for a chess piece, along with a yard sale's worth of assorted paraphernalia. "Something I can show to all my school chums to make them jealous of my American GI beau."

"Am I your beau now?" he asked, trying to sound cool, though he could feel himself blushing.

"Well, we did spend the night together."

"One night doesn't mean squat where I come from."

"You bought me dinner. We danced."

"Technically the British government bought your dinner."

"Go on, let me give it to you." She sounded almost urgent, and he wondered if maybe her distress only came from the realization that they'd be parted soon. He'd certainly been thinking about it. He didn't know where they were being taken, but each intersection they passed was one less with her. They'd only known each other for a day; maybe they'd find, once the bond forged by trauma was tested, they had nothing else to build a friendship on, let alone anything more. But why not try? They didn't have to be *love* letters. They could be *I have been thinking about your mouth a lot this morning* letters.

Gimlet unearthed her logbook from the chess tournament, scribbled her address on the first page, then tore it off and handed it to him. Bucky noticed the agent's eyes in the rearview mirror flick to them, watching her pass the paper over to him.

"Think you can manage that?" she asked, glancing meaningfully at the paper.

Bucky looked down. Instead of her address, she'd written *How much does Mr. Yesterday know about me?*

"Now you give me yours," she said deliberately.

He considered this for a moment, then took the logbook from her and wrote on a fresh page, *They know someone is with me. That's it.*

She looked down at the paper, then back at him. *Promise?* she mouthed.

He nodded.

She settled back into her seat, pulling her hands into her sleeves. She almost looked relaxed, except for her thumbs pushing holes through the cuffs of her cardigan.

Bucky pressed an elbow into her side. "How can I write you if I still don't know your name?"

"I suppose we'll have to remain mysteries to each other."

"You think your friends will believe I'm your beau if

you don't know *my* name?" When she didn't answer, he added, "I guess you could make something up."

"Fantastic," she said, staring out the window. "I'll tell them you're Captain America."

The car stopped with a jolt, almost unseating them both. Gimlet braced herself with a hand against the front passenger seat.

The car had pulled up to a gate, and the driver leaned out of the window to show the security officer at the checkpoint his identification badge. Gimlet glanced out the window again, then turned suddenly to Bucky and seized his hand. "Whatever happens," she whispered, pulling him into her, their faces an inch apart, "don't let anyone take this from you."

"What are you talking—"

"Listen to me." She clapped her free hand over his mouth. "Don't give it to anyone, no matter who they say they are. Or who they tell you they're with. Promise me you'll keep it safe."

He ducked out of her grip. "Keep what safe?"

The driver leaned back into the car, tucking his ID badge into his coat pocket. Gimlet cast a quick glance his direction, then back to Bucky. She took a deep breath, then grabbed him by the front of his shirt and pulled him into a kiss.

For a moment, he was too stunned to move. Her lips were warm, softer than he had imagined. Not that he *had* imagined. It had crossed his mind once or twice over the course of the night they'd spent together. Because she was pretty and ornery and taught him to play chess and they had danced and she hadn't blushed when he'd teased her—instead, she'd teased him back. It didn't matter if they ever saw each other again—she was kissing him, and he cupped his hand at the back of her neck and kissed her in return. She inhaled sharply, pulling herself up on her knees on the seat. Her hand slid around his stomach, under his jacket, and he was light-headed. He could feel his pulse throbbing in his neck, in his fingertips, in every point of his skin where he touched her. *Why,* he thought, *weren't we doing this all night?* Why hadn't she said something? Why hadn't he? Had all her cranky stubbornness been some kind of deranged attempt at flirting? Maybe it was a cultural difference. Maybe he was thick. Maybe . . .

And then he felt something drop into the inside pocket of his jacket.

The driver leaned on the car horn, and Gimlet yanked away from Bucky sharply, wiping her mouth on the back of her hand. He thought for a moment of her red lipstick, and how it must be smeared all over his face, before he remembered she had blotted it. She slumped down in the car seat, her hair mussed and her chest heaving.

So. Not flirting, then.

He could feel the weight of whatever she had dropped in his pocket, and he almost asked her again for her name. It suddenly felt essential for a different reason than it had at the beginning of this drive.

But then the car door beside Gimlet was thrown open and another man in the same dark suit and glasses as the driver appeared. While Bucky and Gimlet had been otherwise occupied, the car had pulled forward through the now-open gate, and several dour-looking men dressed in shades of gray were standing in formation on the pavement, like the welcoming committee at a funeral home.

Bucky opened his mouth to say something, but before he could, the man who had opened the door grabbed Gimlet by the shoulders and dragged her out of the car and onto the pavement.

"Hey!" Bucky lunged after her, but a different besuited man slammed the door in his face. Bucky rattled the handle, throwing his shoulder into it, but even with the lock popped, the door wouldn't budge. "Hey!" He pounded on the window with a flat hand. "Hey! Hey, let her go!"

"I'd let it be, mate," the driver said quietly.

Bucky grabbed the headrest of the front seat to steady himself on the slick upholstery. "What are they doing? What's happening to her?"

The driver retrieved a silver case and began flipping through it. "She's being arrested."

"What? Why?" Bucky yanked the window crank but it was as frustratingly stuck as the door. "You can't arrest her—she hasn't done anything."

The driver pushed his sunglasses up on his forehead and turned to face Bucky. "Young man," he said, in a tone that was more scolding schoolteacher than spy, "that"—he poked the window in the direction of the men who had grabbed Gimlet—"is Imogen Fleming, and she is in possession of some of Great Britain's most valuable secrets."

Bucky froze, his hand still clamped around the window crank. "What?" He looked out the window. Two of the men had Gimlet pinned against the wall, one of them holding her by the neck while the other fastened a set of handcuffs around her wrists. A third was patting her down with invasive vigor, grabbing her by the back of her cardigan and shaking her like he was trying to empty a piggy bank. Her face was tipped up to the sky, mouth open like she was catching rain.

The driver shifted gears, and the car lurched forward along a short drive that led to a sooty brick building. Bucky turned in his seat, staring out the back window until he lost sight of Gimlet in the cloud of exhaust from the car. He slid his hand into the inside pocket of his jacket and traced the shape of whatever it was she had given him. He rubbed his thumb along a sharp corner, flinching at a sudden sting. He yanked his hand from his jacket, and stared at the thin line of blood gathering along the new paper cut. Then he realized.

She'd given him her chess book.

CHAPTER 13
1954

Rostova guides their chopper into a shaky descent onto a helipad in Longyearbyen, the sky pitch-black and the coast of Svalbard a knuckled smudge. The arctic winds and the helicopter blades raise dusty ice from the snowbanks that line the runway. Rostova cuts the engine, and the whir of the motor is replaced by the sound of the gale battering the sides. Frost is already building up along the windows when V slams his metal arm into the door, wedging it open long enough for both of them to climb out.

As they cross the tarmac, Rostova clamps a hand over her fur hat, pinning it in place. V pulls the hood of his coat farther over his face. The fur lining tickles his cheek. He had assumed Rostova's insistence on both of them dressing in four layers minimum before they left was old paranoia left over from the battlefield, but they haven't even made it off the helipad and he is already sure he isn't wearing enough to keep warm. The wind burns his eyes, but the night is clear enough to see the spill of stars overhead. It feels like it's been forever since he saw the sky. He'd never felt as close to it as he had tonight, sitting among low clouds in the chopper.

"You've flown before," Rostova had said, laughing as he'd stared down at the snowy fjords, his face so close to the window he had smudged the glass.

"I don't remember it," he had replied.

Rostova leads the way to the end of the helipad, where a jeep is parked. The headlights flash in greeting. The tires are thick, their treads clotted with muddy snow. As Rostova tugs at the frozen passenger-side door, the driver leans over the seat and shoves it open for her. V, prepared for his own door to be stuck too, almost rips it off its hinges with his bionic arm.

A gasp of dusty air from the car's heaters envelops V as he settles into the back. His coat sticks to the fraying leather seat as he slides across it. In front, Rostova strips off her gloves and presses the backs of her hands to the vents.

Beside her, the driver turns the key, and the jeep's engine coughs to life. "Isn't there a code phrase we're meant to exchange before you let me drive you away?"

Rostova rolls her eyes. *"If ever you have need of my life,"* she says, raising her voice to be heard over the engine.

The driver pulls off her own hood, revealing a mop of curly blond hair and a wide, gap-toothed smile. *"Come and take it.* You look much better now." She taps just below her own right eye, mirror to Rostova's missing one. "You were always cross-eyed before. The patch helps a lot."

Rostova reaches over the console, wrapping an arm around the driver's neck and pulling her into a hug. "Good to see you, *lapochka.*"

"What do I call you now?" The driver throws all her weight behind the gearshift and the jeep rolls forward, snow crunching under the tires. "What is the Party's latest christening?"

"Rostova. You?"

The woman laughs, cupping her hands in front of the vent for a moment, then blowing into them before she grips the wheel. "No more soldiering for me, my friend. I am again my own Oksana Solovyova." She jerks her thumb over her shoulder at V in the back seat. "Who's this?"

"My asset," Rostova replies.

"And what do I call you?" Oksana calls to him, but Rostova answers.

"You don't call him anything. You talk to me."

"Gag order. Got it." Oksana meets V's eyes in the

rearview mirror and wiggles her eyebrows. "*Can* you talk?" She taps her chin, and he realizes she's referring to the mask over the bottom half of his face. "Or is this some kind of bondage gear?"

"Can it." Rostova slaps Oksana across the arm with her fur hat. "You're still a pain in the ass."

Oksana beams. "I knew you missed me."

V stares up through the transparent top of the jeep. A thin vein of green chases itself across the sky, deep and winding as a canyon.

Someone taps him on the knee, and he turns to find Rostova grinning at him. She points up at the sky, her mittens bunched around her fingers. "Do you know what that is?"

"The aurora," he replies. He doesn't know how he knows it—can't remember where he learned it—but it's there. "The Northern Lights."

Rostova looks surprised, and V wonders what she expected him to say. Should he not have known? Is it strange he can't remember *why* he knows? He can't remember anyone telling him. But then Rostova nods, punching his knee affectionately. "You're smarter than you look."

———

Oksana is the captain of a decommissioned water bus with a flimsy sail and a powerful motor that purrs like a jungle cat. When the three of them cast off from the harbor in Longyearbyen, the prow pointed north, the sky is just as dark as when they landed. The snow turns the air hazy, and with the wind skimming the tops of the waves and pushing the storm horizontal, the black water looks like it's steaming.

V doesn't say anything to Rostova or Oksana as they sail. The mask still feels like a hand clasped over his face, suffocating him. He wants to take it off, but every time he fiddles with the edges, Rostova seems to appear at his side like he's tripped an alarm. As instructed, Oksana doesn't address him. Every time he catches her staring at him, he suspects she'll look away guiltily, but instead she winks or touches her tongue to her nose or crosses her eyes, rearranging her face quickly before Rostova notices.

In their first hour on the water, V stumbles across three hidden compartments built into the hull of the boat. "She's a smuggler," he says to Rostova as the two of them sit, huddled over tin mugs of tea in the cockpit.

The red light flashing steadily on the dashboard rouges Rostova's pale skin. "I told you, I have lots of friends in extremely low places." She takes a sip of her tea. "Oksana knows this coastline. She knows these waters. She'll get us where we need to be."

"And where is it we're going?"

"I already told you."

"Told me what?"

She reaches forward, retrieving a piece of jerky from a bag on the console and tearing it with her back teeth. It's so frozen and stale, V swears he hears it crunch as she chews. "I told you. Do you remember me telling you? Think very hard."

He casts back through his memories, trying to remember her briefing before they left the bunker. Rostova watches him, her face lit, but when he shakes his head, she punches his arm. "You never listen to me. The place we're going—it's not really a place. It's a base on the water."

"Whose base?" V asks.

"A group of people who are almost as bad as we are." She tears off another strip of jerky and mashes it between her molars. "They keep to international waters and stay on the move. That's how they avoid detection. We've never caught up to them before."

"How did you find it this time?" he asks.

Rostova starts to look over at him, but then turns her face into her hood. A gust of air leaking in through the windshield ruffles the fur. "MI5 did. We intercepted an informant in Riga with the coordinates before he could give them to an assigned agent." She stares at the dark window for a moment, then reaches into her coat, rooting around for an inside pocket. "Did you take your pills today? You miss a dose, it will scramble your whole brain. I need you sharp."

It seems unlikely there'll be much of his brain left if Karpov keeps doping him, he thinks, taking the blister pack Rostova offers him.

They're for the pain.

What pain?

She misunderstands his hesitation and says, "You can take the mask off. I'll look the other way."

V pulls down his mask and swallows both pills with a gulp of tea. They stick to the back of his throat, and he almost spits them out. He might have, if Rostova weren't watching him.

There is hardly any light on Svalbard. This far north and this late in the year, the day often arrives in darkness, so the entire twenty-four hours they spend on the water is night-black. The snow stops, and Oksana does a radar sweep, searching for the floating base.

"There's definitely something out there," V hears her tell Rostova, both of them inside the cockpit while he sits on the deck, crouching under the overhang to protect himself from the wind. The only real heat on board comes from a wood-burning stove on deck, and he huddles as close as he can without setting himself on fire. "Whether or not it's your ship that doesn't exist remains to be seen."

"How much closer can we get without detection?" Rostova asks.

"Not much. Their equipment will be more advanced than mine. If we can see them, they can probably see us. Our only advantage is that we're much, much smaller, and they aren't looking." V hears the metallic squeak of old springs as Oksana sinks backward in the captain's chair. "How exactly are you going to infiltrate this place?"

"I was planning to dive."

Oksana laughs. "In this weather?"

"I assumed you had wet suits."

"There are no wet suits for cold like this—you'll freeze solid. And you're too far out to swim. You really came all the way here and your plan was to swim?"

"I didn't say it was my only plan," Rostova mutters.

"I'm not going to sit out here freezing my tits off, burning fuel while you try to think of a way onboard." A pause. V presses the back of his non-bionic hand against the smoldering belly of the stove until he feels the heat through his gloves. "Is it . . . ?" he hears Oksana say quietly, and he imagines her jerking her thumb toward the deck where they both know he's sitting.

"No," Rostova replies firmly. "It's me."

"Then get your head on straight. You have an hour, or I'm turning around."

He hears Oksana stomp down to the lower deck, then a few minutes later, she sits down on an empty ammo box next to him. She offers him a beer bottle, already uncapped. "Can you drink with that thing?" she says, tipping the neck of her own bottle at his mask. "You can take it off, you know. I won't tell her."

V says nothing.

"What do I call you?" She takes a drink of her beer, then clamps the bottle between her knees as she rubs her hands up and down her arms. "You're the strong-and-silent type, then, yes?"

"I have orders."

"Oh god. Have they stitched that onto the Soviet flag yet?" She nudges her knee into his. He scoots farther away. "It doesn't have to be your name. Just tell me *something* to call you, so I know what to shout if we get into trouble."

When he doesn't answer, she blows out an exasperated breath. "Fine. When I call for 'Rostova's idiot,' that's you, okay?" She takes another drink. "*Rostova.* Like she's some kind of intellectual. If she ever finishes that damn Tolstoy book, I'll eat her stupid hat. Do you know how many code names I've called her, and I still don't know the name her mother gave her?" She sighs, a burst of frosty air rising from between her lips. Tangles of her white-blond hair fall free from her hood, dark at the roots where the peroxide is growing out. "When was the last time someone called you by your name?" she asks. "Your *real* name?"

He doesn't remember if he had a name before this. That's how it's supposed to be, isn't it? You lose yourself in the cause and the work and the person you need to be to survive. You forget who you once were. Your own identity becomes a liability.

But no one has ever asked him his name before.

"Were you in the war?" she prompts. "On the front?"

He stares at his boots. The end of one of his laces is starting to come unraveled. Should he remember if he was? He must have been.

"I was a sniper," she offers. "With Rostova, in the Red Army. Did she tell you? We served together at Odessa and Sevastopol. I spent two hundred and seventy-six days on the front. One hundred and ten confirmed kills." V raises his eyebrows, impressed in spite of himself, but Oksana waves it away. "It's not as flashy as it sounds. The girls they had shooting were beasts. I was middle-of-the-pack at best. But Rostova." Oksana leans forward and says confidentially, "Three hundred and nine. They gave her an Order of Lenin after she lost her eye, and she threw it in the Moskva. Said she didn't want their medals, she wanted back on the front because she never had a plan beyond that. She didn't leave space for who she could be when she came back because she didn't think she would. There's a cost of the war no one talks about—the ones who didn't know how to come home." She drains her beer, then tosses it into a bucket of fish guts hanging off the ratlines. "People like Rostova are only happy when there's something to fight. The war gave her a purpose. Somewhere to channel it."

"What about you?" he asks.

She claps a hand to her chest in mock surprise, eyes flashing in triumph. "He speaks!"

V raises his bottle to her.

Oksana adjusts her coat, pulling the fur hood forward around her neck. "The whole first year after I came home from the front, I sat in my flat in Moscow, staring at the door with a rifle in my lap, and wishing someone would kick it down. I didn't know what to do with myself without a war. You think I'd be hiding out here, freezing my ass off to smuggle American cigarettes to the Bolsheviks if I didn't need something to do with my hands? Everything is so boring." She presses her thumbs against her lips, a pose like praying. "It can be hard," she says quietly, "to know what's a memory and what's a ghost."

The snow has stopped, and above them, the pale green of the aurora is streaked purple. "If you could forget it all," he asks, "would you?"

She laughs. "If I forgot the war, there wouldn't be any of me left." She leans forward, studying him. The knees of her trousers are soft with wear, the sealskin as purple and shiny as an eggplant. "Not you, though. I think you were something more than a soldier." She wiggles a finger at him, tracing his silhouette against the sky like she's making him a constellation. "I can see it in your eyes."

He looks over the rail, to the sea behind them. Svalbard is still a knuckled swell on the horizon, ice-white through the darkness like a diamond unearthed from coal. "And what if I can't remember who I was either?"

"You will." She pries his untouched bottle from his fingers and takes a drink. "Sooner or later, we all learn what we're capable of."

"Are you two finished?"

V and Oksana both turn. Rostova is standing behind them, arms folded. V looks away, wondering how much she's heard. Does it matter if she did? He didn't say anything incriminating, he reminds himself, though his stomach twists with unmoored guilt.

"Have you solved our access problem?" Oksana replies, bottle against her lips.

"What kind of organization runs this base?" V asks.

Rostova glares at him, and V can hear the reprimand. *You had one instruction.*

Oksana looks between them. "You didn't tell him?"

"He doesn't listen to me," Rostova replies.

"You're cruel." Oksana turns to V. "Does *authoritarian paramilitary subversive terrorists* mean anything to you?"

"Stop," Rostova snaps, turning her hard stare to Oksana. "I need to talk to you."

Oksana takes a drink. "So talk to me."

"In private."

"I'd rather stay here." She pats V's knee. "My name-less friend and I are getting to know each other. I think he might have some valuable contributions to your plan, if you let him take that thing off his face. Do terrorists scare you?" she asks V, but Rostova answers for him.

"Nothing scares us."

Oksana snorts. "Right, you're badasses."

"If we can't access the base," V says, "can we make them come to us?"

"That doesn't make sense." Oksana points her bottle at him. "Explain."

"Radio a distress call," V says. "If they're enemies of the USSR, they'll have an interest in taking us back alive."

"As their prisoners," Rostova says. "Which isn't ideal."

But Oksana holds up a hand. "That could work, actually. You think they'd answer a medical distress call if they thought it was coming from a marooned KGB agent?"

Rostova shrugs. "So what, I punch you in the face and then we send out a mayday?"

"You send it in Russian," V says. "Make them think you're KGB."

"That's not a bad idea, actually." Oksana takes another drink, eyes on Rostova. Her lips stick to the glass. "You're losing your edge."

Rostova glares at her. "They won't take three of us."

"They'd likely tow the boat if they thought it was a KGB craft," Oksana says. "And there are places here to hide. One of us fakes a medical emergency, the other two stow themselves and slip out when they dock us on their barge. At least let me put out a call and see if anyone answers."

"Then we give away our position," Rostova says.

"So? If they respond, we'll have to give them our coordinates. If they don't, we abort." She squints at Rostova. "What's the matter with you? I've never seen you get cold feet."

"I do not have cold feet," Rostova mutters. "I just don't think they'll fall for it."

"Let me put out a mayday," Oksana says. "I'll use the VHF—no one is close enough to receive it except them. I'll make some not-very-subtle references to us being KGB and in grave, mortal danger that has left us vulnerable, and if they answer, we take it from there." When Rostova doesn't answer, Oksana prompts, "You're welcome to dive—watch out for orcas."

Rostova's nostrils flare. She looks from Oksana to V. He can't tell if she's upset he spoke up, or truly unsure of the viability of his plan. Her protestations feel too flimsy to be sincere. Maybe she has instructions he doesn't know about. But it also isn't like her to come unprepared for a job this important.

"Sending out a call in Russian won't be enough,"

Rostova says. "These waters are lousy with Russian fishermen—you'll need more."

"A cipher, then," Oksana says. "Or some code phrase. Something that makes us look KGB."

"I don't think KGB alone will attract them," Rostova says. She presses her fingers against her lips, considering V. His skin itches. "But if you tell them you're part of the Winter Soldier Project, they might bite."

CHAPTER 14
1954

Oksana sends out the mayday twice before they get a response confirming a rescue team is coming. A few minutes later, a blip in the boat's radar starts to throb.

As headlights sweep the water in the distance, Rostova shoves Oksana below to hide, leaving her and V alone on deck. "Take off the mask," she says. "And take off your coat."

"You want me to freeze to death before they get here?" V asks, peeling off the mask and clipping it to the inside of his coat.

"They need to see your arm." She's struggling with the wrapping around a pair of twin syringes. Her hands are shaking, and she curses under her breath when she fumbles. He almost offers to do it for her, but then she takes the wrapper between her teeth and rips it open, extracting one and handing him the other still wrapped in the packaging.

"Take this," she says. "If you can't breathe, inject it into your thigh."

"What are you giving me?" he asks.

"Nothing that will kill you. Well." She hesitates. "Probably not."

"So glad I'm not the one who gets to hide," he mutters.

To his shock, she slaps him across the face. "Don't get smart with me. I let you get away with so much lip. Any other handler would have had you—" She breaks off, clapping a hand over her hat as a gust of wind tries to snatch it. V touches his cheek lightly. It wasn't a strong blow, but it still stings. "Once you get inside," Rostova says, "come find the boat. You remember where it will be?"

She had showed him and Oksana the schematics of the ship they were infiltrating, but the margin for error was still high. "What if it's not there?" he asks.

"Then you find it," she snaps. "Then you and Oksana will find a plane. I'll do the extraction." She unzips his coat, and he shivers as she pulls back his sleeve, exposing his shoulder for the injection. "Please, do exactly what I'm telling you," she says, her voice suddenly soft. "Remember what your purpose is."

"To comply."

"Yes. Yes, that's it." He feels the prick as she injects him, then pulls his shirt down. He expects she'll turn and retreat to her own hiding spot, but instead she puts a hand on his cheek, softly, the same place she slapped him. "Be smart. Don't talk to anyone. Don't deviate from the plan. Understood?" He salutes her, and she shoves his head. "Kiss-ass."

———————

V sits alone on the deck, watching the lights of the rescue boats approach. He had taken off his coat for only a minute before he had started shivering so hard his teeth rattled and he'd pulled it back on. No gloves would have to be enough. His bionic arm would be hard to miss, even if only his fingers were visible. He rubs his shoulder over the injection spot, like that might make the compound spread faster. With the lights of the rescue boats glancing over the deck, he's gone from worrying the chemicals will start to work too quickly to worrying they won't start to work before the boats arrive, and they'll find him cogent and conscious and obviously a trap.

Then he realizes he's shivering in a way that has nothing to do with the cold.

By the time the boat is boarded, V is slumped on his side, gasping, his stomach cramping. *I could have faked this,* he thinks bitterly as he swallows a mouthful of bile.

Flashlight beams arc over the deck, followed by orders barked in German. "Check the lower deck," a man calls. A moment later, someone grabs V by the collar of his coat and yanks him onto his back. "Do you understand me?" the man barks.

"Yes," V manages to choke. "*Ja. Da.*"

"Who do you work for?" When V doesn't answer, the man shoves the flashlight in his face. V throws up his hands, and the light glints off his metal fingers.

The man grabs him by the wrist. V's shoulder twitches where the prosthesis connects to his skin. He holds back the urge to twist this man's arm around until his elbow snaps. Another sharp pain goes through his stomach and he gasps.

"Take him on board," the man calls to two of his sailors. "Make sure he's restrained."

The sailors haul V to his feet, propping him between them as they drag him onto the deck of the rescue boat and into the main cabin. Unlike Oksana's boat, this cabin is well lit behind the dark-tinted windows, and so warm it almost makes the pain in his stomach worth it. The sailors dump him on a table, then are replaced by a medic who checks V's vitals and starts an IV drip and supplemental oxygen. None of the men are wearing uniforms, V notices through his bleary eyes. They aren't soldiers.

Terrorists, Oksana's voice says in his head.

The syringe is tucked in an inside pocket of his coat. The medic has her back turned, and this might be his only opportunity. But he's moving so much slower than usual. He can't get either of his hands to do what he wants, and his fingers are clumsy and shaking.

Just as he manages to get the button on the pocket undone, the man who shone the flashlight in his face suddenly bangs into the cabin. "Towline secure," he calls to the cockpit. "Return to base." He leans over V, peering into his face. "KGB?" he asks.

"Nyet," V chokes.

"Winter Soldier?"

He doesn't answer.

The man grabs him by the shoulder, shaking him. "Where are you coming from? Where are you stationed?"

V can't draw enough breath. His chest feels like it's caving in. He needs the syringe. The tips of his fingers are numb.

A medic appears. "Sedate him," the man barks. "Then start ventilation."

V tries to sit up, tries to protest, but another needle—not the one he needs—is already in his neck. He sinks backward onto the table, the last thing he sees an insignia sewn onto the man's sleeve: a skull surrounded by tentacle arms.

He wakes with a gasp, like surfacing from water.

His chest aches, but he realizes with relief that he can breathe again. He blinks as the world comes back into focus around him. He's in an infirmary somewhere—they must have taken him back to their main ship, just as planned. He can feel the gentle canting. Or maybe he's still dizzy. He's lying in a metal bed, his right arm shackled to the frame with a handcuff. *Stupid,* he thinks, and reaches for it with his bionic arm. . . .

But it doesn't respond.

Is it restrained? Trapped under something? He twists around to look. He still has his coat, and he rattles his cuffed hand, trying to get it loose enough that he can pull back the sleeve and see whatever it is keeping his bionic arm from moving. They must have checked him for weapons, but when he shifts, he can feel the hard cylinder of the syringe still tucked in the lining.

But what the hell have they done to his arm?

"Easy!" A medic appears suddenly, rushing to the bed and rolling V over. "Are you going to vomit?"

"What happened to me?" V gasps.

"You had an allergic reaction. We gave you adrenaline."

"What happened to my arm?"

Instead of answering, the medic says in Russian, "Please rest. I can give you something to help." When he turns for the counter lining the infirmary wall, V notices a patch sewn onto his sleeve: the same insignia the men on the boat had been wearing.

"Who are you?" he asks.

"I'm here to help you."

"That's not an answer."

The medic glances over his shoulder at V, then unlocks a cabinet with one of the many keys on a ring at his belt. "It will be better if you rest."

While the medic's back is turned, V shifts, rolling over so he can reach inside his coat with his cuffed hand. "I feel fine. Let me go."

"You need to stay here." The medic turns just as V manages to slip the syringe into his sleeve.

The medic has a rubber mask in one hand, and he connects the tube dangling from it to a tank behind V's bed. He leans over to secure the mask over V's face, but V bats his hand out of the way. "What is that? I don't want it."

"Soldier. Please."

"I don't want it." The medic leans in again, and V shoves him again, harder this time. "Tell me what it is or don't—"

The medic lunges suddenly, jamming one elbow hard into V's chest. V gasps, his body jackknifing from the impact, but the medic swings a leg up onto the bed and onto V's chest, forcing him back. V turns his head, trying to keep the mask away from his face. The sheets are thin and slick under him, and his feet slip as he struggles for purchase. The medic shifts his knee from his chest to his windpipe, pressing just enough that V gasps. His grip on his syringe slips.

His toe catches a cart at the end of the bed and it topples, sending gauze and scissors and pill bottles flying. A jar of cotton swabs strikes the medic in the ear, and he loosens the pressure on V's chest just enough that V manages to wedge a foot into the medic's stomach and push him off the bed. The medic crashes to the floor, and V doubles over, his throat convulsing as he struggles for air. A combination of blood and saline is spilling down his arm, and V realizes the IV needle has popped out through his skin like stitching. He can't get it with his hands, so he grabs the tube between his teeth and rips it out. The needle flies free with enough force that the plug is yanked out of the bottle. A wash of saline floods the floor.

The medic slips in the saline as he crawls toward the counter, and V notices an alarm button there. He lunges off the bed, forgetting he's still chained and almost yanking his shoulder out of its socket. He's jerked backward, landing hard with his arm twisted up in the chain behind him. The medic grabs the counter, pulling himself up, but V throws out a foot, catching the medic's ankle and tugging his feet out from under him. The medic's chin strikes the countertop as he falls.

V slides the syringe into his cuffed hand, trying to get a better angle, but the medic elbows him in the face, just missing his nose. V reels backward, stunned, and the medic grabs a scalpel from the scattered contents of the overturned tray. He swipes, but V dodges. He swipes again, the blade falling so short that V realizes the medic won't get close enough for him to use his syringe. The next time he swipes, V leans into it, twisting around so the blade bounces off his metal arm. The medic over-balances, and as he reaches out to catch himself on the bed railing, V jams the needle into the medic's eye. He depresses the plunger with such force that the syringe sinks into the medic's skull past the barrel.

The medic convulses, a scream of pain dying in his throat as he collapses. V falls against the bed, winded, his wrist aching where the handcuff is digging in. His bionic arm still won't move.

His ears are ringing, but he can't hear anything outside the door. No alarms. No thundering footsteps in the hall. If he's fast enough, he might get away before anyone realizes he's gone.

The handcuff key is attached to the ring on the medic's belt, and V uses it to unshackle his wrist, then hauls the medic's twitching body onto the bed in his place. V pulls a sheet high enough that the man's face is obscured, then shoves a wad of gauze into his mouth in case he comes around quickly, before refastening the cuff to the man's wrist, chaining him to the bed.

V strips off his coat and pulls up the sleeve of his shirt, studying his bionic arm for clues as to why it isn't responding. He finds the problem right away—an inch-wide bolt that hadn't been there before is jutting out of the diagnostics port. He can't see how it's connected to his arm—it looks magnetized, but when he touches it, it shocks him hard enough that a metallic taste floods his mouth. He grits his teeth.

V opens the cabinets with another key from the medic's ring, rifling through them frantically for something that will get this thing off his arm—or even a clue as to what it is. He feels lopsided and too heavy, the prosthesis dragging him sideways in a way it never has before. He's still dizzy from the fight and the drugs.

He finds nothing to get the bolt off, but instead locates a pistol with three bullets in the chamber. He tucks it into his coat, then turns for the door, realizing just as he reaches for the handle that he forgot to put on his mask.

It's still hooked inside his coat. Suddenly he can feel the shape of it against his ribs, stiffer than it was before, like it's forged from steel.

He doesn't have to wear it. Rostova isn't here, and

these people have already seen his face. And his face doesn't matter. He's no one. Just another Russian agent.

Comply, he thinks. *That is your only mission.*

But he doesn't want to.

He pulls the strap over his head, fastening it in place before tugging his hair out from under it. It takes a moment to adjust to breathing through it—the vents built into the front are open, but something about the item itself, the way it clamps over his mouth and nose, makes him feel trapped. Suddenly he's suffocating again, that man on the boat shoving a flashlight in his face. Water is filling his lungs, the cold constricting around him. His ribs are buckling from the pressure.

V closes his eyes. He doesn't have time to sit here, waiting for his body to catch up to him and stop inventing escalating danger. *It's all in your head*, he tells himself. *There is no water. There is no cold. You can breathe.*

He opens his eyes again, somehow dizzier than before, but shoves open the infirmary door and ducks outside.

The hall beyond the infirmary is bare and industrial. Half the bulbs along the wall are burned out, and the rest are flickering. The ground sways beneath them as the boat cants, and the portholes on the other side are obscured by the frothing ocean. Frost forms around the layered glass like cobwebs.

At the end of the hall, a number three is painted in red on the wall, marking the floor and the location of a stairway. V stops, breathing hard, trying to remember the schematics Rostova showed him—not because he's looking for the boat. He has to get this thing off his arm. There had been an electronics lab marked on the map—floor five. It comes back to him suddenly.

"Hey! Idiot!"

He turns, raising his pistol. The stairwell door cracks open, and Oksana pokes her head out.

He lowers the gun. "Where's Rostova?"

"Finishing the extraction. You all right? You look like you were hit by a truck." When V doesn't answer, she holds open the stairwell door and beckons for him to follow her. "Come on, we need to get to the hangar."

"They did something to my arm."

"You're hurt?"

"No."

"Okay. Then come on." He follows Oksana into the stairwell and chases her up, but pauses when they reach the fifth-floor landing. Oksana stops too when she realizes he isn't behind her. "What are you doing?" she hisses at him.

"I'll meet you."

"That's not the—"

"I'll find you!"

He pushes the stairwell door with his shoulder, the pistol in front of him. The hallway beyond is whitewashed and well lit, with stark halogen lamps glowing along the walls. Two guards stand at the end of it, both with automatic rifles held loosely against their armored torsos.

The taller one manages to shout "Hey—" before V fires.

The bullet hits the man in the knee and he drops. The second guard fires just as V ducks back into the stairway, pulling the door shut behind him so the bullet pings off the metal. Oksana is already gone. V empties the spent shell, ready to fire again, when a second shot echoes up the stairs from below him. He ducks, losing his grip on the door, and it slams shut. He peers over the rail. On the landing below him, a second guard in black armor is crouched, fumbling with something on his belt. V realizes as the man pulls the pin and it starts to fuzz that it's a grenade, some kind of gas already spilling out of it. This guard has a vented helmet and gloves to protect himself, but he still tosses the canister hastily upward, almost fumbling it. It clatters onto the landing at V's feet.

V turns, throws the hallway door open, and kicks the grenade at the guard there, then slams the door again and braces it with his shoulder. He hears the guard hitting it from the other side, screaming to be let out.

V swivels as the guard coming up the stairs fires twice, the first bullet ricocheting off the wall. The second dings V's metal shoulder. The guard raises his gun again, but V swings himself over the rail and drops, his feet colliding with the guard's chest. The guard goes flying, his gun clattering as it strikes the wall. He lunges for it, but V steps on his wrist where it overhangs the step. The *crack* reverberates off the walls, followed by the man's screams. V jams his palm into the man's nose with another *crack*, and the guard lets out a wet moan.

V retrieves the guard's gun, checks the clip, then hauls himself back to the top of the stairs. His bionic arm is dead, but it's still effective when he slams it into the door, knocking it off its hinges.

The hallway is cloudy with smoke. He almost trips over the body of the second guard, sprawled parallel to the threshold.

At the end of the hallway, the door the guards had been patrolling to the lab is marked with a bright yellow sign written in Russian, with German and English below it. To V's surprise, his eyes go to the English first.

DANGER

HIGH-VOLTAGE EQUIPMENT IN OPERATION

ELECTRIC SHOCK HAZARD

DO NOT ENTER WITHOUT PROTECTIVE GEAR

There's a handprint scanner blinking blue beside the door. V grabs the nearest soldier and drags his body to the door. The gas is starting to seep through V's mask, filling his lungs, and he gags. The guard twitches as V yanks off his glove and hauls him by the wrist up to the scanner. There's a pause; then the door unbolts with a buzz.

V knows he should check the perimeter, approach slowly, scope the corners before he moves, but he gets one breath of clean air from the other side and tumbles through the door like a child, falling to his knees and bracing himself as he gasps. His hair falls in his face, tangling with the straps holding his mask in place.

The door shuts behind him, and he hears the locks reactivate.

Silence. He looks up. The room is small—it looks more like a medical facility than an electronics lab, but he remembers the label on the schematic. He pushes himself to his feet, the pistol held in front of him as he starts down an aisle between two countertops. At the end of the aisle, a chair is built into the floor. Restraints hang limply on the armrests, and wires snake from a panel on the side. Behind it, a glowing chamber is built into the opposite wall, webbed by a tangled network of hoses. Whatever is inside bubbles and undulates like a thick soup, giving the room a strange blue heartbeat. Their faint light illuminates a centrifuge and an autoclave, and a set of cabinets lined with bottles.

V tries the cabinet doors, but they're all locked. The glass panes are tempered, unbreakable without the strength of his bionic hand. V finds a set of heavy gloves that dampen the shock from the bolt when he touches it.

He's ready to pry it off between his fingers when someone behind him asks, "Can I help?"

He spins around, flicking the safety off on his pistol, ready for guards or soldiers or an assembly of scientists ready to pour radioactive waste on him.

It's a woman. Alone.

Her blond hair is cut into a bob, and she's dressed in high-waisted trousers and a loose white blouse. She's a decade older than him. Maybe more. It's hard to tell in the bluish light. She looks almost shy as she approaches him, like she's crossing a gymnasium floor to ask him to dance. He trains the pistol on her chest, and she stops.

And smiles. "We can't keep meeting like this."

He doesn't move. Doesn't blink. No indication he doesn't know what she's talking about. Doesn't give her a chance to even think he can be fooled.

"It never gets less strange to see you," she continues. "It makes me realize how old I've got. What is this, three times now?"

He cocks the pistol. "Shut up!"

He hates the way she's looking at him. He's been studied by doctors. Evaluated for physical fitness. He's been examined and scrutinized, but no one has ever looked at him the way she is. Like she knows him.

His grip tightens on the pistol. It suddenly feels

flimsy, a few light strips of metal, no match for his own hand.

She takes a step toward him.

Shoot her, he thinks. But he can't. He can't move. Something in her gaze is pinning him to the floor, muscles shaking like he's fighting restraints.

"Put the gun down, Bucky," she says quietly, and she reaches out, two fingers on the barrel. "We're not going to hurt each other."

"Who the hell," he says, "is Bucky?"

CHAPTER 15
1941

When Mr. Yesterday entered the office, Bucky was already standing. He'd never sat, though a chair had been pulled up to the imposing desk for him. The receptionist had even offered him tea or coffee, his choice, or perhaps just a glass of water, like this was a job interview. Technically, he supposed, it was. They could send him straight from here to a plane back to the United States, and he'd never know where they'd taken Gimlet. Imogen. Whoever she was.

"Mr. Barnes." Mr. Yesterday held out a hand for him to shake. He looked the same as he had in Crawford's office. He was even wearing the same oatmeal-colored suit, and Bucky pictured a whole closet of identical garments, jacket after jacket hanging in precise lines like drilling soldiers. "I apologize for the dustup yesterday. It would seem your arrival in London has been an eventful one, but you have handled yourself admirably. And you're not hurt?" He gave Bucky a quick once-over. "Where the devil are your shoes?"

Bucky looked down. He'd forgotten his feet were still bare. "I stepped in something."

"We'll have to get you some new ones. Please have a seat." Mr. Yesterday took the chair on the other side of the desk, removing his thick glasses to polish them with the end of his tie.

Bucky didn't move. "What are you doing with her? With Gimlet?"

"Who?"

"Imogen. Miss Fleming." Whatever the hell her name was. "She's not involved in any of this."

Mr. Yesterday pursed his lips. "Please, sit down, I'd be happy to explain everything. Well, not everything. Some of it is classified. Would you like some tea? Jane?" he called into the hallway, and a moment later the prim-looking secretary reappeared, holding a pad of paper. "Tea, if you don't mind."

"Oh, I already told her I don't—" Bucky started, but Mr. Yesterday interrupted.

"Please sit, Mr. Barnes. Give me a chance to cast a better light upon your current circumstances."

Tentatively, Bucky took the seat across from Mr. Yesterday. Neither of them said anything as they waited for the tea. Bucky glanced out the window. The liquid sunlight fogged the windows, and from this height, in this office, across from this man and after the disorienting days he'd had since landing here, Bucky felt like he was looking in at a toy-shop window display of a city in miniature, small enough to sit beneath a Christmas tree. A bridge that could fit in his pocket. A cathedral dome the size of a teacup.

When Jane brought the tea, Mr. Yesterday poured two cups without asking. "Do you take milk?" he asked Bucky. "Sugar is a bit scarce these days, but Jane always manages to scrape some together."

Bucky stared at Mr. Yesterday. Steam fuzzed the air between them.

"Milk?" Mr. Yesterday prompted.

"I don't want tea."

"Very well." Mr. Yesterday fished a cube of sugar from the pot with a set of minuscule tongs, and the dissonance of the action with their setting made Bucky's head spin. He felt like he was in a play, the only actor onstage who didn't know the blocking, the lines, or even the damn plot.

Mr. Yesterday tapped his spoon against the rim, then raised the cup to his lips. "I've sent a telegraph to Commander Crawford."

"What?" Bucky sat forward, almost sliding straight off the narrow chair. "Why?"

"He asked to be kept abreast of your arrival."

Bucky bit the inside of his cheek. "Is he going to get updates about everything I do here?"

"I'll let the two of you discuss when he arrives."

"He's coming here?"

"Well, this has become a bit of an international incident."

"Because of me?" Bucky asked.

"Because of the company you stumbled into." Mr. Yesterday opened the top drawer of his desk and withdrew a file folder, which he handed to Bucky. "The young woman you were extracted with is Imogen Fleming. Miss Fleming is the daughter of Edward Fleming, one of Britain's most revered chemists. He was assigned to the US government's Project Rebirth, with the intention he would then bring their findings back here and lead a project to duplicate them."

Bucky flipped open the file. Staring back at him were a series of black-and-white photographs, the first of a young boy holding a trophy. It took him a moment to recognize himself in the background, his face tucked into the collar of his jacket, and Gimlet behind him. He remembered the photographers at the front doors of the museum swarming him and Gimlet as they tried to make their exit. He slid the photos apart. The next was closer, the boy with the trophy almost completely out of the frame. The third was a close-up of them. Gimlet had her face pressed into Bucky's sleeve, and he had one hand raised like he was about to smack the camera from the photographer's hand.

No wonder they had taken so long to send a car to pick them up from the Red Lion. The moment he'd mentioned there was someone with him, they must have been scouring negatives to figure out who that someone was. Bucky and Gimlet had been sitting in prison without knowing it.

"After Dr. Erskine's death," Mr. Yesterday continued, "Dr. Fleming was transferred to an SOE-funded research project called Project Fugue. Our scientists were investigating the treatment of shell shock—are you familiar with the term? *Combat fatigue,* I think you call it in America." Bucky nodded, but Mr. Yesterday still explained, "It's a neurological disorder noted among soldiers returning from the Great War that presents as both physical and psychological symptoms—"

"I know what it is," Bucky interrupted.

Mr. Yesterday took another sip of his tea. Bucky

wanted to pick up his own cup and throw it against the wall. His heart was pounding, and he was tired of being led in circles for seemingly no other reason than so Mr. Yesterday could prove he had a hold on his leash.

"But Dr. Fleming attempted to abscond with the Fugue research—research that was not his—and disappeared. He only popped up again recently when his work was listed on several international black markets. We believe he was seeking a buyer for the stolen research, using his daughter's chess tournaments as cover for these covert meetings."

"That . . . No." Bucky's head was spinning. He wanted to put it down on the desk and go to sleep and wake up after all this was finished. "She told me her father died."

"He did," Mr. Yesterday said, as casually as he had asked Bucky if he wanted milk in his tea. "He was captured by my agents. When he tried to run, he was killed in a firefight. Miss Fleming has managed to evade us thus far."

Bucky pressed a hand against his eyes. He was trying to fit the pieces of this ever-growing puzzle together, but the edges didn't quite align. Gimlet—Imogen—whoever she was—couldn't have been at the tournament as a middleman for her father's illegal dealings. She'd been just as afraid and confused as he had, and she had run too. Or maybe she had been, and stuck with Bucky to maintain her cover. Maybe the dead registrar was her buyer, not Bucky's contact. Maybe it wasn't Gimlet wrapped up in his mission, but the other way around.

"What's going to happen to Imogen?" Bucky asked.

"We'll interrogate her here, then move her to a detention facility in the north." Mr. Yesterday added another lump of sugar to his tea, then asked, "Was there anything she told you while you were together at the Red Lion?"

Bucky stared down at the photos again. In the last one, Gimlet had both her arms wrapped around his, the sleeves of her cardigan so long they covered her hands. "She said a lot of things."

"Anything about her father? Or his work?"

"We talked about . . ." The details of her life she'd shared with him flashed through his mind—dead parents and Fats Waller—as well as the moment of peculiar blackout in which she had begun reciting data points like she was an encyclopedia, but he didn't want to wantonly surrender them to this stranger adding wasteful lumps of sugar to his tea like there wasn't a war on. "Frogs," Bucky said.

Mr. Yesterday glanced up. "Frogs?"

"And music. And chess." He shrugged, feeling suddenly lopsided by the weight of the book she'd hidden in his pocket. "Just talking, you know. Something to fill the silence."

"Did you engage in any other activities with her?"

Mr. Yesterday asked. His teaspoon wobbled on the rim of his cup. "I was told you two shared an intimate moment before she was arrested."

Bucky felt his ears go red. He wanted to shove his chair back from the table and storm out of here. Or at least pick up that stupid little princess teacup and dump the contents over these photographs. He hated the way *intimate* made him feel—embarrassed and young, like they'd been caught necking in the back of the gymnasium at a middle school dance.

He could leave, but there was nowhere to go. And this man was his protector. This was his side.

Before Bucky could say anything, the office door opened, and one of the agents who had handcuffed Gimlet poked his head in. "Pardon me, sir, may I have a word?"

Mr. Yesterday stood, buttoning his jacket. "Excuse me, James, this will only take—"

"Oh, not you, sir," the agent interrupted quickly. "Mr. Barnes."

Mr. Yesterday froze. Bucky twisted around in his chair. "Me?"

The agent nodded, consulting a small pad of paper cupped in one hand. "Miss Fleming says she will cooperate with the interrogation only if it's carried out by . . . well, she actually said, and I'm quoting here, 'Agent Bucky.'"

Bucky winced. Gimlet had been right, he thought—in that posh accent, surrounded by mahogany and brass, it did make him sound like a cartoon squirrel. "What am I supposed to talk to her about?" he asked.

"She says . . ." The agent glanced at his notepad again, then at Mr. Yesterday, who shrugged as if to say, *Go on.* The agent swallowed, then finished, "She says she wants to talk chess."

CHAPTER 16
1954

"**W**ho the hell is Bucky?" he repeats.

"You are," the woman replies. "Or you were. There's less and less of you every time we meet."

"And who are you?"

"Imogen Fleming." Her cheeks dimple when she smiles. "You called me Ginny. You can still call me Ginny. Or Gimlet, though I think you did it just to tease me. Every letter started, *My dear Gimlet,* or *Dear Ginny with a hint of lime.* You had a thousand lines."

"I would never call you anything. I don't know you."

She buries her hands in her pockets and stares down at the floor. Her blond curls whisper against her shoulders as she shakes her head. "Bucky, we've gone through this. You know I won't—"

He fires. The glass pane built into the cabinet behind her cracks. She ducks, throwing her hands over her head.

"Stop talking."

Imogen straightens slowly, like she's thawing out, then reaches up and touches her face. He almost touches his in return, like they're reflections of each other in a mirror. He realizes she's staring at his mask. "That's new," she says. Her eyes dart to his metal arm. "Can I help you with the restraining bolt? There's a kill switch that turns off the electromagnet. I think it's designed so you can't reach it yourself." He keeps his gun trained on her, but nods. "Back in a tick." She turns—*Idiot*, he thinks, *never turn your back on a soldier*—and pulls a drawer out from the small filing cabinet beside the bed. She tosses a cardigan, several mismatched socks, and three toothbrushes on the bed before finally pulling out the false bottom and retrieving a set of heavy pliers. She doesn't hesitate to approach V—not like she should, considering he's armed and dressed in full tactical gear, while she's barefoot and half his size. "Here, turn to the light." She grips the base of the bolt with the pliers and twists. Her face screws up with the effort. Her hair falls in her face, and when she flips it out of the way, he notices puckered white scars running along her temples.

There's a metallic grinding sound, and then the bolt snaps off. His bionic arm wrenches in its socket, and he feels the electric pulse as it switches back on down to his toes. He rolls his shoulder, feeling like he's relocating a joint, and tests his wrists and his fingers. There's a brief delay, but they all work.

"There you are." Imogen tosses the pliers onto the bed, then stretches her fingers back with her other hand. "Now, would you—"

He raises the gun again, now in both hands. "Put your hands on your head and face the wall."

"What?" She wrinkles her nose. "No, I shan't be doing that."

Neither of them move. He has no idea what to do with someone who isn't inspired to fight or flee at the sight of him. She doesn't even look afraid. If anything, she looks cross.

Somewhere in the ship, an alarm starts to blare. Her eyes flick to the door. "I suppose it's too much to hope you've come to break me out of here? For old times' sake."

"We have no old times. I don't know you."

"Yes you do. We met in the war."

"No we didn't."

"We were kids." She sighs theatrically. "Bright, stupid kids. And so pretty. Absolute knockouts, the pair of us. We met playing chess. Well, sort of. I was playing chess. You were joining an Allied espionage program.

Fresh off the boat from . . . Hold on, it will come to me."
She presses her fingers to her temples. "My mind isn't
what it used to be. Virginia, was it?"

He realizes suddenly they've been speaking English
this whole time. She had spoken to him, and he had
answered. He hasn't spoken English to anyone outside
language exams at the base. "You're . . ." He struggles to
place the accent. "American?"

"English, actually, if you don't mind." She waves
a hand. "Call me anything you like, but please, don't
accuse me of being an American." She's still watching
him, a sculptor slowly chipping away at granite. "Come
on. Anything yet?"

"I'm Russian," he says.

"You're not, though. I think you know it, too. It
always comes back eventually, like sunlight through the
shutters. You can never black out the windows entirely."

He squeezes his eyes shut, just for a breath, like that
might wake him. "I don't know you."

"You're an American."

"I'm not."

"An American soldier."

"You're lying."

"And an operative for the US State Department and
the Special Operations Executive of Great Britain. Then
you were recruited for the Liberty Legion. You fought
with Captain America."

"You're lying!"

"Then shoot me!" She flings her arms wide in invitation, and for a moment he thinks she might embrace him. "Shoot me," she says again, and then she laughs. Maddeningly.

"I did not fight with Captain America," he says through gritted teeth. "I would never collaborate with Americans."

"I saw you in the newsreels sometimes. In the background. They kept you out of the papers when they could—cleaning up after Captain America doesn't really make for the heroic exploit the home front needs to keep up hope. And your uniform wasn't as tight as his, which was disappointing for interested parties." She smirks. "I wrote to you once asking if the captain had a girlfriend, and if not, would you introduce me. You didn't think that was as funny as I did. You were always a bit possessive of him. Or maybe of me. I never could tell." She touches her own cheek again. "May I?" She reaches out slowly, like she's extending her hands between the bars of a lion's cage. When her fingers brush his face, his hand flies up, catching her wrist. Her skin is warm, and he can feel her pulse throbbing in her palm.

And then . . .

His first leave home, they met at Coney Island. He waited for her on a bench in the shade of an awning from one of the hot dog stands, unsure if she'd come. The uniform felt stiff and strange—it wasn't his. They'd given

*one to each member of the squad before their leave. "For the perks," Steve
had told him, flicking the brim of his hat playfully. The autumn chill kept
the beachgoers away. The sky was bright, the air off the water crisp and
cold, and when he saw her walking toward him, he stood.*

*She was grinning before she reached him, smile so broad her cheeks
dimpled, and she called across the boardwalk, "It's not quite the Hotel
Astor, but I suppose it will do."*

*He laughed, and she reached to touch his face—to kiss him?—but he
grabbed her by the wrist, reflexively shoving her hand away. His grip was
strong enough he knew it would bruise. But he couldn't remember the last
time someone touched him without wanting to hurt him, and the soldier's
instincts he had spent the last months honing had taken over.*

He let go.

He lets go.

She keeps her hand beside his face, hovering inches
from his skin for a moment before she reaches forward
and hooks her fingers under the edge of his mask. Gently, like she's removing a bandage, she pulls it free. He
takes a breath, like the first gasp after a long swim.

"Hello," she says quietly.

"Hello," she said quietly.

"I'm sorry," he said. "I don't know what—"

"It's fine. Let's sit."

*They sat on opposite sides of a bench on the pier, looking out over the
water. Her dress was green, her coat shabby and plaid. There were holes
in the cuffs of her cardigan where she pressed her thumbs into the wool.
Her cheeks were pink with the cold. Her lipstick was the same poppy red.*

V steps backward, steadying himself on the counter-top, light-headed, his vision blurring. Whose memories are these?

"I . . ." His throat feels swollen, and he looks down at himself, half expecting to see his uniform speckled with sand.

His uniform was speckled with sand, kicked up by the breeze. Music floated up from the boardwalk, the carousel calliope drowned out by the thudding of the rickety track each time the Cyclone dropped. If there had been riders on board, they would have screamed. His toes curled in his boots at the thought. Pressure in his chest, like he'd gulped a mouthful of too-hot tea.

When he started speaking, he couldn't stop. He told her everything. About Cherbourg. The munitions factory in Novara and the snowstorm in Orléans, where he had stayed in a foxhole with Steve all night, soaked to the bone and wondering if it would be the elements that got them before the Krauts could. Steve had recited all the statistics he could remember from Cracker Jack baseball cards to distract them from the cold. He told her he was the only one in their company who still threw up after every parachute jump. About the beaches blackened with blood. The dream he kept having about the German sniper he'd snuck up on and shot through the head. The first time he ever really thought he would die. He told her every story that would never be shared outside the tight ranks of the legion that had lived through it all together. He told her about the blood under his nails that never scrubbed away, and she took his hand anyway. Slowly.

He's gasping.

"What do you remember?" she asks.

They got a hotel room off the boardwalk.

"Touch is a powerful trigger."

When he woke up tangled in scratchy sheets, she was curled into his side, breathing softly. The pillow was stained with her lipstick.

"Come on, Buck," she whispers.

She asked how much longer he had on leave, and he thought of his plans to meet Steve uptown and drive to Washington together, taking the long way so they could see the foliage in full bloom.

He could take the train. He could stay a few more days with her.

"I'm . . ." The words catch in his throat like dry pills, impossible to swallow without pain. "I'm the Winter Soldier."

"Your name is James Buchanan Barnes," she says. "Your friends call you Bucky. You were in a plane crash, and when they couldn't find your body, you were reported dead by the American military. But you weren't dead. You were kidnapped by a secret branch of the KGB headed by Colonel Vasily Karpov and used as a test subject in their ongoing experiments with memory implantation and forced compliance."

He digs his fingers into his forehead. "I would know if I was an American GI."

"The Soviets have been altering and suppressing your memory for over a decade. We've seen each other before." Confusion flickers across her face, chased by pain. "You and your handler—what's her name?"

"Rostova."

"Ah yes, Countess Natalia Ilyinichna Rostova. At least, I think that's the character's name. It's been a long time since I read *War and Peace*. And, like I mentioned"— she touches the scars on her temples—"my mind isn't entirely my own either. I was on the run for a long time. You and your partner found me a few years ago in Amsterdam. Then Marrakesh. God, I hated the heat there. That was . . . I'm not sure. Hydra caught up with me not long after that. You found this place once before but . . ." She lowers her hands. "I'm sorry. It's hard to accurately judge time when you spend most of it locked in a lab while super-Nazis pick your brain apart."

He doesn't remember Amsterdam. Or Marrakesh— he isn't even sure he could find them on a map. He doesn't know this woman, but somehow he remembers the smell of her perfume.

She bites her lip. "It's never taken you this long to remember me before, and I'll be honest, you're break-ing my heart. But I know you're still there. Their drugs and shocks and whatever the hell else they've done to you won't work, because your own memories of who you were—who you *are*—always break through."

"If Rostova and I found you, you'd be dead," he says. His back teeth are clenched together so hard his temples hurt.

But she shakes her head. "Can't damage the goods, darling."

And suddenly he realizes: "We're here for you. You're the extraction."

She holds out her hands, wrists pressed together like she's presenting herself to be cuffed. "Both our brains have someone else's fingerprints all over them."

He had thought Rostova was picking up a file. A piece of intel or a sealed case he'd never know the contents of. Not a mark. He should take her in. He should be forcing her up to the hangar where Oksana is waiting. Finish the job before Rostova has to.

But then she says, "I'm glad it's you. MI5 is likely getting close as well, and I'd prefer not to fall on the sword of some spotty English boy who slept through Eton."

"You have to come with me," he says, but she keeps talking like she didn't hear him.

"Do you know what a desperado is? In chess? A desperado is a piece you know you can't save, so you do as much damage with it as possible before it dies. That's what I told you I was, in one of our letters. You told me I had a very grand opinion of myself. Which I did. You weren't wrong. But every gambit requires a sacrifice."

Something clunks hard into the lab door. V and Imogen both glance toward it.

"Ah, there she is. Rostova." Imogen nods, like this is another predictable plot point, a book she's read before. "You can let her in. I don't mind. But if she knows you remember anything, they'll do it to you all over again.

The drugs and the electroshock and whatever other hell they've put you through to make sure you don't know who you are. You'll be starting over, again. Every time, they get closer to wiping you out entirely. And this—" She holds a hand out to him, like she's encouraging him to stay still before a photo is taken. "This is the end-game." In the glow from the tank behind them, he can almost see another face behind hers, someone younger, but with that same cocked eyebrow and tight, red mouth.

He raises his pistol again, training it on her face. "I do not need advice from enemies of the USSR."

"I'm not your enemy, Bucky."

"Don't call me that."

"It's your name. Your name is James Buchanan Barnes. Your friends call you Bucky."

"Stop it."

"You were born in Shelbyville, Indiana. You have a sister named Rebecca. You hated school, and you could fall asleep anywhere, and you had this particular way of tying your shoes that didn't make sense to anyone else."

"I said stop!"

She steps forward, grabbing the barrel of the pistol and pressing it against her own forehead. He's so startled by the movement he almost loses his grip. "When we first met," she says, "you were wearing the stupidest leather jacket. You thought it made you look tough." Her other hand is on his arm, he realizes, sliding up to his shoulder. He's cupping her waist, without realizing he's moved. "You loved motorcycles and plums and Coney Island."

"Shut up."

"You were a good dancer. You knew the names of the stars. It was always so easy to make you blush. You knew all the words to every love song on the radio."

She slots her finger around his on the trigger. "Do you remember the one about the nightingale? Something about a kiss and a good-bye. I can't recall it anymore." She leans into him, keeping the barrel of the gun pressed to her own forehead as she rests her head on his shoulder. When he closes his eyes, he remembers—*he remembers!*—just for a moment—the taste of her lips. The heat of her kiss. *Ginny with a hint of lime.* "But when the band starts playing, I'll know it's from you."

CHAPTER 17
1954

When Rostova pulls open the door to the lab, she almost shoots him. "Vronsky," she hisses, lowering her gun. "What are you doing? I told you stay with—" She stops when she sees Imogen's body on the floor. "You killed her."

He can feel her blood in his shirt, still warm and sticky, but the material is too dark for Rostova to see the stain. "She killed herself. I couldn't stop her."

Rostova seizes Imogen by the arm and pulls her onto her back, checking for a pulse before patting down her pockets. "Did she take anything?" When he doesn't answer, she snaps, "Vronsky!"

He's doubled over. His limbs are shaking. Someone else's life is flashing through his mind like scenery outside the window of a fast-moving car.

Root beer in a frosted glass. Water straight from a garden hose.

Taking records from their sleeves with the care of handling a kitten.

Bike tires on asphalt.

An oath sworn on an American flag.

"Vronsky, pay attention!" Rostova barks, and he wrenches his body straight. "Did she take anything? A pill or a capsule?"

"No. Nothing." He watches her check Imogen's body, pressing her fingers under her tongue and reaching into her brassiere to feel around.

Bitter tea in a porcelain cup.

A tie looped around his neck, careful hands showing him how to knot it. "Can't believe no one ever taught you before, Buck."

"You were going to bring her in."

"What?" Rostova finishes checking the body, then crosses to the small living area. She tosses the pillows, sending the cardigan folded on top of them flying. V notices the patches on the elbows, sewn and ripped and mended and mended again.

She pulled the sleeves over her hands until her thumbs tore through. She chewed the buttons when she was nervous.

Rostova rips the sheets off the bed and shakes them, then slides a hand under the mattress. She pauses, groping between the springs, then emerges with . . . a book.

Her face splits in a grin. "This," she says, flipping open the cover. "This is what we want."

She reaches into the book and, like a magician's rabbit, holds up a small glass bottle, the adhesive around the cork fuzzy with dust. Inside is one pill.

Rostova tosses him the book. "Hold on to that for me. It's probably nothing, but Karpov will want to decide for himself."

She unhooks a case from her belt and, with the precision and care of someone handling a bomb, transfers the glass bottle into the padded interior. V glances down at the book. The binding is red, and the illustration on the cover so faded it's rubbed away entirely in places. Someone has written over the title again in pen—*One Hundred Great Games of Modern Chess*. He flips the cover, hoping to find the mechanism that had held the pill bottle inside, but instead finds one of the pages of the introduction is dog-eared. The first section is titled, in bold print, "**The Queen's Gambit, Explained, Accepted, Declined**."

A hook catches behind his ribs and tugs. He's falling backward into something he can't remember.

Warm beer and cold roast.

The hotel window with a view of a concrete alley wall. "A five-star view," she had teased. "You sure know how to show a girl a good time."

"Wake up." Rostova claps her hands in front of his

face, and he startles. "Find isopropyl alcohol," she says with deliberate emphasis, and he knows she gave him these instructions already with no response. "They've got to have some here."

The cabinets are all locked, but the doors come off easily with his bionic arm. He can still feel the ghost of an electric current running through it. Maybe the faint buzz had always been there. He had simply grown accustomed to it.

He finds a bottle of rubbing alcohol and slides it down the counter to Rostova, who is pouring tablets she found under the sink into a glass prescription bottle. She uncaps the alcohol, sniffs it, then nods.

"Take this." She unstraps the automatic rifle from her back and hands it to him, then pulls her pistol out of her leg holster. "Put your mask on. Do it! Why'd you take it off?" He pulls his mask over his nose again as Rostova digs up a surgical mask from a drawer and ties it over her own face. "Get the door. There were guards tailing me. They'll be waiting for us."

V positions himself on one side of the door, Rostova on the other. She uncaps the isopropyl alcohol, empties it into the prescription bottle, then screws the cap back on. V waits, both of them staring at the bottle. The mixture bubbles for a moment, then begins to fizz.

"Door!" Rostova shouts. V slams his metal shoulder into the door and the hinges snap. He grabs the handle as Rostova tosses the explosive into the crowd of guards gathered in the hallway and heaves the door over both of them, a shield from the blast.

The bottle explodes. Shards of glass shrapnel bury themselves in the wall. A thick cloud of acrid smoke fills the hall, and V's eyes water. Rostova peers out from behind the door, then motions him forward.

The dozen guards are all on their backs, bloody and moaning. One staggers to his feet and lurches toward them, but V slams him with the door, pinning him against the wall before following Rostova down the hall.

They take the first stairwell they find marked ROOF DECK ACCESS—NO ADMITTANCE. Two flights up, V hears the door below them slam open, and a gunshot ricochets around the stairwell. He almost trips on the narrow stairs, his own feet feeling suddenly too heavy even in his sleek boots.

The door at the top of the stairs is unlocked. A blast of frigid air knocks Rostova a step backward as she tugs it open. V throws a hand up over his eyes to shield them from the snow, scanning the deck. They must have hit a storm, or else the canting of the ship is just stronger here. Even the thick tread on his boots struggles for purchase on the icy boards. Across the deck, a handful of small planes are lined up, their wings dusted in snow. New tracks cut the runway in half.

"Where's—" Rostova starts, but she's interrupted by a volley of bullets pinging off the edge of the roof. V dives behind a searchlight mounted next to the door. On the other side of the stairwell, Rostova takes cover behind a vent spitting white steam into the night. She leans out and fires in return, then pulls back quickly. She catches V's eye and shakes her head. No use shooting back. The wind is too strong, and they are outnumbered.

The gunfire is drowned out by the growl of an engine, and the guards shift their gunfire upward. A plane dips low over the deck, and the guards scatter, leaping out of the way to avoid being struck by the wings. V catches a glimpse of Oksana in the pilot seat, her curls mashed down by the headset.

"She's coming back around," Rostova shouts, and V watches as the hatch door on the side of the plane is thrown open and a rope ladder tumbles down. As the plane starts to dip again, Rostova and V both leap to their feet and run parallel to it along the edge of the roof.

V catches the bottom rung of the ladder with his metal arm and pulls himself up. Below him, Rostova is still running, the edge of the deck getting closer. He hooks his elbow around the bottom rung and leans out as far as he can, stretching his metal arm to her. "Jump!" he shouts, though he isn't sure if she can hear him.

Rostova takes a sudden leap onto the deck rail and pushes off toward the plane. Her hand locks around his wrist, feet kicking wildly for the ladder, like she's swimming.

There's another spray of gunfire, and the plane swerves as bullets strike the undercarriage. The ladder swings wildly, and Rostova loses her grip. V snatches at the air, trying to catch her, but she flails for a moment before crashing back to the deck. She lands flat on her back on the roof of a lookout tower. As she starts to slide, she scrambles for a handhold, but the roof is slick with snow, and she tumbles off the eave and onto the tin-roofed shelter below. Her head slams against the metal.

The plane veers, wings wobbling. The ladder bucks in the storm.

V locks his arm around the bottom rung and lowers himself as far as he can before he drops. His feet hit the deck and he rolls, trying to take some of the impact off his knees, but he still feels the shock waves through his shins.

Behind him, a guard swings his rifle, taking aim, but V charges, grabbing the barrel with his bionic hand before he can fire and bending it in half. The man lets the rifle go, and the sudden change in weight sends V staggering sideways. The guard throws a wild punch, and V blocks it. He catches a glint of metal in the attacker's other hand just before the guard swings a knife. V slams his forearm into the man's wrist, twisting it backward until his grip on the hilt breaks. V grabs it, flips the blade, then catches it high and buries it in the man's shoulder. The guard's shout of pain turns to a wet gurgle, and V knocks him off his feet with a kick to the stomach.

V takes a running leap and catches the edge of the shelter roof where Rostova landed. He hauls himself up, the grip of his metal hand so strong the panels loosen. He grabs Rostova under the arms, heaving her onto his shoulder before he jumps back down over the edge, crouching behind the shelter for cover. Rostova doesn't stir.

The individual shots of the rifles die suddenly, replaced by the rhythmic *thunk* of machine gun fire. V grits his teeth. They won't last long here—automatic fire will tear through the metal shelter in minutes. He scans the sky, but Oksana's plane is gone.

Rostova had taken a rifle off one of the guards they incapacitated with their improvised bomb, and V unhooks the strap from around her, fits the butt into his shoulder, then leans cautiously out from behind the shelter. The guards are spraying the deck wildly, swinging their mounted gun in an indiscriminate arc, and V waits until the shooter pivots, then fires, taking him out with a bullet in the neck. On the ground beside V, Rostova groans, struggling to roll over. She vomits, and

V grabs the shoulder of her coat, nearly lifting her off the ground as he turns her roughly on her side so she doesn't choke. She gags, spitting a mouthful of bile into the snow.

"Stay down. Don't move." He jams the sniper rifle back into his shoulder and leans out from behind the shelter, only to reel backward, momentarily blinded as the searchlight sweeps the deck. He claps a hand over his eyes, vision popping with colors, as the searchlight skims the clouds in pursuit of Oksana's plane. V expels the empty shell in his rifle, then leans into the open again and fires. The man struggling with the searchlight drops.

"You should have left me." Rostova wipes her mouth with the back of her hand.

"You should have told me that sooner." He takes another shot, and the bullet cracks the surface of the searchlight. The beam splinters across the sky.

The purr of an engine rises behind them, and V turns. Oksana's plane is coming toward them, far enough away that the antiaircraft fire can't hit her, but diving toward the sea. She'll just miss the top deck, but the ladder is still dangling from the belly of the plane.

V grabs Rostova by the front of her coat and hauls her into a sitting position. He's not sure she can hold on, so he unhooks the strap from his rifle and wraps it around her wrists, pulling them together before looping them around his neck. The cord cuts into the sliver of bare skin at his throat where the neck of his shirt has bunched, but he's so cold he hardly feels it.

One chance.

He hauls himself up, staggering for a moment before he acclimates to Rostova's added weight, then runs for the ship's rail. Gunfire splatters the deck under his feet. As Oksana's plane dives, V jumps, stretching with his metal arm for the ladder.

Somehow, he catches it. His body jerks, and he feels the circuitry in his shoulder wrench. Oksana pulls the plane out of the dive just before they hit the water, so close that V feels the spray on his face. The ladder bucks, and he struggles to catch the bottom rungs with his foot. He shifts his weight, trying to pull himself and Rostova up, but the tread of his boots is slick with snow. He loses his hold and tips backward, the dark water rising up to meet him.

But then Rostova swings her legs around either side of his waist and hooks her knees on the ladder. The friction slows his fall, enough for him to catch his elbows on her knees and grab one of the rungs. Rostova groans in pain as V pushes himself up, feet on the bottom rung. He grabs her around the waist and hoists them both up.

V pushes Rostova into the plane, then crawls up after her, tugging the hatch door shut behind him before collapsing. Rostova is sprawled on the floor beside him,

chest heaving. From the cockpit, Oksana shouts something, but his ears are ringing. He shakes his head,
trying to clear the noise. Oksana points to Rostova, then
flashes a thumbs-up/thumbs-down. *Dead or alive?*

V rolls over and crawls across the cargo hold to
where Rostova is lying. She has one leg cocked and an
arm thrown over her stomach. Her eyes are unfocused,
and when she coughs, blood splatters her lips. V gives
Oksana a grim thumbs-up.

As the plane dips, V heaves Rostova up into one of
the jump seats and pulls the restraints over her shoulders. She hisses in pain as he tightens them, her head
rolling forward onto her chest.

"Stay awake." He slaps her cheek lightly, and she
raises her head, blinking at him.

"Which one are you?" Her words are slurred, and
the engine is so loud he isn't sure he heard her right.
"Bolkonsky? Or is it . . . Karenin? I can't . . . Stop, stay
still." She grabs his chin, trying to pull his mask off.

He fastens the latch on her restraints, but she pushes
back with strength that surprises him. "I can't remember . . ." Her head lilts to one side, then the other. "I
can't remember who you are."

He catches her hand before she can grab him again.
"It's me," he says quietly. "It's just me."

"I need to see . . ."

"You hit your head."

"Let me see your face. I can always tell."

"Fine." He fastens the restraint, then crouches down in front of her, pulling his mask down around his neck so she can see him. Somewhere on the deck, she lost her eye patch, and V realizes he's never seen her without it. Her damaged eye is milky white, with red veins like lightning strikes running luridly through where the pupil used to be. The lid sags, and the skin under her eye drips like melting wax.

She seizes his face and pulls it close to hers, studying him with an unfocused gaze. Then she slumps forward again, her forehead resting on his chest. "No. Oh, no, no, no."

"What?" he asks, alarmed. He wonders if there's blood on his face, or some injury he hadn't had time to notice. "What is it? What's wrong?"

Rostova droops in her seat. "Too late," she murmurs. "Too late again."

CHAPTER 18
1941

When Bucky entered the interrogation room, Gimlet was already sitting at the metal table in the center, her cuffed hands resting on the edge of the chessboard. Bucky had no idea where they had found it, though this office seemed like it might be the kind of place that would have exactly what you needed lying around.

She was staring at the wall and didn't look at him when he took the chair across from hers. All the furniture in the room, he noted, was bolted to the ground.

"Okay. So." He wasn't sure how to start. Mr. Yesterday's secretary had given him a basic script, let him read it twice before it was taken away and he was shoved in here to face Imogen. He hadn't expected to feel prepared, but he also hadn't anticipated just how different Imogen would feel from the girl he had spent the night with. His T-shirt was stuck to his back, and he resisted the urge to take off his jacket. He still didn't have shoes, and the tile felt warm as summer blacktop against the soles of his feet.

"They told me to tell you the room's bugged," he said finally. "And they're watching."

Imogen glanced up, and Bucky nodded at the opaque pane of glass built into the wall behind her. "Then allow me to send my love and well wishes to the men and women of the SOE listening." She raised her cuffed hands and wiggled her fingers over her head in a wave. "Queen, country, and all that, I hope you're bloody proud of yourselves."

Bucky grabbed her hands, pinning them down to the tabletop. "Look, why don't you just say whatever—"

"What's your name?" she asked.

"What?"

"You know mine." She leaned forward on her elbows. "It seems only fair."

"Fair?" Bucky repeated. "What the hell do you care about fair? You tricked me."

"Did I?"

"I thought you were just there playing chess and got caught up in my mess, but actually you were the mess this whole time."

"You have to go first." She tapped a finger against the board. "White always goes first."

"Is that really what we're doing?" he asked. "Playing chess?"

"Did your handlers give you the impression it would be something different?"

"They're not my handlers," Bucky snapped. The word made him feel like a show dog. "And this"—he pointed to the board—"is a waste of time."

A faint smile tugged at her lips. "Indulge me. I've nowhere else to be."

Bucky wondered what would happen if he refused. Or if he stood up and walked out. What would Mr. Yesterday say? He picked up a pawn, held it up deliberately in front of her face, then placed it two squares forward.

She smiled. "You know, one of the things I like about chess is that there are really only a few ways to start a game. The English opening—this one I taught you." She picked up a pawn and moved it to match his. "Always starts the same, but with every choice you make, the potential for your next move gets more and more infinite. We can't fathom how many different ways our choices split the future. But then, in the end, the outcome is always one of three—you win, or I win, or we draw. It's your turn again."

He moved his knight behind his pawn.

She nodded. "So that's a Dutch variation on the Bird's opening. For your next move, if I may, try a King's Indian setup, with the attack on the black king side. The gamble being, of course, that the King's Indian is not a specific sequence of moves, but rather a system that you permute at your discretion. Of course, if you insist on a Bird's opening, I'll return with a pawn to E-six. The D-five pawn is also playable, as is the C-five. You see what I mean?" She reached over and reset the board, moving their pieces back to their original places. "Do you remember the story I told you, about Edward Fleming?"

"The chess player who wouldn't give in."

He moved his knight first this time. She nodded, a small tic he hadn't noticed until now—that single head bob after every move. "He never conceded a game. Not one, in his whole career. I always thought that was real courage. Real sportsmanship. To keep fighting even when you know you've lost. To fight on your knees, with your face in the dirt." A small crease dimpled the skin between her eyebrows. "When he was eighteen, Eddie was sent to France. He was a clay kicker. He dug tunnels for explosives under enemy lines. It was rotten work. So cold, most of the men lost toes. Eddie was sick all the time. The tunnels were hardly wider than his shoulders, and sometimes he had to crawl on his belly for miles. Sometimes the walls caved in on top of him."

Bucky moved his corresponding pawn. "He was your dad."

The crease deepened. "Well spotted."

"I thought you said he survived the war."

"He came home." She picked up her knight, twirling it absently between her fingers as she studied the board. "That's not really the same, though, is it? He might have been the greatest chess player in the world, but the first tournament he enrolled in after France, he just sat there, staring at the board."

"What was the matter with him?"

She shrugged. "Nothing. Not bodily, anyway. But in his mind, the war didn't end." She set the knight on her board, then looked up at Bucky. "The first year he was home, my father went to five funerals for men in his company. By the time I was born, more men he served with had died back in England than had in France. His best friend shot himself through the head at a Veteran's Parade in Birmingham. My father was there—I was there. It's the only thing I remember clearly from childhood."

"Geez," Bucky murmured.

She glared at the board, though the rattle of her cuffs against the table betrayed her shaking hands. "My father gave up chess. He went to university to study chemistry. He started working on a way to implant memories in the brain—and, the flip side of that coin, how to remove them. He hoped it could be used to treat shell shock."

"Yeah, so I heard," Bucky interrupted. "And then I heard about how he ran away from a government contract and tried to use you to sell his work to whoever forked over the most cash."

Her head shot up. "What?"

"Didn't you . . ." He glanced over her shoulder at the opaque window. "That's what they told me. Your dad's research ended up on an international black market. The sale was happening at the chess tournament."

"I don't know anything about that."

"So why did you go to the tournament?" Bucky asked.

"Because my father registered me for it," she said. "He showed up at my school one day and told me he was going to take me to London for the tournament, then we were going to go to the United States. When he was murdered, I thought that's what he'd want me to do with or without him."

Suddenly it made sense why she'd stayed glued to his side, all the way into the Red Lion and the black car, right up until she realized that, in spite of his accent, he was in London with the SOE. She'd wanted American intervention. Her father may have been counting on an illicit payout to fund the trip, but maybe she truly hadn't known more than their destination.

"Are you sure he wasn't trying to get you there as cover so he could make his sale?" Bucky asked her.

"He wouldn't do that."

"So who was selling his work, then? Who else would have access to it?" When she didn't answer, Bucky prompted, "I can protect you."

She snorted. "No you can't."

"No I can't," he admitted. "But I can help. I can make it easier. Just tell me . . ."

"Tell you what?" She leaned over the board toward him. Her elbow sent a rook flying. "You don't even know what you're asking me, do you? You're nothing but a mouthpiece. What an asset you'll be. You go where they want and say what they want and let yourself be shoved into a locked room with the daughter of a mad scientist they recently murdered so you can scold her about tricking *you*." She slumped back in her chair, then flicked her king, sending him rolling to the edge of the table and onto the floor. "God save the USA."

"I'm nobody's mouthpiece."

"That man—what do you call him?" She pointed at the door, her cuffed hands cradled together in a way that made him think of a pistol grip. "Mr. Yesterday? Did he tell you he shot my unarmed father in the head? I know that's what happened." She twisted around to the window, shouting at it. "I know that's what you did! Better close the curtains next time if you don't want anyone to see you assassinate a civilian, you cowardly, sniveling, filthy piece of—"

The interrogation room door banged open suddenly,

and two agents in suits charged into the room, Mr. Yesterday on their tail. One of them grabbed Imogen by the collar of her cardigan and slammed her into the table, her face pressed into the chessboard. The pieces scattered. She squirmed, furious shouts petering into gasping breaths. The other agent seized Bucky by the arm, pulling him off his chair with such force his bare foot caught one of the bolted-down legs. He yelped, pain shooting through his toe.

Mr. Yesterday stalked up to Imogen, bending down next to the table so his face was inches from hers. "How dare you. There is no low to which the Flemings won't sink. I should have expected it, after your father turned against his country."

For a moment, Bucky thought Imogen was going to spit in his face. Instead, she relaxed enough that the agent holding her loosened his grip. Then she jerked up and head-butted Mr. Yesterday. Her forehead connected with his chin, and he fell backward with a cry of pain. A spurt of blood dribbled from his mouth and onto the floor.

The agent slammed Imogen's face into the table again. The handcuffs slipped up her forearms, and Bucky could see the red welts they had left on her wrists.

Mr. Yesterday pressed the heel of his hand to his lips. "Get him out of here," he snapped.

The agent holding Bucky by the arm dragged him

toward the door. "Hey, wait!" Bucky twisted around, wishing Imogen would look at him. He suddenly wanted, more than anything, to tell her his name. Why hadn't he told her when she asked?

In the hall outside the interrogation room, the agent slammed Bucky against the wall with more force than he felt was necessary since they were technically still on the same side. His chin struck the plaster. He tried to turn, but the agent pressed an elbow into his back, hard enough his spine popped.

"Please don't make a scene," a familiar voice said in his ear.

Bucky froze. All his righteous indignation toward Mr. Yesterday and his goons cooled like a forgotten cup of coffee.

It was the Arbiter.

In a government office, in the same nondescript suit. He worked for the SOE. Or they thought he did. He was pawing at Bucky's jacket, like he was searching for a weapon or a bug or . . .

The chess book was still in his pocket.

The Arbiter would find it—it was in Bucky's inside pocket, but bulky enough that it was hardly hidden. Bucky struggled, trying to throw the Arbiter off him. "Who are you?" he demanded, distraction his only weapon. "Who do you work for?"

"Why would I tell you that?"

"So I don't make a scene."

"I expect your word won't hold as much weight as mine in this office." His accent suddenly sounded too polished to be real. "Leave her to me, and I'll leave you out of this."

"What are you talking about?"

"Imogen Fleming is mine. I own her."

"That's so creepy."

The Arbiter spun Bucky around, pinning him to the wall with a forearm against his chest. "Leave now. Leave England. Don't try to contact her, and I won't involve you."

Bucky tried to elbow the Arbiter, but the man caught his arm and twisted it. Bucky felt his jacket fall open. The corner of the book dug into his ribs, balanced precariously between the heavy leather and his side. If he took a breath, it would fall.

"What the hell do you think you're doing? Release him!"

The Arbiter stepped back at once. Bucky clamped his elbow against his side, trapping the book in place just before it fell, then slumped against the wall, gasping for breath. He doubled over, then, out of view of the Arbiter, shoved the book back into his pocket.

"Apologies, sir," he heard the Arbiter say. "I misunderstood."

Mr. Yesterday was suddenly at Bucky's side, one hand

clamped around his arm. "Apologies, Mr. Barnes, I'm so sorry. Are you all right?"

"I'm fine," Bucky said, the word broken by a wheeze. He hadn't realized how hard the Arbiter had been pressing on his rib cage. "Fine, really."

Mr. Yesterday thrust a finger into the Arbiter's face. "Get back to your desk," he snapped. "And wait for me. Mr. Barnes, please, this way."

Arm still clamped against his side, Bucky followed Mr. Yesterday down the hall. When they reached the office door, he glanced over his shoulder. The Arbiter was still where they'd left him. His eyes met Bucky's, and he pressed a finger to his lips.

Inside Mr. Yesterday's office, Bucky collapsed onto the sofa against the wall. He dropped his head between his legs, struggling to catch his breath. The Arbiter was here—the man who had left a body in the bathroom and chased them through the museum. The Arbiter was *here*—the Arbiter worked for the SOE. The Arbiter was here, and Imogen was here, and he had to tell someone.

Mr. Yesterday crouched in front of Bucky, peering into his face. "Are you hurt?"

"I don't think so."

"I'm so sorry; that was completely uncalled for."

He had to tell someone.

He looked up. Mr. Yesterday's mouth was still bleeding. One of his front teeth had cracked in half where

Gimlet's forehead had connected. The fragment left behind clung precariously to his gums.

He couldn't tell Mr. Yesterday.

Bucky knew it suddenly. The Arbiter was right—there would be nothing but Bucky's word against his. Teenage punk versus a likely decorated government agent was hardly betting odds. Imogen would only tip the scales further against them. He wasn't even sure who exactly the Arbiter was working for, and it was hard to accuse someone of a double cross without knowing what it was they were crossing.

He couldn't tell anyone. Not yet. Not without real proof. If he only had one chance to make an accusation and have it taken seriously, he was going to make it count.

"I'm afraid I need to get to a dentist." Mr. Yesterday sniffed, wet and deep in his throat. "One of my men will take you to the Aglionby Hotel for the night. We have an arrangement with them—you'll be quite safe, and well taken care of. Please do not leave your room—anything you need, the front desk will be happy to bring up to you. Someone will come retrieve you for breakfast."

"What's at breakfast?" Bucky asked.

"Commander Crawford arrives from Washington tonight. He'll meet you at seven a.m." He withdrew a handkerchief from his pocket and spat a delicate wad of blood into it. "Is that all clear?"

Nothing felt clear, but Mr. Yesterday's broken tooth was growing more unsettling the longer he stared at it, and Bucky was afraid one of them would pass out because of it. "Yeah, I got it."

"Is something wrong with your arm?"

"What?" He realized he still had one elbow clamped unnaturally to his side, holding the chess book in place. "Oh. No, I'm just"—he shivered theatrically—"cold."

The hotel room was like something out of a fairy-tale castle—aggressively wallpapered, gold-filigreed in excess, and big enough that the entire first floor of the Crawfords' house could have fit inside. Bucky only took a moment to admire it before he toppled like a felled tree into bed. He was asleep almost at once, but sprang awake what felt like only seconds later to the sensation that someone had a gun to his rib cage. He leaped out of bed, gasping, only to realize he had fallen asleep with his jacket still on, and the chess book was jammed into his side. He had to unpeel it from the pocket—sweat had suctioned the cover to the leather—then tossed both book and jacket onto the duvet.

He thought about lying down again and trying to go back to sleep—maybe this time under the covers and without his filthy clothes—but he was wide-awake now, his heart still racing. He scrubbed a hand through his hair, wincing when his fingers came back greasy. There were dark crescents under the arms of his shirt, and a small spot of blood on the collar. He stripped it off and tossed it on the floor, though his undershirt was just as filthy.

Mr. Yesterday had told him to call the desk for anything he needed. He wasn't sure if this was what he'd meant, but he picked up the telephone receiver by the bed anyway.

There was a moment of silence, and then a woman's voice chirped, "Good evening, Mr. Barnes, this is Jane. What can I do for you?"

"Oh. Hi . . . Jane." Hadn't Mr. Yesterday's secretary been named Jane as well? He'd spoken to her on the phone. He glanced at the clock next to the telephone and realized with surprise it was almost midnight. "Sorry, I didn't look at the time."

"No apology necessary. Is there something I can get for you?"

"I was hoping you had some clothes I could borrow. Just Levi's and an undershirt would be swell—I have a jacket—sorry, it can wait until morning—"

"What size trouser do you wear?" Jane interrupted.

Bucky hesitated. "Really?"

"I'll have a measuring tape sent up. Ring back with your measurements, and we'll have a selection of garments prepared for you, along with underclothes and shoes. Is there anything else you require?"

Some help figuring out what the hell is going on, he considered saying, but he thought sharing national secrets with the concierge might be frowned upon. Even if the concierge was on SOE payroll and probably knew more than he did. Everyone probably knew more than he did.

After they hung up, Bucky stripped off the rest of his clothes, then ran the bath. As the room filled with steam, he retrieved Gimlet's chess book from under his jacket. *One Hundred Great Games of Modern Chess* was embossed on the spine.

The pages were littered with notations in red ink, all as nonsensical as the one he had read aloud in the bunker. He scanned the table of contents until he found what he was looking for: "Kleinman vs. Fleming, 1908." He thumbed the corners, searching for the corresponding page, only to discover that all the pages in the second half were stuck together. It felt like someone had glued the book to a brick. He flipped through until he found the spot where the book became a block, and realized with a jolt that the center had been hollowed out, leaving a small secret compartment in the middle of the sealed pages.

Inside, there was a tiny glass bottle containing one white pill.

CHAPTER 19
1941

When Bucky followed Jane the concierge into the hotel dining room the next morning, Crawford was already there, sitting alone in a banquette booth, staring at the clock hanging behind the coffee counter. When he saw Bucky, he leaped to his feet and charged across the restaurant. Bucky was almost knocked over as Crawford wrapped him in a bone-crushing hug.

"Good god, Buck."

"I'm fine," Bucky mumbled. One of the pins on Crawford's uniform was poking his cheek, but he didn't move. He hadn't realized how much he'd missed Crawford—missed having someone he knew he could trust and rely on—until he saw the commander. The first truly familiar face in weeks.

"I thought I'd have at least a little while to acclimate to the idea of you in active danger, and turns out you got a tail on you your first day here." Crawford pushed back, studying Bucky's face with one hand hooked behind his neck. "You okay? Really?"

"Cross my heart." Bucky held out his arms as proof he was still intact. The slacks and button-up he had found in a garment bag outside his room that morning fit him perfectly. He even had shoes, at long last. They'd left pajamas as well, which he hadn't noticed until they were no longer needed. He'd almost put them on anyway— the silky material felt so luxurious. In these borrowed clothes and with his hair still damp from a shower, he felt like a new person. The previous days might have been a dream.

Except Crawford was still looking at Bucky like he'd been pulled out of a house fire, and he'd discovered a small bruise on his rib cage from where the Arbiter had slammed him into the wall. Imogen's book was still in his pocket.

Crawford clapped a hand on Bucky's shoulder, steering him toward the banquette he'd abandoned. "Come sit down with me, have some coffee. Tea, I guess; tea's what they drink here."

Bucky took the seat across the booth from Crawford. He hadn't realized how hungry he was until he caught a whiff off a passing tray heaped with glossy baked beans and seared, steaming tomatoes.

"Food's on the way," Crawford said, like he could hear Bucky's stomach growling. "Hope it's okay I ordered for you—we're on a schedule."

"You didn't have to come all this way," Bucky said as Crawford filled his cup with hot water. The words AGLIONBY HOTEL were painted in delicate blue script along the rim.

"I did, actually." Crawford flipped the lid on a box of tea bags, thumbing through them like they were a card catalogue. "If our American trainees are being targeted when they arrive in England, that's a matter for the State Department."

"Probably could have been a phone call."

Crawford raised an eyebrow, then laughed. "Probably could have been." He slid a tea bag across the table to Bucky, but when Bucky reached for it, Crawford pulled it back out of his reach. "You're okay, though?" he asked, tipping his head so Bucky was forced to meet his eyes. "Really?"

"I'm okay. A little"—Bucky shook out his shoulders; he'd been holding his muscles tense for so long they were starting to ache—"shaken up."

"I'd expect so. God, I'd be more worried if you weren't." Crawford surrendered the tea bag and picked out his own. "You sleep at all?"

Bucky shrugged. "Some." He'd spent most of the night looking through the pages of the chess book that weren't glued together, searching for some kind of clue about what it was and why Imogen had slipped it to him. He was too nervous to uncap the bottle, but he had placed it on the edge of the hotel room desk, where it sat, backlit by the sunrise, as he stared down the tiny white pill inside. There was nothing remarkable about it. It could have been an aspirin. He had heard of spies who carried cyanide pills in case they were caught, but Imogen wasn't a spy. Not as far as Bucky knew, at least. And if it *was* a suicide capsule and death before divulgence was part of her grand plan, she wouldn't have handed it off to him *before* being taken away for interrogation. It made no sense.

Crawford would know what the pill was. Or at least what to do with it. He could tell Crawford about Imogen, and the book, and the Arbiter, and Crawford would tell Mr. Yesterday, and finally, it felt like everything was truly going to be all right.

Bucky reached into his jacket for the book just as the waitress arrived at their table to deliver a plate of eggs on toast, accompanied by sweaty bacon and halved

grapefruits and fingerling potatoes striped with rose-
mary sprigs. Bucky felt a cloud of warm, herby steam
dampen his face. Crawford thanked her with a smile,
then pushed all the plates toward Bucky.

"Eat something," Crawford said. "You must be starving." As Bucky tucked into the potatoes, Crawford took a
sip of his tea and winced. "I always forget how foul that
black tea is. Tastes like socks. When I was in the hospital
here, they made us drink gallons of this stuff. You took
medicine with tea, not water. I kept thinking I'd get used
to the taste."

"When was that?" Bucky asked.

"After the war," Crawford replied. "Haven't I told
you?" Bucky shook his head. "It's a pretty boring story
as far as war wounds go—I caught a cold that turned
into pneumonia, and they sent me back to England for
a while." He took another sip and shuddered. "They
gave us these god-awful fish tablets. They looked like
they were made for horses—about this big." He held up
his thumb and first finger. "They were always going on
about soldiers not having enough iron in our blood."

Bucky pressed his fork into the center of the egg until
the yolk began to ooze. "Did you have shell shock?" he
asked. "After you got back."

Crawford set down his teacup. "I wouldn't say shell
shock," he said after a moment of consideration. "Not

the way some men do. It took a while to shake the memories, but it didn't get me like it did others."

"Like my dad?" Bucky asked.

"Your dad . . ." Crawford scratched the back of his neck, frowning down at his own reflection in his tea. "Yeah, I think he took it all a little harder. He had nightmares for a long time. Insomnia. He used to call me up at three, four in the morning. I had to start unplugging the phone—not because I didn't care," he added quickly. "But Marcy and I had a new baby, and you can't be there for everyone all the time. I did what I could for him. And then he met your mom and started phoning her in the middle of the night instead."

"Did it get better?" Bucky asked.

Crawford picked up a piece of bacon but made no move to eat it. "I guess so. We never really talked about it. I know he was seeing a military psychologist when he and your mom first married. Something experimental—a drug that was supposed to suppress memories of the front."

Bucky felt the hair rise on the back of his neck. "Was it part of Project Fugue?"

"What? No, that was . . ." Crawford looked around quickly, like he was worried someone was listening, then leaned across the table and said confidentially, "Who told you about that?"

"Mr. Yesterday."

"Of course he did." Crawford swiped at the corners of his mouth with his napkin. "Fugue is something else. Similar research but a different application of it."

"So did it work?" Bucky asked. "The drugs my dad was taking. Did they help him?"

"Not exactly. He dropped out before it really had a chance to kick in. The drugs made him paranoid."

"Paranoid how?"

"He got some crackpot notion into his head that they were using him and the other soldiers to test some mind-control crap they meant for POWs. Wild stuff. He settled down pretty quick, though."

"POWs from other countries?" Bucky asked, and Crawford nodded. Bucky's mind was replaying the moment in the basement of the pub when Gimlet had flipped like a switch and started reciting facts about stolen prisoners and illicit tests. "What did he think they wanted to do to them?"

"Something about wiping out their memories and then conditioning them to be loyal to America."

Bucky dropped his fork. "Is that real?"

"It doesn't quite work like that. And it was after the war—everyone was a little nuts. Lots of crazy ideas were getting thrown around."

"But can the government . . ." Bucky swallowed hard.

The single bite of toast he had muscled down stuck in his throat. "Is there a way for them to change people's memories? Or alter their minds?"

Crawford's brow creased. "What are you asking me, exactly?"

"I'm not asking anything," Bucky said. "But if you can mess with somebody's brain—"

"Not somebody, captured enemy combatants," Crawford corrected him. "It's not like they were lacing a suburban water supply."

"So, it was really happening?" Bucky asked.

"I didn't say that."

"Even if they're enemy prisoners, altering someone's mind is . . ." *Unethical* seemed too small a word. So did *reprehensible*. "Evil," he finally finished.

"Yeah, well, there's a war on, Buck. Manners aren't really a priority."

"It's not manners, it's common decency," Bucky said, appalled. "Especially if you're doing it without their consent. If they want to be our enemies, that's their choice, but taking that away—"

"You think your dad wouldn't have wanted those memories of France out of his brain? Hell, I would have taken that option, if I had the choice. Damn nightmare, the whole thing."

"That's not what I'm say—" Bucky said, but Crawford

grabbed Bucky's wrist, pulling him across the table. A saltshaker tipped when his elbow hit it.

"What you should be saying is nothing." Crawford's voice was suddenly low and sharp-edged, like the snarl of a dog with its hackles rising. "This isn't your job, and this isn't your concern, and if the wrong people overheard you, you'd be neck-deep in trouble. God almighty, why was Yesterday even flapping his tongue about Fugue to you?"

Bucky yanked his hand out of Crawford's grip. The cutlery rattled when his elbow struck the table. "How is it wrong to say we shouldn't be messing around with people's heads?"

"Because if your government wanted you to do that, you would do it without question. That's your job. If you're going to do this work, you're giving up who you are in aid of a cause greater than yourself. If you can't wrap your brain around that, you shouldn't be here." Crawford drained his teacup, then tossed his napkin on the table. "I'm on a plane first thing tomorrow back to the States. I want you to come with me."

Bucky looked up in surprise. "You want me to go back?"

"You want to stay?" Crawford asked, equally incredulous. "After the hell you just went through? You could have been killed. You realize that, right? I'm not going to tell you what to do. You want to stay here and try this thing with the SOE, I can't stop you. But you run that mouth of yours to any of these Brits the way you just did to me, you'll be out on your ass, and I won't be able to help you. I don't want to see you fall at the starting line. You got too much to offer." Crawford ran a hand through his hair. It was grayer at the temples than it had been this time last year. "Come home for a little bit. Let them work out the kinks in their program with someone else. And give this all some time to blow over."

Bucky stared down at his egg. The yolk was congealing, rubbery and cold, along the edge of his plate. Did he want to stay? The Arbiter had warned him to leave now—wash his hands of Imogen and go home. He'd fought so hard to get here that it hadn't occurred to him he could walk away. He'd never thought he was the kind of person an escape clause would apply to. There was no world he could imagine in which this work wouldn't fit him like a glove. But if, two days in, he was already bumping up against questions of morality, he may have grossly misjudged how much his own values aligned with the intelligence forces. This work wasn't supposed to be complicated—there was a universal good and a universal evil. He shouldn't be arguing the ethics of mind control with Crawford after meeting the daughter of a turncoat scientist ready to sell dangerous secrets to the highest bidder.

The thought of stepping back and letting all this be someone else's problem . . . it was a relief. He didn't want to admit, even to himself, that Crawford might have been right intercepting his enlistment papers and telling him to wait until he was older, but maybe he had been right. Maybe Bucky had been wrong about himself all this time.

Crawford retrieved his hat from the banquette seat beside him, then stood. "I gotta get going. Mr. Yesterday's waiting."

"Can I come?" Bucky asked, but Crawford shook his head.

"Sorry, kid. I could tell you it's classified, but mostly it's just boring." He paused, then added, "It's also classified."

"But mostly the boring thing."

Crawford cuffed him affectionately. "Come back to Virginia. Give it a year. Let's get you back in high school. Get you a job, something that's not selling pornos to greenies out of the rec-room library."

Bucky stared at the table. "I'll think about it."

Crawford pursed his lips, and Bucky suspected that he wanted to say more, but he just nodded. "Take it easy for the rest of the day. The front desk can get you anything else you need. Just ring them. Start with something to drink other than tea." Crawford winked, then clapped Bucky on the shoulder one more time before putting his hat back on. "I'll have them send a car tomorrow morning to take you to the airfield. The desk will have the details."

So that was it, Bucky thought as he watched Crawford leave the hotel, pausing for only a moment at the concierge desk. His great foray into military service and heroism, over before it had begun. What was he supposed to do now? Go back to America and forget he'd never had a shot and blown it? Give high school another try, though the thought of sitting in Pre-Algebra with kids four years younger and a foot and a half shorter than him made him want to put the grapefruit spoon through his eye? And then what? If the US joined the war, there'd be a draft. He'd enlist. He'd go through basic training like every other cadet, pack himself in an ocean liner to Europe or Japan or wherever they sent him. End up one more body among thousands, no one to remember his name. But then again, did a hero's death really matter if you died just the same? The only difference between a foxhole and a grave was the name you gave it in your own head.

"Mr. Barnes?"

He looked up. Jane was standing at the end of his table. Or—not Jane. A woman with the same dark hair pulled into the same severe knot as Jane, *and* the same pristine uniform as Jane. They looked so similar that, for a moment, Bucky thought his mind was playing tricks on him.

"Are you . . . Jane?" he asked.

Jane smiled. "Yes, Mr. Barnes."

"The Jane who got me these pants?"

"I'm not at liberty to comment on the origin of your underthings."

A waiter passing their table shot them an alarmed look.

Bucky looked over Jane's shoulder into the lobby. "And the woman at the concierge desk?" he asked, pointing. "Is she Jane too?"

Jane's smile didn't falter. "May I escort you back to your room, Mr. Barnes?"

"Actually, do you mind sitting down for a second?"

Jane perched herself on the banquette edge. "Is there something I can help you with, Mr. Barnes?"

"Maybe. Kind of. I'm not sure. . . ." Bucky scratched the back of his neck. "Who do you work for, exactly?"

"I'm at your disposal, Mr. Barnes."

"Right, yeah, you've made that clear. But if I asked you for help with something . . . would you have to tell anyone?"

"Not if you require discretion, Mr. Barnes."

"You don't have to keep saying my name. Or. You can just call me Bucky."

Jane blinked. "Of course, Mr. Barnes. Anything else?"

No one else was on his side. He might as well be on his own.

"Yeah," Bucky said. "You know anything about chemistry?"

———

The hotel laundry room was long and narrow, the walls lined with porcelain tubs. Brass pipes snaked down from the ceiling, and the tile was gritty with spilled soap powder.

Bucky sat on the edge of one of the tubs, watching as Jane—a different Jane, the Jane who knew about chemistry, apparently—peered through a microscope at the white pill Bucky had given her. The lab equipment looked out of place, wedged on the edge of a sink between a set of irons and bottles of bleach. Beside it, a wireless babbled at a low volume. Jane's only condition to helping him had been that she could keep the radio on in case a more important call came in for her. ("Not that you aren't important, Mr. Barnes, but if I'm absent from my post for an extended period, discretion on the nature of our work might prove difficult.") On the other side of the room, a hot water heater gurgled.

Bucky had accidentally unraveled a seam on his shirt and lost two buttons to nervous fiddling by the time Jane finally straightened up. "Did you figure it out?" he asked, almost tipping backward into the tub in excitement.

"I have identified the chemical compound of the tablet," Jane said, consulting the room-service receipt she had been taking notes on. "But I'm afraid it's not one I recognize."

"What do you mean?"

Jane slid a set of tweezers under the microscope lens, removing the pill from the slide and dropping it back into its vial. "It's not a compound that should exist, scientifically speaking. Based on my deductions, I'd suspect it's a protein inhibitor."

Bucky stared back at her blankly. "I'm gonna need more than that."

"It's a compound that relies on the difference between prokaryotic and eukaryotic ribosome structures to disrupt the generation of new proteins."

"Yeah, that's not . . ." Bucky rubbed his temples, wishing for the first time in his life he hadn't slept through the one chemistry class he'd taken. "Remind me, what do proteins do, exactly?"

"Oh, all kinds of things," Jane replied. "Metabolism, cell replication, oxygenation of the blood, long-term memory formation—"

"Wait," he interrupted. "It can mess with your memories?"

"Theoretically," Jane replied.

"So if you're blocking the things that make memories, could that alter a person's memories?"

"Again, theoretically, yes." She returned the vial to the chess book on the counter, then handed it to Bucky. "But, as I said, I'm not familiar with this particular compound."

"Do you know anything about Project Fugue?" Bucky asked.

"If I did," Jane replied, "I would be expected to exercise the same discretion you have requested of me on this matter."

"Got it."

Behind Jane, the wireless crackled. "Available agent required," said a tinny female voice that Bucky was almost sure belonged to the same Jane he had talked to on the phone the night before. "Available agent required. Prisoner transfer north disrupted by car crash. Two male agents, one female transfer unaccounted for. Northbound on the—"

Prisoner transfer. He knew it was Imogen. It had to be. What other female prisoner transfer would have been interrupted on the way from London?

Bucky watched as Jane scribbled down the address on the room-service receipt. "I have to go."

"Wait." Bucky hopped off the edge of the tub. "Are you going to that crash? Could you take me with you?"

"I am not," Jane replied. "I need to be at the desk."

"Could I go?" he asked.

"I could do nothing to stop you."

"But you could help me get there," he said. "You could draw me a map."

"That would be illegal," she replied, and he felt his shoulders sink. But then Jane added, "However, I'd be happy to supply verbal directions."

"That works. One more thing. Could you get me a motorcycle?"

———

Bucky had driven a motorcycle before. At least a dozen times.

Maybe a half dozen.

Or twice. He'd been on a motorcycle twice.

Once when someone else was driving.

He had *never* driven on the left side of the road, in one of the largest cities in the world, roads rerouted and blocked off, trying to find a car that had crashed in the middle of nowhere before the professional spies did. Jane had assured him that once he got out of London and into the countryside, there was really only one road north. And since she had found him a motorcycle in record time, he was inclined to believe her.

"If anybody asks," he had said to her as she handed him a helmet, "don't tell them where I am."

"Your next appointment is not until six a.m.

tomorrow morning," she had replied, reaching up to fix the strap he had incorrectly fastened. "A car will arrive to take you to Stuart Airfield. As long as you've returned by then, your absence will not be noticed." As he'd straddled the bike, which was a little wobblier than he had expected, Jane had commented, "Mr. Barnes, will you be requiring driving lessons as well?"

"That's low, Jane."

She nodded in straight-faced agreement. "Just an offer."

When he finally spotted tire tracks veering into the woods that rimmed the road, he parked his bike on the shoulder, then followed them on foot. The smell of exhaust was thick in the air.

A little ways into the forest, a black car was wrapped around a tree, hood crunched up and smoking. A man was slumped in the front passenger seat, his head against the dashboard and a dark trail of blood trickling from his skull. Bucky's stomach turned over. He considered taking the man's pulse to see if he was still alive, but he was worried he'd throw up if he got closer. Especially if there wasn't one. The radio had said three passengers, but he couldn't see anyone else. He walked around the car, giving the man inside a wide berth, and noticed the grass leading into the trees was mashed down, as if by heavy footfalls.

He followed the tread so far he started to wonder if

he had been wrong and was actually tracking a heavy-footed deer into an English forest. Then a stone turret came into view, sitting lonely and overgrown among the trees. Ivy had snaked its way between the stones, and the roof had caved in, leaving a jagged smile along the top of the walls. He paused, listening, and over the whisper of the wind through the long grass, he heard the buzz of a transmitter.

Bucky crept around the side of the tower, peering in through one of the empty windows. The Arbiter had his back to Bucky, but Bucky could still see he had set up a wireless transmitter. The earpiece was clamped against his shoulder as he tapped out a message with one hand, the other holding a gun on Imogen. She was sitting on the ground, back against the wall, seemingly unharmed except for a bloody scratch on her forehead. Her hands were tied behind her, and she was gagged, though she was clenching her jaw so hard it looked like she was trying to chew through it.

The Arbiter paused his transmission, and Bucky crept away, breaking into a run as soon as he was sure he was out of earshot. The road where he had left his bike was still deserted. It wasn't exactly the sidearm he'd hoped to have when he faced down a double agent, but anything could be a weapon if you hit someone hard enough with it.

When the motorcycle engine turned over, it seemed

louder than it had been before. He shifted from neutral, jerked the handlebars around, and eased the bike into the forest. He had to build up speed, but the ground was so weedy and uneven, he was afraid the front wheel would hit a rut and he'd go flying. The transmission choked, and he shifted to second, then third. He flexed his foot on the gas. Branches from passing trees whipped at his face.

He passed the black car. Through the trees, he could make out the shape of the crumbling turret. He took a deep breath, then pushed the engine until it screamed.

He burst through the trees at the same moment the Arbiter stepped out of the tower, looking around for the source of the noise. His eyes locked with Bucky's over the handlebars of the bike. He leveled his pistol, and Bucky dumped the clutch, twisted the throttle, then leaned backward, just like he had when he and Rebecca rode bicycles as kids and he'd popped up on one wheel to impress her. He could feel the engine searing through his pant leg.

The bike popped up onto its back wheel and Bucky let go. He sprawled in the grass, blinking stars from his vision, and raised his head in time to see the riderless motorcycle plow into the Arbiter, knocking him off his feet and dragging him backward into the stone wall. The front tire caught on the door, slamming the Arbiter into the frame hard enough that he went limp.

Bucky struggled to his feet. The wedged motor-cycle was belching smoke into the clearing, the engine whining like it was an animal in pain. Bucky coughed, swatting the smoke out of his eyes as he stumbled to the high grass toward the turret. The bike had landed sideways, blocking the entrance, so he hoisted himself up onto one of the window frames. He had hoped to land gracefully, but his shaking arms gave out and he ended up tumbling through the window, landing hard on his backside with a loud *"Oof!"*

It wasn't the heroic entrance he had planned, but he also hadn't expected that, when he turned, Imogen would be somehow free and standing at the wireless set, flipping through the notebook the Arbiter had left on top of it.

She whirled, raising her fist like she was ready to fight. Then she realized who it was. "Well," she said, throwing up her hands in exasperation, "it's about bloody time."

CHAPTER 20
1941

The Arbiter was still slumped over the back of the bike, his face hanging near enough to the belching tailpipe that Bucky momentarily considered shifting him. But Imogen was already jogging away, and he sprinted after her. This man might be a killer, but Bucky wasn't. When he caught up to her, they both broke into a run without a word.

They ran until they were out of breath, then jogged, then walked, then jogged again until they reached a clearing of mossy trees. A small stream wound its way through, slick rocks glistening from under the clear water. Without consulting Imogen, Bucky collapsed onto the soft grass along the bank. His chest was burning, and he could feel mud seeping through his trousers and the elbows of his jacket. Imogen stopped too, stripping off her cardigan and using it to wipe the back of her neck. Her shirt was creased, and her hair had lost most of its curl, leaving tangled waves tucked into her collar.

Bucky stared up at the leaves shimmering with dew, waiting for his ribs to stop aching and wondering how anyone thought a few weeks of basic training was enough to adequately prepare anyone for what was waiting for them on the other side of the ocean.

Finally, Imogen dipped her hand into the stream, then splashed the water over her face and scrubbed her cheeks like she was washing off makeup. Bucky pushed himself up onto his elbows, watching as she ran her hands through her hair, slicking it back off her face, then tied her cardigan over her shoulders. She froze when she caught his gaze, and suddenly it felt like they were once again across the chess table from each other.

"So." He sat the rest of the way up, hooked his arms around his knees, and gave her the sweetest smile he could muster. "Imogen."

She flicked her damp fingers at his face. "Ginny. Only Ginny. No one calls me Imogen."

"Oh, okay, I get it."

"Get what?"

"You make a gimlet with gin. Imo-*gin*. Ginny. That's clever."

"Thank you for explaining it." She pressed her wet fingers to the back of her neck, humming softly. "And your name is James, isn't it? James Barnes? I heard one of the men in the SOE office call you by it."

"You don't have to call me James."

"It's your name."

"Bucky's better."

"You told me that wasn't your actual name."

"It's not—it's just what most people call me. You could too."

She laughed. "Oh, I won't be doing that."

He rolled his eyes. "Why am I not surprised?"

"James is much more dignified."

"So is Imogen." He reached into his jacket and pulled out the chess book. "Did you want me to keep holding on to this for you, or has it been sufficiently protected?"

She started, a sharp sigh of relief escaping between her teeth. "Give me that." She snatched the book from him, pressing it to her chest for a moment before flipping it open.

"I left you a note in the front," he said. "You can read it later. It's real sentimental and garbage."

She froze, staring down at the book. Then she glared at him. "Where is it?"

"Where's what?"

She turned the book upside down, flapping the pages.

"Oh, that." Bucky pulled the bottle with the single pill from his jacket and held it up. "Before I give it to you—"

Ginny didn't give him a chance to finish. She lunged, knees colliding with his chest and knocking him backward onto the soft earth. "Hey!" He wrenched his arm over his head, holding the bottle out of her reach. Her fingers grazed his sleeve, and to his surprise, she grabbed a handful of the leather, pulling herself up with her fingernails digging into his jacket.

"Cut that out!" He rolled out from under her and clambered to his feet, keeping the bottle over his head, the way he used to with his sister when they were supposed to split a candy bar.

Ginny flew to her feet, kicking up turf, and jumped—not up for the bottle, but directly *at* him.

She was smaller than him but still managed to hit him with the force of a linebacker. She wrapped her legs around his waist, hoisting herself up with her hands on his shoulders as she strained to reach the bottle. She started to slide, and grabbed a fistful of his hair for balance.

"Hey—ow! Stop!"

Her hand on his other shoulder slipped, elbow coming down hard on the top of his head. Stars burst at the edges of his vision, and he staggered. His foot slid on an uneven patch of earth, and they both toppled to the ground. Bucky landed on his back, all the air knocked out of him on impact, then *again* when Ginny landed on his chest.

"Hey, stop! Stop it!" he wheezed, shoving her off him, and she pitched backward into a patch of thorny weeds. He braced himself for her to hit him again, but instead, she wrapped her arms around her knees and buried her face against them. She was breathing heavily, and he thought she was only trying to catch her breath, but then he heard a wet snuffle. She swiped a hand under her eyes.

"Wait, no, don't cry." He crawled over to her, holding out the bottle. "Here. I'm sorry, I shouldn't have—"

Her hand shot out, snatching the bottle from him. It took him a moment to realize her face was dry.

"Hey. You tricked me."

"You took something that belongs to me."

"You gave it to me!" He sank backward onto the grass, too exhausted to argue. Almost. "And I was going to give it back." She arched an eyebrow and he added, "After you told me why you have it and what it is. You didn't have to claw my arm off." He touched his nose, checking for blood. "Anyone ever tell you that you fight dirty?"

She picked at a stalk of feathered grass that was stuck to her cardigan. One of her shoes had come off in the brawl, and the knees of her trousers were muddy. "Even if I knew what it was, I wouldn't tell you."

"Wait—you don't know?"

She glared at him. "Do *you*?" When he didn't answer, her eyes narrowed. "You do not."

"I think I do."

"Liar."

"I'm not lying!"

"If you're trying to trick me, it won't work."

"What if I pretend to cry?"

She flung a handful of grass at him. "Give over. How could you possibly know?"

"There was this woman at the hotel—a chemist. I mean, she wasn't staying at the hotel. She works for the SOE, but she was there at the hotel—they put me up in the hotel for the night, but they have some kind of deal with Yesterday. Though Jane seemed like a sort of free-lance dictionary, and it wasn't just—there was more than one of her."

Ginny frowned at him. "Are you having a stroke?"

"She said it's something to do with proteins. Hold on, it'll come to me."

"A protein inhibitor?"

"Yes! That." He slumped backward, exhausted by the mental gymnastics. "That's what it is."

"My father was a neuroscientist. That was part of his

contribution to Project Rebirth. He oversaw the psychological components of the Captain America project. When he came back to Britain, he developed a protein inhibitor to induce controlled memory loss. There was some concern that anyone who came out the other side of the Super-Soldier Program would be so traumatized, they'd have to forget the procedure in order to function."

"I thought your dad didn't tell you anything about his work."

She rolled her eyes at him. "Almost nothing. I'd have to be an idiot not to work this much out on my own. He didn't send me to boarding school until after he'd developed the inhibitor. I suspect things got a bit more secret then."

"So how did it work?"

"The idea was that you'd put a chemical marker in your own memories—like a bookmark before and after something in your brain—and tell the drugs to wipe out what's in between. Then you could go back in and wall-paper that empty space with false memories that weren't linked to trauma."

"You think that's what that pill is?" he asked.

She shrugged. "Maybe. I don't know why he'd give it to me. When he gave me the book, he told me that if anything should happen to him, I was to take it when it was over."

"When what was over?" Bucky asked.

"I don't know. He wouldn't tell me. He said I'd know."

Bucky picked a clump of muddy grass off the bottom of his shoe. "That's unhelpful."

"He never was a particularly transparent man," Ginny replied. "But he was so intense about it, and so serious about protecting the pill and not letting it fall into the government's hands, I just trusted he knew what he was talking about."

"*I* work for the government," Bucky pointed out.

Ginny scowled. "Yes, but you're different."

"Because it's my first day?"

Her eyes flickered to his, a faint smile teasing her lips.

"He said you'd go to America after you won the chess tournament, right?" Bucky asked. "Maybe he was trying to smuggle it across the pond."

"He could have kept it himself."

"Unless he knew something was going to happen to him."

"Then why would he have offered to come to the tournament with me? Wouldn't he have just showed up at my school, given me the pill, and said *Protect it if I get murdered because the government changed their minds about funding my memory wipe programs?*"

"I thought your father worked on the Super-Soldier Program in Britain," Bucky said. "And kidnapped all those prisoners to test things on."

"After he came back to England, when that was

abandoned, he—" She stopped short, staring at Bucky across the clearing with such intensity he almost asked if there was something on his face. "The what?"

"He kidnapped prisoners. Or maybe not kidnapped but coerced them under pretty questionable circumstances."

"Who told you that?"

"You . . . told me."

"No, I didn't."

"Yes, you did, when we were at the pub."

She went on staring at him blankly. "I don't know anything about that."

He stared back, waiting for her to catch up to him. Was she losing her mind? Was he? It had been almost an argument, and then suddenly it was like she was reading names and statistics from a dossier, her gaze flat. What had she said in the moment? He combed back through his memory, trying to remember, but the whole night was a blur of exhaustion.

"I wouldn't share my father's work," Ginny said firmly. "And he hardly told me anything about it. I certainly don't know anything about prison recruitment."

Bucky ran his hands over his face. "Well, he didn't exactly have the moral high ground, since he was trying to sell his research."

She shook her head. "He wasn't."

"He was. That's why the Arbiter was at the chess tournament—that's where your father arranged for their exchange to happen. He wasn't there for me, he was there for you. Did you catch who he was working for?"

"He was transmitting in German." She reached into the pocket of her cardigan and pulled out the crumpled notepad she had taken from the top of the Arbiter's wireless transmitter. "We might be able to pick out a few words, but I don't speak German."

Bucky held out a hand. "I do. Let me see."

"Really? That's unexpected."

"I may not be as smart as you, but I'm not dumb either."

"I never said you were."

She handed him the notebook, and Bucky skimmed it. The Arbiter's handwriting was abysmal, and he struggled to find words he recognized. His vocabulary had felt expansive in a delivery truck in Arlington, but suddenly all he could remember how to say was *Where is the library?* "I think he was transmitting to his bosses. Letting them know he had you and he was taking you . . . somewhere. I don't know this word. There are coordinates. And something about a . . . a code word. Or phrase. Something like that."

"Does it end with *Heil Hitler*?" she asked. "Then we'll know if he's working with the Nazis."

He tapped his finger against the scrawled sign-off. "No . . . it says 'Hail Hydra.'"

"Hydra?" she repeated. "Are you certain he didn't simply misspell Hitler?"

Bucky flipped the page in the notebook, searching for more. "I have a hunch that the first requirement for being a Nazi is knowing how to spell *Hitler*." When he looked up, Ginny had the chess book open, squinting at the first pages. He could see the faint red where her father had underlined phrases. "What are you thinking?"

"What exactly happened when I told you about my father's work?"

"Um . . . We were looking at your chess book. And all the random words your dad underlined and how they didn't make sense. And I was reading it out loud, and then you—"

"You read aloud?"

"Yeah, I was just listing off the words he underlined. Trying to make them make sense."

"Oh my god."

"What? What is it?"

Ginny pressed her thumb to her lips, eyes wide. "It's me."

"What's you?"

"All his research—the research he was selling. All the government secrets he knew." She touched her forehead. "He put it in my head."

Bucky stared at her, uncomprehending. "Is that . . . possible?" he finally asked. "How could he do that without you knowing?"

"That's part of the work he was doing—memory implantation! Something to replace the places you were carving out. Like wallpapering over a hole in the wall. Not a perfect solution, but those memories weren't erased, they were just hidden. Suppressed. There must have been a way to access them—that's what the book is! All the words he underlined—it's the code. I'll bet every section of the book unlocks some different pocket of information he implanted in my mind. That's how he was smuggling the information. Which means . . ." She pressed her hands to either side of her face, like she was trying to squeeze the information out of her head. "He sold me."

"He didn't sell you," Bucky said, but she laughed humorlessly.

"As good as! He was going to go with me to the tournament. He was selling me to the Arbiter—he would have used the code to force all the information out of me, then had me take the pill and I'd just have . . . forgotten any of it ever happened."

Bucky didn't know what to say. He couldn't even entirely tell how she was feeling—she had gotten worked up solving the puzzle, then deflated just as quickly. "You all right?" he asked.

Ginny raised her head to glare at him. "No, I'm absolutely the furthest thing from all right."

"If you need to cry—"

"I am not crying." Ginny dug her fingers into the soil, turning over a handful like she was tilling for harvest. "Maybe I just take the pill now," she muttered.

"What? Why?"

"I assume it will wipe out all the information he implanted, and likely take anything that's happened since then with it. I suspect he wouldn't want me to remember the whole *sold his daughter to the Nazis* bit. Or not Nazis. Pseudo-Nazis."

"I'm not turning you over to Nazis."

"But as long as this information is in my head, it's a danger. I don't want someone like the Arbiter or anybody else prying this out of my brain because he thinks he owns it. Better just to get rid of it."

"You can't do that," Bucky said. "Whoever that guy works for isn't going to stop hunting you just because you claim you don't have what they want anymore—they'll believe it once they rip your brain out of your head and see for themselves, and by then it'll be too late. If you have this information, why not do something with it?"

She frowned. "Like what?"

"Well, to start, you get out of England."

"Are you suggesting I go on the run?" She laughed. "For what—the rest of my life? This isn't a spy novel."

"We'll find someone to help us."

"Who?" she demanded. "I can't tell the British government or ask for their protection. They're already tripping over each other to get this work, and after what my father saw, I can't imagine they'd use it well."

"Then we ask the US. Maybe they'd give you asylum." He wasn't sure if he was using that term right, so he quickly pinned on "Or protection. There's probably someone from the Project Rebirth team who could help you. We ask them."

She looked up from picking dirt from beneath her fingernails. "Oh, it's *we*, is it?"

Bucky felt his neck go red. "Well, I was going to offer you my bedroom once I enlisted."

She looked down at the grass again, pressing her fingers against her lips. He wasn't sure if she was concealing a grimace or a smile.

"I can help you get to the United States," Bucky said. "Crawford and I are flying back tomorrow."

"Who's Crawford?" she asked.

"My dad—kind of. He's like my dad." It wasn't worth explaining, so Bucky pushed on: "He'll help you; I know he will. He's leaving from an airfield outside the city. We could meet him there. It's north of here. . . . Or north of London, I guess." He clambered to his feet, spinning on his heel, tracking the sun. "And if that's east—"

"East is behind you," she said with a sigh. "Good job I was a Girl Guide."

"Good job I don't know what that is. Crawford can help you. *I* can help you. At least come with me that far."

"Fine. Only because I have no other options and don't relish the idea of spending the rest of my life running away from murderous human traffickers."

"That's the spirit." He held out a hand to help her up. When she didn't take it, he prompted, "Give it up. I know you trust me."

She scowled at him. "How would you possibly know that?"

"Because when you thought you were in the weeds, you gave me your chess book, and I kept it safe for you."

She stared at his palm, squinting like she was trying to read something printed there. Then she took his hand, and he pulled her to her feet.

"Your hands are freezing," he muttered.

"And filthy." She held her palms out to inspect them. "Shouldn't have been dipping them in the mud, I suppose."

"Here." He took her hands and slid them into his jacket pockets. "Does that help?" he asked, cupping his palms around her knuckles.

He expected her to pull away, but instead, she hooked her fingers in between his and fell against him, her face to his chest. His skin felt hot, and he was somehow sure he could have traced all the lines of her palms from where they had rested against his.

"What a bloody mess," she murmured into his shirt.

"No kidding," Bucky replied. He wondered what would happen if he opened his jacket and wrapped her in it, their bodies nestled together like quotation marks. For a delirious moment, it felt like she'd melt into him, like metals fused in a forge. Together, they'd emerge as tempered steel. "You're sure lucky I found you—you might be getting your fingernails pulled out by a German psychopath right now if it wasn't for me."

She glared up at him, chin propped against his chest. "Without you, I'd be having my name engraved on the Oswald Shelby Memorial Chess Tournament trophy."

"Right. I ruined your winning streak."

She held his gaze. She was almost a full head shorter than he was, and pressed against him, the height difference felt even larger. He felt like he was looking down on her from a great height. He studied the hard bow of her mouth, the curve of her eyebrows, the circles starting to darken under her eyes. *You have been staring for too long,* said a sensible part of his brain, but he couldn't tear his gaze away. How had he not realized what a knockout she was the moment he sat down across the table from her?

This, that sensible voice scolded, *is not the time for a stupid crush.*

But then Ginny looked at his mouth, and he wondered whether if he didn't kiss her, she might take the initiative. She seemed like the kind of girl who wouldn't give a fig about waiting for the boy to make the first move.

She let her face fall back onto his chest, fingers curling around his in his pockets. "You certainly ruined something."

They hiked until they found the road, and followed it from the cover of the trees that bordered it. When they reached a country town, they stopped at a grocer's and bought a map, two sandwiches, and a Mars bar with the change Ginny dug out of her pocket. They didn't have enough for bus fare, but, when they told him the area they were headed to, the grocer assured them they could arrive by the next day on foot, with time to spare.

They agreed to stop for the night when they reached the ruins of a church that the grocer had told them marked the edge of the county, only about a mile from the airfield. Hanging around a British military base for any longer than they needed to seemed unnecessarily risky, even if they might have gotten a hot meal and a bed before the SOE picked them up again.

The chapel had no roof, and the windows had all been punched out by creeping vines. The stone floor had been tumbled by invading roots, and sprigs of wildflowers curled up from between the cracks. A down of iridescent moss coated every surface shaded from the sun.

Bucky was exhausted. Pain in his heels pulsed up into his legs, and he could feel a sunburn itching the back of his neck. He flopped down in the grass before pulling off his jacket and balling it up under his head as a pillow.

Ginny stood in front of the ruins of the chapel altar, looking around like she was about to address a congregation. "So that's it, then?" she asked loudly. "You're just . . . asleep?"

One of the jagged stones was digging into his back, and he shifted. "Did you have something you wanted to do?"

"No, I just . . ." She blew a piece of hair out of her face, crossing and uncrossing her arms.

"Are you trying to decide if I'm a gentleman?"

He could feel the vibration of her eye roll through the darkness. "You're a cad is what you are."

"You can come sleep next to me."

"But we have this whole great bloody chapel all to ourselves. I wouldn't want to crowd you," she deadpanned.

"Come here." He patted the ground. "I won't try to cuddle you or anything."

A pause. Then she said, quietly, "You could."

"Could what?"

Instead of answering, she stalked over to where he was lying, grumbling to herself as she tramped through the underbrush like an exasperated buffalo. "Cuddle. Such a stupid word. It's infantilizing. Makes me sound like a puppy." She flopped down beside him, pulling the sleeves of her sweater over her hands. "All right, go on, then."

"Go on and what?"

"Don't make me say it."

"Say what?"

She let out another huffy breath. "Cuddle me."

He rolled over, intending to grab her around the waist, fold around her like an envelope, and pin her to the ground in retaliation for the still-throbbing spot on his nose where she'd smashed it while trying to get the book. She'd protest, and he'd laugh and let her go, and then they'd settle down next to each other, close enough to keep each other warm but not so close as to touch.

But she turned at the same time, and suddenly they were face-to-face, nothing between them but a sprinkling of short-stemmed wildflowers.

They stared at each other. The crickets humming in the tall grass made the air between them pulse. She reached out and touched his chin with a reverence that befit the chapel. He looked at her mouth, the soft space between her lips when they parted. He felt magnetized, some pole inside her dragging him toward her. He wanted to be audacious, lean forward and put his mouth to hers with the self-assurance of a film star. He'd take her in his arms, Clark Gable to her Vivien Leigh, and think of something suave and cool to whisper just before he—

Abruptly she scooted up against him, her head pressed into his shoulder and her arms folded against her chest.

Just warmth. That was fine. They'd lie together here all night, silent and parallel like burial plots. It was fine.

But then she shifted. Her fingers grazed the bare skin of his neck. And stayed there.

He couldn't move. He was hyperaware of his own breath, the way it was somehow both too deep and too shallow and so damn loud. Did he always breathe this loud? Why hadn't anyone told him?

"Are you all right?" she asked suddenly.

"Yes." His voice was hoarse, and he cleared his throat.

"You're very tense. It's terribly uncomfortable." She nestled into his shoulder, and he had to work very hard not to think about the way her knee was creeping along his thigh.

Think about something else. Don't think about the way he could see the curve of her breast under the neck of her shirt, or the feeling of her pressed against his side, or—

"Are the stars the same here as they are in America?" he blurted.

And then her warmth was gone. She sat up, hand pressed against her mouth, shoulders shaking with silent laughter.

He sat up too, all his fragile fantasies popped like a soap bubble. "Okay, it was a stupid question," he muttered. "I'm stupid, sorry for asking."

"Oh, come on. Don't pout." She folded her fingers around his arm, like she was keeping him from running away. "You're not stupid. You know that. You just surprised me, that's all."

"With how stupid my question was?"

"No, it was the way you said it. . . . It was sweet, that's all. Like England is a whole other planet."

"It might as well be."

She squeezed his arm lightly, then, when he still didn't turn around, poked him hard in the side.

"Ow! Hey." He scowled, ready to rescind his offer of cuddling up, but then she rested her chin on his shoulder, so close that when she spoke, he felt her breath against his ear. The hair on the back of his neck stood up.

"Ask it again," she said. "I won't laugh this time."

He sighed, throwing his head backward and staring up at the sky, the stars studding it like nails hammered into blue velvet. "What I meant is, when I was little, my dad used to show me the constellations, and I was trying to find them, but nothing looks familiar. And then I was thinking maybe we're on a different spot on the globe, so the way we see the sky might be different."

"That's not a stupid question," she said. "You're asking about hemispheres and how Earth's orbit affects star patterns. It's complicated." She scooted closer to him, until her chin was almost against his shoulder and they were staring up at the same patch of sky. "Which star can't you find?"

"The north one."

She pointed. "It's right there."

"How'd you find it so fast?"

"I learned how to navigate with it, when I flew."

He snorted. "Yeah, right."

"I have a civilian 'A' pilot's license, thank you very much."

"Fancy. Who taught you how to fly?"

"A friend of mine at school was proper rich. She invited me home for Christmas, and when I found out her father was a hobby pilot with his own plane, I about ruined the holiday with all my questions. I thought he'd take me on a ride if I was lucky, but he offered me lessons."

"That was nice."

"I think he pitied me. He wanted to make sure I had some paternal figure in my life, since I was rather low on my own father's priority list."

Her voice was light, but he could hear the strain just below the surface. In the time between sitting down at the chess table and now, her world had exploded. Her family, her future, her own thoughts—all of them stripped for parts. He didn't know what to say—wasn't sure there was anything he could say. He wanted to tell her he was sorry, even though he hadn't done anything except help her pull back the drapes on a dark room.

Then she prompted, "Do you see it? The North Star."

He considered lying but instead said, "No."

"Come off it, it's right there." She sat up, stretching her already outstretched arm, as though she could lean closer to the sky.

Bucky rolled his eyes. "Yeah, pointing doesn't really help."

"All right, then, here." She scooted forward so they were side by side, then wrapped her hand around his and directed it at the sky. "There! Do you see it?"

"I see it," he said.

"Finally." She leaned into him, her back against his chest. Her hands rested on his knees, and he could hardly breathe. He was afraid any sudden movements might send her back to her side of the churchyard. But she didn't move. He trailed his hand down her jaw, tracing the shape of her ear, the curve of her neck, finger not quite touching her skin. When he brushed her clavicle, she shivered.

"If you take that pill," he said, "you won't remember me, will you?"

"Most likely not."

"That's a shame."

"It would give us a chance to try all this again," she offered. "Meet each other under different circumstances."

"What's wrong with our current circumstances?"

"Call me old-fashioned. I'd prefer less government involvement."

"How about I meet you at the Hotel Astor?" he asked. "Think you can remember that?"

She laughed. "I don't even know where that is."

"New York City."

"I've never been. Is it nice?"

"You've never been to New York?" He clapped a hand to his heart in mock horror. "You'd love it."

"Really?" She turned around so she was sitting between his legs, cross-legged so her knees rested on his thighs. "What would I love about it?"

"Well, I've really only been to Coney Island."

"So why don't we meet there?"

"It's not a place you take a girl you're trying to impress."

"Oh, you're trying to impress me, are you?"

"Maybe I am." He reached up to push a piece of hair out of her face, and she caught his hand and held it to her cheek.

"So the Hotel Astor?" Her hands were cold. He wanted to put them in his pockets like he had that morning. He wanted to fold her up like a letter from a lover and carry her inside his jacket, always right beside his heart.

"The rooftop bar," he said. "Corner seat. Me in my dress uniform. You in some slinky green number—"

"Me probably still wearing this cardigan." She leaned back, holding her weight against his. "I'm not a slinky sort of person. Too self-conscious about my stomach."

"You in a suit, then," Bucky said. "White tie and tails. Full Marlene Dietrich. Every head turns when you walk in and sit at the bar. I'll ask the bandleader to play our song—"

"Do we have a song?"

"Sure do. The one about the nightingale."

"Right, of course." She leaned forward, and he caught her other hand in his. "The one that goes *Something, something, something nightingale.*"

"Yeah, that one. And he'll say, 'This next song is for Imogen Fleming—'"

"If they call me Imogen, I refuse to answer."

"'Ginny Fleming,'" he corrected himself. "'This is her favorite song.' Then the lights go down—"

"Aren't we on a rooftop?"

"—and the band picks up with *That certain night*, and you

look over just as the bartender says, 'Excuse me, ma'am, that devastatingly handsome soldier down the bar sent you this.' And then he passes you a gimlet in a frosted glass." He pressed a thumb lightly to her bottom lip. "You take one sip, and you remember it all."

She tucked her chin against her chest, and suddenly he worried he'd said something wrong. He almost let go, but then she pulled their linked hands against her heart. She murmured something so softly he didn't hear, and when he leaned forward, she pressed her forehead against his.

"Don't wait that long," she said, her voice mostly breath. "If you wait for the war to be over, I'm afraid you'll be waiting the rest of your life."

Then she looked at his mouth, and he wanted to kiss her. But those last few inches felt like trying to fill in a canyon by the spoonful. He'd kissed plenty of girls in Arlington, but none of them had ever scared him down to his bones the way she did. None of them had made him want to don white gloves, the sort used to turn brittle pages in an old book. He'd never been this afraid one slip of the hand could ruin everything. He'd never cared if it did.

"If you're gonna forget me," he said, "I'm not gonna worry so much."

He could feel the push and pull of each deep breath

she took. Count her blond eyelashes. See the faint rouge of lipstick still on her mouth, the spots where her irises were veined with emerald.

"Worry about what?"

"Looking like an idiot if I'm misreading signals."

He cupped a hand at the back of her neck and kissed her. She gasped, the sound both surprise and relief, and melted into him, seizing a fistful of his jacket and kissing him in return. Her mouth was open, and when he grabbed her waist, she shifted into his lap, wrapping her legs around him. His palm slid along her thigh, flexing against her.

He felt her fingers tugging urgently at the front of his shirt, and she pulled her lips from his to unfasten the buttons. Her fingers were shaking, and in her haste, one of the buttons popped loose and flew into the dark grass. Ginny hesitated. "Oh no, should I—"

"Forget it."

She laughed, and his heart tumbled like a stone down a hill, picking up speed as it went. This time when he kissed her, his hands were in her hair.

He fell backward onto the stones, and she collapsed on top of him. It felt like the earth would split beneath them. She pushed her hair behind her ears and took a deep, steadying breath. When she reached for his belt, he didn't stop her. He kissed her jaw, her neck, peeled back the shoulder of her blouse and kissed her there. He could feel his pulse in his hands, in his lips, in the chapel stones beneath them. He pressed a hand to her rib cage, counting her heartbeats and staring at the place where their skin met, unsure for a moment how it was that he was here, with her, under the same stars on a different continent, and she was touching him, and she, she, *she*.

After, she lay between his legs, half-dressed, with her head on his chest, and he traced the bones of her cheek, her jaw, the bridge of her thin nose, the corners of her mouth. She rested her chin on her hands, and with her face above him, there was nothing but her and the sky. The stars wreathed her—not a girl, but a constellation— and he remembered a book he'd read when he was young that said the brightest objects in space naturally exist in the darkest depths. She fell asleep curled up against him, and he watched the sunrise to the rhythm of her low breathing. *Fierce light*, he thought, as dawn erupted over the sky, *always claws its way through darkness.*

CHAPTER 21
1954

V wakes with a jolt. It takes him a moment to remember he's in the dormitories back on Svalbard, where ship crews sleep while their boats are docked. Oksana had brought them here after they landed. She'd fed change into a meter until the lock on the door to a private room clicked open, installed V inside, then went to see to Rostova. He had meant to wait for her to come back, but as soon as he let himself stretch out on the bottom bunk, he'd been asleep. Now he sits up, his muscles putty and his ribs aching. A fur blanket he must have pulled on top of himself while he slept slides off his shoulders. His arm throbs, and he reaches to rub the pain from it, only to realize he's reaching for his left arm—his prosthesis.

He raises his fist, watching the faint light from the overhead bulb glancing off the chrome plating. For the first time he can remember, it doesn't feel like his. Phantom pain shudders through a limb that is no longer there, so real and present that, for a moment, he's sure he could draw a map of what were once his veins, the whorls of his fingerprints, the curves of his nails, the swells of his knuckles. He can feel them all as he looks at his bionic arm, like shadows on a double-exposed filmstrip.

His skin itches. He's sweating. He strips off his coat and the thermal shirt under it. When he tosses them onto the floor, something bounces from the pocket of his coat and it takes a moment for him to realize it's the book they found in the vault. There's a coin of dried blood on the cover, dirt brown. He can't remember if it was there before. He turns the book over in his hands, tracing the title again with the tip of his finger.

One Hundred Great Games of Modern Chess.

He flips the book open, searching for a table of contents, but finds instead a note written in English. The paper is rippled and the ink is faded, but he can still make out the words, along with a date from 1941.

Gimlet—
It would seem I got attached.
Write me at Camp Lehigh.
xx Bucky

"Good morning."

V startles. Oksana is standing in the dormitory door, wearing Wellington boots caked with mud and a Nordic sweater several sizes too big for her. "Ah, look at you, you have such a nice face." She taps her cheek, and he touches his own. He isn't wearing the mask.

"Where's Rostova?"

"Resting. She's fine," Oksana adds quickly. "But she shouldn't travel for a few days. Especially if she's the one piloting the plane. She really knocked her head." She tosses a rucksack onto a chair at the end of the bed and begins to rummage through it. "Can I look you over as well? That jump into the plane alone probably broke something."

"Are you a doctor?"

"No, but I can tell why something's hurting."

"I'm not hurt," V says. He can still feel the shape of his missing limb, but short of digging up and reattaching what was once there, he isn't sure there's anything to be done about that. Some pain, he knows, simply has to be survived. When Oksana reaches into her bag and he hears the click of surgical metal, he reflexively shrinks backward. He feels suddenly exposed, his body strange and unsuitable for anyone else to see.

Oksana notices, and pulls her empty hands slowly from the bag. "Can I check, just to be sure? No instruments." She wiggles his fingers in demonstration.

V slides to the end of the bed until his legs are hanging over the edge. Oksana rubs her hands, warming her fingers before she presses them into V's sides. Her exam is quick and painless—she checks his ribs, prods vital organs for perforations and pain where it shouldn't be, puts gentle pressure on his joints and along his bones. She even has him roll up his pants and pull off his knee-high thermal socks so she can check his toes for frostbite. When she gets to his metal arm, she pauses, her hand glancing off the silver panel at his wrist like she's testing the heat of a pan on the stove. "Does this come off? Or is it a—"

"Don't touch it," V says, and Oksana withdraws, obviously relieved.

When she's finished, V pulls his shirt back on, watching as Oksana dips into the bag, coming up with mismatched brown bottles. "I have a few different things I can give you for pain, but I need to know what you're on." When V just stares at her, uncomprehending, she adds, "In case they don't mix. Aren't you . . ." She trails off, waiting for V to finish the sentence. When he doesn't, Oksana laughs nervously, running a hand through her matted curls. "You don't make things easy, do you?" She taps two fingers against the inside of her elbow, then nods to the corresponding place on his. "Are you a junkie?"

"What?" V pulls up his sleeve and studies his arm,

noticing for the first time a network of tiny pinprick scars clustered at the crease. He stares at them. The realization that he doesn't remember where they came from is sinking in like blood into soft earth. Had he been injected with something onboard the Hydra base? He can't remember. There are so many of the tiny freckle-like scars—he can't possibly have forgotten them all. Was this part of the treatment he had undergone when he was first brought from the front into Karpov's care? He had been injured, he knows that. He had lost a limb and almost died from exposure. Surely there had been some kind of intravenous drip or adrenaline injection required to keep him alive. But this looks like they brought him back from the dead a dozen times.

He turns his arm over, studying the webbing between his fingers, then the blue veins at his wrist. "What are these from?"

Oksana glances up from her bag. "You're asking me?"

"I don't remember."

"Some of the garbage you get on the street eats your brain," she says. "Maybe you got a bad batch."

V stares at her. "There are drugs that do that?"

"What? Shake your brain?" She scratches her own arm, like it might be catching. "Sure. Seizures. Hallucinations. Memory loss. Take your pick."

"Are there more?"

"What—injection sites?"

"Where else would they be?"

"The junkies I've met—when their veins collapse, they inject into their feet or their groin. Sometimes the backs of their knees."

V pulls up his shirt, twisting around to see his torso as he searches for more patches of those pink scars. "Do you see any?"

"What am I—"

"Are there more scars?"

Oksana ducks her head, eyes darting to the door, and he realizes that, for the first time since they met, something about him has made her nervous. Maybe the arm. Maybe the track marks. Maybe the sudden manic insistence she check him all over for signs of drugs he doesn't remember taking. Maybe all three.

He doesn't care.

"Check my knees." V leaps to his feet and pushes his trousers down, turning so Oksana can see the backs of his legs. "Are they there?"

"It doesn't work like that," she says.

He turns. "Like what?"

Her gaze glances over his bare legs for a moment before she looks away again. "You don't forget every time you ever shot up. Or that you did to begin with. You might lose bits and pieces here and there—days, maybe, or months. But it's not . . . It's not like that. If you were a doper, you'd remember it."

That trickle of pain runs down his bionic arm again. No, not his bionic arm, the arm that was once there. The arm he no longer has. He rolls his shoulder, like the pain is just a kink in his wiring and he might readjust the circuitry.

There's a soft clink of glasses as Oksana replaces the pill bottles in her bag. "Were you taking something for the gunshot?"

V rounds on her. "What gunshot?"

"I won't tell Rostova if you are."

"What gunshot?" he says again, and his own voice startles him. He almost doesn't recognize it.

"Are you . . ." Oksana bites her lip, eyes flicking to his calf, and he follows her gaze.

There's a bullet wound on his leg.

It's healing—but not healed. The skin around it is still red and shiny. It can't be more than a few weeks old. Maybe less.

He doesn't remember getting shot.

How can he not remember getting shot?

Oksana reaches into her bag again. "I can give you something. Would you like me to—"

"Leave," he snaps, and he hears her gratefully exhale. V locks the dormitory door behind her, then lurches to the sink in the corner of the room, catching himself on the edge of the basin. It cracks in his metal fingers. He stares at his reflection in the spotted mirror over the sink. He can't remember the last time he looked at himself this way. Were there mirrors in their bunker? He can't remember ever consciously looking in one. When was the last time he saw his own face?

It feels like looking at a stranger. Or a photograph of someone he once knew, but whose name he can't remember. He touches the cleft in his chin. His lips. The bump in the bridge of his nose and the curve of his cheekbones. They all feel strange and unfamiliar. He doesn't remember the pattern of his stubble. The tilt of his eyebrows. The hard angles of his face.

Or where the bullet in his leg came from.

He strips off the rest of his clothes, then steps back so he can see his whole body in the mirror, searching his reflection for more foreign scars.

He finds a spot on his back, near where his bionic arm is fused to his skin. There's a ropy scar there, like a knife had gone in between his shoulder blades. He finds another on the back of his neck, pink and small, and a puckered line on the bottom of one foot. The inside of his thigh is spotted with patches of discolored skin. They look like burns.

He collapses onto the floor, knees pulled up, head between them, struggling for breath. He feels like a stranger, a pretender wearing someone else's clothes. He stares at his hands, opening and closing his fists. The blue veins in his wrist pulse, and he finds another scar there, a thin white line running parallel to his wrist, like a chip of bone poking through his skin.

I don't know who I am, he thinks. His heart clatters in his chest. Breath comes in sharp, erratic gasps. *I have lived lives I do not remember.*

Unbidden, the memory of the woman in the lab rises in his mind, but she looks different. Younger. How can he see her younger if he's never met her before? How can he know what she looked like when she was seventeen? How had he looked at her and thought her hair was shorter than it had been the last time he saw her? He hadn't thought it in the moment, but suddenly, staring at his hands, he remembers her like she once was.

Imogen Fleming.

Ginny with a hint of lime.

He has forgotten his own name, but he remembers hers.

He retrieves the book from where he dropped it beside the bed and flips through it again, searching for any clue beyond that cryptic message in the front. He finds the hidden panel in the back from which Rostova removed the pill and discovers a thick postcard wedged into the binding there. He pries it out and studies the image on the front—a towering brick building that a script banner declares THE HOTEL ASTOR—NEW YORK CITY. He flips the postcard over. The edges are soft with age, corners starting to peel apart. It feels petal-delicate in his hands.

The back is stacked with stamps and postmarks, addresses written and rewritten, squares of paper pasted on top of each other. One postcard sent back and forth for years: Ginny to James and back again, over and over, the postmarks chasing each other around the world. Someone—whoever had first sent the card, he imagined—had written a message on the opposite side that neither of them had obscured. Three words, one question, traced over again in a different color of ink when they grew too faded to read.

Wait for me?

CHAPTER 22
1941

Bucky had hoped Stuart Airfield would be a crowded military outpost, ferry pilots and special-duty clerks and RAF officers roaming in droves, so that if they walked with a quick pace and their gazes ahead, he and Ginny would be able to get lost in the crowd. Instead, the airfield was only one hangar, a tin shack built onto the side overgrown with ivy, and a radio tower jutting out the top.

"Are you sure this is the right place?" Ginny asked as they lurked in the trees that rimmed the runway. There were no planes—just a jeep parked in the shadow of the hangar.

"Not a clue." Bucky held up a hand to shield his face

from the sun as he peered across the tarmac. "Someone's here—or they were and left their car."

"I was hoping for a plane," Ginny said. "That didn't seem much to ask from an airfield, yet here we are."

"Were you planning on hijacking it?"

She shrugged. "If necessary."

A sudden screeching split the air, and they both jumped. Ginny sank back in the undergrowth, but Bucky leaned forward. The sun flashed off the hangar doors as they slid open. It was almost too bright to see, but he could make out the dark silhouette of a plane parked there, waiting for takeoff, and, under it, a pilot doing his preflight checks.

"That's Crawford!" Bucky grabbed Ginny by the hand, pulling her to her feet. "That's him."

He tried to drag her from the trees, but Ginny dug in her heels. "Are you sure?" she asked, her voice pinched.

"Pretty sure I know what he looks like." He reached to link their fingers, but she jerked away like he had burned her. "What's the matter?"

She took another step back, the brambles snagging her trousers. "Maybe I should wait here."

"Don't be silly. Come on." This time, he held out a hand and let her take it, then led her in a sprint across the runway, both of them ducking low like they were dodging fire. They slowed as they approached the hangar, and Bucky shouted, "Crawford! Hey!"

The figure under the plane turned, and Bucky waved.

Crawford dropped his clipboard.

"Good god, Buck," he said, jogging over to meet him and Ginny at the hangar doors. His face was shiny with sweat, and his eyes were rimmed with dark circles. "What the hell are you doing here? They said you missed your car. You weren't at the hotel. The SOE is tearing up London looking for you. Geez, I gotta phone them. How'd you get here?"

"I took a different route." Bucky pried his fingers from between Ginny's and put a hand on her back, encouraging her forward. "This is Ginny Fleming. Ginny, this is Sergeant Commander Nicholas Crawford."

Ginny ducked her chin with a little wave. "Hello."

Crawford looked between them. "Fleming . . ." he said slowly, like he knew the name but couldn't remember from where. "You're . . ."

"Imogen Fleming," she said, then added with uncharacteristic shyness, "Pleasure to meet you."

"Look, we can't explain much," Bucky said. "But we need to get Ginny to the US."

Crawford blinked. "Excuse me?"

"She's coming back to the US with us." Bucky was bouncing on the balls of his feet, buzzing with the adrenaline of having made it and finding Crawford. They were all getting out of here, together. It had worked. "Her dad was a scientist who got killed by the SOE, and there's some bad people looking for her. They're the ones who sent the man to the tournament. He wasn't there for me like we thought—he wanted Ginny!"

A familiar crease appeared between Crawford's eyebrows. "Slow down."

"We're taking Ginny back to Arlington with us." Bucky snapped his fingers playfully in front of Crawford's face. "Come on, Nick, try to keep up."

Crawford didn't smile. He retrieved his clipboard from the ground, brushing gravel off the paper. "That's not possible."

"This is a Thunderbolt, isn't it?" Bucky pointed at the plane. "There's room for a third. We can take her with us."

"It's not a question of . . ." Crawford trailed off, pinching the bridge of his nose. He turned to Ginny, giving her what he might have hoped would be a smile but looked more like a grimace. "Miss Fleming, do you think you could wait for us in the office there? Maybe you could make some tea while I have a word with Bucky."

"I don't want to make tea," Ginny replied. Bucky could feel her fingers creeping around his wrist, the same way they had when the two of them had been photographed at the chess tournament. "I'd rather hear what's being said about me behind my back."

"Well, how about we promise not to say anything until we can say it to your front?" Crawford put a hand on Bucky's shoulder, prying them apart. Bucky half expected

Crawford to nudge Ginny toward the office with his foot like he was keeping a stray dog out of his yard. She started to protest, but he said over her, "Miss Fleming, please, this won't take long. By the time you've got the water boiling, we'll be finished. Then we can all sit down and have a chat over tea like civilized people."

Before she could raise more protestations, Crawford dragged Bucky out of the hangar. Bucky glanced back at Ginny, but the sun was too bright to see anything more than her silhouette against the bright chrome belly of the Thunderbolt.

Out on the tarmac, Crawford shoved Bucky roughly away from him. Bucky almost laughed, thinking Crawford was about to pull him into a headlock and give him a good-natured scolding about running off without telling him where he was going.

But then Crawford snapped, "What the hell were you thinking, bringing her here?"

Bucky looked up. Crawford was staring at him, face set, arms folded across his chest.

"She needs our help," Bucky said. He tried to stand straight, but he could feel his shoulders rising, like he was bracing for a blow. "She has to get out of England. There are bad people after her. If she stays here—"

"She was in *government custody*," Crawford said, his voice trembling with barely suppressed anger. "How'd she . . . You know what? Don't tell me. I don't want to have to lie at the trial. Christ, Buck." He flung the clipboard, and it bounced on the tarmac. Bucky flinched. He'd never seen Crawford angry like this, not even the night Bucky had punched Johnny Ripley at the soda fountain. Crawford turned away from him, hands knotted together behind his neck, shoulders heaving with the effort it took not to yell. "No."

"No what?"

"The answer is no. We're not taking her anywhere. I'm phoning the SOE to come pick her up."

"You can't do that!"

Crawford rounded on him. "At the very least, I need to call off all the agents they pulled from the field to turn London inside out looking for you. Don't you ever think?"

"You don't understand—there's a man, I think he might be a double agent. He was at the chess tournament. He had some kind of deal with Ginny's dad—"

"Stop, are you hearing yourself?" Crawford grabbed Bucky by the shoulders, shaking him hard enough that he bit his tongue. "No. She's not coming with us. I could give you a thousand reasons why, but what's the point—you won't listen to them. You never listen. This isn't about you and some pretty girl you've taken a shine to. There are lives at stake here, and you're wasting time that could be spent on real agents who need real help."

"So her life matters less because she doesn't have a government stamp of approval?" Bucky wrenched himself out of Crawford's grip, resisting the urge to rub his arms.

"I'm saying she is not your problem, and she's not your responsibility," Crawford replied. "You have disobeyed the SOE. You've made a mess—an expensive mess—because you think you know better than the people in charge. We're calling the SOE to retrieve her, and then you're coming back home with me."

"But Ginny—"

"James." Bucky flinched. Crawford used his name like a weapon. "As your commanding officer, I'm ordering you to step down."

Bucky raised his chin. "You're not my commanding officer."

Crawford started toward the office, but Bucky blocked his path. Crawford tried to step around him, but Bucky moved with him, and Crawford leaned backward, laughing humorlessly with his hands hooked in his pockets. "Don't start with me, kid."

"I'm not letting you call them."

"You're making a mistake, Buck."

"Doesn't look that way from where I'm standing."

"Bucky." Crawford's hand drifted to his belt, hovering over his pistol. "Move."

He wouldn't shoot me, Bucky thought, but a cold shiver of uncertainty ran through him.

Crawford took a step toward him, and Bucky raised his fists, falling into a boxing stance. The way Crawford had taught him. "I won't let you take her."

"Put your hands down," Crawford snapped. "What do you think this is? One of your schoolyard scrapes?"

If that's what it came to, Bucky was ready. He could scrap with the best of them.

Crawford shook his head. "Cripes, Buck. Put your hands d—"

His words were cut off by a gunshot.

Bucky flinched, throwing his hands over his face. Crawford must have moved so fast that he fired his pistol before Bucky noticed he had reached for it. He looked down at himself, waiting for blood to soak through his shirt. Hadn't the men at Camp Lehigh told him that sometimes you don't feel the bullet until long after it's found its mark?

Then Crawford staggered. Bucky looked up as the commander fell to his knees. He opened his mouth, and blood flooded his lips. He gasped once, a wet rasp like a stopped-up drain. Then he slumped onto the tarmac.

Bucky lurched backward. His whole body went numb. He couldn't make sense of what he was seeing. Crawford, with blood seeping through the back of his shirt. Crawford, on the ground. Crawford, not moving. Crawford, dead. He couldn't be dead. He was just here, and it couldn't happen that fast.

It took a moment before he registered the growl of an engine and looked up. A military truck with a canvas back rolled to a stop ahead of him. The driver's-side door banged open, and the Arbiter lurched out, his semi-automatic pistol still aimed at Crawford's body. He fired again, the bullet snapping into the back of Crawford's skull. Crawford's body jerked, blood splashing onto the runway. In the sunlight, it looked like spilled oil.

Bucky wanted to close his eyes. He couldn't see against the blaze of the sun. He couldn't take a breath. He couldn't stop staring at Crawford's body. He wanted to look away from Crawford's body. He'd never stop seeing Crawford's body.

The Arbiter unloaded the magazine from his pistol, then clipped a new one in place. When he pulled back the barrel, it crunched like bone breaking. He raised his gun, pointing it at Bucky.

Bucky grabbed Crawford's pistol and dove under the Arbiter's truck, rolling under the belly just as the Arbiter fired. The wing mirror shattered. A second shot popped the left front tire. Bucky wiggled onto his stomach, pushing himself up on his elbows. The under-carriage of the truck was still hot, and he choked on the smell of exhaust and dust. Something damp was soaking through the knees of his slacks, and he thought he must have rolled into a puddle of petrol from the truck. Then he realized it was Crawford's blood. Bucky gagged, clamping a hand over his mouth so he didn't vomit. He fumbled with the pistol, almost dropping it as he pawed at the safety. His palms were sweating.

He heard a shell clatter to the ground, and watched as the Arbiter circled the truck, his shiny shoes reflecting the sun. Bucky clutched the gun, following the Arbiter's shadow as he moved, ready to fire. There was another shot, and Bucky flinched. Another one of the tires popped. The left side was out, and the truck sagged. Bucky rolled out of the way as the undercarriage sank toward him, the still-searing machinery singeing the shoulder of his jacket. Another shot, and the back right tire began to deflate. Bucky realized suddenly that, if the Arbiter shot out the last tire, he'd be crushed under the truck. He'd be burned black by the hot engine as he suffocated slowly, his rib cage folding in on itself before it flattened.

There was still enough space that he could wriggle out under the only tire still inflated, but he could see the Arbiter's shoes waiting there for him. His shadow across the tarmac raised the pistol, waiting. He was letting Bucky make a choice. Pick how he wanted to die.

When Bucky didn't move, the Arbiter fired again, three times into the slowly flattening back tire. The vehicle sank a little lower. Bucky tried to move, but his foot was caught in the suspension, the truck's weight slowly pressing on his toes and driving his heel into the ground. He screamed in pain, the bones in his foot bending backward until the top of his foot was almost flat against his shin. He gritted his teeth, fighting to stay conscious, trying to think through the panic and the pain and *think, think, think*!

Then there was a crunch. The pain magnified until his vision spotted, then abruptly went out like a light, replaced by a dull pulse up and down his leg. Which somehow seemed worse.

Bucky grabbed the truck's bumper, trying to pull himself out. A hot pipe was pressing down on his exposed ankle, and he couldn't feel it, but he could smell his own flesh burning. He lost his grip on the pistol, and it skittered under one of the collapsed tires, wedged between the rubber and the pavement.

The Arbiter crouched down, peering under the truck until his face was level with Bucky's. "You were warned," he said. "Now where's Imogen Fleming?"

Bucky gritted his teeth, wishing he had a better retort than the whine of pain that escaped him.

"I'll find her with or without you," the Arbiter said. "Last chance."

Bucky spat at him. His mouth was dry, his throat leeched by the fumes of the truck, so it didn't travel nearly as far as he knew he was capable of spitting, but the Arbiter caught the spite behind it. He stood up. "Very well."

Bucky scrambled, clawing at the asphalt as he tried to get free. One of his fingernails ripped, blood running down the back of his hand. He could see the Arbiter's shadow on the tarmac as he straightened, raised his pistol, and aimed at the last tire.

But before he could fire, the Arbiter suddenly dove out of the way. The rumble of an engine cut through the blood thumping in Bucky's ears. Someone had fired up the Thunderbolt, and a moment later, the wing crashed through the canvas-covered back of the truck. It caught the cab, dragging the truck onto its right two wheels. As the truck tipped, Bucky clambered out from under it on his elbows. Every time his leg struck the pavement, a fresh wave of pain doused him. He was going to throw up. Or pass out. Or both. Probably both. The palms of his hands were shredded and bloody, cuts studded with gravel.

The Thunderbolt's wing tore free from the truck, and Bucky threw his head back, squinting at the cockpit as it trundled by. Ginny was behind the controls, hair askew under the headphones she had haphazardly jammed on. The collision with the truck had robbed her of any speed, and the plane wasn't taxiing fast enough to take off. She'd have to turn around, or she'd never get off the ground.

Bucky looked around wildly, trying to see where the Arbiter had gone, wondering if Ginny had managed to squish him when she caught the truck. But then Bucky spotted him crouched, hidden from Ginny's view behind Crawford's jeep. His pistol was cradled against his chest, and Bucky realized he was waiting for Ginny to come back around before he fired. He must have thought Bucky was somewhere under the smashed truck—he wasn't looking for him anymore.

Bucky's own pistol—Crawford's pistol—was still lodged under one of the truck tires. He could see the gleam of the sun off the barrel, like the flash of a dropped nickel. Bucky crawled forward, stretching to reach it. It was jammed so tight he was sure that, even if he got it free, it would be too bent to shoot. He could hear the plane coming back around, the engine getting louder as Ginny pivoted at the end of the runway and started back around.

The Arbiter sprang up from behind the jeep and walked confidently into the center of the runway. He leveled his pistol with the cockpit of the Thunderbolt barreling toward him and opened fire. Bullets bounced off the bottom of the plane, climbing toward the windshield. One struck the fuselage, and a jet of smoke began to spill out.

Bucky threw all his weight against the truck tire, tugging at the pistol until it finally came free. The barrel was scratched, but not visibly dented—though if there were any flaws on the interior, no matter how small, the whole thing might blow up in his face. He checked the magazine. There was one bullet left.

The gunfire stopped, and Bucky heard the clatter of a magazine hitting the ground. The plane's engine was screaming toward them, the propeller kicking up a cloud of dust.

The Arbiter raised his pistol again and took aim at the cockpit, just as Bucky pulled himself up with the support of the truck tire. He forced his smashed leg to hold him, though it trembled so badly he wasn't sure he could stand straight, let alone shoot.

But he'd fight to his final pawn. He had come too far to concede.

He took a breath. Leveled his pistol as the Arbiter aimed at Ginny.

Bucky fired.

The bullet struck the Arbiter in the neck. He crumpled to the ground just as Ginny pulled up hard on the controls. The Thunderbolt lurched into the air, the wheels barely clearing the fallen truck. The wings wobbled for a moment before the plane straightened out, then sailed into the sun, light glinting off the domed cockpit as she climbed.

And Bucky couldn't stand up anymore.

CHAPTER 23
1941

Bucky spent three weeks in a London hospital, and after two operations to repair the shrapnel the Arbiter's truck had rendered into the bones of his foot, he was ready to go full Billy the Kid and bust his way out. He was bored, exhausted from pain, and feeling more and more misplaced by the day. No one from the SOE came to check on him while he was laid up, or even debrief him about what had happened at the airfield. The only thing the British intelligence office seemed to want to do with him anymore was get him out of their country.

Virginia was worse—the same isolated loneliness and bone-deep exhaustion, except with no morphine. The Crawfords' house was tomb-quiet. Mrs. Crawford had taken Bucky back in without hesitation, assured him over and over that of course he was still welcome, still part of their household, she would do whatever she could to help, it's what Nick would have wanted. Some days she said it with her eyes full of tears, other times with a blank, glazed-over stare, and he didn't know which was worse. He needed out of their house—out of Arlington, by any means necessary. He'd hop a Greyhound and ride it in circles around the country until he was old enough to enlist if that was the only way.

The doctor at Camp Lehigh assigned Bucky rehabilitative therapy on base with military specialists, which meant that, two times a week, for an hour that seemed to last for days, his foot was wrapped up in elastic bands and stretched in ways that made him shout incoherent strings of curses at the obviously sadistic doctors. Breaking his foot hadn't hurt this much. None of the operations had hurt this much. Those first few days without the morphine had been cake in comparison.

At the end of every session, the severe therapist left him lying sweaty and exhausted on a hospital cot, tremors of pain running all the way to his hips, with instructions to flex and then point his toes for five minutes before he was excused. Usually, he lay still with his eyes closed instead, trying to focus on the colored spots behind his lids and not the pain or the memory of Crawford falling to his knees or Ginny's plane disappearing into the sun.

The rehabilitation was horrible, but at least it was somewhere to be and someone expecting him. Something to do that wasn't asking the secretary yet again if any mail had come for him, praying she'd hand him a letter with Ginny's name on the envelope. He'd left her his address. He'd told her to write.

But if she had taken that pill and erased her father's implanted memories, she might not even remember who he was. She'd see a note from a stranger in the cover of a half-shut book.

Bucky stared up at the dimpled ceiling of the communal recovery room, rolling his ankle every time someone looked his way, like he had a reason to still be there. He hated being in the Crawfords' house. Even being in the barracks with the soldiers was a painful reminder of how much he didn't feel like he belonged with them anymore. He was tired of being asked what had happened to his foot, reciting a lie about a plane crash that had killed the commander, then trying to pretend like he wasn't seeing Crawford's blood soaking his knees as he lay under the truck.

From the cot next to his, someone coughed. "You okay there?"

Bucky raised his head. Another soldier had sat down, the ice pack pressed to his chin starting to melt down his arm. Even though the man was sitting, Bucky could tell he was tall, with broad shoulders and thick quads that strained the seams of his standard-issue uniform. In spite of his build, his face was boyish, giving him an overgrown look, like a weed left to flourish in a fertilized field. Maybe it was the fresh-cadet haircut. It made everyone look like a baby.

The soldier gave him a sheepish smile. "You got quite a vocabulary. In quite a few languages. I think I heard English, German, Russian, and . . . French? You know more than just curses?"

"Not in French," Bucky replied.

"Where'd you learn German?"

"From a Swiss deliveryman. I'm not a Nazi," he added, and it came out more defensive than he meant it.

"No, of course not." The soldier raised his empty hand. "You enlisted?"

"Not yet."

"So what happened to your leg?"

Bucky sat up, wincing as he reached under the bed for his shoes. "That's above your pay grade."

"Figures." The soldier readjusted his grip on the ice pack, and another sluice of water darkened his sleeve. "You need a hand?" he asked, nodding toward Bucky's shoes.

"I got it." Bucky clenched his teeth as he pulled his boot on over his injured foot. He would have left it off, but there was snow on the ground. He had woken that morning to find the whole camp dusted white.

"I'm still finding my way around," the soldier said, "but if you need someone to lean on—"

"I'm fine." Bucky pulled too hard on his laces and a jolt of pain ran up his leg. He swallowed a whimper. The soldier looked ready to offer himself as a crutch again, so Bucky quickly asked, "Are you enlisted?"

"Just got here."

"How'd you end up at Camp Lehigh all the way from Brooklyn?"

The soldier laughed, ears going red. "Rats, is it that obvious? I thought I had the accent under control."

"You sound like a shoe-shine boy."

"Come on." The soldier swatted playfully at Bucky. "It's not that bad."

"Say *penny for a pape, mistah?*"

The soldier grinned. He looked familiar—something about the line of his jaw, though Bucky couldn't place where he'd seen him before. "You ever been to Brooklyn?" the soldier asked.

"I've been to Coney Island."

"Did you ride the Cyclone?" The soldier slid to the edge of the cot, elbows on his knees as he leaned forward eagerly. "Last time I went, they wouldn't let me on—I was too short."

"What were you, four?" Bucky muttered.

The soldier shrugged. "I haven't always been this tall."

"You mean you weren't born six foot five?"

"Six two, actually."

"Well, I assume you're doing it all in heels."

The soldier stared at him for a moment, then grinned again. The right side of his mouth quirked first, giving his chiseled face a momentary asymmetry that was so charming Bucky smiled too. "I heard you were a smartass," the soldier said. "Or maybe a pain in the ass. I can't remember which."

"Who's telling you about me?" Bucky asked.

"That's above your pay grade." The soldier pulled his legs up onto the cot, sitting cross-legged. He was so broad that he made it look like children's furniture. "When are you enlisting?"

"I don't know. They offered me a medical deferment for when I turn eighteen on account of my foot. I might take it."

"You sound like you've already gone and come back."

"I sort of have." Bucky rubbed his neck. "I don't know if I'm cut out to follow orders."

"You'd rather be calling the shots?"

"I'd rather have a say in what's getting shot at," he said. "And whether or not we're even aiming in the right direction. I'm not a fascist, I swear," he added quickly. "German aside."

"Of course you're not," the soldier said. His eyes were the blue of a gas-range flame, and Bucky felt himself leaning toward the warmth. "All that means is you've realized the world can't be neatly divided into good guys and bad guys. That's the first step. Now you can quit worrying about doing what's right and start focusing on doing what's needed."

Bucky squinted at him. "Who are you, exactly?"

The crooked smile returned. "You ever hear of the Army's Able Company?"

"No."

"Good. That's exactly how it should be. You mind if I pass you on to Rex Applegate? I think you should meet him. William Fairbairn too."

"You want me to look them up in the phone book or something?" Bucky asked.

"No, they call you." The soldier stood, tossing the ice pack onto the cot. Whatever swelling it was meant to be keeping down seemed to have vanished entirely.

"Looks like your chin's all better," Bucky said.

"I heal quick." Those blue eyes flashed, like he was sharing a private joke with himself. Bucky wanted to know what it was. He wanted to be in confidence with this enigmatic stranger.

He didn't want him to leave.

Get a grip, he scolded himself. He was so desperate for a friend, he had latched on to the first blue-eyed stranger who smiled at him. Well, second. He forced himself not to think about Ginny.

"Hey—good luck out there. Whatever happens." The

soldier stuck out a hand, and Bucky shook it. "Maybe we'll see each other again."

"When the Able Company gives me a call?"

"Hopefully sooner than that."

"Barnes!" someone called, and Bucky turned. One of the secretaries was standing in the door, scanning the recovery room. When she spotted him, she waved a postcard in his direction. She was too far away for him to make out the photo on the front. "Mail for you."

"Be right there!" He turned, but the soldier was already walking away, his jacket slung over one shoulder. "Hey!" Bucky called, and the soldier stopped. "I didn't get your name."

"It's Rogers." That smile again. "Steve Rogers. And you're Barnes, right?" He glanced at the door where the secretary was still waiting.

"James Barnes, yeah."

"Anyone ever call you Jim?"

"No, but they call me Bucky. You can . . ." The words jammed in his throat, and he coughed. "You can too. You can call me Bucky."

"Nice to meet you, Bucky." He gave Bucky a small salute as he turned. "Take care of your feet—and listen for the phone!"

CHAPTER 24
1954

The nurse at the bunker is new—a broad-shouldered girl with red hair and a lazy eye.

V sits still on the infirmary exam table as she checks him, moving only when he's told. The cold from the metal is seeping through his thin trousers. He waits for her to ask about the bullet hole in his leg.

She doesn't.

When she's finished, she rolls an IV drip on a stand from the corner and ties off his arm. His skin prickles, a feeling like the hackles rising on a dog's back. He stares at the spot on his arm she douses with iodine, trying to see the dark pinpricks from past injections there, but he can't find them anymore. Had he imagined them? The memory of Svalbard is slowly fogging over, like an island disappearing into the horizon. Oksana had told him . . . What had she told him? Then he and Rostova had . . . Where is Rostova? He hasn't seen her since they landed . . . has he?

"What is that?" he asks. The nurse pauses, and he adds, "In the drip."

She's not supposed to tell him. He's not supposed to ask. She's probably new, and still follows rules. The nurse before her . . . hadn't she also had red hair?

"It's glucose," she replies without looking at him.

"Why?"

"To stabilize your blood sugar. The instructions come from Dr. Karpov," she says, her trump card dropped on the table before he can ask anything else. "Quick pinch." She jams the needle into his arm, and he flinches, though he hardly feels it. The reaction belonged to someone else, a man without track marks speckling his arms. He stares at the glass bottle suspended above him, light reflecting and refracting through the clear liquid. "Lie back, please," the nurse says. "And try to relax."

He stretches out on the table, though his body feels taut as a piano wire. He's a fox in a forest, and though he can't yet see the dogs closing in, he can hear them baying from the dark trees. He tips his head, watching as his distorted reflection in the glass does the same. "Did you know there are frogs that survive polar climates by allowing themselves to freeze?" he asks.

The nurse looks up from her clipboard. Her eyes narrow, but her voice remains flat. "Is that so?"

"It's because of glucose." Out of the corner of his eye, he sees her set down her clipboard, then slide open a drawer. "They replace the water in their bodies with glucose. It keeps their cells from breaking down."

"Where did you learn this?" she asks.

He watches as she punctures the top of a sealed bottle with a syringe. When she draws back the plunger, golden liquid fills the tube. Her lips move, like she's counting out the dosage. He's too far away to read the label on the bottle, but he thinks suddenly, *She's going to sedate me.*

"I don't know." His arm feels heavy—he's not sure he could bend it. When he swallows, he tastes stale beer. He can feel the bubbles in his chest.

It's like there's a record playing in the next room—sometimes he picks out a lyric or a melody line, and he knows he's heard it all before—once he could have sung along—but now he can't remember what the song is called.

"Don't do that."

He's picking at the medical tape holding his IV in place, and the nurse is glaring at him. He hadn't realized he was doing it, but he doesn't stop.

"I said don't do that."

She stalks over to him, the full syringe still in her hand. He expects she'll try and pry his metal fingers away from the tape, but instead, she slaps him across the face.

It stuns him. It shouldn't stun him. He's been struck before.

"I don't want this," he says, shaking the IV tube so the bottle rattles on its stand.

"Karpov said—"

"I want to talk to Karpov."

"That's not an option."

Why is he arguing? He is not supposed to argue with any of the staff. His instructions are to comply, comply, always comply.

He's tired of complying.

"Let me talk to Karpov," he says again.

The nurse ignores him.

"Hey." He grabs her arm with his bionic hand. "Did you hear me? I said I want to—"

Without warning, she jams the syringe into his neck.

The shock steals his breath. It feels so much bigger than a thin needle as it slips under his skin. It's like she stuck him with a knife. He can't breathe. He can't breathe—no, he *isn't* breathing; it feels like he can't breathe around the intrusion. Like one deep breath might drag the needle and whatever is inside it deeper into him.

The nurse's finger bounces off the plunger, and he thrashes under her like an eel, knowing she'll hold on. The needle snaps off in his neck, leaving her with a dribbling broken syringe.

The nurse swears, then tosses the broken ampoule on a nearby tray. V is still gasping. He can still feel the needle inside him, wobbling under his skin. "What was that?" He can taste it in the back of his throat—metallic and bitter, like sucking on pennies. "What was that?" he demands again. "Tell me."

But the nurse is at the counter, depressing the red button on an intercom. "Breach in infirmary," she says calmly into the microphone. "I need assistance with the Sold—"

"Don't." He lunges off the table, grabbing her by the arm. The microphone slides off the counter and dangles by its cords, bouncing. Static shrieks. "Tell me—"

She elbows him in the face, hard enough to send him staggering. He crashes into the exam table, and the nurse shoves him back down on it. There are restraints hanging off the table—were they always there?—and she's trying to catch his limbs and tie him down. "I need backup!" she shouts at the door. She's strong—stronger than V expected. And he feels slow, every movement like wading through mud.

He grabs the IV tube and rips it from his arm. Immediately, he feels lighter, though whether that's a trick of his own mind or not, he isn't sure. The nurse snags one of his legs in a strap, pinning it to the table, and he grabs the IV tubing and wraps it around her neck. She gasps for air, tearing at her throat so frantically she draws her own blood. She takes a sloppy swing at him, and he yanks the tube. She overbalances, loses her footing, and falls, striking her head on the edge of the table. She slumps to the floor, and V lets go of the tube. It falls loose around her throat like a necklace, leaking glucose onto the tile.

V staggers to his feet. Distantly he can hear an alarm ringing. He bolts for the infirmary door, only to find it locked. He slams a fist into it, but even the bionic arm hardly dents the thick metal. This room was meant to keep him in. This whole bunker was built to be a prison cell. *His* prison cell.

He turns in a circle, looking around the room. It's like he's never been there before—has he? Everything seems new. He notices for the first time—maybe, maybe not—a panel of opaque glass behind the table. He'd seen something like that before, in an interrogation room. In London.

Ginny Fleming, her lipstick blotted. A broken tooth—not hers.

He runs at the glass, taking one leap onto the counter before throwing himself through the window with his metal arm up to absorb most of the impact and shield his face. The glass shatters, and he crashes onto the floor on the other side. His ears ring. The air around him feels resonant and prickly.

He lies still for a moment, confirming he isn't injured, then sits up. He looks around, shaking broken glass from his hair. He's smashed into an observation deck, with high stools so the occupants can look down into the infirmary. It must have been one-way glass, something that could be used to watch him without his knowledge.

He staggers to his feet. There's a door on the opposite side of the observation deck, and he stumbles through it. The sound of breaking glass is still echoing in his head, building into a roar like an engine slowly approaching.

Beyond the deck, a large cylindrical chamber is suspended above the floor, surrounded by a tangle of cables and gleaming silver canisters. Beneath it, a board with straps like a medical stretcher hangs vertically on a pneumatic crane. The machine hums softly, like it's warming up. V examines the control panel, trying to work out what this machine is for. There are five sections, each labeled in raised lettering—SECURITY SYSTEMS, ANALYSIS, VITALS, SYSTEM POWER, and CRYOSTASIS. Beneath CRYOSTASIS is a temperature dial, the lowest setting labeled –196° C. He feels something wet and cold dribbling down his neck, but when he swipes his hand there, it comes back dry.

Beside the control panel there's a desk, with a single

file drawer resting on top. V wrenches the drawer out of place with his metal arm and flips through the documents inside. Each folder is labeled with a different date.

The first reads:

1945, Initial Procedures and First Cryostasis

He flips it open to find a medical chart, starting with a list of vitals, followed by an injury report.

- *Arm, left, missing below the elbow, extensive bone and muscle damage between elbow and shoulder, amputation at humeral head recommended*
- *Broken back*
- *Fractured clavicle*
- *Fractured femur, right*
- *Fractured ulna, right*
- *Fractured tibia, left*
- *Fractured knee, left*
- *Fractured skull, parietal bone*
- *Punctured lung*
- *Ruptured spleen*
- *Frostbite, extensive tissue damage*
- *Hypothermia*

He winces in sympathy. What poor soldier had been brought to this place with their body so uninhabitable?

And what psychopath had decided to try to save them? It must have only been prolonging the inevitable, stretching out the final days. He flips the paper, scanning for a time and date of death, but his gaze snags on a procedure list.

Arm, left, amputated at shoulder. Bionic technology framework installed. Awaiting prosthesis.

A twinge of that phantom pain runs up and down his arm. A lost piece of himself reaches out through the darkness. A memory of ice. Ghosts whispering behind bright lights. An arm that was no longer his, stretching for . . .

At the end of the surgical report, someone had scribbled a series of dosages alongside the words *placed in cryostasis for accelerated recovery. Recommended storage temperature −196° C.*

Cryostasis. He doesn't know the word, but he can feel the cold. It's already in his lungs. His joints. He lives with it, always dormant just under his skin. He'd simply never known the source until now.

He flips through the rest of the files, thumbing the tabs.

1946, Code Name Bezukhov—First Injection

1946, Code Name Bezukhov—Second Injection with ECT

1946, Code Name Bezukhov—Third Injection with ECT, Supplemented with 300 Milligrams Phenobarbital

1946, Second Cryostasis

1948, Code Name Bolkonsky—First Injection, Revised Formula

1951, Code Name Levin—First Injection, Revised Formula, Supplemented with Phenobarbital

1953, Code Name Kuragin—First Injection, Revised Formula with ECT

1953, Code Name Karenin—Second Injection, Revised Formula Version 2 with Ketamine and 1500 Milligrams Sodium Pentothal Intravenously with Saline

They aren't him. They're all him.

Each one tells a different story of a life he doesn't remember living. Places he can't remember, people he doesn't know he's met. In every one, it was him and Rostova, him and Rostova, chasing something around the world. Something no one ever gave a name to. One folder mentions Marrakesh. Another, Amsterdam.

Subject made contact with Imogen Fleming. Subject was sedated on site and returned to base. Brain scans indicate increased activity in the hippo-campus. It is advised he be placed in cryostasis until formula has been revised. Under SIGNATURE OF AUTHORIZATION is Karpov's name.

A different report: *One hour after first dose of ketamine administered intravenously, subject experienced seizures and vomiting. Placed on supplementary oxygen to elevate vital signs. Blank-slate proce-dure recommended upon stabilization.*

Another:

Revised formula supplemented with bitemporal electroshock therapy effective at suppressing retrograde memories, though implicit memories were adversely affected. Subject experienced intense physical pain upon receiving treatment. Subject likely would not survive more therapy at this dose, and formulation is ineffective without supplementary electroshock. Blank slate recommended.

Another:

Subject stole a scalpel from the infirmary and attempted to make a self-inflicted incision at the radial artery of the right wrist. Subject returned to cryostasis. Current formulation is ineffective.

He braces himself against the desk, struggling to stay on his feet. All the forgotten pain is suddenly bearing down on him again. The walls that had so long enclosed him are collapsing, and now there is a sky. A horizon. A whole damn world. How many lives has he lived? How many times has he died and been brought back to life? How many days has he spent here, locked underground and frozen over, his memories wrung from him and his brain reassembled in the aftermath? How many hot lights has he writhed in pain beneath, and how many cold ice baths has he surfaced from, gasping at the first breath after years—*years*—of his life have been taken from him?

In the newest file, there's a report about an incident in Riga.

Subject made contact with MI5 agent, code name Yesterday, in Riga. Yesterday shot subject in left thigh, bullet removed in the field and further treatment given back at base. Full recovery expected. Higher dosage of temporary suppressant recommended, taken twice daily orally, to be administered by Agent Rostova. Additional tactical gear issued to conceal identity and discourage verbal communication. Blank-slate protocol not recommended.

The scar on his leg itches. He had been shot in the field on a mission, and he can't remember it because they'd doped him up. For years, they'd pumped him full of whatever drugs and electricity and gas it took until he forgot who he was.

All for what?

The last file contains only one piece of paper, and he almost drops it when he unexpectedly finds a picture of himself paper-clipped to the front. The photo is taken from an overhead angle, looking down on his mangled body on an operating table. He looks like a corpse. His stomach heaves, and he flips the photo over on the desktop before turning to the paper under it.

PROJECT: WINTER SOLDIER

Subject: James Buchanan Barnes

Known Aliases: Bucky, Canary, Desperado

Known Affiliations: Liberty Legion, The Invaders, US Military, US State Department, British Special Operations Executive, Captain America, The Able Company

Citizenship: United States of America

Born: 1925, Shelbyville, Indiana, United States of America

Known Relations:
- George M. Barnes (father, deceased)
- Winnifred C. Barnes (mother, deceased)
- Rebecca P. Barnes (sister, location unknown)

Status: MIA, Reported Dead by US Military: 1945, London

Assets:
- Hand-to-Hand Combat
- US Military Training (extent of supplemental education unknown)
- Speaks English (fluent), Russian (fluent), German (fluent), French (semi-fluent)
- Counterintelligence Instruction by US Military, SOE, OSS

Super-Soldier Serum: Negative

"Well," says a voice from behind him. "This is unfortunate."

V whips around, reaching for a weapon he knows he doesn't have.

Karpov stands on the opposite side of the room,

flanked by a group of his guards in full combat armor. Their rifles are held low, but their fingers rest on the triggers. Karpov steps forward, and a shard of glass that V must have shaken from his hair cracks. It sounds like breaking ice. A warning before it all caves in.

"Obviously this was not the way I hoped you'd find out," Karpov says, gesturing vaguely around the lab. "Ideally . . . Well, ideally, you never would have found out at all."

V tosses the file onto the floor between them, and it slides along the tile. Karpov stops it with the toe of his loafer.

"What have you done to me?" V demands.

Karpov picks up the folder, dusting off the front and shuffling the documents inside until they align. "We did what was necessary."

"Necessary for what?" V spits.

"For your survival."

"Stop lying to me."

Karpov flips open the folder, studying the single page with his thumb pressed to his lip, like he's never seen it before. "My department is creating the perfect soldier, agent. *You* will be the perfect soldier."

"Who am I?"

"You are the Winter Soldier," Karpov says firmly. "Who you *were* is irrelevant."

"But I was . . . someone!" His voice cracks. "I was someone else. I was this person—I was James Barnes—I had a life and a country and a family! And you took that from me."

Karpov waved a hand. "Without me, your life would have been small and unimportant. You would have been one more soldier who died on the front. One headstone among thousands. But you and I together, Soldier—we are making history. You are the first of a new kind."

"What if I don't want to be?"

"Then you should have died," Karpov says flatly. "Believe me, there were days I wished you would. But you kept stubbornly refusing to. You wanted this. We both knew you were destined for more than a life as Captain America's pathetic sidekick."

"Why don't I remember anything?" V asks. He wants to tear at his heart, fall to his knees in an operatic performance of madness. "What did you do to me?"

One of the guards raises his rifle, but Karpov holds out a hand, then takes another step toward V. "During the war, there was a race to create the first superhuman soldier. A man strong enough and dedicated so completely to his cause that he would die before he'd falter. The Americans tried with their captain."

Blue eyes flash in V's mind. A tilted smile. The smell of aftershave. The taste of spearmint gum.

"The Germans had Zola and his Übermensch,"

Karpov continues. "Hydra and their Infinitas Agenda. Only I saw the fatal flaw in each of these projects. They allowed their subjects to retain an identity beyond their role as an agent of their country. They all caught on eventually, after their soldiers died or went rogue. Now they chase my tail, pretending they too have always known the truth." Karpov presses the heels of his hands together, fingertips brushing. "To unmake a person, you must erase their memories. Those are the things that make us who we are. And a soldier should be nothing but a weapon. I had ideas of how this might be achieved—we had done experiments during the war. Nothing achieved quite the desired effect. And then we found you." He spread his arms to V and smiled, like a father welcoming back a prodigal son. "Fallen from a plane and left for dead in the icy waters of the English Channel. You had no memory of who you used to be, but you retained all your motor skills, speech, senses. It was perfect. Your memories might have come back in time—concussion-induced amnesia isn't always permanent. But what would that have mattered? Without us, you would have died in the ice. We saved you."

"And when I started to remember?" V asks. "That's happened every time, hasn't it?"

Karpov's lips twitched into a mirthless smile. "It won't any longer, thanks to the formula you retrieved for us. The British chemist Edward Fleming developed a drug that alters the temporal lobe so as to make memory retrieval impossible. We hadn't been able to duplicate it without a sample. But now that you and Rostova brought back the dose that Imogen Fleming never took, we will be able to reverse-engineer the formula and duplicate it. Hydra never could. The stupid Americans never could. But you and I, Soldier—together we will take the first steps into this brave new world."

V feels the backs of his legs hit the desk. He had been retreating without realizing it. "Why are you telling me this?"

"Because you won't remember any of it," Karpov says, and flicks two fingers to the guards flanking him. "You'll be sedated and placed in cryostasis until we're sure the formula is ready. The sample you brought us should be all we need to get it right this time." He smiles again, and says, with sincere reassurance, "We won't have to do this again."

As they advance, V realizes that the guards' guns must be loaded with tranquilizer darts, not bullets. They can't kill him—Karpov won't let them. And even if they had been instructed to shoot to kill, there is nothing more they could take from him. They've stripped and scrubbed him so many times already.

He's begged for death. He's held the knife to his own wrist.

But this time—maybe for the first time—he wants

more than the death he has evaded again and again. He wants to pick the locks. He wants to see the sky.

One of the soldiers raises his gun, but Karpov puts a finger on the barrel. "Wait." He turns to V, tipping his head toward the laboratory door. "Come on, Soldier. This doesn't have to be an ordeal." V doesn't move. Karpov's lips twitch. "Don't fight it."

But that's the only thing they've ever taught him how to do.

"It's nothing you haven't survived before," Karpov says.

He is tired of surviving. He wants to live.

Before they can move, V grabs one of the thick tubes connecting the cryostasis chamber to the floor with his metal arm and wrenches. The bolts holding it in place spring free, and a blast of frigid air, white and crackling with cold, gushes out, spraying the soldiers and Karpov. They all shrink backward, and V leaps over the desk and runs. The concrete under his feet is damp and slick, and veins of white ice are creeping across it from the spraying cryo hose.

On the other side of the laboratory, he spots a vent in the ceiling. He takes a running step up, his foot wedged against the wall hard enough to propel himself upward. He catches the grate with his metal arm and rips it out of its frame, then hoists himself up and into the narrow shaft beyond.

"Don't let him get away!" he hears Karpov shout, but he's already running, crouched low, his back scraping the top of the ventilation shaft. There's a clatter behind him, but he doesn't look back.

Ahead of him, the shaft splits in two directions, and he picks the left without knowing why. There's a pop behind him, and something strikes his metal arm. They followed him. They're firing at him. Another pop— this one falls short and bursts against the heel of his boot. He twists around. Two of Karpov's men clamber after him, guns awkwardly wedged in front of them. V abruptly changes direction, diving back down the shaft, sliding toward the guards. They try to adjust their aim, but he strikes them before they have the chance. The first guard is crouched, and V knocks his feet out from under him, then slams the man's head into the wall of the vent. The second soldier is fighting with his rifle, struggling for a clean shot. V grabs the barrel, crumpling it against the ceiling, then deals the man a sharp uppercut to the chin. The guard reels, and V snatches up the first guard's rifle and unloads a tranquilizer into the second's chest. He slumps, motionless. V considers taking the gun with him, but tranquilizer darts are worthless, and the guns are bulky and will only slow him down. He keeps going.

His back is already aching from the crouched angle of the run, and he remembers suddenly the sound of his spine cracking when he hit the ice. He can feel every point where his bones had snapped, like a course plotted on a map. He remembers the fall. He remembers losing his grip, the cold moment when he realized there was nothing he could do, and fight turned to fear. This was how it ended.

But it doesn't have to be that way now. From here forward, no one decides his fate but him.

A chugging *thunk* bounces down the shaft, followed by a *whoosh*. The vent around him fills with hot, rancid air. He doubles over, coughing, lungs convulsing. Whatever they filter out with these vents, they must have reversed the valve so it's all flooding him. His eyes burn, and he pulls the neck of his shirt up over his nose and mouth, though it does little to help. He needs his mask, he thinks, and lets out a hysterical laugh. He needs to get out of here.

The shaft climbs upward at a sharp right angle. He stares up at the slick chute. There's nothing to hold on to if he climbs or catch himself against if he falls. The air around him is getting hotter. The metal walls of the air vent are burning hot. The soles of his boots are melting—he can smell the rubber.

There's another clatter behind him, and he turns in time to see a panel pop open in the floor. Someone tosses a flash grenade through it, and it rolls toward him. V grits his teeth and looks up the vertical chute above him.

He can see one spot almost six feet overhead where a panel has come loose. If he catches it just right, it might loosen enough that he could use it as a handhold. He can't jump to reach it. He can't even get a running start.

He wedges the toe of his boot against the bottom of the chute, presses his back to the other side, ignoring the heat burning through his shirt and the blood pumping through the burn scars on his shoulder—*freezer burn*, he thinks wildly. Just as the grenade explodes in a corona of light, V shoves himself upward, stretching out with his metal arm. He catches the edge of the loose panel, and it peels away from the wall like a skinned piece of fruit. He slams his back into the chute, his feet pressed to the other side, and wedges himself in place with his boots braced against the loose panel. Beneath him, he can hear the soldiers climbing into the vent, searching for him.

He stretches again, digging his metal fingers into the wall until he creates a dent. He pulls himself up, then switches his fingers for his foot, weightless for a moment before he pushes himself up like the divot is a rung on a ladder. He keeps going like this, hand over hand, even when he hears the soldiers below him, shouting to each other. The exposed skin on his hand is starting to turn red and blister from the heat.

Finally, the chute above him bends and he heaves himself up, expecting another tunnel, but instead he falls. He tumbles, weightless, through the empty air, and he remembers the plane. He remembers a voice—Steve— it has to be—who is Steve?—but it's Steve's voice, *Bucky, let go! You have to let go—*

And then he hits the snow, just a few feet below. The fall knocks the breath out of him, but when he opens his eyes he's staring at the sky. *The sky.* Wide and gray, the clouds pulsing with the dregs of a storm. Snow is falling. He can feel the soft flakes on his face. He sits up and realizes he has rolled out of the shaft and tumbled out onto the roof of the underground bunker, buried under heavy drifts. The only hint it's there are the fingers of steam stretching up from the vents, weaving drunkenly toward the sky.

V stumbles to his feet. The cold seeps through the burned soles of his boots, soaking his socks, and he gasps with relief. Beyond the bunker, the tundra stretches, a wild, unfriendly landscape broken only by distant ice caps. He takes a breath, and it fogs white against the sky. For a moment, there seems to be no difference between the sky and the earth. It's all just an endless expanse of gray, gray, gray. Vertigo grips him, and he almost tips over.

The whole damn world seemed upside down.

The song again—like a record through thin apartment walls. He can't remember where he heard it, but he tastes salt and the stale smack of melted ice, and his vision floods with the image of a skyline, a city seen from a rooftop bar.

Me in my dress uniform. You in a white tie and tails.

The song is drowned out by the growl of an engine. V drops low reflexively and crawls to the edge of the bunker roof, just in time to see two snowcats barreling out of the garage. He'll never get out of here on foot. There has to be a base—something more than just this bunker buried in the snow—where he and Rostova left in their plane. Why can't he remember it? Why can't he remember where they left from? Where they were going? They were going to Norway. They went to—

No, they had gone to Riga. They'd gone to Riga to find a man at a bar, and he'd been shot. V had killed the man in an inky moonlit park—no, Rostova had killed him. When they returned, the doctors here had done something to V, something to his memory. They had forced him to take pills and covered his face. How many other missions has he been sent out on that he can't remember? How many people has he killed? The cold stings his eyes, and he drags his hand over them.

When the next snowcat careens out of the garage, V drops off the bunker and onto its roof. The impact is bone-rattling, and he's sure someone in the cab must have heard it, but no one sticks their head out the window to check. He waits until they're far enough from the other snowcats that they can't be seen, then reaches down and smashes in the windshield with his metal hand. He swings himself inside, the flimsy roof crumpling in his bionic grip. There are two soldiers in the cab, both wearing headsets. The passenger recovers quick enough to flip a switch on the dashboard and start calling into the mouthpiece, "We have the subj—"

V rips the headset cables out of the dashboard and whips them around the man's neck, yanking him out the broken windshield and out of the cab. His body tumbles into the snow. The second man—the driver—reaches for a gun between the seats, but V stamps hard on his hand. He feels the bones crack, and the man screams.

Something hits him from behind: a third man he hadn't seen crouched in the back seat of the snowcat grabs him around the waist, tackling him. V loses his balance, and they both tumble forward onto the hood of the snowcat. The guard lands on top of V, an elbow pressed into his windpipe. V gasps for breath. The snowcat's treads spit needles of snow in their faces. He can feel the sting on his exposed skin. His vision is spotting. He can't breathe. He tries to pull his bionic arm free, but it's wedged in the grill on the front of the vehicle. He can't get it loose.

The soldier fumbles with the pocket of his parka, trying to get a tranquilizer.

V wraps his legs around the man's waist, then, with his arm still wedged in the grill, lets himself tumble over the nose of the snowcat, toward the snow. The man flips with him, surprised by the sudden shift in weight. V swings himself under the belly of the snowcat, his bionic arm a fulcrum, but the soldier falls into the path of the treads. For a moment, their tracks in the snow are bright red.

V bounces a few times against the hard-packed snow, struggling for breath, before he manages to hook his foot up into the engine, suspending himself long enough to rip the grill off the front of the snowcat; then he drops to the ground.

The snowcat jolts, but keeps plowing forward. V sits in the snow, gasping, waiting for it to turn around, but instead it keeps going, leaving him behind until it's swallowed by the storm.

He shakes the grill from his bionic arm as he stands, tossing it into the snow. He can't see the bunker any-more. He can't see anything—the wasteland is still and quiet. He takes a deep, cold breath and feels free for the first time in his memory. However fleeting or flawed that memory might be, it is his. He starts to run, hope thrumming in him, brighter and stronger for having died again and again and again and still risen anyway. He will survive. He will make it out of this alive. He will meet himself again.

And then the tundra's stillness is cracked by a gunshot.

V keeps running, thinking for one ecstatic moment they must have missed. He's still on his feet. He's still moving. Then he sees the blood splatters blooming in the snow around him like a field of poppies. He had heard stories about the red poppies in Flanders. His father had told him. His father had been in Europe during the Great War, and after he came home, he never once slept through the night.

V has been shot—not with a tranquilizer, but a bullet, in the same spot he'd been shot in Riga. Adrenaline carries him a few steps more than he might have gotten otherwise, but his leg collapses under him, folding like a tripod. He crashes to the ground and snow envelops him, gusting down his shirt and melting in a frigid stream down his back.

He shoves himself up on his elbows, wiping at his face. He squints across the gray landscape, trying to work out where the shot came from, but he can't orient himself. It's too much nothing. He can't remember which direction he was facing before he fell. Even his footprints and those blossoms of blood in the snow have already been obliterated by the wind. The remaining snowcats are too far, the rumble of their engines bouncing across the landscape so it feels like they're closing in on him. They're nowhere. They're everywhere. *This is how men drown*, he thinks, *when they can't tell the sea from the sky. This is how I drowned.* Some other life of his had ended this way.

This one won't.

V struggles back to his feet, dragging his leg after him as it leaks blood. He can cover the trail. He has to get away from here. He can find shelter. He can fight through the pain—he's made it through worse. He'll tourniquet his leg. He'll hold his skin together until the bleeding stops. He's survived the cold before, what's once more? All he needs is somewhere to hide. Somewhere to—

A low snowdrift ahead of him bursts apart. He thinks at first it must have been another shot, this one wide, and he almost turns, searching for the sniper. Then he sees the silhouette climbing up from where they had been lying on their belly in the snow. Their gray-and-white tactical suit renders them almost impossible to see in the snow. He'd been running straight toward them without knowing.

He stumbles, trying to turn, but his boots are too heavy, and his feet are numb. He can feel blood dripping down his leg as the sniper jams the rifle into their shoulder and aims again.

"No!" V throws his bionic arm up over his chest. "No, wait—"

The second bullet buries itself in his other leg, a mirror to the first, and he collapses onto his back. A dusting of snow settles over him, so light it's like he's fallen into soft sugar. He stares at the gray sky, watching his breath rise to meet it. He hears the click of the spent shell kicked from the rifle. Snowflakes catch on his eyelashes, melting against the heat of his skin and running down his face and into his ears.

James Barnes, he thinks. *I'm James Barnes. My friends called me Bucky. . . . Stevie called me Buck. . . . Ginny called me . . . Ginny called me . . .*

The sniper stands over him, unwrapping her balaclava, but he already knows.

Rostova holds up her thumb and forefinger in the shape of a gun and points them at the space between his eyes. *Bang.*

He's panting from the pain and the cold. His lungs feel like they're shrinking inside him, and he can't get a deep breath. Each one comes out a short, wet gasp.

He came down with pneumonia in the Dolomites. Steve wrapped them both in a coat and held him until his fever broke. . . .

Rostova unhooks a chain from her belt, pulling it taut between her hands to break the coating of frost on the metal. He tries again to push himself away, but his elbows sink into the soft snow and he collapses again. Rostova presses a heavy foot onto his chest, pinning him in place. He grabs her boot, trying to shove her off. He feels his ribs crack under the pressure. His grip falters. His ears pop.

His sister at the community swimming pool, asking him to count the seconds while she held her breath underwater as their mother dozed in a lounge chair on the deck. They would all pink in the sun. Dry skin peeled off them like paint all summer.

Rostova shifts her boot from his chest to his bionic arm, pinning it down just long enough to slot a small key into the shoulder port used to run diagnostics. There's a whir, a shudder so deep it feels like the individual cells of his body break apart for a moment, and then he can't feel his arm anymore. The phantom pain that haunted him in Svalbard returns, somehow more real and immediate than the bullets in his knees. His stomach heaves.

Spiked punch at an Army dance, catching Steve's eye across the gymnasium over the shoulder of a pretty WAF pilot with her head against his chest . . .

Rostova yanks both his arms over his head and wraps the chain around them. She's going to clip him to her belt and drag him back to the base, like he's an animal carcass brought back from a hunt.

"Don't you want to muzzle me?" V chokes out, the words rasping and spiteful.

Rostova jerks the chain hard enough he feels his right shoulder pull in its socket. He screams. His lungs are burning.

Smoke from their campfires that stuck in his hair for weeks. When he met Ginny in a Dublin bar, the first thing she said, even before she kissed him, was "You smell like smoke," and he replied, "You smell like gin with a lime twist. . . ."

"Did you know?" he asks.

Rostova's hand slips, and the chain tumbles into the snow. She doesn't move to pick it up.

"You did," he says. "You knew every time, and you never told me."

She has known more versions of him—has more memories of him—than he has. She knows what he looked like with his hair cut short, the lines of frustration in his face as he relearned combat drills with a bionic arm, names he doesn't remember her calling him. She must have seen the way his eyes looked when he'd start to remember, and she must know what it looked like when those memories were snuffed out again.

Rostova pinning him to the ground, wrestling a scalpel from his hand. The white tile under them already slick with blood . . .

Rostova stares at the horizon. Snow collects on the top of her hat, and the wind ruffles the fur. "Please, stop talking."

"How did you never tell me?"

"Stop."

"How did you look me in the eye every day and tell me you had my back—"

She snatches the chain up from the snow, dragging him into a sitting position and starting to pull his body through the snow. Pain explodes through both his legs—he feels like his bones are splintering. The bottoms of his feet throb, and he isn't sure if it was the heat or the cold that burned them.

"You let me trust you," he chokes out. He's so cold he can hardly speak. His jaw rattles. "Again and again and again."

She wrenches the chain again. "Shut up!"

"I saved your life."

She stops. Turns her face to the sky and laughs, so quiet he sees her misty breath before he realizes she made a sound. "You did. And you always did. No matter how many times, they never wiped that stupid hero complex out of you."

"Was it worth it?" He pulls himself up, muscles seizing, and grabs the hem of her coat. She turns sharply, but doesn't shake him off. "You took my life and my past and my family and my country and my mind. Look me in the eyes and tell me you're proud of yourself."

She doesn't. "I did it for my country."

He laughs. His throat is raw, and he tastes blood. "You have to do better than that."

She drops the chain, and he collapses back into the snow. He can't feel the cold anymore. That's a warning.

In their three-week survival course outside Nome, their company learned the warning signs of hypothermia. Pinky kept calling it "hypothyroidism" by mistake.

Rostova pulls a pistol from her coat and empties the magazine before retrieving a tranquilizer dart from her belt. "I have no regrets."

"You should," he replies.

She looks down at his blood on the snow. The barrel of her gun. "I know."

He stares up at her, watching her fingers guide the capsule into the chamber. "What's your name?" he asks suddenly. "Your real name—it's not Rostova, is it?" She spins the chamber, stopping it sharply with her thumb. "It doesn't matter if I know, does it? When was the last time you told someone your real name?" He's so tired. The cold is already in his bones, and he feels weightless. He could sink into the snow. He could let himself be swallowed up by this uninhabitable terrain. He'd become a part of the landscape, dormant until the next soldier stumbled across the tundra. But instead he says to her, "I'm James. James Barnes. I think my friends call me Bucky."

"Rostova!" A snowcat careens to a stop behind them—V hadn't heard the engine. Karpov clambers from the driver's seat.

"What's your name?" V asks again.

Karpov is struggling toward them, a hand raised to shield his face from the snow.

It takes all V's strength, but he pushes himself forward and grabs Rostova's wrist, the one holding the gun.

She stiffens but doesn't pull away. His sleeve falls back, far enough that the white scar on his wrist is visible, like a vein of ice wedged into his pulse point. "Kill me," he says, his voice breaking. "Don't make me do it again. Kill me before you give me back to him."

"Rostova!" Karpov shouts.

"You understand, don't you?" he says. "What it's like to not belong to yourself anymore?"

"Rostova!"

She takes a deep breath of the snowy air, and doesn't flinch when the cold strikes her lungs. She tips her head back and says to the sky, "Masha."

"What are you waiting for?" Karpov screams.

"My name is Maria Ekaterina Nikolayeva Popova," she says. "But my mother always called me Masha."

There's a gunshot. V and Rostova—James and Masha—both look to the pistol in her hand, then the blood creeping over the front of her white tactical suit, another poppy in another field.

She falls so slowly, like a feather riding the breeze. She lands in the snow with her face beside his, close enough he can see the individual snowflakes nestled in her hair. When she opens her mouth, blood floods her lips. Her breath rattles. The space between each one grows longer and longer. She reaches out and touches his cheek.

The wind drifts over them, covering their footprints and their blood, the shapes of their bodies in the snow and the memory of every bullet they ever took for each other across all the lifetimes only one of them could remember. Soon there will be nothing left of either of them, but for a moment they are both still there. The world around them is still and silent and pristine white all the way to the horizon. A blank slate.

For a moment, it's just Rostova and Vronsky.

And then just Vronsky.

"Dump her body," he hears Karpov call to his soldiers. "Take the subject back to the bunker. The cryostasis will proceed as planned."

CHAPTER 25
1954

He returns to a foggy consciousness strapped to an operating table, staring into lights so bright that he can still see them when he closes his eyes. His head throbs. He can't feel his legs, and he can't raise his head high enough to see if they're still there. Something holds him in place, and he doesn't have the strength to fight it.

They've removed his bionic arm. The socket is swaddled in a protective gauze, rubber edges sealing it against his skin. There's a tube in his other arm, and he can feel the cold already, under his skin. He feels soaked to the bone. Doctors float at the corners of his vision, talking softly. Their faces are covered by surgical masks and their eyes obscured by heavy lenses. They look like ghosts. One of them bends over him with a pair of thin-nosed scissors, and he feels a sharp pinch at his neck. A moment later there's a soft plink as the doctor drops the needle he extracted onto an offered tray.

Another doctor smears a cold gel over V's chest, then attaches a sensor. A machine begins to beep in time with his heart. The rhythmic throb seems far too slow. He hardly feels conscious, though he's aware of what's happening around him, and he can feel it all—the scrape of the tube they feed into his nose, the burning drops they put in both his eyes that turn the world lavender, the latex fingers shoved into his mouth, checking roughly under his tongue and in his cheeks before a rubber mouth guard is forced between his teeth.

"If he's ready," says a voice, Karpov's voice, "you can begin lowering the temperature."

The fight floods him again.

He won't go back. He can't—he won't go back into the ice. He won't lose himself again. He's clawed his way back through the darkness, from beneath the surface and the cold, and broken through every damn time—and he will not surrender this hard-won ground. He will not be their lab rat. He will not be their soldier. He will not be honed and tempered, weaponized like newly forged steel.

He will fight on his knees with his face in the dirt. He will never concede.

He tries to sit up, but the restraints are too tight, and there are so many of them. There are too many tubes and wires and cables tethering him. His muscles shake, and pain ricochets through him. His eyes throb. He tries to say something, but he can't force words out through the mouth guard.

Karpov's face swims into view above him. Through the film of whatever they put in his eyes, the doctor's skin looks red. "It's easier," he says, patting V's cheek, "if you relax."

But he wasn't raised to concede. Rostova had never taught him how. George Barnes had never taught him. Edward Fleming had let the German chase his king for hours, refusing to resign. He wants to kick the restraints off his legs. He wants to rip them from the table and wrap them around Karpov's throat. He wants every man and woman in this room, everyone who has raised a finger to him, to watch him rise from this table. He wants to see them fear him.

The scissors the doctor used to remove the needle from his neck are resting on a nearby tray, close enough that they must not think him capable of moving. The ice is already solidifying in his veins, but if he reaches . . . If he stretches . . .

Karpov tilts his head to confer with one of the doctors. Another doctor removes the IV drip from V's arm and covers the spot with a gauze pad, then turns away.

He feels the pull all the way to his shoulder as he stretches toward the scissors, his fingers barely brushing the handles. Karpov is right there. Karpov, who made sure V knew how to kill without wasting time on remorse. Who gave him Rostova and told her to teach him where to stab a man so that he bleeds out before he hits the floor. The restraint is rubbing V's skin raw, but he keeps stretching. The scissors twitch on the tray when his nail catches a ridge in the handle.

He thinks of Rostova. *Masha.* He thinks of every code name she called him. Maybe they never told her his real one. How many times had she turned away when they shoved tubes down his throat and let the ice close around him? How many pills had she slipped him even though she knew they were eating his brain like moths through wool? He thinks of Ginny Fleming putting her hand on the barrel of his pistol, their love a graveyard where nothing stayed buried. He can picture her—not hollow-cheeked and pale in the Hydra lab, but as she was when he first met her. Her pin curls and her oversize cardigan. He had kissed her. They had danced. She had dropped a book in his pocket, and he had held her hand before they parted. The sunlight on the runway had been so bright that day.

His finger catches the handle of the scissors.

He flips it into his palm, and the cold metal against his skin jolts him awake. It gives him something to focus on, a sense to sharpen the others. The color starts to return to his vision. He can breathe without gagging. He rotates the scissors between his fingers, lining up the point with Karpov's thigh. All it will take, when the doctor turns, is one hard jam into his leg.

Karpov shifts his weight, leaning onto his back foot.

One step. That's all he needs.

One step closer, and it's over.

Then one of the doctors grabs him by the chin and yanks his face forward. He's blinded for a moment by the lights, and then a heavy rubber mask is shoved over his nose and mouth. He tries to turn his head, but there's a hiss as gas is released, and his vision turns milky around the edges. He wants to hold his breath, but he isn't even sure he's breathing anymore. He can't seem to locate his lungs in his body. The scissors slip from his grip.

"There you go," Karpov's voice says. "Something to help you relax."

He can't relax. He has to fight. He has to stay awake, he has to remember.

"Countdown commencing," someone says. "Ten."

He tries to pull against the restraints, but he's already turning to smoke, floating away inch by inch, though somehow the pain remains. His whole body is phantom limbs.

You have to remember, he tells himself, digging his finger-nails into his palm, desperate to stay awake. *When you wake up you will remember everything. You will not forget again.*

"Nine."

Your name is James Barnes. Your friends call you Bucky. You were born in Shelbyville, Indiana. . . .

His vision fuzzes. The lights overhead are getting brighter, individual bulbs blurring into a long streak like the tail of a comet.

You are James Barnes. Your sister's name is Rebecca. Your mother's name was . . .

"Eight."

Your mother's name was . . .

He's shivering. He can't hear the electric beep of his heart anymore.

"Seven."

James Barnes, James Barnes, James Barnes, don't forget it, don't forget.

The room is full of ghosts. Everywhere he looks, there are nothing but rags and shadows.

"Six."

Bucky. They call you Bucky, your friends call you Bucky. You have to remember it all.

"Five."

Remember the smell of motorcycle exhaust and heat off the blacktop and the particular golden glow of Midwest wheat fields at sunset.

"Four."

And snowcapped mountains from above, flying under the stars in the seat behind Steve. The aurora turned the windshield purple and pink.

Remember the mints and crumbs and ticket stubs always at the bottom of her purse. She never threw anything away.

"Three."

And the standing water in your boots . . .

Your mother's purple hydrangeas shedding petals across the lawn . . .

The bleached sheets in the motel in Queens, the first time you woke up screaming and Ginny held you . . .

Remember who you were.

Remember who you are. . . .

"Two."

Don't let them take it again. Don't let them—

"One."

Mackenzi Lee

MACKENZI LEE holds a BA in history and an MFA in writing for children and young adults from Simmons College. She is the *New York Times* best-selling author of the Marvel Rebels & Renegades series, which includes *Loki: Where Mischief Lies* and *Gamora and Nebula: Sisters in Arms*, as well as the Stonewall Honor-winning historical fantasy series The Montague Siblings. She is also the author of the nonfiction book *Bygone Badass Broads*, a collection of short biographies of forgotten women from history. In 2020, she was named one of *Forbes*'s 30 Under 30 for her work in bringing minority narratives to historical fiction. She works as an independent bookseller, drinks too much Diet Coke, and has a Saint Bernard dog that's more popular than she is.